SAVAGE WILD GODS

THE SAVAGE WILDS
BOOK THREE

SEAN FLETCHER

For those who gave these savage Wilds a chance. Let's enter together, one last time.

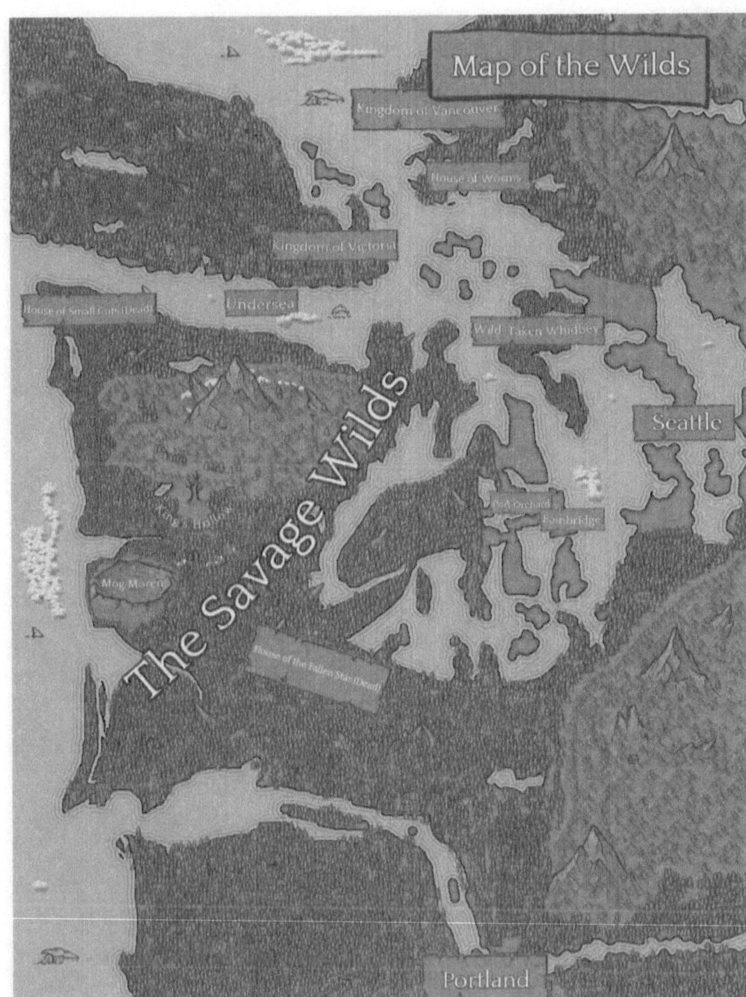

Map of the Wilds
Kingdom of Vancouver
House of Worms
Kingdom of Victoria
House of Small Cats (Dead)
Undersea
Wild Taken Whidbey
The Savage Wilds
Seattle
King's Hollow
Port Orchard
Bainbridge
Mog Moren
House of the Fallen Star (Dead)
Portland

“Rage, rage against the dying of the light.”

Dylan Thomas

CHAPTER ONE

I was convinced the universe had a sense of humor. A sick one.

Had someone once told me that I, a girl from Seattle, would one day be the Empress of a forgotten people, would one day discover that I wasn't human, I would have laughed in their face. And, depending on how I felt and who they were, maybe hit them for telling such a stupid joke.

Now, as I followed General Tenia, *my* general, deeper through to tunnels of the Below to meet with an awakening god, I was starting to believe a joke like that wasn't stupid enough.

Thanks to the dim blue light from the surrounding crystals, I missed the tunnel's sharp decline and stumbled. General Tenia smirked as she glanced back at me.

"Watch yourself. The Below tends to have rocks underfoot."

The three guards she'd ordered to accompany us snickered. I pushed off the slick wall, squeezing my hands into fists. It'd be petty, but the urge to lash out for such a remark burned through my veins.

"Noted," I said curtly.

General Tenia chuckled and kept moving. Out of all the subjects I'd inherited after taking Sotera's throne, she hated me the most. It didn't matter that I wasn't to blame for the state the Below was in. Had I fallen and broken my neck, I had no doubt she'd be delighted I'd died without making too much of a mess.

I rested my hand just over the inside of my left forearm. Sliver, the sword I could fashion out of my own crystal bone, lay just beneath my skin. The farther down we went, the more I kept a watchful eye on the guards at my back. General Tenia had told me they were necessary. I agreed not because I believed her, but because I had to believe I could defend myself regardless of what I was up against. I was Empress, after all.

"Long live the Empress of Glass." Rune's voice, mired in threat, curled through my head. In my memory, I imagined the warm brush of his breath as he whispered the words into my ear. I wondered if he would grieve if my own foolishness and naivete got me killed barely a month after my coronation.

Mostly, I wondered how hard he might laugh.

"How much farther?" I asked, trying to get my bearings. General Tenia was one of the few still alive who knew the way, and I already had little trust in her. The air down here was cold enough to prickle the hair on my arms and growing colder still.

"You'll know when we're there," General Tenia answered. "Empress," she added as an afterthought. "Grislehaut will make sure of that."

The narrow tunnel briefly opened into a larger chamber, and we emerged at the empty underground city where Sotera had forced me to use my magic to create monstrous crystal beings; the same beings she later used to collapse the earth beneath Seattle.

Now, half of this city—and much more of the Below—lay

crushed beneath corpses of skyscrapers, crumbled asphalt, and the twisted metal and shattered glass of cars. There were human bodies buried among the rubble, but there was no reaching them. Already King Bendeti had flooded so much of the cavern floor with seawater we'd had to take a boat to even reach where we were. The air smelled thickly of salt.

One of the guards spits onto a half-buried street sign. "May they all rot."

I was beside him in an instant, hand pressing over his heart. The magic of Those Below thrummed through the crystal of his body, begging me to take it. Begging me to kill him.

"Take that back," I warned.

He tried to escape my touch, eying my hand as though it were a sword. "Apologies, Empress! I only meant— They—"

"Those above didn't do this. Your former Empress did. The humans aren't our enemy."

"Perhaps not. The same can't be said about the High King of the Wilds," General Tenia drawled.

I whirled on her. "He's an ally, too."

Though only part of her face was flesh, General Tenia managed to impressively arch a single eyebrow. "I suppose that's why he hasn't answered any of your requests to meet with him. Silence is the response an *ally* would give."

It'd only been a month. How many times had I told myself that? Only a month since I took the throne of Those Below out from under Rune. A busy month where I was sure he'd been consolidating more allies and preparing against the surprise threat Father Dumas and the worshippers of the Mother Tree now posed. All that and an awakening god, of course.

Rune's lack of an answer had nothing to do with me. Nothing to do with how I'd stabbed him in the back and stolen the one thing he craved above all else: power.

"Are we going to keep gawking at the scenery, Empress?" General Tenia jerked her chin at the collapsed city, causing the metal pieces clasped in her hair to clink together. "I know how you enjoy the view."

Every word she spoke reeked of insubordination. I should punish her. Draining the magic from Those Below was the least of what I could do. But as of yet, I couldn't bring myself to be as bad as the Empress I'd replaced.

Maybe that mercy would be what finally killed me.

We reentered the narrow tunnels. Soon, the cold air was joined by an unnatural stillness, putting me on even higher alert. The Below as I knew it always moved. Thermal geysers belching searing steam, pools of bubbling magma, glittering fields of sharpened crystals.

Here, as the darkness grew absolute, there was a threat to the quiet.

"Come closer," it beckoned. *"Come and meet your end."*

I raised a glowing hand, casting sickly light around the tunnel, and tried to gauge which direction the worst of the danger was coming from. The guards had stopped.

"What are you doing?" General Tenia barked at them.

"Can't you feel it?" one of the guards said, eyes wide. "We can't go any farther. Sotera told us never to get too close. She—"

"Is dead," I said, putting as much newly gained authority into my voice as possible. "And stopping now won't fix anything. We need to go farther in."

"You three remain here," General Tenia said.

My eyes snapped to her. "Why did you bring them, only to leave them behind?"

She held my gaze but didn't answer. She didn't need to. Working with silver-tongued Rune and fighting plenty of those who wanted me dead had built a distrusting scab over my heart. I'd already puzzled out her plot for myself. A problem I'd have to deal with sooner rather than later.

I jumped as one of the guards shrieked. She'd thrust out her hand, its shadow dancing crazily off the wall. "What's happening to me?"

"By the Deep..." General Tenia murmured.

The woman's hand was dissolving bit by bit into the air, as though she'd dipped it into a vat of acid. No matter how much she shook it, her body continued unraveling.

"Make it stop. Make it stop!" the guard continued to shriek. She drew her sword and tried to line up the edge of the blade with the base of her wrist. She raised it high and only stopped when one of the other guards grabbed her. He looked at me, expression pleading.

"What do we do?"

The air stirred farther down the tunnel, though there was no breeze. The longer I looked at it, the more my vision twisted, spots dancing across my eyes. If I didn't do something quick, I had no doubt I'd start unravelling, too, body and mind.

I summoned a needle of crystal and pricked the inside of my palm until it bled. The sudden bite of pain chased away the gathering brain fog and gave my magic time to ground me. The parts of my body that had begun to blur and fade away sharpened once more.

"Go back up, all of you," I told General Tenia. "I think you'll be fine if you get far enough away."

She cocked that same eyebrow, though I couldn't discern whether she thought me stupid, brave, or suicidal. Maybe all three. "And what do you plan to do?"

I continued walking down the tunnel. "What I came here for: visit a god."

In truth, I had no plan. If Rune had been here, he wouldn't be worried. He'd sweet talk Grislehaut—

I pricked the inside of my palm again. Enough. I'd lost him and the wildlings who'd become my friends. And if I blamed them for abandoning me, then I had to blame myself twice as much.

Though my body remained sharp and grounded, Grislehaut's aura continued dissolving my surroundings. The surface of the rocks was stripped away like cast orange peels. The stone beneath my feet was crushed first to fine powder and then to nothing at all. Obsidian dust twinkled in the air like starlight.

At the end of the tunnel were two enormous crystals, crossed like a giant X. A promise of death past this point.

I stepped between the X and into the chamber beyond where I was forced to stop.

There was pitch black, and then there was this—the absence of light, as though the very idea of it had been devoured. Whatever texture had once been on the floor, walls, and ceilings had been scoured to smoothness, like how a room would appear before someone started decorating.

Though I wasn't entirely human, that human sixth sense told me to *run now.*

I tamped it down and tenderly reached out a hand until I could feel the silken cold as it brushed up against a veil of black. My sixth sense reached a keening pitch, and this time I heeded it. Any farther beyond that veil and I knew I'd turn into nothingness as well.

"Gah!"

I stumbled back as a spike of pain pricked my mind. Something that was more intention than thought bubbled up, unbidden, too fast for me to stop. The intention formed thoughts, which then formed words.

"Welcome, tiny mortal," Grislehaut said in a voice that rattled my crystal bones. "Come and greet your ruination."

CHAPTER TWO

Once the pain had subsided, I steeled myself against the dark. "That isn't how you greet your Empress."

Nice one, Val. Don't reprimand your very mortal general but give lip to a god.

Grislehaut didn't laugh. He didn't grow angry. I wasn't sure he was capable of such basic emotions.

More of his intention manifested into words. "Have you come to free me?"

"No."

A long, dangerous pause. "Then what is it you want?"

Many things, some of which I couldn't have, and most I didn't deserve. Grislehaut had been down here an unfathomably long time. It was only because of Sotera's meddling and Father Dumas's treachery that he was waking up at all. But if he could slumber for eons once, he could do so again.

"I need you to go back to sleep," I said. "This isn't your world. This isn't your time."

I staggered back, clutching my head as a swell of seething

anger pummeled me. I guess emotions like that weren't beneath him, after all.

"I was before time." Grislehaut words nearly split my skull. "Before the stars filled the sky, before saltwater overflowed the seas, before the Below filled the vacuum of the earth and the Wilds covered it."

When his words leaked away, I found myself on one knee. A great pressure weighed on me, waiting to see what I'd do.

"Run, run, little mortal," Grislehaut whispered. "Like all the others, see the folly in your struggle."

"Not me," I gritted out. "I need you to listen."

"Then you're very brave. Or very stupid."

Seemed both this god and General Tenia thought they had me measured.

While still on a knee, I surreptitiously glanced around the chamber.

Though most of the room was nothing but a gaping blackness, there *were* more crystals like the ones outside the chamber ringing those parts of the ceiling the darkness hadn't swallowed up. These crystals had vicious points turned inward. All of them were dim. All of them looked weak. They might be one of the few things keeping Grislehaut confined here.

At one time I might have been able to regrow them, but now Grislehaut's presence was too strong. Already in my short time here, the darkness had spread, testing the boundaries of his underground prison.

I stood and took a step back, my body leaving behind an afterimage that took a worrying amount of time to vanish.

"Is this what you do?" I asked. "Break things apart? And then what? What's the point?"

"And then all things will renew, as they always have. Life and death. Cycle and rebirth. It is the way of all things."

That didn't help me. A being with no motivations except to *exist* and destroy couldn't be bargained with.

For not the first time I wondered why Father Dumas had sought to free Grislehaut in the first place. Was he just that crazy? Or did he think he could ride out the destruction and claim what was left in the aftermath?

"What do you want?" I asked. "What would it take to make you go back to sleep?"

"I am inevitable," Grislehaut said. "But want... You already have the one thing that I want. The one thing only you can give."

"And that is...?" I demanded when he didn't elaborate.

"I think not. Not until I've seen things through. Not until all is gone. Then I will take it, whether you want to give me what I desire or not."

I dared to take a step closer to the dark. "Tell me what—"

"I can feel them above," Grislehaut said. "Crawling on the skin of the earth like fleas. I will devour them all."

I longed to drive Sliver into the dark mass. But as long as the chamber wasn't breached, I had a little time to figure out another way to keep him down here. I started backing away.

"Once all is done, then you will give me what I want," Grislehaut said. "That is a promise."

His presence drew back like a leech being removed. I braced myself on the wall to catch my breath before stepping through the crystal X and starting the climb back up. Every step away from Grislehaut's chamber left me feeling more whole. But though he was being held for now, my worst fears had been confirmed: He was growing stronger. We were running out of time.

General Tenia and the guards weren't farther up where I'd left them. They didn't seem to be in the tunnels at all.

Frowning, I picked up the pace, tracing our path back until I emerged on a shore of a shallow sea, courtesy of Bendeti. The boat we'd taken here lay beached among the fine rocks. General Tenia was helping the guards push it into the water. Her mouth fell open when she saw me.

"I know you went through all that trouble to leave me for dead," I said. "Sorry to disappoint."

"Hold!" General Tenia snarled at the guards. She removed the metal cudgel from her waist and hefted it with practiced ease. "It would have been easier if you had died in there. No mess, no questions. The fact that Empress Sotera ever saw you as a threat—"

"She's just Sotera, and she's dead," I said, taunting. "I'm your Empress now."

With a roar of rage, General Tenia came at me.

Sliver was already in my hand—the crystal blade thinly slicked with blood from where I drew it from my forearm.

I deflected her first swing and then her next. I danced away as she spun and used the momentum to strike at my head. The club whistled inches from my skull as I ducked. She'd clearly had decades of training. If she connected with any part of my body, even once, my crystal bone would shatter.

"Stop dancing, *Empress*," General Tenia spat. "You have no spine. No desire to do what's *necessary*."

She punctuated her final words with three brutal swings, and though I blocked, each one wore me down more than the first. The last blow sent me reeling back, radiating pain all up and down my arms. Anger spurred me. I wasn't fighting back because I was weak; despite her hatred of me, I *needed* her.

"What will it take?" I tried not to pant. I'd recovered from my time as a prisoner Below, but still my weakness peeked through at the most inopportune times. "What do I have to prove to earn your loyalty?"

"If you have to ask, you never will," General Tenia said. "But maybe die. Die, and give up this pretense that you care about us. Die, and leave Those Below to their own destiny."

She dropped back, seeking a weakness in my stance before starting a new series of blows. Not even my training with Rune and General Forcheck could prepare me for it. It was an assault that could only be met with equal brutality.

I twisted my hand. A sliver of crystal shot from the ground and pierced the meat of her calf. Tenia faltered with a scream, collapsing to a knee. I twisted my hand again and the sliver of crystal drew back.

"Coward," she said. "Dirty, cheating coward."

"I'm not some honorable ruler from long ago," I said. "I'll do whatever I must to *win.*"

"Kill me, then." General Tenia turned her neck so that it would be all too easy to slice through. "I've already failed one Empress. I've lost my usefulness."

"I'm not going to do that," I said.

"Spare me your coddling mercy and kill me!" General Tenia barked.

I met her murderous gaze. "Despite what you think, I am one of you, one of Those Below, and I care what happens to them—what happens to everyone—more than Sotera ever did."

"Don't you talk... Keep her name out of your mouth," General Tenia growled.

I was suddenly bone and soul tired, my limbs so heavy I wondered whether I'd sink the boat should I step aboard.

I offered General Tenia a hand. Since becoming Empress, I'd tried to keep her busy away from me, giving her little time to plot my demise. That had clearly not worked.

"Keep your enemies close," Marian had once told me. "Easier to stick a knife in their ribs that way."

Then she'd laughed.

"I need your help to make this better. For all of us," I said. I reached out. "Please?"

General Tenia glared at my offered hand as though it were a snake rearing to strike. I knew what I was doing was stupid. The world I was part of didn't respect kindness and concessions. General Forcheck would have berated me for exposing my vulnerable underbelly.

But I couldn't rule the same as Sotera. There had to be a better way.

"I..." General Tenia started to rise. She reached for my hand. "I suppose."

She twisted a little to the side. Years of Wilds-honed reflexes had me backing out of range of the knife she swung around with her other hand.

I freed myself from her grasp. Magic surged to me, and I wrapped it around her body and *squeezed*, exactly the same way Sotera had done to me.

General Tenia screamed and collapsed, thrashing. I continue squeezing, and her screams tapered to whimpers.

I shouldn't stop. She'd try to kill me again if I let her.

I shouldn't stop. Mercy wouldn't save me.

I lowered my hand.

General Tenia lay there, panting. My heart thumped too loudly in my ears.

You enjoyed it, though, didn't you? Bloodthirsty little Empress.

"I don't want to hurt you," I said to General Tenia. "The last thing I want to do is be like Sotera."

General Tenia spat gritty black water onto the stones—Those Below's version of blood. "Too late. You already are."

I HAD the guards row back to the palace under threat of doing to them what I'd done to General Tenia. Bendeti's rising water had forced almost all of the city of the Deep to evacuate, but the palace's throne room remained just above the water's surface. It also remained almost entirely empty. I'd sent everyone who wasn't necessary or an ally to higher chambers with the rest of Those Below.

The boat thumped against the stone at the base of the palace and I stepped off.

"Get some rest, and get someone to look at that calf wound," I told General Tenia. "Then speak with General Estmar about what else he might have found about Grislehaut."

General Tenia wiped away more gritty black liquid from the corner of her mouth. "And should I send another request to meet to the High King?" she asked, tone mocking.

I imagined my messenger kneeling at Rune's feet. I imagined him sneering at my request before throwing it aside. I didn't think I could take the anxiety of waiting any longer.

"No, no more," I said.

With a curt nod, General Tenia led the others away, and I was alone. I spotted a sharp gray fin cutting through the ever-rising water. It cruised closer to the boat, and I hurried away through the stone archway and into the palace, taking the steps up to the main floors two at a time. Almost immediately Raki, one of Sotera's servants who'd taken care of me while I was a prisoner here, appeared. He looked slightly panicked, the colored growths of rocks along his arms and legs more flushed than normal.

"Visitors," he said in that soft, curt way of his. "Lords. Throne room."

The news startled me more than I'd have liked, but I couldn't pretend I hadn't been expecting something like this. There were very few Lords of Rune's Wilds alive or sticking around, if any. These must have been the Lords of the other Wilds, drawn to the conflict in ours like buzzards to carrion.

"Thank you," I told Raki.

"With you?" he asked.

I hesitated, before shaking my head. "You don't need to be there. But thanks."

He gave a shallow bow and hurried off, disappearing into one of the palace's many hidden pathways that only he knew. When I'd first become empress, I'd debated asking him to join me down here in the place that had hurt him as it had me. But with all the wildlings returning with Rune, I'd been left with few options.

Still, as I strode down the palace halls and entered through a pair of enormous double doors into the throne room, I still felt bad. It didn't help that this very room was where his sister had died. I still recalled Qell's blood spilling across the magnificent floor after Sotera had driven a hand through her chest. In fact, I could almost make out dark stains across crystal, caught in the cracks from Grislehaut's tremors.

I shouldn't have brought him back. I shouldn't have done a lot of things.

Two figures stood on the dais at the far end of the room, their backs to me. One, the man, leaned forward, hand outstretched to touch the cold arms of my crystal throne.

"I wouldn't," I said loudly. "Like the Wilds, things down here have bite."

The pair jerked around. I waited for them to break the silence, wishing I'd stopped by to change into something more resplendent and befitting an Empress. Old habits were hard to break, and I'd chosen to visit Grislehaut in functional jeans and a hoodie. Functional but underwhelming.

Like the viceroy butterfly, intimidation can warn off hungry predators. One of General Forcheck's many kernels of wisdom I hadn't yet taken to heart.

At last the woman bowed low. "Empress of Glass, I am Tannis."

Tannis's skin was the color of sun-parched rock, hair a sandy tan and frizzed as a tumbleweed. Her dress was pinned with cactus spines and thistle, and every time she moved, the fabric dusted silt across the floor.

"We're so grateful for having an audience with us," Tannis went on.

"Not that there were many waiting," the man said. "It seems your palace is quite...empty." He, too, finally gave a bow. "I am Sulien."

He was enormously broad shouldered, with a head too small and ears that curled like whorls in a tree's trunk. Delicate white roots streamed off the elbows of his immaculately trimmed coat, sewn from beast skins and the snarling to teeth of what might have been a wolverine.

"I don't need anyone with me," I said, not sure if that made it seem like a strength or a weakness. "And I'm curious what two Lords of Wilds far from here are doing in my kingdom. In fact, I'd love to know what they're doing anywhere close to these Wilds at all."

"We had an offer we'd like to discuss with you," Tannis said.

They parted as I stepped through them, up the dais, and settled into my throne. I tried to recline lazily as I'd seen Rune do, to show both control and airy indifference at the same time. Perhaps I was imagining it, but Tannis and Sulien didn't seem as intimidating as the former Lords Mordecai or Jezaline.

Maybe they were better than they'd been. Or maybe I'd changed.

Still, they weren't here to make friends. The Wilds and Below both stood in a precarious position, and they were here to rip away what chunks of it they could.

"And what is this offer?" I said.

Tannis and Sulien exchanged a quicksilver look, and I had no doubt they'd talked in length about how this might go. Perhaps they'd discussed the best way to take advantage of an Empress newly crowned.

"We're here to make an alliance," Sulien said. "To unite our forces with yours."

"We want to take the Wilds here and establish our own kingdoms," Tannis added.

I forced myself to let the silence build before saying, "And what happened to your Wilds that you need to take a piece of these?"

"All, not a piece," Sulien said and didn't elaborate.

That told me all I needed. Either they'd been cast out of their Wilds or had been on the bottom of the food chain and wanted to claw their way up here.

"We'd heard," Tannis said haltingly, "that this Wilds has been in conflict, but that the worst of it has passed."

I couldn't help giving a wry smile. "I think you've been drastically misinformed."

They shifted uncomfortably.

"Rather than trying to take High King Rune's Wilds," I said, "Why don't you join him as an ally? Or an advisor?"

"Do you really think he'd listen?" Sulien said. "Did he listen to you?"

"That's not what I asked," I snapped a little too forcefully.

Tannis took a step forward. "We've heard many things since Rune became High King. For instance, if he wanted advice, as you suggest, then he shouldn't have disbanded the Council of Loam."

"*I* disbanded them," I said.

They blinked, clearly caught off guard. "The High King gave you permission?"

No. No he had not. But all these Lords needed to know was that I wasn't someone to be tugged around as they were trying to do. "The Council tried to connive behind Rune's back. I took care of that. It's difficult, you understand, to have a Council when the councilors themselves are dead."

They looked disconcerted now, and I tried not to wince. I'd wanted them to understand who they were dealing with, to see me as more than someone who could be threatened. Instead, I might have scared them off from revealing anything more.

"What about Rune?" I asked. "Have you discussed your demands with him? This is my kingdom. You want his."

Sulien's face twisted in annoyance. "Do you really think we could ask him—"

"What if we struck a deal, Empress?" Tannis interrupted. "We'll give you information we have, information you want. And in exchange you will help us out with what we have planned."

Once I could play around with promises, holding oaths to others by the threat of my blade or retribution. As Empress, my words had power and couldn't be given away nearly so easily.

"I promise to listen to your offer," I said. "That's all."

Sulien swelled with anger, but Tannis held up a hand. "And if you find what we have to say useful, then you'll help us?"

"Your information," I demanded.

"We're not the only ones moving to depose the High King," Tannis said. "An attempt will be made to remove him soon, which is why we need to move fast. If we do not establish some semblance of control before he's dead, then it will be a long line of slaughtering every single person who thinks they have claim to the Wilds after he's gone."

They had no idea how many I'd already killed to help Rune take his throne in the first place. They had no idea how far in over their heads they were.

"Who is moving to depose him? When?" I asked. Did Rune know? Could I—would I—be able to warn him?

Sulien merely smiled, and I cursed my over eagerness. "We can tell you more in time, *if* you decide to help us."

I rearranged my expression into something resembling disinterest as I sank back into the throne. "And how do you plan to get a head start on taking Rune's Wilds before he's removed by someone else?"

Sulien reached into his coat and closed his fingers around something. "We were hoping you'd help us. What if you had a way to hurt Rune? To cut him where it hurts the most?"

Keeping my voice even, "Why would I want to do that?"

Their smirks told me my disinterested façade wasn't working.

"We heard you took the throne of Those Below out of a kindness to him," Tannis said. "So that he wouldn't have to suffer the cold and dark as you have."

"Such a noble effort. But Rune didn't see it that way, did he?" Sulien said.

They had me there. I'd often wondered, for one who always seemed a step ahead, how Rune had missed my intentions. Maybe he hadn't. Maybe he hadn't cared. To him, power was paramount, and I'd stolen an entire kingdom's worth of it.

"We're very familiar with those like Rune," Tannis said. "There are many Lords such as him in the Wilds where we come from. They align and woo and love and promise anything to get what they want. But the moment the object of that affection gives up what they desire, or doesn't act as they want, they cast them aside. Or worse."

"And that's why we're offering you a way to ensure he can't do the same thing to you," Sulien said. "Or get back at him if he already has."

I wasn't as mad at them for suggesting such a thing as I was at myself for considering it. What a thrill it would be to hurt Rune in the same way he'd hurt me. To stop having to be afraid of him, as much as I was afraid of myself.

"We have something that could weaken even the High King of the Wilds, enough to bend him to your command." Sulien uncurled his fingers. Resting atop his palm was an amulet, carved of a pulsing heart gem and caged with finely smithed bands of palladium. It glittered dangerously in the light.

"There are beasts in our Wilds who grow to immense size, turned even more ferocious by eating the flesh of a wildling," Sulien said. "To get a heart gem such as this requires it to be carved from their chest while they're still alive, on the darkest night of the year. Only something like this could temper the power of the high king. We will give you this, and we will give you the words to use to trigger its spell."

"It will not give you total control over him, strong as he is," Tannis warned. "But it will stop him and his magic long enough for you to overpower him. When he's under your control, you can make him suffer as you see fit, but don't wait too long to kill him or we won't have time to establish our rule before others are made aware. And when you are done, break his crown, and let only yours remain."

She nodded to my brow where my crown sat, made half of crystal—blended with opal, jasper, and sunstone—and half with jeweled berries and lavender blooms dusted with silver. I'd almost forgotten it was there.

"It should be easy to slip Rune the amulet," Sulien said. "We've been told you are close with him—"

"*Was* close," I said.

"Was," Sulien echoed, sounding less sure now.

"Still, you could gift it to him," Tannis said. "And when he's out of the way, we could gift you a piece of the Wilds for your own."

When he's out of the way. They talked about killing Rune so casually. As though he were some terrible Lord, rather than savage, wild, kind Rune. Rune, who, in those moments of despair when I couldn't imagine being alone any longer, I admitted I still cared for more than I liked.

These Lords stood here and plotted his death, and I was letting them.

"It'd be a simple thing," Sulien said as I started to rise from the throne. He held the amulet out, as though I would eagerly snatch it from his hand. "If he doesn't care for you any longer, then at the very least he trusts you, so getting close won't be a problem—"

Sulien stumbled as the floor cracked beneath his feet. I called on more of my magic. The walls shook. Crystals sprouted in a threatening ring around me, their vicious points facing toward Sulien and Tannis.

I drew more magic until I was left shaking and forced myself to stop. I couldn't risk showing any more weakness. My outburst had nearly revealed my terrible secret: I should have had all of Sotera's power, but I had a fraction of that. My power felt strangled, and my middling connection to the Wilds felt blocked.

"Get out," I said, voice blessedly strong. "And before you try to kill a High King, figure out who it is you're asking for help."

A smirk lifted one side of Sulien's lips. "We already did."

He hung the amulet on the point of one of my crystals.

"We'll leave this here, along with the word to activate it, in case you want a little more time to decide."

"But not too much time," Tannis added. "Otherwise, it will be too late for any of us."

They didn't look the least bit intimidated by my display; they looked like they'd found exactly what they were looking for, even though I hadn't agreed to what they wanted.

At the end of the throne room, Tannis looked back. "Even Empresses could use more power. You know how to get it. You know what you have to do."

And before I could refute her, they were gone.

CHAPTER THREE

I was still shaken by the time I retreated back to my room, the one place in the entire Below I felt safe. Mostly because I could lock myself in with crystal over the door. Nothing short of a full-on coup from General Tenia was getting through that.

Today, I wondered if it would be tested.

I hadn't bothered decorating the sparse room, and there was nothing but the basics: a bed, an end table, an armoire, and new, clear windows that allowed me to see the place I supposedly ruled over. No homey touches. I hadn't wanted to believe I'd be staying here long.

I took a moment to sit on the bed. The brief burst of power had taken a lot out of me, more than I wanted to admit. I removed my crown and turned it over in my hands, watching it gleam.

Maybe I was weak because I hadn't consolidated my power like Rune had, destroying his throne and concentrating all the Wilds' magic into him. Or maybe Rune was somehow blocking me. The Wilds, the Below, the Undersea, all were intrinsically connected. And since the crown I wore was composed of both the Wilds and the Below, maybe if Rune was gone, I'd have access to all the magic I wanted.

My eyes drifted to the bedside table where I'd tossed the amulet Tannis and Sulien had left. Against the onyx stone, the heart gem stood out like spilled blood.

Why had I kept it? I couldn't—wouldn't—kill him, though at one time I'd wished to.

But what if I didn't have to? The Lords had said the amulet would take away Rune's power. If I did that, would it make him less terrifying? And if I did that, was I doing it because I feared him as a potential enemy? Or did I fear him because of how he made me fee—

I stood. I had to keep moving. If I stopped to think, even for a second, it'd give my doubts a chance to pounce.

I removed my hoodie, splattered with the black silt of General Tenia's blood. Within the armoire I took out the only thing hanging up, a coat stitched with living greenery. Down here it had started to wither, cut off as it was from Wild magic.

"I understand that," I muttered, pulling it on. The moment it settled over me, the vines hugged me close, as though drawing strength from the trickle of Wild magic I still had.

I tucked my crown into my pocket, turning it so the thorns didn't prick my side. I never liked having it on, and going up to the Wilds as an Empress now wouldn't help me. I wouldn't be going for an official meeting; I'd be sneaking in.

Should I send another request to meet? General Tenia's mocking voice bounced around in my head. I could send a million requests, but it seemed Rune wasn't going to listen to a single one. If he was going to ignore the next one, I was going to make him do it to my face.

The rational part of me knew this was a massive mistake. This was more than sneaking in to steal heart gems, the way Rune had first found me. I was a ruler now, sneaking into another ruler's kingdom, even if that ruler was Rune. *Especially* if that ruler was Rune.

But the other Lords' insistence that he would be deposed soon called for drastic action. He needed to be warned.

There was a soft rap on the door. When I removed the crystal lock and pulled it open, Raki stood there, looking abashed. Behind him stood the priest of Those Below, Tibald, the one who'd been there for my impromptu coronation.

"Empress," Tibald said, hobbling past Raki and giving me a bow. He was a sickly, thin man, half his body scabbed with sunstone and half his jaw frozen in crystal. "At last I found you."

"You found me," I said, voice dull. With dozens of rooms in the palace, I tended to switch every couple of days for added peace of mind. I never told anyone except Raki for a reason. "*Why* have you found me?"

Tibald had the dignity to look a little embarrassed. "I asked young Raki to escort me to you. I know you, ah, like your privacy, but this was of vital importance. Something you should have been informed of immediately following your ascension."

Though there was no sunlight down here to give me any indication of the time, I knew that it was night in the Wilds above. My best chance of staying undetected long enough to actually reach Rune wouldn't last forever, and every passing day was a greater chance of him getting attacked.

"Can it wait?" I asked.

"Many things can wait," Tibald answered. "But not everything should."

I sighed. "Lead the way."

"Apologies," Raki whispered as I passed. I gave him a reassuring pat on the growths of rocks covering his arm and followed Tibald.

"Why are you just coming to me about this now if it's so important?" I asked Tibald as we walked. His shuffling gait made me impatient to run ahead as he led us through the winding halls of the palace.

Tibald gave a flourishing wave of his hand. "You had other things to occupy your attention. Normally a new Empress has many to help her settle in to her new role. You had very few."

"I had nobody," I corrected, though that was my fault more than anyone else's.

"That is more accurate, I suppose," Tibald conceded. "But between that and dealing with Grislehaut, I figured that this could wait for a time, but no longer."

I considered him. I didn't know the specifics of what religion he served or what he actually did around the palace, only that he'd stayed and hadn't seemed a threat. More than once I'd yearned to ask him for advice, but he'd served Sotera, and I still couldn't fully trust anyone who had.

Tibald led me down a winding staircase of glazed glass. Around and around we went, my annoyance growing every second, until we reached a doorway covered with razor-sharp crystals so tightly interlocked there was no hope of getting past.

"They are nigh indestructible," Tibald said. "Only the current Empress and her blood descendants are able to pass them."

I rested a hand on the crystal and felt a thrum of power vibrate through my arm. The crystals retracted, and we were able to step through. I held in a gasp.

The walls were panels of lustrous black minerals—onyx, obsidian, flecks of cobalt, and veins of lapis blue, all reflecting the light from a dozen crystals floating at various heights. Each were as big as my head and exquisitely carved. I could make out nearly imperceptible threads of light running between each of them.

The crystals didn't feel dangerous, only mesmerizing, and I hastened to take a cautious step in between them. The threads of light vibrated, as though sensing my presence, but nothing terrible happened.

"It is rather astonishing, isn't it?" Tibald was looking around the room with the sort of awe that told me he'd never seen the inside. "Sotera would often lock herself in here for hours at a time. Most often near the end."

He looked at me as he said that, as though I were directly responsible for her death. I nearly had been—I'd *tried* to be—but Father Dumas had made the killing blow. It was just one more of the many things I resented him for.

I circled the nearest crystal, taking in how each angle changed the reflection of the light. "What is this room?"

"I don't know." Tibald shrugged, his shoulders grinding like two pieces of slate rubbing together. "I have never been allowed in. It is my job as head priest to show this to the next ruler, but I was not granted entrance or made aware of its purpose."

Something that Sotera used must have some use to me, especially if she sought it out frequently. Maybe it was simply a place of sanctuary. There *was* something soothing about being in here. Or maybe it held some power I had yet to figure out. Not that whatever it was had done her any good in the end.

"The earth remembers," Tibald said. "I did hear Sotera muttering that a couple times upon leaving this chamber. Perhaps that will help you."

"Not a bit," I said, though I tucked the information away. I met Tibald's eyes, determined to try to make, if not another friend, then at least one less enemy. "Thank you, Tibald. Your

Empress and I didn't always agree, but I'll do my best to use this room well."

Tibald gave a stiff bow, so low it was impossible to see his reaction. "As the Empress wills it. I only hope it serves you better than it did her."

I hoped it did, too.

I suddenly looked up at the ceiling. My connection to the Below was telling me there was someone above here to see me. Someone who was desperate to meet.

"I have to go," I said, sweeping past Tibald.

One of the first things I'd done upon becoming Empress was create a chamber between the Below and the Wilds, a place those on the surface could easily find. Creating it had used so much magic that I'd been sickly for two days after, and not once since I'd done so had anyone come to visit, human or wildling.

I walked into the smooth-sided auditorium. Less than ten feet over my head, through crystal and rock, I could feel the thrum of magic crisscrossing the surface. Close, so, so close.

I missed the Wilds. I missed the green. I missed its dangerous, alluring magic.

I missed Rune with the intensity of a shattered bone. I doubt he missed me all that much. Maybe he missed the chance to get even.

Perhaps he had come here now to do just that.

But when I saw who waited at the bottom of the chamber stairs, my heart leapt. Peyton, my once-guardian, gaped up at me. The lines of her face were drawn and tired, like she hadn't slept in the month since I'd seen her.

"Val," Peyton said, awed. "They weren't lying!"

I felt like a kid getting caught sneaking back inside after a night out. *This isn't what it looks like, I swear. I'm just pretending to be Empress for a bit of fun. It's no big deal.*

Then I saw who stood beside her.

Gracie—the woman I used to traverse the Wilds with, as close to a true friend as I had in the human world—looked as shocked to see me as I was to see her. Her freckled face had paled since I'd last visited her in Seattle, but at least it wasn't the paleness of someone dead, as I'd thought her to be. Her hand dropped from the knife strapped to her side.

Then she crossed to me and squeezed me so tight it was impossible to breathe. When she let go, my face was wet. "You survived the fall," I said. "You survived Sotera."

Gracie let out a breath. "Barely. I didn't have time to grab any of my stuff before they were forcing us out of the city." She sighed. "I had just finished decorating it the way I liked, too. But Val..." Her eyes narrowed, as though trying to puzzle me out. "You were there when Sotera collapsed the city, weren't you? You saw the whole thing."

I was part of it, I wanted to say. *I didn't do more to stop it.* "I'm glad you got out okay. Are both of you all right?"

"We're fine. We've been staying in Castle Rock," Peyton said.

Castle Rock, one of the only surviving human towns within the Wilds. Once, I'd assured those who lived there that Rune would be okay with them staying. I had to trust that Rune followed through on the promise not to hurt them.

He wouldn't. You know him better than that. At least you used to.

"I've been so worried," Peyton said. "Things have been so crazy I didn't have time to get away before now, and nobody I asked seemed to know where you were." She frowned. "But what are you doing here? Why are you meeting us?"

I withdrew the crown from my pocket. If possible, their eyes went even wider.

"I should have known," Peyton murmured. "There were rumors..."

"*I* wouldn't have guessed that," Gracie said. She threw a look at Peyton. "Does this mean... Does this change things?"

"Change what?" I said.

Peyton was silent a long time, staring at my crown until I slipped it back into my pocket.

"You should put it on," she said sharply. "Let everyone know who you are."

"Not everyone is friendly because of that," I said. "Why are you down here?"

"I have to confess that, as much as I wanted to see you, we were looking for the new ruler of the Below. We were hoping, whomever they were, they'd be more amicable than Sotera." Peyton gave a strangled laugh. "We couldn't go to Rune. The wildlings are too busy with their own wars, and he wouldn't help him anyway."

"Help who?" I asked.

"Joshua."

At hearing my stepbrother's name, a hand gripped my stomach and squeezed. "He hasn't come back yet? I thought he'd gone on an assignment for the Department of Fringe Affairs."

When Peyton seemed unable to elaborate, Gracie placed a comforting hand on her back. "That's not technically true. Joshua told us he had something to do for the DFA, but when we got worried and started asking some of them, nobody knew what we were talking about. Nobody even had a clue where he might have gone. Not even Leah."

Leah, Joshua's second-in-command and someone who meant much more to him than that. When she'd told me she didn't know where Joshua was, I thought she'd been lying, unwilling to reveal anything to me, someone she didn't trust in the slightest.

"And he's been gone since then," I murmured.

Shame filled me. The last few times Joshua and I met hadn't been on the best of terms, and I hadn't considered looking for him since. I'd assumed he could take care of himself.

"I can ask around some more," I said. "Maybe someone's lying. He could have been sent on a top-secret assignment."

"There's no need," Peyton said. Her breathing stuttered. "Not anymore."

My stomach tightened further. "Peyton, where is Joshua?"

"The Department of Fringe affairs got word a couple days ago," Gracie answered when Peyton couldn't. "Joshua's been captured by King Bendeti of the Undersea."

CHAPTER FOUR

After Peyton and Gracie left, I parted the last few feet of earth and, for the first time in a month, stepped back into the Wilds.

Relief rushed through me, so palpable my head spun, and I nearly sank to my knees. Just above the immense tops of thick trees, faint stars blanketed the dawn-lit sky like shattered crystal. As I walked, the gold-red eyes of beasts followed me or scurried out of sight into the underbrush. Each step filled me with sensations I'd so dearly missed: the smell of sweet fruit and lingering mist, the brush of rough moss draped from low-hanging boughs.

But for all the joy of coming back, I couldn't relax too much. I had to meet with Rune, whether he wanted to see me or not, but Peyton's visit and General Tenia's continuous betrayal told me I had a couple things to do before then. And I wasn't welcome in the Wilds any longer.

I hadn't walked for more than ten minutes before the back of my neck prickled. I whipped around, starting to draw Sliver, to find branches, thorns, bones, and insect carcasses drawing themselves together around a four-legged beast that had been invisible a moment before.

"Erebus," I breathed. "You found me!"

Erebus gave an agreeing growl. *I did,* he seemed to say. *No thanks to you.*

"I couldn't bring you down there," I said. "I couldn't let you be trapped." *Along with me.*

I moved closer and cautiously parted brambles to scratch Erebus beneath his chin, pretending he was a dog instead of a beast twice the size of a wolf, with thorns for teeth. Erebus seemed to enjoy it, giving off his least-threatening growl.

"I have to find someone," I said, looking around as though the answer would fall from the trees. I also had to move fast, and without Rune to summon a path to walk, I was left with few options. "Do you know where Marian is?"

I do, Erebus seemed to growl. *But why do you need to find her?*

"I need allies, and I trust her." Whether she'd see me or not was a problem I'd deal with when I got there.

Erebus went entirely still, as though rooting himself to the very Wilds. A moment later he dipped his front legs low, allowing me to slide onto his back and grip the snarl of roots at the rear of his neck.

The Wilds blurred as Erebus took off, moving so fast from shadow to shadow that tears streamed from my eyes and I had to tuck my face near the mint along Erebus's back to keep my whipping hair from catching on a passing branch.

More than once I feared that Erebus would suddenly stop, throwing me off, and I'd find Rune and his wildlings blocking my way. More than once I didn't dread the hypothetical encounter as much as I should.

Eventually, Erebus slowed enough for me to pick my head up and see we'd stopped at the edge of a sunny glade sprawling with wildflowers white as snow, yellow as pollen, red as blood. Everything seemed serene, and I felt like an intruder about to desecrate a holy shrine.

"Thank you, Erebus."

He growled. His debris dropped to the forest floor, and a moment later the cold feeling of his shadow settled itself near my collarbone.

I dared to step out of the trees and strode on the worn path through the flowers toward a small but homey cottage in the center. It looked Wild-grown, not built over any prior human dwelling. Steam rose from small pools of hot springs at its back.

I'd nearly reached the front door when Marian came limping around the side of the cottage. The lower half of one of her legs had been replaced with sinuous white roots like a fibrous prosthetic, stark against her dark skin. She gripped a cane wrapped in delicate flowers.

She saw me. Stopped. Nearly dropped the basket of tender young greens and roots she must have collected. An unreadable expression crossed her face.

"Marian—"

Marian limped inside. The door shut firmly against me.

I sighed. I hadn't expected this to be easy. And I couldn't pretend I deserved a welcome reception, not after what happened.

Still, I approached the door and knocked. "Can we talk? Please?"

The door seemed to stiffen. I started to knock again before it gave in and opened slightly.

"Not sure why you're asking, *Empress*," Marian's muffled voice answered.

The door opened all the way by itself, and I walked inside. "I'm just Val, you know that."

Marian scoffed from somewhere at the back of the house. "And I'm just a helpless little forest nymph. Whatever you have to say to make you feel better, Empress."

Inside was magically more spacious than the exterior. There were no stairs, but instead ramps and small lips that were easy to clear. A small reading nook was to my left, set before large, sun-lit windows and shelves of scavenged human books. The ceiling rose two stories overhead, strung with vines and nests filled with singing birds.

"Rune made this for you?" I asked in awe.

"Know anyone else capable?" Marian was unloading the items from her basket at a woven table, handing bundles of what she'd collected to the vines as they reached down to help her.

When she was done, a vine grabbed the basket and hung it alongside other household items above. Marian brushed past me to the reading nook. "What do you want?"

I pulled my eyes away from the vines. "I could just be coming to see you."

Marian gave a harsh laugh. "A social visit? Please. You and Rune always want something."

Selfish, both of you. Marian had told me once. *Everyone wants something for themselves.*

I feared she might still be right.

A couple of the vines shooed me aside and started rearranging the items in the cupboards. I was forced to stand in the doorway of the reading nook, trying to think of something to say.

"You left Rune after all. You'd talked about doing so, but I didn't think you actually would."

"There was no reason for me to stay. Not as useless as I was." She gave me a look filled with such venom I nearly recoiled. "Not after what happened with Olette."

Olette, the wildling girl entrusted to my care. I had only been able to watch as she'd been impaled by Sotera. Her body had transformed into a menagerie of animals as Mother Mal preserved her spirit, and I'd been left with a profound sense of guilt ever since.

"Does Luella—" I started.

"Luella knows what happened to her daughter," Marian said. "She sent an echo bird asking for Olette soon after you took the throne. But *you* weren't here to tell her what happened. I had to do that. Was that planned, by the way? Taking the throne?"

"Would it make it better if it wasn't?" I asked.

Marian's smile was falsely sweet. "Not at all. I'll bet you're regretting it."

More than she knew. "I did it to protect Rune. I didn't want to."

"But you did. And now Rune's pissed. And now here you are, asking me for..." Marian waved her hand. "Whatever it is you want."

"Knock, knock."

The front door sprang open by itself, and Cassius walked in. The smile on his face beamed nearly as much as his copper hair. He carried what I recognized as a flask of pain tonic, the kind General Forcheck brewed.

"I got your latest deli—"

He froze when he saw me. "Val! Does..." He peeked outside. "Does Rune know you're here?"

"Good to see you too," I said. "And no. I'd prefer it stayed that way."

"I told you I could get those for myself," Marian snapped at him. "I have to have *something* to do."

Cassius just smiled and let a vine carry the tonic away. "Sure you do."

"How's the High King's army?" I asked. Cassius, along with his grandmother General Forcheck, had been working to get the separate wildlings factions into a unified fighting force.

Cassius hesitated, and I wondered if he believed I was asking to get info on an enemy.

"Just tell her," Marian snapped. "You really think she's going to march up here and face off against you?"

"They're doing well enough, at least when they believe they'll be fighting King Bendeti or Father Dumas," Cassius said. "Others are scared, mostly the ones who never truly stopped believing in the wildling religions. After all, you can be as well-trained and strong as possible, and it won't do anything against a god."

"Rune means to take on Grislehaut?" I said.

Cassius gave me a strange look. "Don't you?"

Of course I did. Alone. I'd assumed that was what Rune had resigned me to, but now I wasn't so sure.

Cassius moved to the kitchen and started rearranging a few things he apparently didn't think the vines had properly tucked away. I was happy to see him here, and not just because he was visiting Marian. His haunted past had left him with a bloodlust that most wildlings who'd endured as he had never truly escaped. If he'd found some solace from that here, then I was happy for him.

Cassius finished straightening up. "Well, if you two are busy..."

"You're not leaving yet, are you?" Marian said as he stepped back outside.

Cassius poked his head back in, smirking. "Would you like me to stay? Again?"

Marian glowered at him.

"I'll keep making myself useful until you're done," Cassius said.

"That's impossible," Marian called. Her gaze snapped to me. "Rune doesn't know you're here? Like, at all? Have you talked to him once since you took that stupid throne?"

"I tried. Apparently, he doesn't want to talk to me."

Once, Marian would have been happy about that, wanting Rune for herself as she had.

Instead, her frown only deepened. I waited for her to berate me about how Rune and I *deserved* each other and all our strife, as unsettling and true as that might have been.

"Are you happy here?" I asked when Marian returned to sulking instead.

Marian looked out the window, and it was as though she was alone again, left with only her peace. The glower on her face smoothed the wrinkles and scars, transforming her into a girl ten years younger, a girl who hadn't been forced to endure the things she had. Who hadn't survived all that, only to get a fraction of what she'd been promised.

Then her expression clouded again.

"I was happy," she said. "Until about five minutes ago."

I let the sting slide over me. "If you are, then I won't ruin that. This is the least of what you deserve."

"You make the sound like a threat." She snapped her fingers at me. "Are you going to say your piece or what?"

"I was," I said. "Until about a minute ago."

Marian's scowl deepened. "Then say it. This is *my* place now, and nobody will ever claim I'm not a good host. I don't want you complaining later that I didn't at least listen."

As briefly as I could, I told her about all that I'd dealt with since becoming Empress. About General Tenia's treachery, the Lords pressuring me for my help. About Grislehaut, and how, despite having hundreds of subjects, though they were scattered and mostly civilians, I was more alone than I'd ever felt.

By the end I felt scraped raw, and Marian's expression hadn't shifted in the slightest.

"I need people I can trust, who have my back," I said. "I trust you. Even if you hate me, I trust you."

Marian snatched a bottle of tonic from a vine that carried it over. I winced as she downed half of it, remembering its bitter taste all too well.

"Have you actually gone back to visit Mother Mal?" I asked.

"That damned meddler? What for?"

I shrugged. "I feel I need to. To check on things."

"What's the point?" Marian asked. "It's a graveyard, just like every other place in the Wilds."

I stood. It was clear my time here was at an end. "I need to make things right. Rune and the Wilds aren't out of danger yet. None of us are."

Marian took another swig. "That stopped being my problem a while ago. I've paid my penance more than most."

"I agree," I said.

"Where are you going?" Marian called as I headed to the door. The entire house seemed to turn toward me, to watch what I'd do next.

"I have to find someone," I said. "Someone close to me."

Marian's cane thumped on the ground as she pushed herself up. "You're thinking of doing something stupid, aren't you?" She sneered. "You think you're being so *valiant*, so *selfless*. But what you're really going to do is get whomever it is killed. You either have to keep people close enough to protect them or keep them away so they don't get hurt. But you can't bear doing that, can you? It's all about what you want."

"I agree. I'm tired of hurting people." I glanced back at her. "But if you ever think I'm worth helping again, I could really use you."

Marian leaned on the table, fiddling with the handle of her cane. “Please. I’m useless. I can’t help anyone.”

The door opened on its own, and I stepped outside. The sun had warmed the sky, burning off the mist in the glen. Deep in the surrounding trees, an animal screamed.

“Maybe I’m not the only one who needs to stop being selfish,” I said.

Marian glared daggers at me. “More people are going to get hurt,” she called as I walked away. “More people are going to die. And you won’t be able to stop it, no matter how hard you try.”

I knew that as certain as anything, and the reality of it ate away at my heart.

CHAPTER FIVE

Cold dread and a sense of impending death settled in the pit of my stomach as I summoned Erebus and directed him toward where I could enter the Kingdom of the Undersea.

We kept along the coast, making it easier to stay headed in the right direction and less likely that Rune or other wildlings would try to stop us. If not for being up here without permission, then to try to stop me from doing something I'd doubtless regret.

A few miles before I had to stop, I leaned down and shouted over the wind, "I need something here, Erebus!"

Erebus ground to a halt. I dismounted and stole into the grove of small trees. Growing in sporadic clumps at their base were rows of thick, tuberous plants. General Forcheck had once brought me here, showed me these plants, spirvelt, in preparation for fighting the Undersea if Bendeti ever flooded the land.

I knelt and, with a crystal knife, cut a few of the tube-like stalks free. They were thick and waxy, and if swallowed, they gave the ability to breathe underwater. For a short time, at least.

"Use these for defensive purposes only," General Forcheck had cautioned. "Only a fool or someone with a death wish would attack a king in their own kingdom, especially the Kingdom of the Undersea."

I finished tucking the spirvelt into my jacket. I didn't have a death wish. I guess that made me a fool.

I settled back on Erebus and urged him toward the northwestern-most point on the peninsula, a place humans had once called Neah Bay, and the shoreline closest to where I could enter the Undersea. During my times poring over maps with Marian and Cassius, discussing advantages and weaknesses of the various kingdoms, another thing I'd picked up was the most likely location for King Bendeti's palace. If Bendeti had Joshua prisoner, the most likely place to find him was in the cold, dark waters at the mouth of the Salish Sea. There, Bendeti could be closest to the Olympic Peninsula and what had once been Victoria, and attack either whenever he wished.

After twenty more minutes of riding, Erebus stopped us at the edge of the Wilds and retreated near my collarbone. I stepped out on a rocky shoreline. Salt spray frothed over the black rocks. I swore I caught the silver crest of a fin farther out in the darkened waves.

Now that I was here, panic caught up with me, clamping down on my lungs as though I'd already descended to the bottom of the ocean. I had no idea what I was doing. There was an improbably small chance this would work. Yet asking Rune to help me save someone he'd tried to kill—and had tried to kill him—on more than one occasion seemed laughable. Even the DFA was incapable of rescuing Joshua now that he was in the clutches of the Undersea. It was either me or leave him there to rot.

Before I could reason myself out of it, I withdrew one of the spirvelt and took a bite. It tasted as appetizing as cardboard, and its rough edges scraped my esophagus as I swallowed.

I stood there for a few minutes, waiting for something to happen. Maybe the Wild magic had stopped working for me. Maybe it had rejected me as much as Rune—

Pain stabbed into my neck, so sharp I wondered if I'd been pierced with an arrow.

I fell to my knees as my breathing constricted. I reached for the skin on my neck where the worst of the pain was. The tips of my fingers found small holes, rigid along the edges, as though the spirvelt had stabbed straight through and stinted it open. Small bubbles like blisters bulged from the skin, sensitive to the touch.

My need for air grew even more desperate, and I clambered toward the waves, determined not to drown on dry land. I waded in as far as I could manage before casting myself in headfirst.

The dark water crashed into me like a weight being dropped on my chest. The cold wrapped my limbs like chains, and it was only when I allowed myself to sink to the bottom and touch the sand that warmth started to seep back in.

The water was a sea-glass green so dark it was difficult to see more than ten feet in front of me. But as I began moving along the bottom, the water transitioned to a languid blue. If I stayed near the bottom—closer to the Below, I guessed—the cold didn't stab quite so much, and even the saltwater didn't sting my eyes. I could also move reasonably well, mostly unaffected by the whims of the currents. I certainly wouldn't be a match against any of the Undersea or Bendeti himself, but I wouldn't be entirely helpless, either.

I kept moving. The bare ground near the shore gave way to shallow canyons between boulders, covered with spires of rosy coral and crusts of urchins. Fields of sea grass waved in the current while crabs scuttled between my feet. I could see, in the darker depths, the enormous outline of a whale, followed by a clicking call.

I headed in the direction I thought was right, following paths of current-strewn sand. General Forcheck had never told me how long the effects of spirvelt lasted. I could only hope I'd be able to find Joshua and get him out in time.

I emerged from the next canyon and immediately ducked back inside. A patrol of Bendeti's guards, clothed in lobster-shelled armor tipped with dogfish spines, zipped past, dragged behind gray, bullet-sleek sharks. I waited until I was sure there were no others behind them and took off running, kicking my feet to gain extra momentum. They had to have somewhere nearby they were coming from.

I crested the next reef and floated to a stop, a surprised stream of bubbles pouring from my neck.

In the distance was Bendeti's palace, carved out of an enormous mound of sea rock. Shipwrecks, from galleons to metal cruise liners, circled the outside. Their masts and iron sidings acted like palisades, keeping out anyone foolish enough to attack.

I kept to the sea floor and crept closer. The palace had few walls, and inside I could see an auditorium with pearl floors. Gentry floated amongst each other, all of them glittering with scales, gold, and ornaments they'd likely scrounged from the sunken vessels. Multi-colored fish and crawling octopi dotted the castle walls, and in deeper water, sharks circled.

I ducked as more guards swam by, and I watched to see where they'd go. If Joshua was in the palace, there would be little to hide me.

Instead, the guards veered toward a kelp forest reaching over a hundred feet toward the thin sun at the surface. Within I could see metal chains attached to floating cages. I kicked toward it, my heart speeding up.

I easily lost myself in the kelp and hurried along the bottom, staring up at each of the cages I passed. I recalled Zuri, Xander's beloved, telling us she'd been trapped in one of these, left shivering and alone for days on end. And she was one of the Undersea, more used to the brutal cold and dark.

I moved faster, checking cage after cage. A graveyard full of skeletons littered the sandy bottom, and my stomach tightened as I stepped over each one. Something I hadn't let myself consider until now seeped into my thoughts: Joshua could already be dead. I could already be too late, a month too late.

Then I saw familiar blond hair splayed against the bottom of the next cage. The current tugged it to and fro, though the rest of his body remained deathly still.

I kicked off the bottom until I could grip the side. "Joshua!"

My voice came out accompanied by a stream of bubbles, and each time I opened my mouth there was a moment where the water rushed in and pressed on my lungs; it felt like drowning. "*Joshua*!"

Joshua didn't stir for a moment. Then he uncurled his shivering body to look at me.

"Val?"

A bubble had been fastened over his mouth, and with every gasping word it deflated and was slow to refill. There went my plan to feed him spirvelt. He'd begin drowning the moment that bubble ruptured; this deep, and in his condition, not even Wild magic would save him then.

"You're..." Joshua's chest fluttered while the bubble took an agonizing long time to refill. "...here."

"And you're hurt," I said.

Joshua cracked a tired grin, so unlike the confident, cocky one I knew. "I'll admit I've been better."

He sat the rest of the way up, and I squeezed the bars tighter to keep from recoiling.

Bendeti had already been to him, perhaps multiple times. A thin cloud of crimson leaked from Joshua's left arm. It looked shredded, as though shaken in the jaws of a shark. His face was puffed with bruises and dotted with infected spots where someone had repeatedly jabbed poisoned barbs.

"You shouldn't be here," Joshua said. "If Bendeti catches you—"

"I already know that," I said. "I'm here to get you out."

A pause, longer than was needed for his air bubble to fill. "Why?"

"That's a stupid question. You're my stepbrother."

"Not lately. Lately we could barely call each other acquaintances. Are you here as my stepsister, or for that High King?"

I was amazed he could still muster the energy to say Rune's title with such disdain. I removed the crown from my jacket pocket and showed him. "I'm here for you, as your family. And I'm not entirely helpless."

Joshua stared at the crown. "It's true, then. Father Dumas said you'd taken the throne, that it could ruin things."

I tucked that tidbit away, for when we were both out of here and Joshua didn't look as though he was on the verge of death. "Is he why you're here?"

Joshua lay his head back, exhausted. "When I went to see him, I didn't know how involved he was yet. Didn't know what he was capable of. I was DFA, supported by the government, and he knew me. But none of it mattered, especially since Sotera had practically destroyed Seattle by that point. The second I found out that he was working to free a god, the moment I told him to stop, he gave me to Bendeti as a gift for their new alliance."

Joshua squeezed his eyes shut. "I was such an idiot, Val.

Peyton was the believer, but I let Father Dumas get away with so much, thinking it was harmless. He had vast knowledge about the Wilds, so I even let him get involved in DFA affairs. Whenever something seemed off, I bought his every assurance that he was just a harmless priest worshipping a dead religion. We both know now he was anything but. Father Dumas had a plan from the start. He was even there when you were created."

Bubbles trickled out of my mouth as I gaped. "Created. Like...he's my father?"

Joshua's chuckles turned to racking coughs. I double-checked no guards had swum by to check on us.

"Nothing so crude," Joshua said. "When I was a kid, I thought you had another mom and dad, ones the Wilds killed. Of course I believed that. I was a kid, and anything different would have been impossible. You were human after all." He met my eyes. "We both know better now, don't we?"

You never had any parents, Peyton told me once. *Not as far as we know.*

"It doesn't matter who my parents were," I said. "It doesn't matter that they weren't human. That doesn't change the fact that you're my stepbrother—"

Joshua was shaking his head so hard he created a new current. "That's not what I'm trying to say. You—"

He was struck by another bout of watery coughing. Speckles of blood sprayed the inside of his air bubble.

"Whatever it is, tell me later," I said.

"You and I both know there won't be a later," Joshua said sadly. "I'm a hard man to kill, but I know when I'm finished."

I pulled at the bars as though I could wrench them apart. "Stop talking like—"

"Listen to me, and listen closely." Joshua pulled himself up. Face to face, the full extent of his injuries was impossible to ignore. He wouldn't last much longer down here. "You listening?"

"I'm listening," I said.

"It won't just be Grislehaut. All the Wild's gods are wanting to return, just like in the days before."

"Before the Forming," I finished. "The Cataclysm."

"I'm sure Rune told you that," Joshua said. "I don't even think Bendeti knows what he's helping with. Grislehaut will be the start. Once he's free, it'll be a chain reaction. Every god that the wildlings didn't slay, all those beings that hid in the dark places of the Wilds, biding their time, every single one that wants the world to go back to the terrible way it was, they'll come back. They'll destroy everything. Whatever Grislehaut doesn't decimate they'll take for themselves. There won't be any place left for you."

"Then we'll stop Grislehaut," I said. "Together. Now back away from the bars."

"Val, no." Joshua tried to catch my sleeve. "I'm not making it out of here. But I need to tell you something, and you need to leave."

"Shut up and step back," I said, drawing Sliver and raising it above my head.

"Val—"

He fell back as I sliced at the lock. It took a couple hard swings, but eventually the door swung open and I wrested my shoulder beneath Joshua's. He resisted at first before letting his head sag against me.

"You should leave me," he murmured. "After all I've done to you—all we've done to each other—you should leave me to rot. But I'm glad you're not."

Together we floated out of the cage.

Right as one of Bendeti's guards came around the kelp.

He startled and gaped at us. Then he cut through the water

toward me, spear leveled. With Joshua at my side, I barely managed to twist away. The guard flipped around in an elegant loop. Right as he brought his spear around, Joshua kicked out at him, ramming him off kilter. As the guard tried to reorient himself, I drove Sliver through his throat.

The guard gurgled a stream of bubbles and blood before going limp. I pulled my sword and let his body slowly drift to the ocean floor.

"We need to go," I said. "The blood will bring the sharks."

"Them, or worse," Joshua agreed.

I was reminded of the sea serpents Bendeti had summoned against Rune. Suddenly, every deep shadow was a coiled, slick body. A gaping cave of teeth.

"Val, I can't move fast enough," Joshua insisted, but I ignored him, leveraged myself under his shoulder again, and started moving swiftly across the ocean floor.

"My stepsister, the Empress," Joshua said. "It has a fitting ring to it. What's it like?"

"More trouble than it's worth," I said.

"I'm proud of you. If I don't get to say anything else, I wanted to say that."

"Stop making it sound like you're dying."

Joshua grimaced, a small trail of blood leaking out from between his teeth.

We threaded through the kelp forest and then between the canyons of rock, heading as fast as I could carry us back toward shore. Killing the guard seemed to alert the ocean that we were intruders, and it felt as though the current itself tried to hold me back. Fish began to gather, and wolf eels poked their heads out of holes in the rocks and bit at my ankles. I sliced the heads off the ones I could reach, leaving an even more obvious blood trail in our wake.

"Val, wait," Joshua warned, right before I stepped out of

cover and in plain view of an entourage of guards. They were pulled by more sharks and flanked by schools of sharp-toothed fish. In the center was a lone orca, and on his back...

"King Bendeti!" I hissed, shrinking back. There was no mistaking his seaweed-like hair, his blue skin the color of a drowned man's. There was certainly no mistaking the gawdy dressing of glittering shells and pearls. "What's he doing here?"

"This *is* his kingdom," Joshua said.

"You know what I mean. Why's he headed toward the cages?"

"Perhaps coming to visit me." Joshua peeked out. His expression darkened. "In fact, I know that's where he's going. Father Dumas is with him."

As the group floated over us, I spied Father Dumas on the back of Bendeti's orca. Bendeti must have granted him the ability to breath in a way different than Joshua because there was no bubble over his mouth. He'd removed his usual cloth cap, and his long hair danced in his wake. On one hand he'd affixed a gauntlet glowing with power. One of the heart-gem infused weapons he'd created.

"I still don't understand." King Bendeti's words floated down to us. "You had the girl and that ridiculous high king right where you wanted them. If you'd killed them, then we wouldn't be having this problem!"

Father Dumas gave an acquiescing nod. "I'll admit that was an oversight. I wished for them to be there at the end to see it. I didn't anticipate them being any more trouble, the girl especially."

"There's always trouble when it comes to Rune," Bendeti snarled. "And that girl is even worse. If I'd been there, I'd have cut their throats and fed them to the waves. I want that boy king dead. What happens to the girl is your concern."

"Which is why we're going to speak to her delightful stepbrother," Father Dumas said. "He's been Below. He may know how best for you to flood it."

"You'd better ask good questions. He doesn't have long."

A school of fish had risen from the reef beside us and begun to circle the procession. Bendeti waved a hand at them, as though placating a crowd of adoring citizens. "I hope you don't need Rune for anything else. I've already taken steps to ensure he will die."

"Is that right?" Father Dumas said, looking amused.

"It was simple to engineer, really," Bendeti said. "In a way, your oversight provided the opportunity. His downfall needed to be from within. From someone close. He and that new Empress will end up destroying each other. He'll be dead by the end of the night."

"And why would she do that?" Father Dumas said.

"She wouldn't. But she won't be around to stop it."

The school of fish around Bendeti circled more frantically. King Bendeti cocked his head. His smile grew predatory, like a shark fixated on his prey. He turned toward our hiding spot. "In fact, I aim to ensure she won't."

"Val, go!" Joshua urged.

I had already taken off deeper into the canyon of rocks as Bendeti's procession started to turn our direction. Now I could see Bendeti's plan in perfect clarity. Joshua had been bait. They'd likely let slip that he was here, knowing I'd be told and stupidly come to save him, bringing me into their clutches and drawing me away from Rune. Drawing me away from whomever King Bendeti had sent to kill him.

"Faster," I said to Joshua. It might have been easier to move near the ocean floor, but as we sprinted toward the next cluster of coral reefs, Joshua wheezing at my side, a long shadow passed overhead.

I drew Sliver and stabbed upward on instinct, spearing through the open mouth of a shark as it charged at me. I tugged my sword free and sliced at another circling. Behind them, I could see Bendeit's guards forming up, a pod of orca flanking them. Bendeti's expression was hungry as he commanded them toward us.

"Val, leave me," Joshua panted. "They're too fast. You'll never get away with me holding you back."

"Shut up," I gritted out and then kicked us into an inlet of coral, tucking us out of sight where nothing but the smallest of fish could reach. Joshua's chest was heaving, his eyes glassy.

"Can't...breathe."

All the running had nearly depleted the bubble around his mouth, and it wasn't refilling. I looked frantically around. I could make out the streaking rays of the sunlight pouring from the surface. Just ahead, across a fifty-yard stretch of white sand and sea grass, was the shoreline. We were so close.

"We figured you'd come, *Empress*," Bendeti's mocking voice drifted to me. "Your heart was always too soft for what needed doing. Your beloved Rune is likely dead now. I wish I could have seen the look in his eyes as you gave the killing blow."

"Come out, child," Father Dumas said. "It's over now. You don't need to make this worse."

"Tell them to go to hell," Joshua said. "Father Dumas especially."

"Stop talking," I said. "Conserve your air."

"It won't be enough. I have enough left to tell you—"

"Joshua, stop, I don't want to hear—"

"I spoke with Rune, after you gave me the hint about Sotera attacking Seattle."

Shocked, I nearly missed the sleek shadow of a shark as it cruised by. I sank farther into the cover of the reef. "*You* went to see him?"

"He found me." The corner of Joshua's mouth quirked up. "Don't look so shocked. I'm thickheaded, but I came around in the end, enough to talk to him, at least. He cares for you. I think you both care for each other more than you'll ever admit. More than I'd ever admit, at least."

His breathing had grown shallower. I tucked him close as he began to shiver. "Guard yourself, Val. Please don't let yourself get hurt."

No matter how much I held him, Joshua's shivering wouldn't stop. The shredded cuts on his left arm had started bleeding again.

"Val," Joshua said quietly. "I need you to kill me."

"We're getting out of here." I checked outside the reef. More sharks and barracudas had begun to circle. Bendeti, Father Dumas, and the rest of the guards were nearly on us, flanked by the orcas. Bendeti was waving his hand, and currents whipped through the reef, trying to push me from cover. We didn't have long before I couldn't resist him anymore. "We're almost to shore."

Joshua only wheezed in response. His bubble of air was nearly gone, and after that he'd die a slow, agonizing death as water filled his lungs.

Just like me, I realized, struggling to take my next breath. My throat was growing tight. When I brought my fingers to my neck, I could feel that the holes had started to close. I had minutes left, maybe.

"I'm nearly dead already," Joshua said. "But I won't let them chew me up. You can make it quick. You can make it painless."

I at last let his words register.

"I *can't* do it." My throat tightened even more. My tears were hot against the cold current. "I won't."

Images flashed through my mind: Joshua's still-living body

toyed with by orcas or picked apart piece by piece by fish, one tiny bite at a time while Bendeti kept him alive.

Joshua stared past me, to the light of the surface. "This is as good a place as any. I can see the sun. Better than that damned cold." He gripped my sleeve. "Before he gave me to Bendeti, Father Dumas said something: When he is one, he will sleep."

I shook my head. "I don't know what that means, Joshua."

"I think it has to do with Grislehaut. Father Dumas thinks you can do something to stop him, something he didn't see before, and that scares him. You have to get Grislehaut to go back to sleep."

I'd already tried that. It hadn't done any good.

"Strike hard and true." Joshua's eyes softened. With a trembling hand, he found my cheek, found the warm tears running there. "I'm so, so proud of..."

"Search the reefs," I heard Bendeti order. "Turn over every rock and slither through every crevice. Flush them out."

The last of the bubble over Joshua's mouth vanished. He started to hyperventilate, his eyes going wide. When he spoke, nothing but bubbles escaped, but I could read his lips.

Please Val. Please...

My fingers were wrapped in the back of his shirt. *Strike hard and true.* It'd been one of the first lessons Joshua taught me in the backyard those summer mornings when Peyton wasn't around. He'd patiently showed me how to grip a knife and then a sword. I'd barely spoken during those first few years, but those lessons were as good as any communication. The time he'd spent with me said how much he loved me.

Strike hard and true. Not even enemies deserve to suffer.

I placed a shaking hand over Joshua's chest, steadied it against his flesh. I made sure he could see my lips. "I love you."

Then, feeling as though I was cutting off a part of me, I shot a sliver of crystal straight through his heart.

CHAPTER SIX

"I said to flush her out!"

Bendeti's voice meant nothing to me. I couldn't breathe. Not just because the spirvelt had almost run out, but because it felt like my lungs, my heart, and everything else inside me had been ripped out. My tears were hot against the cold water pressing my skin. My rage was a building inferno.

Nothing but a thin trickle of blood leaked from the hole in Joshua's chest. His glassy eyes stared up at the surface, his lips frozen in a final soft smile. I looked away. If I didn't, I might choose to die here with him.

Aware of Bendeti and his sea creatures closing in every second, I quickly tucked Joshua's body deeper into the crevices of the reef where he wouldn't be found. I would return when all this was done and bring him home.

"Come out, girl," Bendeti taunted. "I'll make it quick."

He'd do no such thing. But then, were I in his situation, I wouldn't either. After what he'd done to Joshua, that was a promise.

I crept to the edge of the reef. My best hope still lay in

getting to shore, but it'd be nearly impossible with how surrounded I was. I needed a bit of time.

Another shadow drifted over me, and I twisted to see a shark darting for me. I barely had enough time to drive Sliver through the bottom of its open jaw and up into its brain. I held tight as its death throes eventually subsided before drawing a crystal knife and slicing it down the rough skin of its belly. I let it go and intestines and a cloud of blood bloomed through the water, quickly taken up by the current and creating a smokescreen of red.

As one, the rest of the sharks swarmed this new feast. Through the red haze, I could see my path to the shore was momentarily free.

As Bendeti roared at his creatures to forget the meal and go after me, I took off. My feet dug into the sea floor, kicking up the sand and sea grass to obscure my escape. A sudden current pummeled me sideways. I managed to right myself in time to see a second whirlpool form at my back. Bendeti had dismounted his orca and was shooting toward me with terrifying speed, a malicious hunger on his face. He thrust his hand out, and a jet of water gouged slashes in the sand. Part of it cut my arm. More blood spread.

Through the stinging cuts and failing air, I had nearly made it to shore when some of Bendeti's guards cut me off. His sharks circled closer but didn't strike, waiting for their master's command.

Bendeti laughed. He looked back at Father Dumas. "I will say this, human, you have insight. Her stepbrother was the best gift you could have given me." To me he said, "You failed to see that you were nothing without Rune, and you are nothing now. Not even being an Empress will change that."

I glowered at him, trying not to show my desperation as my air slowly leaked out.

"I could let you drown," Bendeti mused. "But I've learned already the consequences of not doing the job properly. You have been a thorn in my side from the very beginning, and now with you and Rune gone, there's nothing standing in my way."

A whirlpool swirled in the center of his palm, growing larger by the second. He aimed it at me. "Goodby—"

Rune had told me once that there was no place the Wilds couldn't reach, only places where its magic was weakened. Here in the desolate depths of the Undersea, I'd felt the magic of the Below right beneath my feet. Now I called it to me.

Spears of blue crystal erupted from the sand, cleaving fish and flesh alike. Sharks turned belly up, their skulls pierced. Bendeti's guards fell, skewered through their lobster-shelled breastplates.

One of the crystal spears pierced Bendeti's arm, and his whirlpool whipped off track. The worst of it shot past me like a boat motor chopping the water, and the residual force shoved into me like a bus.

I was launched the rest of the way to the surface and cast onto the sand, landing hard enough to punch the last of the air from my lungs. For a moment I clawed at my throat as the lingering spirvelt vanished, before I could at last gulp mouthfuls of sweet air.

Sopping and shivering, I swayed to my feet and limped toward the relative safety of the Wilds' trees. A sucking sound made me look back.

The surf had retreated, building to an enormous wave three stories high. At its crest was Bendeti. Even from here I could feel the rage of his gaze directed at me.

I'd barely started running before a wave hit the shore.

My feet were swept out from under me. Saltwater and sand filled my nose and threatened to drown me a second time as I was pummeled into a tree. My back hit bark, and I let out a gurgling scream.

Then the water retreated, and I was dropped to the ground. My spine twinged unpleasantly.

"Erebus..." I managed, crawling to my knees. "I need you."

"I know that didn't kill you," Bendeti called.

I blinked a dozen times until my vision cleared and I could make him out on the shoreline just beyond the edge of the trees. His guards were headed my way, scanning the trees for any sign of me.

"You're too disgustingly resilient to die so easily," Bendeti continued. He made a gesture to something I couldn't see. "But this should do the job."

I stumbled to standing, feet sinking into the soaked pine needles and mud. "Erebus?"

A shadow passed over the tree beside me. Relief seeped into my bones. "Thank goodness. Hurry, we need to—"

The words died in my throat as the head of a sea serpent, neck thick as a telephone pole and scales the color of the darkest depths, curled around the other side.

I held in a scream and pressed myself against the trunk, not even daring to breath. I imagined the serpent's yellow, slitted eyes flicking this way and that, seeking any sign of movement. The cold shadow of Erebus crawled to the spot on my collarbone. I swore he was trembling.

Wait, I urged him. *Not yet.*

Erebus let out a growl.

The serpent snapped our direction, and Erebus lunged off me. On instinct, I drew Sliver and brought it down on the thinnest part of the serpent's neck, trying to aim each strike between the cracks of its interlocking scales. Blood sprayed across my front. The serpent hissed and wrenched its head back before darting forward again. The tip of its fangs scraped the top of my arm, burning like a stream of fire. I threw myself aside, and it drew back toward the sea, still hissing.

"Bring her to me." Bendeti seethed. "Let me rip her into pieces!"

The serpent struck from behind. I managed to turn just enough that the side of its gaping mouth clipped me before closing around the tree where I'd stood and biting it in half.

I hacked again, trying to aim Sliver inside the earlier gouge I'd made. The serpent attempted to draw back, but it had trespassed in the Wilds and the Wilds had lost patience. The trees themselves closed in, holding its head in place.

I put everything I had behind one final swing. At last, the serpent's head was cut free and hit the forest floor, the severed end of its neck steaming.

Erebus growled approvingly. Bits of the serpent's fallen scales joined the forest detritus that covered his exterior. He knelt to let me on.

Time to go.

I gaped at the serpent's sightless yellow eyes before Bendeti's roar of anger shook me from my trance.

I slipped onto Erebus's back and gripped tight. "Run. Now."

THE DAYLIGHT WAS strong enough that even with sticking to the shadows beneath the trees it wasn't long before Erebus couldn't go any farther. He barely gave a growl of warning before the ferns and tightened thorns of his front legs were unraveling. I pitched forward, nearly slicing my cheek open on the edge of a serpent's scale and landing hard in the dirt. Erebus's shadowy form curled near my collarbone and growled an apology.

"It's okay," I reassured him. "You did good."

Truthfully, it was lucky he'd thrown me off here, wherever here was. I'd been so desperate to flee from Bendeti I'd automatically directed Erebus deeper into the Wilds, rather than down Below where I could recover and plan how I might approach Rune. Or perhaps I'd done it intentionally. Despite how much Rune didn't want to see me, I needed to warn him. I needed to make sure he was safe.

Riding on Erebus had somewhat dried my clothes, though a salty film caked my skin. Dozens of cuts from coral and Bendeti's assaults stung every time I moved. I bit my lip and hurried as fast as I could deeper into the trees. I had no idea where Rune had settled, but I knew I wouldn't have to look long. Here in the Wilds, something found you eventually.

Sure enough, less than ten minutes later there was a flutter like a bird taking flight, and Pitius, one of Rune's spies, was suddenly perched on the branch overhead. Her eyes widened.

"What are you doing back here?" she breathed, voice wispy.

More wildlings peeked out from behind her, some tall and bent like willow branches, others with skin like green saplings, all of them expertly blended with the scenery. I recognized a few, though it was impossible to tell whether they thought me friend or foe. I could take another step and find three arrows in my chest.

"I need to find Rune, Pitius," I said. "I think he's in danger."

The wildlings stirred. Pitius's brow furrowed, crumpling the persimmons in her hair. "I don't understand. You were just there."

I blinked. "What are you talking about? I just arrived."

"When I left camp, Rune was speaking to you, and I thought whatever you had to say was done." Her voice pitched higher. "*You* came to find him, Val. He said you summoned him."

For a moment I gaped at her, a terrible realization dawning on me. "But that wasn't..."

Before I could finish the thought, Pitius vanished in a flash of leaves, and then I was running after her, throwing aside the branches and thorns that tore at my clothes. Bendeti had pulled some trick. There was no other way I could be in two places at once.

In a way, they'll end up destroying each other. He'll be dead by the end of the night.

My lungs burned. My abused body begged me to stop, but still I kept after Pitius as she flickered through the tops of the trees. All too soon I could sense others hidden around us. Wildlings shouted as I ran past where they'd been positioned to keep watch, hopefully at the edges of Rune's camp. They converged on me.

"It's Val!" I yelled, hoping at the very least it'd make them pause, if only for a moment. "A friend!"

Not entirely true, but the claim was enough to slow some. But not all. I cut right, barely evading a pair of knives thrown at my head.

I could make out a clearing up ahead with more wildlings waiting for me there.

I cut right again. I needed a vantage point, somewhere I could get words to Rune without taking a knife or arrow in my back.

My eyes traced an enormous tree, one of its leafy branches reaching across the clearing. I scrambled up the rough bark. The stinging cuts from the Undersea screamed at me, and more than once I tore the skin of my fingertips off.

The leaves up here were thick enough I was able to obscure myself at the end of a limb. I peered below.

Rune's new camp mimicked King's Hollow, where the old throne of the High King once sat. Enormous fir and maples dipped into cerulean blue lakes, encircling a cleared center.

Rune sat at the head of the hollow. He'd crafted a new throne, this one less gawdy than the first. There were no jewels, gold, crystal, or thorns. All that power belonged now to the crown atop his head.

Rune himself lounged back, legs crossed on the arms in a pose of ostentatious indifference I'd never quite managed to mimic. His expression was smug as he scrutinized the figure kneeling before him.

It was me.

I gaped at myself. I was here, and I was kneeling in front of Rune. Whatever magic had made it possible had impersonated every detail, from my clothing to the scars along my arms.

I leaned forward, still trying to make sense of things. I hadn't felt any brush of enchantments as I raced in here, which meant this camp must have been so brand new they didn't have time to cast them. Rune was more exposed than he could have ever guessed.

Rune leaned forward. His smirk had turned to a frown. He said something I couldn't hear, and fake-Val raised her head. From this angle, I could just make out a slight glisten on her skin. Like tiny crystals. Like salt.

It was one of Bendeti's spies. Some were shapeshifters, good enough that one just like this had once tricked me into revealing secrets about Mother Mal to a fake-Rune. Good enough that Bendeti had used the same trick to exploit Rune and my relationship a second time.

Rune said something again, this time louder. Pitius landed at his side, a moment before the wildlings I'd evaded earlier found me. One crept closer, raising a sword point toward me.

"Don't move," he warned.

"She what?" Rune said, ear cocked to Pitius.

The moment he looked away, fake-Val plunged a hand into her jacket, withdrawing a knife made of hardened sand and flecks of glass. She leapt at Rune.

I threw myself from the tree, Sliver in my hand, landing hard enough that I swore my femurs jammed into my ribcage. Rune had already drawn spewing thorns from the earth and created a shield to protect himself.

It wasn't fast enough.

Fake-Val's knife flew just past his throat, and I swore my heart stuttered to a halt in my chest. I brought Sliver down, and fake-Val screamed as I cut off her hand. She whirled on me, enraged.

"He promised me you'd be dead!"

"I'm surprisingly hard to kill," I said.

More of Rune's wildlings surrounded the clearing. Fake-Val hissed as she hid her hand, but already I could see the seawater dribbling from it, turning red like blood. Her expression transformed into agony.

"Who is this?" she screeched. She held up her falsely bleeding stump. "Look at what she did to me, Rune! Kill her!"

I snarled as I leapt at her, but she managed to evade me. "If you can't tell the difference between the two of us, then you deserve to be attacked," I yelled at Rune. "Take a good look."

Rune's eyes flicked between us both. "Two Vals. I'm having trouble deciding if this is my wildest dream or most terrible nightmare."

"You know me," I pleaded. I raised my arms in what I hoped was non-threatening enough to not get me shot full of arrows. "Rune—"

"She's going for her sword," Fake-Val yelled. "Kill he—"

Cold spray speckled my face. I tasted salt on my lips.

Fake-Val stumbled back, shocked, as Rune withdrew a thorn as long as my arm from her gut. He smiled wickedly.

"Looks like I chose right."

Fake-Val stumbled back and then recovered. "Whether it be a High King or an Empress, one of you dies tonight."

She charged me. My stomach felt as though it were ripping in two as I summoned crystals between us, trying to slow her down. Up here the pain was worse, like fire through my veins.

Fake-Val slipped around my defenses, and then I was helpless as she regrew the hand I'd sliced off and brought her fingers together into a knife-sharp point. I raised Sliver up as she plunged it at my chest.

A spear of ice appeared through her throat at the same time Rune punctured her chest with another thorn. Fake-Val gurgled, eyes wide. She slumped down Rune's thorn before her body erupted into a fine, misty spray, further coating my face and tongue with salt.

"Looks like you're more useless than I thought, *Empress.*" Marian pushed through the surrounding wildlings. She glared at them. "None of you could have made that shot? And you expect to protect the High King?"

I spun on Rune. "You were *guessing* which one of us was real? You could have killed me!"

"As you said, you're hard to kill," Rune answered, not looking the least bit disconcerted. "And I knew from the moment that fake entered my domain that it wasn't you. Though I was curious about what it had to say."

"And if you were wrong?" I asked. "If you hadn't been able to tell it was me?"

Rune gave a throaty laugh. "I'm wrong about many things, but I would never be wrong about that."

He stared at the spray coating the grass and then up at me, his gold-red eyes filling with fury. Only now, with the high of battle wearing off, did I realize the predicament I was in. I stumbled up, prepared to run.

You can't keep running. Not from him. Not forever.

"Val?" Rune's voice was a hard question.

As though compulsion had grabbed my limbs, I froze. My heart beat a frantic rhythm, each thump painful. Had I believed that saving him would change things back to the way they were?

No, I'd wanted this. I'd wanted to force Rune to confront me after a month of silence.

I straightened and turned back. More wildlings surrounded me, including the shocked faces of Cassius and Raquel the beastmaster. Others were perched on trees or slinking through the underbrush, covered in cloaks of feathers and moss and living greenery, complimented by silver bands and flakes of gold that glinted as sharply as the weapons they carried. They were dazzling and dangerous. An entourage fit for the High King of the Wilds.

Rune stepped before them all. Now that I allowed myself a good look at him, he was even more dazzling than any other, his smirk sinister and alluring in equal measure.

"That fake kept trying to get me alone," Rune said. "If I hadn't guessed it was just trying to kill me, I would have thought it was for other reasons."

My face flamed. Rune's smirk grew.

"How unfortunate it was a fake. You were groveling and making so many delicious promises." He gave a shallow, mocking bow. "Now, Empress, you will tell me why you're in my kingdom."

CHAPTER SEVEN

My mind had gone horribly blank. In my imaginings of our meeting just like this, I'd had a dozen clever things to say, accusations to make, promises to lie about. In every fantasy I'd been in far more control than I was now. I could apologize. I could demand a formal meeting, as I'd tried to do a half dozen times before. I could ask him if everything had changed between us, or if there was still a chance to salvage what little we had—

"Val?" Cassius asked. He was looking quizzically at me, and I realized I'd been staring at all of them for the better part of a minute.

"It's good to see you all," I managed. "Glad most of you are still alive."

"I believe I asked for an explanation," Rune said, voice pitched low. The underbrush crowded me further, barring my every escape. For as much as I lacked control over my own magic, apparently Rune didn't have the same problem. "You shouldn't be here. So why are you?"

In those same fantasies, I'd imagined him uglier and

meaner than he ever was, something to make me feel better. Unfortunately, he was even more savagely beautiful than ever, lips cocked in a villainous grin, as though waiting to devour whatever I said next. His circlet woven of silver thorns, raven's feathers, and jeweled berries was brazenly crooked and snarled within his hair. His gold-red eyes drank me in like a parched man stumbling across an oasis. When he tilted his head up, I caught the glint of a scar along the hollow of his throat.

"Your time Below has taken your speech away," Rune said. "What a shame. I always thought your sharp tongue was your most dangerous weapon."

"I request a meeting," I breathed out, finally managing to get my lips to work. "As Empress of Those Below, I request a formal meeting with the High King of the Wilds."

"And what would the high king get out of this?" Rune said, not missing a beat.

"I *saved* you," I said, exasperated. "I should get an audience."

"Technically, you already got one," Rune said.

Marian rolled her eyes. I didn't grace his answer with one of my own but held his gaze. I knew he was mad, but at some point that had to end. We had bigger problems to deal with than our own petty grievances.

"Rune," I said. "I'd like to speak with you."

"Is being a ruler not all that you wished?" Rune said, eyes narrowing. "Do you hope to make a new deal and bargain for more?"

"You know why. I've spoken with Grislehaut, and he's growing more powerful by the day. We need to figure out something before Father Dumas finds a way to free him."

For the first time, I saw a flash of surprise in Rune's face. "You spoke with him? Is that possible?"

I winced, remembering Grislehaut's icepick-like pain in my

skull. "I assure you it is. Now can we talk, or are you going to keep sticking your fingers in your ears every time I send an official summons? I wouldn't have snuck up here if you'd have stopped acting like a child and answered me the first time."

I sought out familiar faces behind me, trying to feel as though I wasn't alone in this. But even if my former friends were here, they couldn't do anything. It was up to him.

"Leave us," Rune commanded the others.

"Are you sure that's a good idea, my High King?" one of the wildlings asked. She glared at me. "What if she's up to something?"

Rune scoffed. "Of *course* she's up to something. We both are. That's what makes this fun. Now go."

With one final glare my way, the other wildlings started dispersing. Marian limped over to me. Her eyes sought out my bleeding side. "Is that fatal?"

"I'll be fine. How'd you know I'd be here?"

"How'd I know you would come see Rune?" she asked. "You two are drawn to each other like stormfronts, and only slightly less destructive when you meet."

I wasn't sure what to make of that. "Thank you for coming back. I know you didn't need to, but it means more than I can say."

Marian managed to scoff in a way that made her sound both embarrassed and so, so done with me and my requests. "Don't make me regret it. I only hope there aren't too many more attempts on your life. They get exhausting."

I told her how to reach the Below and where to find Raki and General Tenia; then she, Cassius, and the rest bled back into the greenery and Rune and I were alone. He jerked his head, and I followed him. After a few minutes walking, we reached a mirror-still stream reflecting the stars at the edge of a moonlight-washed glen.

"I'll ask you again: what are you doing in my Wilds?" Rune said. "Was the power you took not enough? Have you come to ask for more?"

I'd expected him to be mad. He even had a little right to be. "As high king you gave me a promise once," I said. "You gave me a home here. Safety. Security."

"*As long as those last*," Rune finished. "I remember that part of my promise, too. And what if those promises have run out?"

"Have they?"

The weight of his gaze settled over me. "That depends," he said at last. I didn't dare ask him what it depended on.

He stepped closer, and I was reminded of a time not too long ago when I yearned to touch him, to want the slide of his lips over mine and the searing press of his hands against my back and hips. For a wondrously terrible moment, I thought he was going to embrace me in that same way. Then his expression darkened, and I understood. We'd hurt each other again. This time perhaps more than could be fixed.

"You look..." Rune appraised me. "Like you're missing the sun. Like you haven't had a full night's rest." One eyebrow cocked. "Like you've spoken with a god."

I tried to keep the venom from my voice. "I wonder why that is."

"Then you got what you asked for when you made your choice to take away Sotera's thron—"

"Let's *not* do this, okay?" I said. "It was mine to take as much as it was yours. If anything, I deserved it *more* than you, so if all you're going to do is throw blame around, then we have nothing to talk about."

We eyed each other, both bristling with anger.

"You won't answer any of my official summons, so I had to come here," I said.

Rune waved a hand. "I've been busy. Ambitious humans,

rising gods, the surviving Lords of my Wilds as hungry for power as new chicks are for a meal. They want more land, more from me."

"I'm aware. In fact, some Lords from other Wilds just visited the Below."

I wished Rune looked more shocked about that than he did. He hadn't reach the dizzying heights of High King by being dismissive of potential danger. "I'm sure they had some very interesting propositions for you."

I recalled the amulet sitting on the bedside table in my room. The one I hadn't thrown out yet.

"They'd like to remove you. Very soon," I said.

"Then they'll need to get in line," Rune said. "There are others who are trying to beat them to it. As you saw, some were here tonight." I could see his mind putting the pieces together. "What's strange is that Bendeti is free to try to kill me at any time he wants. So why now, moments before you show up?"

Before I could pull away, he took one of my arms that had been sliced by Bendeti's whirlpools. An ache that had nothing to do with my injuries shivered over me as he ran his fingers across the cuts.

"These wounds are encrusted with salt, and not from the spy who tried to kill me," Rune said. "What have you done?"

"I took away one of Bendeti's bargaining chips," I said. "I learned that he meant to attack you and foiled him. Again."

Something I swore might have been pride flickered in Rune's eyes. "You have a knack for bringing ruination to every plan he has. Still, I can't imagine anything so important to risk going to the Undersea..."

I wouldn't tell him what I'd done to Joshua. Not yet. I still hadn't fully come to grips with it myself.

After I didn't fill in Rune's silence with answer, he dropped my arm and disappeared back toward his throne. He returned a moment later. "Kneel at the stream bank."

"Excuse me?"

Rune's grin was petulant. "Please, Empress. It'll be easier."

I tried to look as dignified as I could as both of us sank to our knees in the soft grass. The sound of trickling water worked to soothe my raging thoughts and the exhaustion of the last few hours. Joshua's death—and my part in it—was like the ache of a fractured bone; it was there in the background, dull but sharp and unbearable if I rested too much focus on it.

Rune pulled out a purple salve I saw Keen of the Mysts use. This he applied on the worst of the bruises I'd received, which were starting to yellow. I tried to distract myself with the beauty of the low-hanging moon as he blended eclipse flower for the pain with grubber's root for potential infection and started applying the mixture to the worst of the cuts.

"The salt will sterilize them enough," I murmured and then hissed as he put another fingertip on the worst of the cuts.

Rune said nothing. I could still feel anger radiating off him. If he wouldn't be bothered to talk, then I would ask what I came here to ask, and he would have to deal with that as he would.

"What happens if someone manages to..." A lump rose in my throat. "What happens if all those trying to kill you succeed? You're carrying the power of the entire Wilds with you."

"I'm not entirely sure," Rune said, as though the thought of him dying and all that power being released was a moderately distracting quandary. "General Forcheck told me that, after the last high king was killed during the Sundering, there was the Night of Knives. When the high king's crown rotted into the dirt and the throne refused to accept a new ruler, all those desiring his power stood over his body and piece by piece carved him and ate—"

"Enough, Rune," I said.

Rune smiled wickedly as he finished rubbing salve over the last of my cuts. "My power will go to everyone. It will go to no one. Maybe those ambitious Lords of the other Wilds who visited you will get their wish."

"Grislehaut won't stop at just destroying the Below," I said. "You know that. We have to figure out whatever Father Dumas has planned now that he and Bendeti are working together."

Rune took his time methodically tucking the last of the healing materials away. "I think you have it well enough in hand. You deal with your problem, and I'll deal with mine. You need to return to the Below."

I tried to grab his wrist as he stood, but Rune was too quick. I wanted to scream. I wanted to pull my hair out. "We have to work together, Rune!"

"We did, once," Rune said. "We had an alliance, but that's gone now."

"Why have you really been ignoring my summons?" I demanded.

He turned back, and our eyes met in the dark. For just a moment, I swore that one dripped black like ink, the other a vibrant blue. The residual consequence of him donning the crown of both the Below and the Wilds Sotera crafted. The one I currently held.

I got to my feet, wincing a little at the remaining aches. "Give me the truth. Why have you been ignoring *me*?"

"There was a reason I told you not to take more power than you could handle," Rune said, sounding as though he was trying to restrain himself from yelling. "I told you not to take the throne of Those Below. Do you know why that was?"

I was left gaping for an answer other than the most

obvious one. "You always want more power. *Always*. You didn't want me taking that away from you."

Rune shook his head, the ghost of a smile tugging at the corner of his lips, like I'd missed an obvious joke. "I wasn't sure if your summons were for me or what I could do for you." His expression sobered. "Sometimes I don't recognize you anymore. I don't think you do, either."

Then he was gone, leaving me stunned. It was only a while later, when I was on my way down Below, before I realized he'd never answered his own question.

CHAPTER EIGHT

The moment I returned Below, I retraced my steps to the crystal chamber beneath the palace. I'd guessed right, and much like the shards of magic-charged crystals Qell had once used to heal my bones, so too the luminous glow of this room had some healing properties. And I needed it. I had a deeper ache within, like I was a doll and my stuffing had been pulled out.

I sank against one of the smooth, dark walls. The salve Rune had used to heal me—now dried—tugged on my skin as I pulled my knees to my chest and pressed my forehead to them.

Only here, alone with no one to listen, did I let myself cry.

I cried for Joshua and his lifeless body tucked at the bottom of the sea.

I cried for what Rune and I had done to each other, that we couldn't even speak like we once had.

I cried for myself and the chasm of loneliness that threatened to swallow me up. To all the world-ending problems I didn't have answers to.

Someone whispered.

I pulled my head up, wiping at my eyes, and cocked my head toward the impenetrable walls of spikes that guarded the room's entrance. Had someone called my name? I could still hear faint whispering, but not from out there.

I turned my attention to the floating crystals. There were still nearly invisible threads of light stringing between each one.

I got to my feet, not taking my eyes off the crystal. "Is someone there?"

The crystals bobbed and twinkled. *Come play*, they seemed to say. *Come see all that we truly are.*

While Tibald the priest may have had no clue about the function of this room, I had a few guesses, knowing Sotera as I had. The crystals could have been an old way to transport royalty across the Below, or once maybe even above.

More likely, they were used as a way to spy wherever she wished. Sotera had managed to grow crystals along thin chasms in the Wilds long before she made a move against Rune. Perhaps she'd used those to see what was happening before she struck.

I approached the nearest crystal, hand outstretched. Could I see what Bendeti and Father Dumas were up to with this? Could I see what Rune was doing, even if he wouldn't see me?

I touched the nearest crystal. My fingers buzzed.

It began spinning without warning, nearly pummeling the side of my head. I ducked, but the others were spinning, faster and faster, pulling my magic from me like a thread unspooling.

"Stop!" I cried, unsure of what else to do. "That's enough!"

I grabbed the next one swinging by, and it halted in midair, nearly yanking me off my feet. Voices erupted around me.

"—have one chance, even if there are consequences."

Sotera stood beside me. In an instant, I drew Sliver and backed away.

Sotera and the voices vanished.

I looked about the empty room. Now that I wasn't so panicked, the details of what I'd just seen were starting to register. That had been Sotera, but she'd looked as ghostly as a faded memory, the imprint of what she'd once been.

The earth remembers. I did hear Sotera muttering that.

The crystals didn't spin the next time I touched them, and Sotera's sudden appearance didn't startle me so much. Her ghostly visage stood within a crystal room of the palace reflected on the onyx black walls. Sotera finished speaking to someone I couldn't see before walking out of the room, and the image faded.

The earth indeed remembered. These must have been her memories; perhaps the memories of all the rulers before me. A way to unburden their thoughts, leave behind lessons—or warnings—for those after them.

I pushed the crystals to the left, ready in case they tried to take my head off again. Back and back I rewound the memories until someone I'd never seen before appeared. I paused and the scene began playing out.

"—this can't work!" Sotera said.

I was shocked by how young she looked. Though her face was still inhumanly beautiful, there was no cruelty pinched at the corner of her eyes. Her flesh was pale and partially see-through. The crystal half of her body hadn't yet been marred by spiderwebbing cracks.

"Grandmother—" Sotera tried.

"That's Empress Lavena," the old woman snapped. "Especially to you."

Sotera bowed. "Empress, we have no idea what a god could want."

Empress Lavena, an older, crueler version of her granddaughter, laughed. "What do all beings want? Power, that's what. And since it's trapped down here as we are, then it also wants freedom. So while we're stuck together, why *shouldn't* we use it?"

I slowly removed my hands from the crystal and walked between the two of them while Sotera bit at her lip, worried the sleeves of her coat.

"He's a god of the Wilds—"

"The very Wilds where we should be!" Empress Lavena spat. In two strides she'd crossed to Sotera and ripped at her hair, forcing Sotera to her knees with a cry. "We belong up there, not them. If it weren't for their treachery, we would be! So don't come mewling to me about it being 'right' or the consequences of what might happen."

Empress Lavena threw Sotera aside. "I don't know what will happen if we try to use Grislehaut's power to free us. But I *do* know what will happen if we *don't*. Show me your arm."

Sotera shrank back. "I won't."

Empress Lavena moved toward Sotera, and she flinched back and relented, pulling up a sleeve. Though these were memories and long past, I held in a gasp at the yellowing bruises along the flesh parts of her arm and partially melted crystal along the other. Someone had beaten her, badly, and pressed hot metal, or worse, to the rest.

Empress Lavena pulled the sleeve up farther until the few splotches of Sotera's flesh began fusing with crystal. "How long until the crystal consumes you? How long until we're nothing but statues that can barely breathe?"

Empress Lavena dropped Sotera's arm in disgust. Sotera hurried to push the sleeve back down, taking care to ensure it covered every inch.

Her grandmother watched her do this, a cold gleam in her eye. "Are those marks the work of your new husband, or are you going to tell me they were training accidents again?"

Sotera tilted her chin back.

"Answer me," Empress Lavena said. "Is he cruel?"

Sotera's lip quivered. "He's vicious. More than you can imagine. Nothing satisfies him. Nothing except seeing me in pain."

"Good. Then he is turning you into what you need to be. The weak will not thrive down here."

Empress Lavena sneered. "That is why your mother didn't survive. That is why I've been saddled with her equally spineless child. And if this doesn't work, when I die, all of the Below will be doomed to your incompetence."

"I'm not weak like her," Sotera said through gritted teeth. "I'm *not.*"

"Good." Empress Lavena appeared pleased. "Then you just might survive."

I looked away, unwilling to see more, and the crystal spun to the right, moving forward in time. As much as I'd despised Sotera, it was still tough to watch someone treat her in much the same way she'd treated me. Maybe she had because she sought to make me stronger. Maybe she hadn't known a better way.

The crystals stopped, and Empress Lavena stumbled back into the room. I was startled to see her covered in burns and splintered cracks along her arms. But she was smiling. In her hands she cupped wisps of blue magic that looked light as air, with a bright white core at the center. Though the magic flickered when she moved, like a fire in a strong wind, it didn't go out.

"I've done it," she said.

Sotera had stood the moment she'd entered. Her eyes were wide with fear. "It's not possible."

"Only to small minds and the weak," Empress Lavena

snarled. "Send the guards away. Now!" she snapped at Sotera, who hastened to step out.

Empress Lavena lay the wisps of blue on the floor. They didn't disperse but stayed collected together, centered around that white core. The magic danced in Empress Lavena's eyes, flickering over her triumphant expression.

She began muttering words. The entire room shook. Though I couldn't see it, I was sure the entire palace, the entire city of the Deep, the entire Below, shook as well. It was tectonic plates shifting. It was the earth ripping apart.

It was only when an enormous roar sounded, one that tore through my mind more than my ears, did Empress Lavena fall silent. Everything stopped shaking, and a terrible, horrible foreboding filled the silence.

Sotera stumbled against the door. Her face was terrified. "What have you done?"

"You down here?"

I blinked. It took me a second to realize the second question came from the present. As though reading my mind, the crystals dimmed and the memories blinked out of existence.

Marian waited for me outside the room.

"That gritty old priest told me where to find you," she said.

I stared at her, trying to remember what she was doing here. *I* had asked her to come, that was right. At the moment, my head was filled with little else but Sotera's memories.

Marian frowned at me. If possible, she looked concerned. "You there? You haven't been sleeping, have you?"

Focus, Val. There would hopefully be time to break down everything I'd seen later. "I haven't been doing a lot of things."

As though a dam within had broken down, a swell of emotions raced to the surface. I threw my arms around Marian.

"What're you—" Marian raised her cane, as though to fend off my affection.

"I'm glad you're here," I murmured into her shoulder. "Even if you didn't want to be."

Marian didn't hug back, but she did relax. "I couldn't let you get in that last barb without doing something about it."

I released her, and Marian took in the room behind me. "You haven't made up with Rune, have you? If you had, he'd be here instead."

"I want you with me, too," I said firmly.

Marian cocked an eyebrow, waiting.

"But, no, we haven't made up," I admitted.

"Didn't think so. You two work best together." She looked a bit sour saying the words. "Always got things done. He told me once—"

Marian's lips puckered, as though Rune's words weren't hers to tell. I could guess a few things Rune said about me recently, none of them pleasant.

"Well, he's not here, and he won't speak with me," I said. "I'll make do with what I have."

"And how exactly do you plan on stopping a god from rising?" Marian said. "You have a plan?"

No, I did not. I didn't even have a clue where to begin. I would continue scouring Sotera's memories later, but I had little hope they'd reveal anything useful. Sotera had been desperate to escape before Grislehaut's rise. If she hadn't found anything, likely I wouldn't either.

Marian began limping back up the stairs with me close behind.

"I didn't come just to say hello. General Forcheck's here to speak with you, if you want. To give counsel."

"*Here*? Below?"

"That's where we are, isn't it?"

"I didn't think Rune would allow her to help me."

"Let's just say he didn't *not* tell her to come. So she insisted, if only for a short time."

I was shocked but delighted. To have the famed General of the Killing Green and now General of the High King here to help wasn't a small thing. I'd taken her presence for granted when I'd been with Rune. I'd taken so much for granted that I wouldn't now.

"We'll meet her in the throne room," I said.

Marian turned the corner and stopped. "Who are you?"

General Tenia stood there, hand resting on the cudgel at her waist. She sneered at Marian. "I see another insect has infested the Below."

"Marian's helping," I said. "Since my own subjects seem unwilling to."

Marian gave me a questioning look. General Tenia forced herself to give the smallest of bows, her expression growing grave. "There's something you should—"

"You can share it with all of us," I said, brushing past her. "In the throne room."

General Tenia gave an indignant snort. "I have more important matters. Empress."

"Maybe you do. I won't command you to join. But I want you there. You know the Below far better than me, and I could use as much wisdom as I can get."

General Tenia clearly looked as though she were trying to come up with any excuse to disagree but couldn't help appearing pleased. "For a moment, then."

General Forcheck was already waiting for me in the throne room. Though I wouldn't dare hug her, the appraising, almost kind look she gave me was enough. She made a slight bow, as much as her old joints would allow. Her heavily wrinkled face split into a wide grin.

"I see you've done little to warm the place up. Perhaps a

nice throw rug could accent the walls. At the very least, it could cover the cracks."

I couldn't help smiling back, grateful at her attempt at levity, terrible as it was. "You'll have to bring me a catalog next time you're here, and I'll put in an order."

"General of the Killing Green," General Tenia said with some respect as we all took places around the crystal table in the center of the room. "If half the stories I've heard are true, I suppose I can only be grateful we aren't meeting in battle."

"You must be fierce yourself if the Empress has requested you here," General Forcheck answered.

Not her most subtle flattery, but General Tenia appeared pleased regardless before reverting to her usual stern displeasure. "King Bendeti has increased the flow of water down Below," she said without preamble.

"Then he'll drown this place just a bit faster," Marian said.

"He's concentrated it." General Tenia looked pointedly at me. "He's working on flooding the chamber where Grislehaut resides."

"He can't drown a god," I said.

"He's not intending to," General Tenia said. "I believe he means to break the chamber and old magics keeping Grislehaut trapped within it."

"A place infused with power," General Forcheck guessed. "I'm sure this chamber is specially strengthened with wards, enchantments, and conjurings built within the framework. Not easily broken by themselves, but if the very structure they've been infused with goes, then there's little for the magic to latch onto. And you, Empress," she said to me. "You can't reinforce the chamber itself?"

I could barely use any strong magic of the Below without consequence. Something I didn't feel comfortable sharing with General Tenia watching me closely.

"No, even if it weren't already underwater."

"How much time do we have?" Marian asked General Tenia.

She braced her hands on the table, thinking. "Bendeti has a great sea, but the chamber is vast and the Below even more so. We had three weeks before this. Now? A couple weeks, maybe, before the chamber gives. Killing King Bendeti would stop it, or at least give Va—The Empress time to secure the Below."

General Forcheck looked delighted. "It is good the High King of the Wilds shares your thoughts on who needs to die. Killing is an elegant solution, though I'm obviously biased."

"It doesn't make sense," Marian said. "Bendeti and that stupid priest are going to free Grislehaut and destroy *everything*."

"I don't think the human believes it will destroy *him*," General Forcheck said. "Either that or he doesn't care. That's the thing with zealots; either they believe their lives are worth far more than others, or far less. Both are equally dangerous mindsets."

"We need to kill King Bendeti first," I said. Even voicing it aloud seemed too monumental a task, but I had to see a clear path forward, *something* that didn't make me feel hopeless. "After that... I don't know."

"We move to kill the human priest, obviously," Marian said.

"I'm not sure how that'll stop Grislehaut," I admitted.

"Killing kings and killing Lords is your specialty, Empress of Glass," General Forcheck said. "Why not take the next step to killing gods?"

General Tenia gave me a surprised look. I wondered if she'd heard of what I'd done before facing off against Sotera. I doubted it would change her opinion of me.

"Get Those Below to higher chambers," I told her. "Make sure they're as far as they can be from the rising seawater."

If possible, General Tenia looked even more shocked, though she quickly composed herself. "There isn't much higher we can go."

"I will show you," General Forcheck said. "There are places close to the surface. As close as you can get without talking to High King Rune, which I will do."

"I'll do it," I said, holding in a sigh. "I'm Empress; it has to be me."

"I was under the impression that you two just spoke," General Forcheck said. "And yet here I am instead of him."

"Let's put it this way, Rune didn't say I *couldn't* speak to him again. Only that he thought we had nothing to talk about. That's as open an invitation as I could ask for. He respects you, General Forcheck, but he'll want to hear the begging from me."

General Forcheck laughed. "I daresay he would, though I doubt he'll get much. Very well, let's start getting Those Below above and worry about the High King's anger after."

"Very well," General Tenia said. She turned to go.

"I'd like you to keep an ear open for anyone else trying to make an attempt on my life," I called after her. "That includes you. I need you to have my back if we're going to keep Those Below safe."

General Tenia smirked. "I will do you the courtesy of announcing my next attack." She bowed, and I could almost believe it was sincere. "As the Empress wills it."

Marian laughed the moment General Tenia had left. "I like her."

"She didn't expect you to care, Empress," General Forcheck said. "Despite her treachery, you haven't killed her. You might have yet learned some diplomacy that doesn't involve blades."

"And you think I'm stupid for that?" I wondered.

General Forcheck raised her cane in a mini salute. "Not at all. May it keep the knife out of your back for one more day."

I couldn't bring myself to even crack a smile. "Tell me, General Forcheck, as the one here with the most wisdom."

General Forcheck cackled. "Just say that I'm old, Empress."

"Am I...forcing things that aren't meant to be by asking for alliances? Is it better to be alone and safer or together but unsure of who has your back?"

"You've already begun to answer that question for yourself. Your tenacity never had doubts before this; don't let it start now, against a foe such as a god."

That wasn't as clear an answer as I was hoping. "What happened the last time Grislehaut was free? What happened during the Cataclysm?"

Even Marian looked somber as General Forcheck weighed her words. "I believe the name says it all. I am sure of this: none of us want to find out."

CHAPTER NINE

Now that I'd somehow got Marian on my side, if only for a bit, my confidence was at an all-time high. I was going to need it, and I was determined to keep the streak going.

Since neither Marian nor I could create a path to quickly transport us, it took an hour of uncomfortable riding on Erebus's back before Marian and I left Rune's Wilds. Marian had directed me to a place along the coasts, where Xander had told her he'd be staying with his former group, the Mysts.

"He's just as pathetic as you," she'd told me when I'd asked for Xander's whereabouts. "Came sneaking back into Rune's Wilds once I'd settled into my new place, begging to speak with me again."

"And did you?"

"I still haven't forgiven him," she'd answered. "But I don't want to slit his throat anymore, either."

I heard Marian yell for us to stop over the whipping wind, and I urged Erebus to a halt. Marian stumbled off and shrugged away my help as he melted back into our surroundings.

"This it?" I asked.

Marian finished dusting off her legs with the tip of her cane and looked around. "Looks like the place."

We'd entered a grove of moss-draped trees dusted with dew and smelling of mint. Fire scarred the trunks, and thickets created narrow channels of greenery, easy to slip into and vanish. There was no sound except for the wind and the crunch of pine needles beneath our feet.

"Keen," I called out. "I'm here to speak with Xander."

"You realize this is a terrible idea," Marian muttered. She hadn't stopped scanning the trees. "Keen's alliance with Rune—and technically you—is over. He holds no allegiance to anyone."

I was well aware. And while I didn't think Keen would full-out attack me, I wasn't going in as unguarded as Marian seemed to think.

I called for Keen again, and almost immediately the air stirred. Cloaked figures in gray fabric that looked like collected clouds emerged quicker than a breath around us. I found Keen, his usual irksome smile on his face, lounging on a branch just overhead. His hair was a thunderhead of silver-gray, his entire body transparent as a light shower.

He made no sound as he landed in front of me and brushed his cloak aside to give a sweeping bow. "Greetings, Val. Or should I say, *Empress*. I didn't think we'd ever see you again."

"You only hoped you wouldn't."

Keen nodded in agreement. "That, yes. But mostly I thought you'd be dead by now.

"So you've told me before," I said wryly. "I'm here to see Xander."

"Who needs to talk to me about what?" Xander appeared behind him. The last I'd seen of him had been in a stuffy, noisy Thai restaurant in what remained of Seattle. Out here his wildness was more apparent than ever. Nubs of horns curled from his head, creating whorls in his hair. He must have grabbed a bow on the way out to see me, and his heavily calloused fingers were wrapped around it. Two deep, scarred gashes scored his left cheek—the reminder Rune had carved on his face that Xander was a traitor and would be killed the moment he returned to Rune's Wilds.

The very thing I needed to convince him to do.

Xander's face broke out in a smile when he saw me. "Val! And looks like you persuaded Marian to leave her cozy abode. Not sure how you managed that."

"With thinly veiled insults and the guarantee that she'd get herself killed if I didn't step in," Marian grumbled.

"I was hoping to speak with you, Xander," I said.

"Of course," Xander said. "Unless..." His expression darkened. "If it's anything to do with Rune, I can't help you."

"Can we talk about it?" I hated how pleading my voice sounded.

"I'll let you stay for a short time," Keen said. "Even outside Rune's Wilds, there are dangers, and you seem to attract more than most, *Empress*."

Xander's eyes widened, and I realized my newly acquired title was information he might not have received yet. "It seems we have a lot to talk about."

"You could help us, Keen," I said. "Work to make everywhere less dangerous. You were invaluable to Rune, and now you could be invaluable to me."

Keen's smirk was indulgent. "Flattery? How different from the threats and knives you used before. But no, I don't think so. I've heard what slumbers deep in the caverns of the Below. We Mysts know when to fight and when to cut our losses and run."

"There might not be a place to run if we don't fight," I pointed out.

Keen's smile grew. "Threats of a different kind, then. Let us each choose our own path and see who survives in the end."

He vanished into the trees. Xander parted the greenery, and Marian and I followed him to a common area with a stump for a table, glazed with use. Zuri, Xander's beloved, emerged from a nearby pool. She shot him a questioning look.

"Val has a proposition for me," Xander said.

"Then the very least we can do is listen." She gave me a hug, her body chilly as the coastal wind. "We both owe her everything, after all."

Not that long ago, I'd saved Zuri from Bendeti's clutches in a way I hadn't been able to save Joshua. There was nothing more I could do for Xander to sway him to my side now. My words would have to be enough.

Zuri joined us at the table, taking sips from a bowl of sea water with salt crusted on the rim. Xander returned with some food; freshly skinned beasts, their heart gems removed in a way only a wildling could do without causing the meat to rot; and charred tubers and bowls of sugar-glazed flower petals. Zuri insisted on serving us. I noticed she piled more food on my plate than the rest, so much that I had to politely tell her to stop.

"So it's true you took Sotera's throne," Xander said after we'd eaten and my stomach felt full to bursting. "I suspect Rune wasn't too pleased with that."

Marian's eyes flickered to the scars on Xander's cheek. "How do you think he took it? He's refusing to speak with her."

Xander took his time chewing. "One thing I learned about Rune is that, when it comes to those who betrayed him, he hurts them only a fraction as much as they've hurt him."

That didn't make me feel any better. I'd filled him in with the details he missed since being exiled, about what Father

Dumas had unleashed with Grislehaut, about the different factions all vying for our destruction.

"I want you to come help me," I said to Xander. "I have few allies, and I need people I can trust to see this through."

Xander mulled this over, spearing the tubers with a fork. "I don't want to leave Zuri. I trust that Keen won't hurt her, but he failed to protect her from Bendeti the first time. I don't want it to happen again."

Marian snorted. "Zuri, you can come along. With Bendeti flooding the palace, you'll be more at home Below than any of us."

"Will it be safe?" Xander said.

"Nowhere's safe," I said and then lowered my voice. There was no doubt at least one of the Mysts was trying to listen in. "Keen thinks he'll be free of Grislehaut if he just moves fast enough. He doesn't understand this isn't just some new Wild Lords he can evade and ignore swearing allegiance to. Where does he think he'll go?"

"He spoke of Wilds far from here. Places like—"

"What was once Sacramento?" I said, and Xander's stunned expression answered for me. "Yellowstone? Yosemite? I've already had Lords from some of those Wilds coming *here*, seeking safety *here*. Keen might be less conspicuous there, but it's no guarantee." I took a breath, readying the killing stroke. "You could join him and keep running. Or this could be your penance for what you did to Rune, and to me. I'm sure always being on the run isn't something you envisioned with your love, and Zuri, I'm sure you'll agree."

Xander's brow furrowed. "Now you're fighting dirty."

"And what wildlings did I learn that from?"

"I didn't envision a lot of things, but at least if we stay with the Mysts, there's a better chance we'll survive."

"Even if that were true, it'd only be temporary."

"It *has* been difficult," Zuri admitted, and I felt my chances of this actually working creep just a fraction higher. Zuri clasped Xander's hand tight, looking at him. "And at least around here, we can easily get the seawater I need."

"I'd get that for you anywhere," Xander said firmly.

Zuri gave a soft smile. "Of course you would. For me you'd seek an ocean in the desert. But some places *may* be easier to find it than others. I know the coast and water *here*."

"Have you spoken with Rune about this, Val?" Xander said. "You think he'd allow me back?"

"He's not the one asking, I am." I drew my crown from my coat and laid it on the table. Both Xander and Zuri eyed it with awe.

"You'd be under me," I continued, "and as such, my domain is yours. And, if you're comfortable with it, whatever alliance I make with Rune would be yours as well."

"It might be difficult to make an alliance with someone who won't speak with you," Xander said wryly, but there was no hiding the spark of hope in his eyes. Despite what he'd done to Rune, despite his willingness to abide by his exile, it was clear he wished to be back at the side of the wildling he saw as his brother, in the place they'd both shed blood to liberate.

Zuri stood. She gave Xander a peck on the cheek. "I'm feeling a bit parched. Make whatever choice is yours, love. I will follow you wherever."

Xander nodded distractedly. "She misses the sea," he said when she'd left. "It is not the same out here, in these Wilds, as it was where we were. No matter how violent Bendeti's Undersea, no matter how treacherous staying nearby becomes, it's still home."

Marian shot me a look, and I knew she was thinking of my desire to fight alongside Rune again, no matter our animosity.

For Xander and me both, the ache of wanting to be beside something that might cause us pain was frighteningly similar.

"What are your chances, really, of winning?" Xander asked.

"Better with you there," I said. "But not good. They've never been good. You know that."

He nodded, smiling. "The odds have never been ours."

"The chances will also be higher if Rune aligns with Val," Marian said. "Which he'll probably try to do sooner than we think."

I raised an eyebrow. "You seem awful sure of that."

"You think he *won't* try?"

"Why would he? He seems to hate me."

Marian looked at me as one might a poor, stupid beast. "And you really believe that?" She shrugged at Xander. "Guess I'm the idiot then."

Xander scratched at one of his horns. "Rune's never been easy to read. When he says there's no chance of something happening, then it's not the craziest to assume he means forever."

I recalled Rune's whispered breath tickling the back of my neck as we lay together on the cold floor of a cabin, his arms wrapped around me to keep us warm.

Maybe the feelings that love and hatred evoke are not so different.

My body was hot, as though I were still wrapped in his arms. I moved so that the chill could resettle on my skin. "You're both not making any sense."

"Do you think Rune might try to kill me right away?" Xander asked, and the mood immediately soured again.

"I'm not sure," I answered honestly. "But I'll protect you. I give you my word."

"Then I'll go with you," Xander said at last. "If, at some point, you ask Rune about ending my exile, if only for Zuri's sake." He peered up into the canopy. "I thought I'd be content with his choice and what I'd done. It's selfish, but I feel things are coming to a close, and I want to be by his side when they do."

"You did try to betray him," I pointed out. "And it might make him appear weak if he rescinds on his choice."

"He's high king, he can do whatever he wants," Marian said. "Do you honestly think anyone's going to tell him no?"

"He might still be mad," I went on.

"*You* tried to kill him," Xander answered. "More than once. More than me! And yet look how that's working for you."

Terribly, I wanted to say. *Incredibly terribly*.

"I'll try talking to him," I said. "But I can't promise anything."

"I'd rather it be you asking, more than anyone else," Xander said.

I wasn't sure what to make of that.

I stood, itching to return Below. With things as tumultuous as they were, any time away felt like rocking a house of cards, waiting for the entire thing to fall. "Discuss with Zuri. Come as soon as you're able."

I left Marian to catch up with Xander and walked deeper into the maze of green tunnels until I felt the heavy sensation of being watched by multiple pairs of eyes.

"Voya, I need to speak with you," I said.

No one leapt down to answer me at first. I'd expected that. The Mysts would want to show me that, though I might be Empress, they were those for which grand titles meant nothing.

"Voya—"

A girl appeared out of thin air. She cocked her head quizzically as though to say, *Yeah, what do you want?*

I withdrew a small crystal vial I'd fashioned and held it out. "If you can, I need some Magora venom."

Though the venom didn't work on me, it was as strong as any wildling compulsion. Believing I was under its spell, Keen had once made me dance with him, my hands wrapped around the back of his neck, intimately close. He'd supposedly been testing my loyalty. Really he was testing how important I was to Rune. How vulnerable I could make the High King.

Rune's expression had remained aloof throughout, but I'd seen the secret hunger in his eyes as he'd watched us spin. A hunger we were both still hurting each other with.

If injected, the venom should compel someone to reveal their secrets. Something I had a feeling I'd need more of in the future.

Voya looked off into the trees, as though receiving an unspoken command. I waited, vial outstretched, until she opened her mouth. A centipede as long as my arm scuttled out. It reared its segmented body level with my face, venom-tipped pincers clacking together.

Voya made a small click with her tongue, and the Magora lashed out. It struck the vial and injected so much venom that some of it sloshed over the side and tingled where it touched my hand.

I quickly wiped the excess venom off, stoppered the vial, and tucked it away. "Thank you."

"Don't thank us yet."

Keen frowned down at me. "I hope you know what you're doing, asking Xander back. If he dies, it's on you."

"Believe me, I know," I said. "You don't have to fight, but you could spy for me. Find out when Bendeti plans to strike against Rune."

"I don't think so," Keen said. "You're an Empress now, and

I'm only here for myself. I did you favors once, and I plan on staying out of anyone's debt as long as possible."

I shrugged. It'd been worth another shot.

"But I have a request for you, Empress," Keen said. "If you survive, rule differently than others have before. Take a chance to be better, and maybe things will *be* better."

I recalled Rune looking at me, horrified, after I murdered one of his Councilors for betraying him. The underhanded way I'd stolen his power. The thrill I got as I killed the Lords and drove Sliver through the chests of those who deserved it.

"I'm not sure I can be better," I admitted. "But I'll try."

THE RIDE back on Erebus was chillier than before, and by the time we arrived down Below, small crusts of ice had begun forming on the dew-soaked hem of my coat. Cursing, Marian hobbled off toward her room the moment we stopped, only to return seconds later, looking vindicated.

"Throne room," was all she said.

My apprehension mounting, we both made our way there. Had the Lords returned with more forceful demands? Had Bendeti broken through another part of the Below? I wished childishly for General Forcheck to return, if only to have someone with more experience at my side.

But when I pushed through the double doors, all thoughts left my head.

Rune was waiting for me.

CHAPTER TEN

"What are you doing here?" I blurted out.

Rune elegantly rose a single eyebrow. "Strange. I seem to recall, very recently, you were *desperate* to speak to me. I wonder if that's changed."

I sucked in a sharp breath to keep from spouting off the first thing that came to my mind, something that would definitely bring this conversation to a quick end. "I asked once, and you refused."

It was then that I noticed Rune wasn't alone. Wildlings stood sternly at his side. Wolves, composed as much from greenery as they were from shock-white fur, guarded his flanks. He'd brought an entire entourage fit for a High King, just to deliver this stupid message. Likely just to embarrass me.

His attendants made my own lack of any all the more apparent. I brought my chin up and swiftly ascended to my throne. At least up here, looking down at his stupidly smirking face, I could regain some semblance of control.

"It is my turn to ask," I said. "What are you doing in my Below?"

I had meant for the question to make him uncomfortable. Instead, he didn't try to hide his smirk as he and the other wildlings bowed. It was as though he thought this all a game, and he was indulging me playing Empress.

"I bring an invitation," Rune said. "I'm here to invite you to the midnight revel."

Marian's jaw dropped. I took my time crossing my legs to pretend I was considering this.

"I learned a lot of things when we were aligned," I said. "But not what that is."

"Then you would be among a great many, including wildlings, who don't know. Before the Sundering, in the days where we still had High Kings, it was a celebration to the gods and spirits to watch over the new ruler and give them guidance. To reconnect us to the Wilds."

"A...celebration?" I echoed.

"A party," Rune admitted. "Dancing, drinking, merriment. *Fun*," he added as my face clearly showed further confusion.

"Fun," I repeated. "I didn't think *fun* was possible in the Wilds. Do you really think now's the best time? What about Bendeti? The other Lords? What about Grislehaut?"

"And to that I say what better time to dance in the face of death? After all, sometimes the only fun worth doing is the kind that makes others miserable."

"And you want to do this," I said, still not believing it.

"It will be excruciating," Rune lamented. "But I'll somehow manage. I'll manage even better with you—The Empress of Those Below—in attendance. We were supposed to do the revel after I became High King, but we were a bit busy. Think of it as our first official collaboration as allies."

"Allies," I repeated again, since being a parrot seemed all I was capable of at the moment. "Why?"

Rune blinked. I'd finally managed to catch him off guard. "I think it would be in both of our best interests if we were to align—"

"That's not what I meant."

I was on my feet, descending the dais. A faint rumble sounded in the Deep, and I realized it was my fury that had caused it, the tight hold on my magic briefly slipping free. No, he couldn't come sauntering in here, pretending that he hadn't scorned me for the better part of a month, acting as though nothing had changed.

Rune held his ground, a bit apprehensive, as I approached him, close enough that I could speak without the rest of the wildlings hearing.

"You decided to offer this *grand* invitation only after I begged you?"

"I wanted to see how sincere you were," Rune murmured. His eyes flickered to the throne. "I'd already lost so much to you."

I held his gaze, wrestling my anger under control.

"You hurt me," Rune said, as though confessing a secret. "In more ways than one. It was childish, and it was wrong, but I wanted to hurt you back. Seems I did."

"Seems you did," I said. "You're an ass. An absolute ass, you know that?"

"Thoroughly, with how often you rightly remind me."

I opened my mouth to flat out refuse his offer. He clearly needed me—or believed he did—and by asking, he'd handed over an opportunity to hurt him back. I could do it, strike painfully for all the time he'd ignored me.

Or...

"I accept," I said through gritted teeth.

Rune's expression was half delight, half surprise, though I wasn't sure he could have been as surprised as me. "Excellent. It's in two days' time. I'll—"

"But I need to know, why did you really ask? What are you really after?"

For a moment, I saw a flash of desire in his eyes, before it was shuttered behind his cold mask. "To recompense. To build an alliance. And..."

His hesitation burned the air. I couldn't help giving a smirk of my own.

"Ah. There it is. Dancing just for the fun of it? What are you really plotting?"

"General Forcheck believes that Bendeti means to invade the Wilds when the moon is at its most full and the tide's reach the greatest," Rune admitted. "Bendeti and his Undersea horde have languished in the dark and cold for too long, and they mean to stay this time. He'll come for the Wilds, come to kill me, and then he'll come for the Below."

Rune stepped closer. "He'll come for you, the jewel that slipped his grasp. He would not be the only one who knows the pain of losing you."

Heat spread across my cheeks, and I had to remind myself that I was still furious with him.

"The moon will be fullest and the tide highest the night after the revel," Rune went on. "We will celebrate and enjoy, and then we will prepare for war."

"And why shouldn't I let you fight him by yourself?" I said.

"Tell me you don't care," Rune said fiercely. "Pretend, as I have tried, that you're okay with me facing what's coming alone."

Like many things—my power, my influence—I was reaching the limit of what I could pretend to do. I couldn't pretend much longer to be Empress without help. I couldn't pretend much longer to have total control over my magic.

I couldn't pretend that I detested Rune, that I didn't want to be with him anymore.

"I have some stipulations," I said, gratefully bringing us back around to safer subjects like a coming war, rather than my long-buried feelings for him. "You'll let Those Below into the Wilds."

"Those that remain of Sotera's army?" Rune said with some surprise. "I thought many were killed or left."

"Many," I said. "She had less than we thought, but there are still those loyal to the current Empress. As loyal as I can hope they'll be. We'll need them. And I want the civilians who aren't fighting up there as well."

"Done," Rune agreed, far easier than I thought he would. I was prepared for him to make things difficult, as was his way. "The Wilds are vast. Surely we can find a place for them."

"Good." I still didn't trust his motives or believe he was being entirely honest with me. I supposed that was something we had in common. "I'll have dinner brought for you and the others."

Then I left, making it clear I wouldn't be joining them.

I NEEDED TIME TO THINK. To breathe. A moment to escape the swirling thoughts fluttering through my mind like a colony of bats.

I found a protruding outcropping of rock that looked over the Below and the city of the Deep. When I'd been Sotera's prisoner, I'd had a prison cell with a similar view, but something about it now brought a source of comfort. The city of the Deep—built of slabs of obsidian, petrified wood, jade, and agate—still stood tall against Bendeti's watery onslaught despite being mostly submerged. Saltwater lapped at the upper two tiers. I swore, in just the time I sat here, it had risen another half foot. I thought General Tenia's prediction a bit off.

Even if Bendeti was flooding mostly Grislehaut's chamber, I guessed it'd be less than a week before nothing but the Undersea could exist down here.

I pulled my legs farther from the edge as shark fins circled the waters beneath. Something enormous with tentacles and a clacking beak splashed in the dark.

I sensed Rune's approach, a tingle on my skin, before I heard his soft footfalls. I didn't want to see him. I was pretty sure anything I said right now would come out angry.

Still, I scooted over to make room. Rune gracefully sat beside me—close, but not too close. He peered into the water directly beneath, to the massive crystal graveyard of Those Below shining weakly from the murky depths.

I waited for him to speak, but he seemed content merely sitting with me. The silence wasn't entirely comfortable, but it was welcome, like a scratchy blanket that I could wrap around myself.

"You left me," I said, unable to contain it any longer. "For a month I was here alone, fending off animosity and assassination attempts from those who were supposed to be helping me."

Rune shifted but waited while I got my thoughts under control.

"*Now* you show up and expect us to be friendly again. And I want to be, really, I do, but I don't know if I'm sure how to anymore. Not with you."

I turned and was surprised to see sadness cross his face. "I know you're mad, Rune. I did what I thought was best to protect both of us, but... I guess I just made things worse."

"Not without my part in it you didn't," Rune said. "All my life I've solved problems with rage and violence. But I couldn't—I wouldn't—use those against you. So, instead, I wielded distance and chilly indifference." He looked away, as though embarrassed. "I believed, if only for a little bit, that you'd use the power you gained against me."

I stared at him, jaw slack. "Maybe at one time, but after what we'd been through together... How could you think that?"

"You know of my past, Val. I've had only bad experiences with those using their power to hurt me, and even with you I'm embarrassed to say that same fear is hard to kill. So I cut you off before you could get the chance.

"In some ways, I delighted in how I hurt you, and I believe you delighted in hurting me somewhat, too. It's not right what I did, but it's the truth, and I'm beyond wanting to lie to you."

I thought again to the amulet the Lords had given to me, the one currently tucked deeply in my pocket. The one I could hand to him to rob him of his power and hurt him in whatever way I wanted. I wouldn't delight in *that*.

"You told me that as High King you had to rule different, had to be different," I said. "That has to apply even when you're not ruling."

"And to you," he reminded me. "You have to be better, too."

I wished I was as good a person as Rune seemed to think. Maybe then I could become someone who deserved the things I wanted.

I was about to tell Rune exactly that, but when I looked at him, his one eye wept black like ink, the other shining a vibrant, threatening blue.

"Rune!"

Rune turned away, blinked a few times. When he looked at me again, his face was the same as I'd always known.

I shifted to my knees. "I'm not imagining this. What's wrong with you?"

"There's nothing wrong." He said it with so much of his usual authority-bordering-on-arrogance that I almost believed him.

I *would* have believed him if I didn't know him so well. Didn't know the strain at the corners of his eyes that meant he was putting on a strong mask for others.

"No." I reached up and took his face in my hands. Rune's breath stilled.

"What," he said, "are you doing?"

"If you won't tell the truth, I'll discern it for myself."

"Val..."

Whether by the forcefulness of my examination or another reason entirely, Rune's protests tapered off. I turned his face to either side, seeking anything that would give me a hint as to what wearing Sotera's crown had done to him.

Finding nothing, I sat back, my hands still firmly cupping either side of his face. "There's something wrong with me, too," I admitted. "Not to the same effect, but my power over the Below is weak. It *hurts* sometimes to use its magic. And though I should have some control over the Wilds thanks to the crown, I can't seem to get a handle on it."

"Because of me," Rune said. "Because of my magic. We both wore the crown that Sotera created, the one woven of the Below and the Wilds."

"The one that nearly killed you," I murmured. "That's still killing you."

Rune waved a hand. "And you as well, but that's just technicalities. But while you saved me—thank you for that, by the way, you can rub it in later—while you wrested the crown from my head and took the power for your own, that combining of those two magics has affected you, too. My magic of the Wilds is polluted, and since you took the throne of the Below, your magic here has become polluted too."

"And it's killing us," I finished.

"Little by little," Rune agreed. "But it won't kill us as quickly as others will if we're without sufficiently strong magic. If those power-hungry Lords, Bendeti, or anyone else who wanted to off us knew we weren't at our full strength, well..."

"What can we do about it?"

Rune was quiet so long I thought he hadn't heard me. "Rune—"

"There might be a way," Rune said.

His eyes glittered a gold-red so intense I swore they were peeling back every defense I could have set against him. I realized I was still holding his face in my hands, fingertips barely brushing the sharp lines of his jaw, the faint curl of his hair. I drew back, if not a bit slowly, and both of us seemed to exhale.

"What way is that?" I asked. "I'm not giving you the throne of the Below, if that's what you were wondering."

"I wouldn't dare suggest it," Rune said. But whatever he *was* going to suggest seemed hard to conjure. He opened and closed his mouth a few times. A laugh bubbled from my throat.

"Are you...*speechless*? Let me guess, your solution is terrifying."

"In its own way," Rune said cryptically. "There are old magics of the Wilds and the Below, and right now they are at war, stopping the other from being fully free."

Rune turned until he, too, kneeled before me. "The Below has been long trapped by the Wilds, and those like Sotera and others who felt wronged by that have turned the Below's magic against us. It must work together now. These old magics must know that there is no reason to fight any longer, just as *we* must know that. And in order—"

"Rune?"

Cassius was coming over. He looked apologetic. "Don't mean to interrupt, but we have to get going. There's a lot to prepare."

"Just a sec," I said. "Rune, what were you going to say?"

But Rune was already on his feet. "Another time."

"No, *now*. I want to know—" I started, but Rune took my hand, kissing it in a way that was shockingly intimate.

"Later. We will have a lot of time to speak later, now that we're speaking to one another at all."

"And whose fault is that?" I said.

"Ours," he said simply. "Ours."

Cassius had turned to give us some privacy, not that it mattered to me. I was past the days where I had to hide how I felt about Rune from others. Now, it seemed, the only one I continued to pretend in front of was myself.

Cassius gave me an excited grin when we were done. "Guess we'll see you soon at the revel, Val. Try to talk it up for Marian, if you can. She's agreed to come but doesn't seem all that excited."

"Give her someone to murder," I said. "That will cheer her up."

"Perhaps there *will* be someone to murder," Rune said. "After all, it will be a night to remember."

Of that I had no doubt. Just hopefully not for the wrong reasons.

CHAPTER ELEVEN

I had barely a knock of warning before my bedroom door swung open and Marian swept inside. There'd been so much going on lately I'd not only forgotten to change rooms but apparently forgotten to lock it.

"Good, you haven't picked what to wear yet," Marian said.

We were heading up to the Wilds for the revel in less than an hour. Most of yesterday I'd been in contact with General Tenia about how the move to the surface was going.

Slowly, had been her curt reply. *We need more time.*

Which meant we needed King Bendeti dead, which meant I'd stayed up most of the night convening with Xander and Marian about how to accomplish that. Short of a likely disastrous assault on the Undersea, we'd come up with nothing. And up until the moment Marian walked in, I'd still been poring over strategies and maps, wracking my brain for something we'd missed.

I looked down at myself. "I'm wearing this," I said.

Marion took me in, from the Wilds-spun coat over a thinning long-sleeve shirt, to the pair of jeans Gracie had gifted me, though they were getting so many holes it looked as though I'd fallen into a pit of vine vipers.

"No," Marian said at last. "You're not."

"We're going to fight the Undersea," I said.

"*After* the revel. You need to look nice *during* it. What?" she said when I stared at her.

"Cassius asked *me* to convince *you* to enjoy it, not the other way around. He's excited you're going."

A pleased expression flashed quicksilver over Marian's face before she ripped open my armoire and started thumbing through my scant clothing piled at the bottom. "You have nothing here."

"I move a lot," I admitted.

"Stop that," she admonished. "You're the Empress, and you shouldn't be running scared. I know you and Rune are trying to 'be better' or whatever, but there are those for which no amount of forgiveness is enough. If they threaten your life, take theirs."

I sat on the bed as she continued pulling dresses, pants, and jackets out, shaking her head and putting them back.

"You seriously don't have anything?" Marian said, exasperated.

"I still don't think dressing up is that big a deal," I muttered.

"You don't want to look good? Not even for Rune?"

I did. I didn't. I wasn't entirely sure *how* I wanted him to see me. Desirable? Powerful? Threatening? Did I want to make him realize who he'd almost given up as an ally, or as a...

Bendeti would not be the only one who knows the pain of losing you.

Marian let out another scoff of disgust as she reached the last of my things. There was another knock at the door. This time it was Raki. He held up a small, folded pile of fabric.

"For the revel."

I carefully unfurled it and held in a gasp. It was a luminous dress glowing with a soft light around the edges. One of Sotera's, I remembered, sewn from the silk of the Below's glow worms and speckled with glitters of lazulite that, when turned, twinkled against the black fabric as though I wore the night sky.

"You went into Sotera's room to get this?" I asked Raki. After a pause, he nodded.

I wasn't sure how to feel about him going into the room of the woman who'd put him through so much, who'd murdered his sister. Wearing this could be a painful reminder. Wearing it could also be flaunting that whatever hold Sotera had over us was no more.

The determined glint in Raki's eyes said he agreed with the second sentiment.

"Thank you," I said. "It's perfect. The black will even hide blood."

That got a small smile from him before he left me to change. I quickly slipped out of my old things and into the dress.

"How does it feel?" Marian asked when I stood before her.

I spun. Despite its beauty, I hated the flimsy, light feel of the silk. The first time I'd ever worn a dress was at the behest of Sotera, when I felt like little more than her doll.

The next was when I nearly gave myself over to Bendeti as his queen so I could try to murder him.

Perhaps there will be someone to murder.

"It's perfect," I said at last.

"Good. Because it looks good. Now come over here and I'll do your hair and makeup." She held up pouches of powders and clasps full of creams. "I brought my own since I didn't think you wanted to adorn your face with rocks."

After she finished and left to get ready herself, I was delighted to find the dress had small pockets tucked within the folds of the fabric. I slipped in an easily concealable knife.

The amulet the Lords had gifted me glittered like jeweled blood on the bedside table. The words I needed to use to activate it danced in my head.

Hurt him. Hurt him before he hurts you. Because you know he will.

How easy would it be to slip it into his hand or pretend it was a gift for the revel? How thin was that line I had to cross?

"He's changed," I said aloud. "We both have."

The dark voice snickered at my naivete.

I slipped the amulet into one pocket where it settled, heavy and foreboding. It was a safeguard. A backup plan. Nothing more. Not for Rune. Never for Rune.

I threw the Wild-spun cloak over my bare shoulders. The dress by itself looked good, but I wouldn't be freezing to death for the sake of fashion.

Last, I put the crown of the Below on my head and used my reflection in the crystal wall to get it straight. As the saying went, I looked dressed to kill.

Though who or what remained to be seen.

MARIAN, Xander, and a dozen of my soldiers, those who'd remained after I'd become Empress, waited for me in the chamber between the Below and the Wilds. Xander clutched Zuri's arm so hard her blue skin was turning white. If I was nervous, he looked downright sick.

"You're with me," I said. "Rune will respect that."

Xander tried to smile, though it came out a grimace. "Does he know I'm coming?"

I couldn't recall if I'd mentioned that to him. "It'll be a surprise."

"Oh good. We know how much he loves those."

Marian limped to the center of the chamber and knelt to place a single tendril of thorns onto the floor.

"Rune infused it with magic, but I'll need your help," she said to me.

I drew on my magic to the point where I felt sick and pushed it into the thorny tendril as Marian did the same. The thorns spewed outward and curled into a standing circle. Within moments the green deepened and a dark path led to the other side.

I took a deep breath and walked through. Flower stems curled around my fingers to lead me; leafed branches brushed across my crown.

Empress, they seemed to say. *Welcome back. Are you going to stay?*

We emerged within Rune's new palace.

He'd settled north of what had once been Olympia, building lush walls and pillars of green atop and within the corpses of what had once been houses, manors, commercial buildings, and a rec center. A dozen of my reflections glittered back at me as we passed panes of colored glass beneath trees ripped through brick and overhanging the smooth promenade. Through all the sparkly beauty was a wide glen.

Dozens of wildlings mingled around languid blue pools and tables piled high with freshly hunted beasts and newly conjured delicacies. As we entered, the wildlings' eyes turned on me—some curious, others filled with disgust, and still others terrifyingly full of hope. I wished I'd worn more. I wished I could exude more confidence.

I stood frozen for a moment, unsure of what to do, until Rune slipped from the crowd, flanked by Cassius and Pitius.

Rune's eyes met mine. His weren't curious or filled with disgust or hope. They were as hungry as a starving man at a feast. "The Empress has arrived."

I gave a small bow to match his. "Along with guests."

Xander stepped out from behind me, swallowing hard. "High King Rune."

Rune's expression shifted from surprise to fury. "Correct me if I'm wrong, but I thought I told you to never return to my Wilds."

He lifted a hand, and the pleasant music and bright spectacle of the revel dimmed. A number of Rune's soldiers appeared in the surrounding trees. The enchantments I'd felt brush across my skin as we'd entered curled around my body, waiting for his command.

"I—" Xander faltered. "Rune, we—"

"Was that mark on your face not enough?" Rune hissed. "Are you trying to test me, now of all times?"

"Xander's with me," I said firmly, stepping in front of him. "As High King, you can respect the wishes of an Empress, and I asked him to come. Therefore, Xander's not breaking your command so much as following mine."

Pitius glanced nervously at Rune while he stared at me. As the seconds passed, I swore he started to appear almost pleased.

Rune held out an arm. "Walk with me, Empress."

The sudden switch to civility surprised me. I made a show of turning to the few of my soldiers who'd accompanied me. "I want it known that Xander is aligned with the Empress of Glass. Anyone who messes with him will have to deal with *me*."

My soldiers bowed and dispersed among the revelers as the merriment and festivities started up again.

"Everything will be fine," I muttered to Xander and Zuri. "You'll see."

"If you say so," Xander muttered back.

Rune's eyes glittered with wicked delight as I took his arm, careful not to stray too close to him as we began to walk.

"Did you find something funny in me giving orders?" I challenged.

"Anything but," Rune said.

Chilly silence filled the space between us. Just as I was wondering which of us would concede and break it, Rune said, "So, was that *your* test, then? Did you dream of seeing my surprise?"

I tried to keep my voice even. "That's bold, assuming I dream about you."

Rune's grin was half delight, half threat. "Touché. Things are still tenuous, Val. I merely wanted to ensure this wasn't some small way to undermine—"

"You have to stop thinking that everything is about you," I snapped. "I need Xander, someone I can trust."

I looked pointedly at him. "You want him back, too. Don't deny it."

"Am I that easy to read now?" Rune muttered.

I risked touching the top of his arm. "No. You never make it easy. But I like to think I'm better at reading you than most."

Rune looked strangely pleased at that. "What do you think?" he asked as we glided through the revelers. Those dancing paused to bow to us, or maybe just to Rune. As we passed, I caught some giving me sideways glances filled with barely concealed disgust. There were minor Lords in attendance and even humans, though not Peyton nor anyone I knew.

"How many do you think would kill you?" I answered.

Rune snorted. “Hopefully not as many as before. But still more than I’d like.”

Glowing bats, like fattened fireflies, dropped ripened fruit into outstretched hands. People laughed. Someone sang a warbling tune that made my head spin if I listened too intently for too long.

Everything *looked* fine. But like the prettiest things in the Wilds, like the wildlings, like *Rune*, those that looked the most beautiful were often the most dangerous. I couldn’t help feeling that this, too, was all a farce; that something terrible was going to happen. Like we were flaunting in the face of danger.

“You’re tense.” Rune stopped us outside a cluster of wildlings colored like amber sap, congregated around whom I assumed was a minor Lord. “Just for a little bit, we can let things go. This is a night for dancing. It is a night for whispered promises, brazen flirtations, and broken hearts.”

“It could also be a night to weep,” I said. “And if we’re not careful, a night to bleed.”

Rune’s smirk was equal menace and delight. “Calm yourself. Tomorrow, when the moon is highest and Bendeti’s tide arrives, you will get your bloodshed. But not tonight.”

“And Bendeti will be coming with a vengeance, no doubt about that,” General Forcheck said, hobbling over. She took a swig from one of the many brewed tonics she carried, and I smelled licorice and peppergrass on her breath. “Something got the king of the fish riled up.”

General Forcheck gave me a significant look, her smile baring slightly pointed teeth.

“Yes, you never explained exactly what you did to upset Bendeti so much, Val,” Rune said.

“I evaded him yet again,” I said. “You should be happy;

when Bendeti comes, he'll finally want to kill me more than you."

"And why would that make me happy?" Rune held my arm close. "I feel there's more to the story than that."

"Joshua is dead." I hadn't meant for the words to slip out, but the moment they did, the relief was immense, like unburdening part of a heavy load on another. "I killed him to save him. I know you hated him. Maybe you can be happy about *that*."

Rune, more than almost anyone, could understand what it meant to kill those he loved. In Mog Moren, the place of his imprisonment, his cousin Vanesi had forced him to slit the throat of his best friend among others, forging him into who he'd become. I wished I could say that what I'd done to Joshua had tempered me into something more dangerous. Instead, I only felt more brittle.

"I hated him," Rune agreed at last. "But I don't delight in what you had to do, or your grief."

You could have prevented it, I wanted to yell. If he'd stood by me from the start, then maybe I could have saved him. Maybe... Maybe... Maybe...

But if I was mad at him, then I also had to be mad at myself. And if we were heaping blame, then I had to be careful not to be crushed by my share of it.

"Prepare well for tomorrow, General Forcheck," I said. "At the very least, we can make Bendeti work for his vengeance."

"As the Empress wills it," General Forcheck said before hobbling off.

A flute picked up a trilling song, followed by chimes, and soon a merry tune filled the glen. Some of the wildlings began to dance, alone, in pairs, or in groups, unfettered by the stares of those watching. I was a bit shocked at first. However, before the wildlings knew nothing but war and struggle, I knew they'd reveled in the delights of song, dance, and drink rather than violence.

Without warning, Rune swept me into his arms.

"Dance with me," he said. "Those who want to gain my favor or talk more politics are on their way."

"You'd rather have me stepping on your toes than plotting ways to kill your enemies?" I said, more breathlessly than I'd like.

His gaze met mine, and there was something indiscernible within. My mind went blank. If this was his attempt to make me forget, if only for a little bit, what I'd done to Joshua, then it was working, and I was grateful.

"I didn't know you could dance," I continued.

"You know how to fight," he said. "It's much the same, but with less elegance. The upside is that if you mess up someone isn't liable to kill you."

And with that we were swept into the throng. I was aware of the other dancers around us, but whether because it was Rune or my imagination, they all peeled away, until we were alone within the crowd.

Rune wasn't wrong; it felt like fighting. The exchange of steps, Rune taking the space I conceded before I took his space back in kind. Give and take. Back and forth. Though we didn't have blades, every time our eyes met, I swore there were sparks.

I was intimately aware of his hand resting on the thin fabric covering my hip; on our hands clasped tightly together; of my own hand grasped around the back of his neck, brushing against the bristly curls of his hair beneath his crown. I recalled in vivid detail the last time I'd run my fingers through that hair, and my cheeks flushed further.

Rune leaned in closer so that his breath tickled my ear when he spoke.

"Tell me when you want to stop."

Laughter surrounded us. My feet twisted and slapped the ground, barely evading Rune's. My heart thumped louder, harder, leaving no doubt that Rune heard it. Maybe he felt it resonating through his body. Maybe that was why he intertwined our fingers tighter, to feel it more fully.

I didn't want to stop. I was out of control. The both of us were hurtling toward an unknown edge. I knew we would go careening into the abyss, but I wanted to, if only for a moment, feel the sensation of flying.

"High King Rune."

We jerked to a halt, and I had to blink to bring my swirling surroundings back to earth.

Tannis and Sulien, the two minor Lords from the other Wilds, stood in our path, looking sullen. Rune's grip tightened on my hand, almost to the point of pain.

"You might have noticed, but we were in the middle of something," he said. His voice was light, but there was an unmistakable undertone of threat woven within.

"We've been trying to speak with you," Sulien rumbled, steeling his broad shoulders.

"And I've been avoiding you. I have other things to steal my attention tonight."

Both the Lords' eyes flickered to me. Rune knew I'd met with them before. But I wondered, with growing dread, if he knew the specifics of what they'd asked me to do.

"We will make this short," Tannis said curtly. "We wish for you to give us some of your Wild to rule over as our new kingdoms. We will serve as your new Lords and perhaps on the Council of Loam, should you decide to revive it again."

"Would you also serve me exactly as the Council of Loam before did?"

"Of course," Sulien said stupidly, before realizing his

mistake and giving a hasty half bow. "But only as advisors. We would never dare undermine your authority in any way."

"Of course you wouldn't," Rune said. "You wouldn't get the chance. The last Lords who made up the Council made similar promises. Tell me, do you know what happened when we discovered what one of them had been up to?"

This time Sulien chose his words carefully. His eyes flickered to me. "We'd heard stories..."

"Then you've heard enough to know that, however bad the Wilds you fled from were, staying here would be even worse for you."

"Empress—" Tannis grabbed for my arm. A crystal knife was immediately in my hand, and I lowered the point at their shocked faces.

"Careful," Rune purred. "I'm not the only dangerous one here. No, despite your pretty assurances, you would be no different than the Lords I usurped, gluttons for power whispering promises of allegiance in my ear while sinking a knife into my back."

Tannis's lips trembled with the strain of holding her tongue, her chin set in a proud tilt. Sulien looked stunned, as though they'd anticipated Rune at least listening to them.

For the first time, I saw these Lords for who they truly were: beings not so different than me, young, inexperienced, desperate. And while that didn't make them any less dangerous should they be against us, they could still be useful. They at least deserved a chance.

"Prove yourselves," I said.

"What?" Sulien growled.

"If you want to show High King Rune that you're serious, then prove yourselves loyal to him first. Serve beside him in the coming battles. Shed blood."

Tannis's face curled into a sneer. "I didn't leave one war just to join another."

"No, only to gorge yourself on what remained after it," Rune said dully. "That much is obvious."

"It seems to me the High King should divvy up his Wilds, while he still has the ability to," Sulien said.

The pools behind us bubbled. The sconces of everfire lighting the glen dimmed, as though the trees had reached out their canopies and cast everything in darkness.

"I am the Wilds, and the Wilds are me," Rune said, voice pitched dangerously low. "Unless you plan on trying to cut me down right here and ending up beneath the dirt, we have nothing more to speak about."

"Why would we try to sever your rule?" Tannis said, sneering my direction. "There are others who would gladly do that job for us."

Both of them vanished into the crowd. My skin crawled as Rune's questioning gaze turned on me.

"Val," he said. "What were they talking about?"

Tannis wouldn't have revealed what we'd spoken about unless they already believed I wouldn't betray Rune. They'd gotten in one last barb to set us against each other in a different way.

"Val?" Rune pressed. The darkness had receded, and Rune's power with it, but I didn't feel any safer.

I could lie. Let the guilt consume me, Rune's questions be damned. But here, in front of him, keeping what I'd considered doing to him a secret no longer seemed possible.

Those around us were staring, so I pulled us over to a small ring of stumps, scattering clustering of gold-red-eyed creatures who lingered on the edge of the revel. There I slowly withdrew the amulet.

"They gave this to me. They told me the magic words to

activate it and told me to give it to you to weaken you. And once you were weak, they told me I should..."

I didn't need to finish.

"I never intended to give it to you," I hurried to explain.

"And yet you could have," Rune said, voice cool.

"But I *didn't.*"

Yet here it was with me, a solid reminder of my lingering mistrust of him.

Rune looked truly sad. "We can't seem to stop hurting each other, can we?"

He filtered back into the revelers, reminding me that I was far better with knives than with words, though I could have used both to cut Rune equally deep.

"Rune stalked off pretty quick," Cassius said, joining me. "Everything okay? You didn't step on his toes one too many times, did you?"

"Everything's fine," I lied.

To stay distracted from my myriad thoughts, I went over to one of the tables of refreshments, a log covered in vibrant mushrooms and blooming vines of bleeding heart. A hole cut in the side trickled a sweet-smelling drink.

I took a cupful and swallowed half in one go, feeling better as the oaky, slightly burning sensation caked my throat. I tried to keep my eyes off Rune as he made his way through the revelers, talking with some, subtly threatening others. No doubt General Forcheck had informed him that he had to do *some* politics tonight.

Raquel the beastmaster came over to ask about Erebus, who was currently off hunting somewhere. A couple more wildlings I vaguely remembered warily approached to introduce themselves. Their nervous twitching and fumbling flattery reminded me of when Pitius had brought my belongings from Seattle. That had been equal parts an attempt to make me feel at home as it was an offering to keep them safe from my wrath.

I plastered on a smile and tried to be as sweet as possible. Between conversations I downed more of the burning liquid, all the while cursing myself.

When the night had grown long, Rune ascended a tree he'd grown from a sapling in a matter of moments, the branches cradling him as he looked over his subjects. From where I stood, I couldn't quite make out what he was saying, hopefully something about unity. Something about a new age with a better, kinder ruler. Maybe I was only hoping to hear that.

When he was done, Rune and everyone else turned toward the languid blue pools at his back, faces tilted to the night sky.

"They're waiting for the gods and spirits to arrive," Xander said. He and Zuri had escaped the center of the revel and remained around the outside. Better for them. Rune might have let what Xander did pass, but there were undoubtedly others here who weren't as forgiving. "I've heard in the past, back before the old High King was killed, the entire sky was lit with color. Every benevolent god and spirit from the greatest depths of the Wilds would attend to support the new ruler."

I looked to the sky again. It remained empty and dark.

"It was a nice gesture," Zuri said sadly, patting Xander's arm. "Maybe one day they will return again."

Xander gave a tight nod. "Maybe."

My gaze brushed over the revelers. Some also looked expectantly toward the sky. Others whispered in their tight groups, shooting looks at Rune.

My eyes were drawn to a figure lingering on the outskirts. They had a hood pulled up, but not enough that I couldn't see the mucus-like coating of her skin, writhing with black leeches.

My breath caught. My blood pounded in my ears. There

was only one wildling I knew who looked like that: Erena, from the long-dead House of Worms. The last I'd seen of her she'd abandoned the Council of Loam and led Sotera into the Halfway and straight to Mother Mal. She'd been the catalyst behind Olette's death, and afterward I'd been too weak to prevent her from slipping through my grasp.

I was still gaping as Erena turned away and slid back into the surrounding trees.

"Xander," I said breathlessly. "Tell General Forcheck there are enemies here. Tell her to prepare."

Xander immediately looked around, sizing up possible threats. "Where?"

I searched the trees but couldn't make out any sign of Erena. "I'm not sure. Zuri, get to safety. Xander, take an elevated position."

He and Zuri hurried to obey without another word. Trying to stay as subtle as possible to avoid panic, I drew a crystal dagger and slipped around the outside of the revelers. Most were shaking from their stupor of staring at the sky and starting to dance again, to sing, to drink. I caught Idwal, one of Rune's spies.

"Stay by Rune," I commanded. "Stay close to him."

He looked wary to obey me, as though doing so would be betraying Rune like Xander had. Regardless, I was relieved when he scurried off to do as I asked.

I strode into the trees. There were more partygoers mingling deeper within. Likely those who'd found someone they wished to share a more private venue with. I quickly found one of my soldiers, watching the privacy-seekers with a bored expression on his face.

"Did a woman in a cloak come through here?" I asked.

The guard nodded toward the revelers and said in a

drawling voice, "You might have noticed that many with cloaks have come—"

He straightened when he saw it was me. "Empress! Apologies. I—You'll have to be more specific."

The other revelers had moved closer, silent as falling leaves. I couldn't distinguish Erena's shape from among them. She'd been able to vanish quickly before, and I had no doubt she'd done that again. Though why was she *here* of all places?

I held in a frustrated sigh. "If you see a wildling with leeches on her face, alert me immediately. And keep your eyes open—"

There was a hiss, a sharp pain in my cheek, followed by a meaty thwack.

The soldier stumbled back. His hands clawed at the fleshy part of his throat where an arrow with vanes of dried seaweed and a shaft of spines protruded. He gurgled blood and fell.

I dropped to the forest floor as more arrows zipped overhead. My face was right beside the dead solider. Close enough to see the veins in flesh purpling. Poisoned. I dabbed the cut on my cheek and was relieved to see it come away with only red. If the arrow had cut me any deeper, I'd be dead, too.

I risked peering from cover. Those that I thought were revelers had shed cloaks to reveal armor of lobster shell, coral, and shields inlaid with pearls. Their eyes were dark and wet, and they gnashed mouths of sharpened teeth. I smelled salt on the air.

The Undersea had arrived early.

CHAPTER TWELVE

I withdrew spears of crystal from the earth. Propping myself up, I hurled them at the closest of the Undersea before taking off back toward the revel. I didn't make it far before a rushing wave of water hit me at the back of the knees and brought me to the ground.

My vision spun. I hit my head and for a moment swore I saw Joshua's bloated, dead face swirl in front of me before I hit a tree and came to a stop.

I rolled over, sputtering water. I'd just gotten to my feet right as Undersea soldiers plunged from the surf. They were shark-skinned beings with fin-like knives and nightmarish rows of gnashing teeth.

"Tasty, tasty girl. Come closer and let us feed on that pretty neck."

I lunged to the side as they snapped at me. I covered one arm in crystal to deflect their knives before drawing Sliver. "Come any closer and I'll bite right back."

One of them hissed. He skated through the ankle-deep water toward me.

With a swiftness that clearly surprised him, I evaded and stabbed him in the gut and up through the heart. He hissed again as he died, and I hurled him off, right as a sharp pain pierced my side. I'd given up too much ground for a killing blow, allowing the other one to slip through my defenses.

I screamed before cutting him down.

More of the Undersea were streaming from the trees, along with enough sea water that soon we'd all be swimming.

Clutching my bleeding side, I took off as fast as I could toward the revel. Roots squirmed at my feet, drawing themselves together and intertwining into a near-impenetrable wall.

With my middling Wild magic, I kept the roots in front of me from closing completely and leapt through to the other side. I bit back a scream as I landed hard, before getting to my feet. Rune finished waving his hands like a conductor, and the roots tightened fully against the coming onslaught.

"The Undersea," he guessed, looking at me.

"Early," I agreed.

His expression was fury and bloodlust. "Then let me give them a warm welcome." His eyes flickered to the blood coating my hand, drenching the side of my dress. "Val, you're—"

"Focus on them," I said. "I've survived worse."

Whatever concern Rune was going to voice was lost as Bendeti's wave slammed against the root wall. Trusting that he was going to be all right, I pushed aside screaming, panicked revelers, searching for Marian.

I found her giving Cassius a firm kiss before he ran off to help the others.

"I need healing," I said.

"Of course you do," she said. But she'd already withdrawn her healing pouch. Her fingers moved deftly to coat my wound in a mixture of mashed eclipse flower and petals, before running her glowing hand over the worst of the damage. A wry grin split her face.

"You were right, that dress does hide blood well. There." I sighed as she finished up. "I know you won't listen, but don't move too much or it'll start bleeding again."

"Lead everyone who's not fighting back into Rune's palace," I said. "Our—my—soldiers will help Rune."

Marian pulled one of Rune's wildlings over and repeated my instructions before returning to me. "You want me to be useful, *Empress*, then let me be useful, not a babysitter." Frost coated her fingertips. "Let's turn some saltwater red."

Rune's wildlings and my soldiers were forming up at the root wall right as the Undersea broke over it. General Forcheck was shouting orders, an expression of murderous delight on her face. I saw Tannis and Sulien fleeing toward the palace and grabbed Sulien's arm.

"If you want to give Rune a reason to help you, then prove it now."

He freed himself from my grasp and backed up, eyes wide. "We have nothing worth fighting for here. Maybe we would have if you'd listened to us."

"Leave them," Marian said in disgust. Her eyes narrowed over my shoulder. A cloaked figure had emerged from a black pool of mucus coating the ground and began stalking toward Rune. "Wait... I know that slimy face."

I took off after Erena, Marian close behind. We ran past waves crashing over the root wall, carrying Undersea soldiers, past the sound of clashing weapons and hiss of cast magic. A shadow cloaked everything into further darkness as, at the far end of the glen, a beast so enormous it had no discernable shape emerged from the trees. Rune brought his hand down, and the beast mimicked his movement. Scores of the Undersea went flying. Even more were crushed to death.

Erena had drawn a knife from her cloak, angling it at Rune's exposed back. The leeches on her face writhed in excitement. I tried to shout a warning, but all that came out was a frantic, panting breath.

Then a shard of ice flew past me. Erena barely had time to step back and avoid it. She snarled when she saw us.

"It was too much to hope you'd be dead!" she spat.

I raised Sliver as Marian took my other side.

"I remember you," Marian said. "You showed Sotera the Halfway. You're the reason she killed Olette."

Erena sneered. "I only wish Sotera had done more. But Bendeti will finish the job. He'll bring things back to the way they should be."

I was ready when Erena came at me, but I wasn't prepared for when she vomited black ichor. The liquid hissed when it hit the ground, and I stumbled back to avoid its spray. I parried her knife, but Erena spit more ichor, keeping me at bay, before lunging at Marian. Because of Marian's leg, Erena must have thought her little threat, but Marian twirled with all the wildling grace she used to have. Her expression was bottled rage distilled into a singular goal: to kill the one who had hurt Olette.

With another flourish, Marian escaped Erena's next strike and smashed her cane across the side of Erena's knee.

"You'll pay for that," Erena hissed.

The moment Erena came at Marian again, I scored a hit on her other side. Erena's dagger went flying. She backed up, snarling.

"Give up," I said.

"We'll meet another time," Erena promised. "Until then, fear every shadow. You never know where I'll be lurking."

I lunged, but Erena anticipated that. She skirted out of range, and I felt sharp stinging on my arm and looked down to find a few of her leeches had attached themselves to my flesh. They pulsed, shoving liquid into my veins, before I cut them off. Erena giggled.

"That was for the House of Worms. Die slow, die painful. Rune will never get what he wants."

"She's going to—" I yelled.

A mixture of mucus and leeches pooled at her feet, and Erena started to sink into it. She'd only made it halfway before the pool froze as solid as the first hard frost. Erena jerked to a halt.

"She's mine," Marian said.

Erena screeched, clawing at the ice until the tips of her fingers bloodied. Her eyes widened as Marian moved purposefully toward her.

"A trial," Erena gasped. "I demand a trial. It's what the Council of Loam would have done. Rune was furious that it was disbanded, that it didn't follow his new laws. He wouldn't want this—"

A knife made of ice appeared in Marian's hand, and she lopped off some of the leeches on Erena's face. Erena's pleas pitched higher until Marian yanked the woman's head back and cut her throat so viciously she nearly removed Erena's head.

Erena's body slumped forward, leaking black across the ice. Marian stared at the body and slowly her own began to untense. "I feel better now. Thanks, Val."

The rest of the Undersea was in full retreat, chased back over the root wall. The glen was soaked in seawater swirling a myriad of colors. My body felt itchy and dry.

"Let's help the others—"

My legs gave out. I numbly tried to stand again, sloshing water everywhere, only to have my entire body collapse fully, submerging half my face. When I blinked at the arm where

Erena's leeches had attached, I could see my veins bulging with black poison.

"Damn," I muttered.

Marian was screaming for Rune, was screaming at me to stay awake, and don't you dare fall asleep, Val, don't you dare close your eyes, don't you dare leave us–

Her words sounded far away, pounding like a bad headache. I opened my mouth to assure her that I was totally fine.

Darkness wrapped slender fingers around my ankle and pulled me down.

CHAPTER THIRTEEN

I hurtled into dreams.

Father Dumas was laying me down at the forested edge of the Wilds. I tried to move, but my body felt syrupy and unresponsive. Drugged, maybe. My left arm was splayed out to the side, and Father Dumas hovered over it, a feverish look in his eyes. He held aloft a small knife, the hilt engraved with strange markings.

Don't, I wanted to cry.

He plunged down, and drops of blood spilt like jewels across the ground, dampening the leaves, soaked up greedily by the soil.

"Must be true... *Must* be..."

Father Dumas peeled back my skin, and his face shone with mesmerizing blue light. He gave a triumphant laugh.

Then Peyton was there. She drew bleeding scratches down her cheeks as she screamed. "*What have you done?*"

"We had to be sure." Father Dumas didn't sound the least bit consoling. "We had to know. And we were right!"

Peyton sobbed harder, and if I could have moved, I wanted

nothing more than to wrap my arms around her and hold her tight.

"What—" Peyton cleared her throat. "What is she?"

"The key to everything we need. The power to save or destroy. But she must never become that powerful. She must never know how strong she can be."

"Why not?"

"Why not?" Father Dumas laughed as though Peyton were a child who'd asked a silly question. "Because if she does, she'll be the end of us."

The dream shifted, and I sat atop a blanket at a picnic in a beautiful clearing filled with birdsong. A bountiful spread of slain beasts, sugared fruits, and drink spread before me, but all of it was rotted and reeked. The Lords of the Wilds I helped Rune kill sat on the other side: Mordecai, Jezaline, and Aleki, along with Rune's cousins, Vanesi, and her brother Cobb.

All of them were rotten, too. Wilted flowers drooped from where their eyes should have been, and worms crawled through the holes in their paper-thin skin. Vanesi had smudges of ink across her throat, and the fleshy parts of her body that hadn't turned to crystal had begun to melt like wax.

"The Wilds consume all, but they didn't take us." Mordecai laughed like the jester he was dressed as, poofy sleeves and all. "Your High King was so vindictive he wouldn't even let us rest, and the loam spat us straight back out."

"But we forget," Jezaline said mockingly to me. "You *love* him. The murderer, the killer."

"He was always a willful child," Aleki said. "He liked to make others hurt."

"You think I sent him to Mog Moren because I hated him?" Cobb said. "I did it to protect us. He couldn't possibly love anything enough to save it. The same is true for you."

Vanesi stood over me. The flesh part of her face had

continued to melt. Her mouth widened as her chin dipped to her chest, until it looked like she was howling in agony.

"I'll make it easier for you," she said. "And far less painful."

Before I could scream, she drove a sword through my chest. I fell and fell until I hit the ground and shattered.

I was in a million pieces spread across a dark void. In the center was nothing but a soft cocoon of light and a woman I couldn't make out within. The darkness pressed in, testing the edges of the light, and if I could, I'd have shouted a warning.

"You are not the sister I once knew," Grislehaut said. "Nor the god that was."

"She is gone," the woman answered. "I am here to take her place."

"Then you can rule with me. We can make this world new."

"One day, perhaps," the woman said. "But not yet."

The darkness pressed further in, nearly puncturing the sphere of light.

"If not, you'll be destroyed too. Not killed, but made nothing."

"I will stay as I am," the woman said. "Just as you must stay as you are. You must stay. Stay..."

"STAY WITH ME."

I felt myself in Rune's arms, rocking back and forth to the rhythm of his steps. He'd tucked me close, carrying me as easily as he would a pillow.

Through the tar-thick haze of my thoughts, I could make out the night sky reflected on the surface of a small pool of water. Rune was speaking to it. Pleading, at first, and then demanding. Moments later, a raspy, high-pitched voice answered.

"Only one thing will heal her," Rune said. "And I'm not asking."

When I temporarily drifted back into consciousness, I was sprawled across soft grass, the tips tickling the back of my neck. My limbs felt as though someone had injected boiling water into my veins. I tried to raise my arms. Dark purple had swollen the veins beneath my skin near to bursting.

"Lie still."

Rune stood over me. Blood splattered his front.

"You're hurt..." I slurred.

His scowl deepened. "The blood isn't mine."

"Oh." My stomach lurched at that. "Then am I...?"

"Stop talking. Save your strength."

How similar this was to the last time we were in the Halfway. Sotera's curse had nearly ripped me apart from the inside out, and only Rune's swift intervention had kept me alive. Rune even wore a similar expression, frustration mingled with fear.

When reality snapped into focus again, I realized Rune had removed his blood-covered coat, pulled back his sleeves. He was washing blood from the hot, sharp pain in my arms and in my gut. Each time he drew back, he was covered in even more blood, and his scowl deepened. He vanished from my sight and returned a moment later with water cupped in his hand. With gentle fingers he tilted my head up and poured it against my barely open lips. Most spilled off either side, but some made it down my throat. I sputtered before swallowing.

"More," Rune demanded, tilting his hand.

"More will kill her faster than her injuries," a familiar voice said. "That water is not meant for mortals. You have to accept that she might not make it."

"She will survive," Rune said firmly. "She's stronger than that. So much stronger."

A scoff. "For your sake, for all your sakes, I hope you're right."

I AWAKENED an unknown amount of time later. The sensation of molten lead in my veins was gone. Only a dim hum of discomfort remained.

I sat up and the soft bed of grasses and tufts of sandwort that pillowed my head retracted. When I stood, I nearly pitched over into the bi-colored pool of life and death nearby. It was vacant of Xin's spear-riddled body, and for that I was grateful. One side bubbled with a vicious, dark liquid that smelled of meat gone bad. The other was startlingly clear.

My first coherent thought was of Rune. I didn't remember much about what happened after Erena poisoned me. But I remembered him. He brought me to the Halfway. He fed me water from the pool. He kept me alive. Again.

I spotted him by the edge of the ghost-white trees, peering into them at the vague, phantom forms of animals and grander beasts passing by deep within.

I knelt by the edge of the clear pool. Mother Mal had specifically instructed Rune and me never to drink the water, only to use it to heal our injuries. Yet Rune had fed it to me, I was sure, and I was somehow still here. And I felt a terrible thirst for it now.

I carefully scooped some into my hands and drank cupful after cupful. My head buzzed with a sharp warning. If I didn't stop, I wouldn't ever take another drink again. When I stood, my world swayed even more crazily than before. I fell to my knees, disoriented.

"Much more of that and you'll finish the job Erena couldn't," Rune said.

He sat beside me. To my undying embarrassment, I leaned into him, head still spinning. "I just need a moment. I'll be fine in a sec."

"I know you will be."

Rune wrapped one arm around my shoulders to hold me up. With the other he raised my own arm. A dark, angry crimson had dried over my forearm in an erratic pattern, as though someone had taken a razor blade and traced it from elbow to wrist.

"Erena's poison ruptured your veins," Rune said. I felt the low growl of displeasure rumble through his chest. "You literally would have bled to death from the inside out."

I managed to turn my head enough to look at him. "Why do I get the feeling you're blaming *me* for that?"

"Do you understand how close... If I hadn't reached the Halfway in time..."

He was furious, but clearly trying to restrain it. "I blame *us*, Val. If my connection to the Wilds had been stronger, I could have prevented Erena and Bendeti's soldiers from ever entering the glen. He wouldn't have dared attack me at all. If *your* connection had been stronger..." His frown deepened. "If only you'd listened—"

"If only I'd listened to you and let you take Sotera's throne?" I finished.

He looked away. "Yes."

"If I'd have done that, then we'd probably both be dead."

Rune pursed his lips. With a twirl of his hand, a thick, waxy leaf appeared between his fingers. Green sap dripped out when he broke it apart, and he rubbed this on the smears of crimson along my arms. With each stroke the dried blood thinned and wiped off.

"I can't keep almost losing you because of my—our—weakness," he murmured.

"I don't know if that's our choice," I said. "To be together is to risk losing each other."

"Unless being together meant we became stronger, not more vulnerable."

He looked at me. I refused to break his gaze. I wouldn't shy away from these growing feelings, the ones I was surer with every passing day Rune also had for me.

At last Rune returned to my arms, using more waxy leaves to gently wipe away the rest of the blood. I marveled at the domesticity of the movements. How strange that the same hands he'd cut throats and ordered deaths with, could also be used for something so tender. I'd seen his tenderness before, directed at me and others closest to him. But the way he easily revealed it now was disarming. *Distressing.*

Rune reached the crook of my elbow, and his fingers brushed against the pocket of my dress and the shape of the amulet within. I removed my arm and closed a fist around the red heart gem.

"I never should have taken it."

"You thought it could be useful," Rune said. "I only wonder *why*. Are you still frightened of me?"

"No." The answer came easily, but I had to bite my tongue to stop the rest of the words from tumbling out: *I am frightened, but for a different reason than before.*

Rune cupped my cheek. "Hold still."

There was a sharp sting when he rubbed the rough pad of his thumb over the slice in my skin where the Undersea's arrow had grazed. There was a pleasant buzz, and the small cut closed up as he ran his thumb back and forth.

He didn't remove his hand when he'd finished. I thought of how it felt to kiss him. More than that, I thought of how it felt to be *known* by him, utterly and completely. Once, we'd shared a mutual hatred of one another. That had shifted to a connection of shared wounds.

Surely the fondness we felt could be built on more than pain and misery. Surely we could build something together that was beautiful. Find things in each other that we actually liked.

How to do that I didn't know. But I wanted to learn.

Rune cleared his throat. "I have a proposition—"

"I see Hob has still failed to properly discern whom to let into the Halfway."

The bark of the Mother Tree peeled back, and Mother Mal emerged from within.

I'd nearly forgotten how tall she was, how slim her willowy, branchy arms were, which tapered to claw-like fingers and spotted with dormant flower buds. Her head was a slender beast's skull sporadically splotched with flesh. Her human-like eyes took me in, unreadable as always, but if I peered at them too long, I was sure I'd find the eons she'd been alive stirring beneath.

"Good thing Hob hasn't learned," I said. "Someone has to be there to let guests in." Then, remembering who I was speaking to, followed up with a, "Thank you for letting us in, by the way."

Mother Mal partially opened her skulled mouth in what could have been shock, or more likely her version of a wry grin. "Humility. Perhaps the pool of life and death fixed as many of your most irksome flaws as it did your injuries."

I highly doubted that.

Hob was tucked behind her cloak, a knobby-limbed, gangly creature with a beard of moss and nails like eagle claws. The severed head of Kaffa, the enormous snake that had once curled around the base of the Mother Tree, had been removed.

The long coils of his body had become one with the Mother Tree's writhing network of roots.

Olette had stayed with them here, once. A somber child who, for a brief moment, found happiness in this place outside places.

Rune got to his feet. I took a moment to mentally brace myself before standing beside him. The woodland clearing wobbled a little but righted itself quickly enough.

"You didn't appear at the Midnight Revel," Rune said. "I'm too bitter to believe any of the gods of old would actually show themselves—if they were even still alive—but I assumed you'd be there. Perhaps you're too far gone, too damaged."

"There was no place for me," Mother Mal said. "Not yet."

"What about Olette?" I said, finally forcing myself to say her name. I gestured to the Mother Tree. The lapis-blue veins that choked the trunk, the ones Sotera had infected it with, were so dull they were nearly black, a benefit of Olette's spirit. "You saved her spirit, kept it safe here. Wouldn't she be at the revel? Hasn't she become part of the Wilds?"

"In more ways than you realize," Mother Mal said. She stared at me, as though trying to discern whether what I was asking would bring what remained of Olette to further harm. I'd brought Olette here so she'd be in the care of a being who'd raised children of her own. Even after death, or whatever state Olette was in now, I was pleased to see Mother Mal's desire to protect her remained.

"She isn't yet ready," Mother Mal said. "She is being reborn."

"Reborn?" I imagined Olette's damp, rotted body rising from the loam, her eyes nothing but rotted flowers, her skin full of holes. "What does that mean?"

"There is a legend one of my tutors told me about the gods of the Wilds," Rune said. "It says that many of them were once mortal but gifted immortality through magic and circumstance."

"And have all your tutor's lessons come to pass?" Mother Mal said.

"That remains to be seen. What also remains to be seen is whether you're creating new gods. Before the Forming there were gods and great beasts aplenty. There was also untold death and destruction. I won't have that again, not in my Wilds."

Mother Mal leaned forward as though genuinely curious. "And how far would you go to ensure that never happens again?"

I could see it. Rune closing the distance between him and Mother Mal. Rune driving a knife into her chest. I could also see it not making a bit of difference.

"Life and death is a circle," Mother Mal said. "What was lost can never be found again, but something new can take its place. And sometimes that new thing is different than what had come before. All it needs is a little time, a little tending, and it can grow anew, even grander than the first."

It was as though a veil had been drawn from my eyes and I could see the Mother Tree for what it actually was: a birthplace of gods. In my brief vision, the roots coiling at the base of the tree stretched. Smooth depressions appeared within them where a child, and beings much, much larger than that, might have curled up, tended to by their attentive Mother Mal.

Pieces slammed together in my head so hard my eye twinged. "Grislehaut... He's one of your children, too, isn't he?"

The entire clearing went still.

"Be careful of what you speak, and to whom," Mother Mal said.

The more I thought about it, the more I was sure I was right. "He is," I insisted. "You said you raised Rhasahlyn the

Gentle and Nieriati the Bloom Tender. They're ancient forces of the Wilds, just like Grislehaut is. You raised him, and you can help us stop him. You can keep him from destroying everything."

"Children can grow unruly," Mother Mal said. "They can even grow vengeful. What makes you think he wants to see me?"

"You sealed him away the first time, didn't you?" Rune said, though it didn't sound like a question.

"That was another time, another age."

"But you can do it again," I pressed.

"There are reasons he can't be placated this time, at least not by me," Mother Mal said. "I will not speak to him. And you would do well to stop asking me to."

I glared at her. Mother Mal had never changed her mind or deviated from what only she believed as the way things were meant to be. She hadn't stopped Sotera from killing Olette or Vanesi from barging in here and killing everything. She forever remained immovable from whatever grand plan she wouldn't let the rest of us see.

"Then how can we stop him?" I asked, dejected. "And don't say you don't know. You might be the only one who actually does."

"All that you need to end the greatest threat is within you."

I nearly screamed in frustration. Mother Mal always spoke in half-truths, but I was over it.

"But there is something you can do for me," Mother Mal continued before I could rant at her. "That seed planted within you has done its job, and now it can be returned."

My hand instinctively went to my chest. Mother Mal had once gifted me a seed plucked from one of the flowers along her arm. That seed had nestled deep within my chest and remained there ever since, anchoring me to the Wilds and its magic.

Rune glared at Mother Mal. "That seed kept her alive. It's bound to the Wild half of Val's crown."

"*Val* is bound to the crown," Mother Mal corrected. "The seed has played its part. Return it now, Empress of Glass."

"I might be bound to the crown but my magic here is weak," I said. "I can't give it up."

"Soon that might not be your choice. At least now I'm giving you one. I want what is best for the Wilds, and if that means I must do its will rather than mine, then I am okay with that. Surely, as a ruler, you understand such sacrifice?"

"So you'll do what's best for the Wilds and screw anyone else, right? You let Olette die, but it's fine because the Wilds wanted it?"

Darkness pressed the edges of the clearing. The Mother Tree's branches groaned as they reached down and stopped just over our heads, as though restrained from strangling me. Rune stepped to my side, but I wasn't cowed by Mother Mal's display of power. She couldn't bully me into getting what she wanted.

"The Wilds always give," Mother Mal said. "But to do so, it must take."

"We have a war to get back to," Rune said. "Your unruly child grows stronger by the day, and since you won't, somebody has to calm him."

I waited for Mother Mal to trap us here until we did as she asked, but that wasn't her way. She never forced anything. She gave false choices, and eventually, no matter what you did, she got what she wanted, whether *you* wanted it or not.

"Hob will lead you out," Mother Mal said.

"We know the way," I said curtly.

We stepped over the smashed crystal of what had once

been tightly knit brambles guarding the entrance of the clearing. The moment the Mother Tree was out of sight something deep below my feet rumbled, possibly Grislehaut stirring. We were running out of time, and one of our best options, one of those who would understand the most, refused to help.

"There will be another way," Rune said.

"How can you be so confident?" I said.

Rune flashed me a grin, though it didn't quite meet his eyes. "Sometimes confidence is all I have. That, and you. You haven't let death claim you yet, and if you refuse to stop fighting, then I certainly can't."

There was something wholly unlike hatred in his eyes. I was flushed, unable to speak.

"Such a brazen attack by the Undersea can't go unpunished," Rune continued. "It's time to end the king of fish. He thinks he'll be safe even on land because of the high tides. He will strike, again and again, until the full moon fades. But now that he's strongest, that will make us stronger, too."

We took another step through a pool of still water reflecting starlight and back into the Wilds. Rune summoned a path of beckoning green and a dark destination. "Let's go kill a king."

CHAPTER FOURTEEN

After I changed back into my normal clothes, we returned to Rune's green palace to find most of the revelers who'd survived the Undersea's assault soaked and shivering amongst the repurposed human dwellings. Some hovered around crackling bowls of everfire, rubbing their hands. Their glittering eyes followed Rune and me as we moved back toward the glen.

Bendeti had been thorough. The entire glen was flooded with seawater up to my knees. Bodies of Undersea soldiers that hadn't been dredged drifted listlessly, occasionally bumping into one another. The trees around the edges were already starting to wilt, either from the amount of salt or Bendeti's magic.

"My Lord Rune."

Pitius knelt before us. One of my soldiers stood beside her, rubbing the top of his crystal hand in nervous habit. He was younger, his face not yet wrinkled and cracked by age or suspicion.

"Kelar," I said, remembering his name. "I'm glad you're okay."

Kelar seemed shocked that I'd known he'd existed at all. He lowered his bow even farther, until I worried he'd break the crystal along his back. "My Empress, I'm honored!"

"He's honored," Rune echoed, raising an eyebrow at me. "What is it, Pitius?"

"We've acquired a prisoner from the Undersea," Pitius answered. "We thought that you might like to interrogate him."

"I may have a few questions," Rune said.

"I could join you, Empress," Kelar said. "I briefly worked under the one who oversaw Sotera's prisoners. He always got them to talk."

"And did you like the work they did?" I asked.

Kelar's face fell. "I will do whatever I'm asked."

While I wanted allegiance and help, I needed to temper any blind loyalty or fanaticism that would turn me into someone like Father Dumas. I put a hand on Kelar's shoulder.

"I'll take care of this. Work on burying the dead." I glanced at Rune. "I'm sure the high king wouldn't mind us cutting into the earth."

"We're allies now, aren't we?" Rune said. He waved a hand. "You can carve into the ground all you'd like, and the Wilds won't take vengeance."

"Dig deep, give them the burial they deserve, Kelar," I said.

Though rarely could Those Below shed actual tears, Kelar's eyes glazed a little. "Of course, Empress. Always."

After Kelar rushed off, Rune stared at me with an expression that was difficult to read. He'd seen me giving orders before. But like Those Below, perhaps he was starting to truly see me as an Empress, with real weight behind my commands. Was he reconsidering being upset at what I did? Likely he thought it even more of a mistake he'd let me go through with it.

Pitius led us deep into the palace, to the top of a circular well with about a dozen porticoed floors, a thousand steps leading down, and row upon row of cells. This dungeon could hold a hundred prisoners, at least.

"Believe it or not, it was here when I arrived," Rune said. "A delight and hobby for the Lord who used to live here, I'm sure. I don't intend to ever fill it."

"We never intended to do a lot of things," I said sadly. "But already it's coming in handy."

They'd put the prisoner in the very first cell, at the bottom of a pit with smooth, damp walls. I could make out the shape of him below, curled up in a couple inches of water.

"He wasn't injured when we caught him," Pitius said. "We think he was trying to run."

That caught me off guard. With all the brutality Bendeti had shown me and others, I hadn't considered that there would be those under his command who didn't want to fight or were scared to.

"Is that true?" I called down to the prisoner. "Were you running?"

His dark, wet eyes blinked up at me, but he stayed silent. Half his lobster-shelled armor was missing, as though he'd been in the middle of shedding it when he'd been caught. He didn't look much older than me. Seemed this war was fought by the young.

Rune leaned precariously over the edge. "I'm curious, what would you do if your king was dead? What would you be instead of his soldier?"

Still, the prisoner remained silent.

"We're running out of time, Rune," I said. "Bendeti has to have found somewhere reasonably close by to hide, and we need to know where."

I drew a crystal needle from my wrist. I fingered the glass vial in my coat pocket. "Bring him up here."

Rune did so without hesitation, manipulating the earth so that it rose the entire floor to our level. The prisoner lurched forward, as though to shove us out of the way and make a run for it, but thick roots sprang from the walls and held him fast.

"*Stay still,*" Rune said, voice thick with compulsion. "*Answer our questions.*"

The prisoner opened his mouth. Nothing but a grating hiss came out.

Then he slumped, panting with exertion. Rune asked again, and again to the same effect. No doubt Bendeti had trained his soldiers to resist such wildling magic. But he hadn't prepped them for everything the Wilds had to offer.

I dipped the tip of my crystal needle in the vial of Magora's venom. The prisoner thrashed as I drew close, until Rune's words stopped him. I pricked the side of the prisoner's neck, deep enough to ensure the venom made it into his bloodstream.

The result was immediate. His already dilated pupils swelled to twice the size. The veins of his neck popped with the strain of trying to hold himself back and failing.

"Where is Bendeti?" I said.

The prisoner gnashed his teeth, foamed at the mouth, tried to bite his tongue, but eventually rasped, "King's Hollow."

"Of course he is," Rune said. "I'll bet he couldn't wait to take what he thought was my throne. How many soldiers did he bring?"

"Less than a hundred. Even less than that now," the prisoner said. He swallowed, as though trying to shove the words back down. "It was supposed to be quick. You were supposed to be unaware. That was what the human priest said."

"Father Dumas knew you were going to do the revel,

Rune," I said. "I should have guessed. I'm sure he knows more about the gods of the Wilds than you do."

"Yes, he's becoming almost as big a pain as Bendeti." Rune stepped closer to the prisoner. "And who will the Undersea follow when Bendeti is dead?"

"Another," the prisoner said. "His daughter."

I was surprised to hear that Bendeti had any children, anyone who might potentially love him. "And will she fight us?"

"I don't know," the prisoner said. "Few have seen her. She keeps to her own palace deep in the Pacific, far away from Bendeti."

"Likely why she's still alive," Rune said. He spoke a word and the compulsion fell away from the prisoner, though I was sure the Magora's venom would take some time to wear off. "We'll push on Bendeti tonight, not give him any chance to recover."

"You don't have long."

The prisoner's head was tilted, mouth frothing. "I heard them talking. My King believes that Val will soon no longer be the Empress of Glass."

"I'm sure he thought I'd be dead by now," I said wryly.

"No, he believed you'd give it up. That Rune would give up his throne of the High King."

"Then he doesn't know me well at all," Rune said.

The prisoner's words rankled me a bit. Though becoming Empress had happened due more to necessity than desire, I couldn't see any instance where giving up my place would make things *better*.

"What should we do with the prisoner?" Pitius whispered once Rune had lowered him back into the pit and we'd left the cell. I knew what she was really asking, and Rune did too, judging by the way he frowned at the ground, considering.

"Give him more seawater and food. Leave him down there, at least until the worst of this is over."

Pitius nodded and went to do just that.

"Are you sure?" I asked. "At one time you would have killed him. One less liability."

"Are you sad about that?" Rune said.

I wasn't. I wanted a Rune who would do what was necessary—*whatever* was necessary—to keep us safe. But he had to be better. We both did.

"Maybe he can still prove useful," I relented. "And maybe if we keep him alive, when all this is done his friends and loved ones won't hate us enough to try to kill us back."

"I love your optimism," Rune said. "Even if it's misplaced."

King's Hollow smelled of seawater, old magic, and blood.

Rune had obscured his wildlings and my soldiers, and I crouched beside him, Marian, Xander, and Raquel, searching for our prey.

Like the glen near Rune's palace, the Hollow was submerged in a foot of water. It flooded the underground tunnels, lapped against the raised platform where Rune's now-destroyed throne sat. Bendeti's soldiers patrolled the outskirts or lounged beneath the glass-covered awnings where wildlings had once lived.

I pointed. "There."

Behind the throne, atop a once-clear lake turned brackish, were islands of sprawling green. Bendeti relaxed atop the nearest one.

"Our prisoner was right about how many soldiers he brought," Rune murmured. "We have the numbers."

Though the prisoner hadn't said it aloud, I got the impression there were more like him who didn't want to fight. Much like killing the Lords of the Wilds, if we could remove their king, it was possible others would surrender.

"I can sneak around," I said to Rune. "Take out Bendeti before anyone notices, like I tried to with Sotera."

"Tried to," Rune emphasized.

One of my biggest failures. Something I was determined not to repeat. "She was waiting for me. Bendeti is not."

"And who's to say this isn't another trap? The prisoner could have had the idea planted. He could believe he was telling us the truth."

What if, what if, what if. So many uncertainties.

"To kill the snake, we have to remove the head," Xander said.

"While I'd normally like to slaughter each and every one, the less we have to fight, the less we have to lose," Marian added.

Rune's expression was part bemusement, part frustration. "Seems time away from me has brought out everyone's gentler qualities."

Marian scoffed. "Erena would disagree with you, were she not missing her throat."

I touched Rune's arm. "I can do this, Rune. Circle the Hollow, cut off any escapes. Give me time to move close to Bendeti, and I'll do the rest."

Trust me, I wanted to add, as though we hadn't done anything *but* that since the day we met.

"Bendeti can't get away," Rune said. "No matter what."

"I'll help make sure he doesn't," Marian said.

I drew Sliver, the gleaming blade perfectly weighted in my hand, eager to draw blood. "He won't."

"Raquel," Rune said.

Raquel pinched the earth together and summoned a half

dozen wolf-like creatures made of dirt and rock, their eyes glittering with life. "On your command, Rune."

Rune's hand caught mine as I started to draw away. He looked as though he wanted to say something else, and the possibility of what it could be made my stomach clench with a mixture of apprehension and want.

"Make him hurt," Rune said.

My hand felt colder as I removed it from his. "I will. Marian, get closer to me. Erebus, cloak us."

With a low growl, Erebus moved from the crook on my collarbone and spread over Marian and me like a cold blanket, until my world turned grayscale and we'd become part of the shadows.

As Rune and the others silently circled the Hollow, I slipped far around until I'd made it to a vantage point above the islands where Bendeti sat. I wished I had the poison-filled ink pods that Xin from the Halfway had once given me. They'd nearly killed Bendeti once, and I was sure it could have easily finished the job this time.

"Look beneath the water," Marian whispered in my ear. "That's where he'll try to go."

Coral columns had risen from the bottom of the pool where schools of fish, a couple sharks, and even an orca circled. Down there must have been somewhere he could escape. No way he could bring all the sea life in without a relatively large back door. I would have one shot to stop him.

"The moment I jump, leave me," I said to Erebus. I readjusted my footing, waiting for the perfect moment.

I didn't need to wait long.

Surging like a creature from the deep, enormous trees burst from beneath the islands, shattering the coral columns, shoving fish and shark alike aside until the trees breached the surface. Moments later wildlings surged from the undergrowth in all directions to surround the soldiers of the Undersea. Waves of blue clashed with waves of green. Bendeti leapt up, shocked. He made a break for the water.

"Now, Erebus!"

Erebus sloughed off me as I leapt to the edge of the pool right as a thin layer of ice froze its surface, temporarily stopping Bendeti from leaping in. He swung around, snarling, "Kill them!"

"Go!" Marian yelled.

Bendeti's soldiers moved tenuously toward us. I skirted around them, stepped lightly across the ice, and jumped the last few feet to land in front of a startled Bendeti.

"You bi—"

I pulled the amulet the Lords had gifted me and slammed it against Bendeti's chest. As his fist crashed against my ribs, I wheezed out the words to activate it. His limbs drooped. His skin temporarily lost its dull shine.

"Wha—What did you do to me?" he gasped.

I struck with Sliver and managed to score a hit to his shoulder, parting flesh and spraying blood into the water. A weak wave knocked me to one side, allowing Bendeti to back away from my next attack.

"This was all a trick," he hissed, clutching his wound. "Father Dumas kept you alive to kill me, made me out as your worst enemy so you wouldn't focus on him."

"You did that yourself," I said. "And don't worry, Father Dumas is next."

"You little fool. He's already won. He won the moment he freed that god."

I'd been so focused on Bendeti I hadn't noticed the ice covering the water had thawed. Bendeti leapt in, magically propelling himself into the depths. Toward escape.

I raced to the water's edge right as a shark beached itself, snapping at me. As it tried to squirm back into the water, I plunged Sliver into its eye and twisted. It flopped a few more times before lying still.

Panting, I filled my lungs with air and plunged after Bendeti. The water was cold enough to freeze my capillaries, and I had to blink away the salty sting before I could see anything.

An orca, its body full of arrows, drifted listlessly past me, blood seeping from its wounds. The schools of fish swirled behind Bendeti as his current carried him to the darkness below, and no doubt out toward the sea. Once he reached freedom, it was over. He wouldn't risk coming onto land again, and Rune and I would have to always keep one eye toward the sea, for as short a time as we were alive.

My lungs were starting to burn as I found the Below's magic near the bottom of the pool, felt it reaching for me. I pulled until it was painful and then pulled some more. The earth here was already weakened from the enormous crevasses Sotera had created. All I had to do was reopen them.

I unleashed my magic. My insides felt as though two hands had pried me open. The space behind my eyes spiked with pain as my vision went white.

The earth split apart beneath Bendeti.

The water began swirling around me as it was drawn down, first a gentle tug and then an irresistible force. I was flipped end over end, barely managing to right myself in time to see the whirlpool I created suck Bendeti in. His eyes were wide and confused, as though he couldn't believe the very sea he once controlled had betrayed him. He screamed curses at me that were lost as he was torn through the split in the earth. Over the roil of water rushing through my ears, I thought I heard the crack of his legs and arms as they were twisted into unnatural positions by the force of the water.

I slammed into the side of the pool and nearly blacked out. Using instinct more than skill, I willed the crystal within the earth to fuse my hands in place and then my arms. Rock parted, creating a pocket of air. I shoved my face into this as deep as possible and took desperate gulping breaths. My muscles and bones screamed in agony as thousands of gallons drained Below, trying to take me with it. I focused only on taking shallow sips of air, of keeping myself fused to the wall.

What might have been two minutes or two hours later, the ceaseless pressure faltered and then slowed to a trickle. Eventually it wasn't water pulling me down but gravity, and I found my feet dangling over nothing. Moving was agony, but inch by inch I started crawling up the side, stopping once to rest and look down.

A hundred feet below, through the fissure I'd created, lay dozens of those from the Undersea sprawled in all manner of broken poses. In the center of them, as though the focus of a macabre art display, was the King of the Undersea.

Bendeti had been impaled on crystal, his open mouth full of water that dribbled down his cheeks. His skin had begun to dry out, even more blue in death. I swore he was still glaring at me.

"Take my hand." Xander was reaching down toward me. "Quickly, before you lose grip."

With great effort, I took one of his calloused hands. He easily pulled me up, grinning.

"Long live the Empress of Glass. Long live the king killer."

CHAPTER FIFTEEN

Now that I wasn't forced to hold on for dear life, I began to shiver with a combination of fatigue and cold. My lungs felt seared like I'd sucked in clouds of ash.

Xander helped me up the sharp incline around the drained pool until we reached King's Hollow, now a hive of activity.

"I need to go see about the others," Xander said. "Will you be all right?"

Breathing too much still hurt so I waved him off with a nod. He'd barely left before Rune landed from above. He was covered in blood and scores of small cuts. To my shock, he scooped me into a hug so tight I let out an undignified "Eeep!"

He drew back, his eyes dark, lips tilted in a reprimanding frown.

"Don't tell me how stupid that was," I said.

"I assumed you already knew. Though I suppose it can only be called stupid if it doesn't work."

Now there was something proud in his smile, something wholly un-Rune-like that I was seeing more and more often.

"Get some rest," he told me before I could puzzle over it too much. "I'll deal with the aftermath."

"*We'll* deal with it," I insisted. "You're not the only ruler here—"

I stumbled, and it was only because Rune held me firm that I didn't fall on my face.

"As agonizing as it might be, listen to me and rest," Rune said.

"What about you?" I said, flushing with embarrassment. "Don't pretend like you're fine."

I expected him to deny it, but Rune turned away, wincing. He put his hand to his eye, and when he drew it back to look at me, a black liquid stained his palm.

I grabbed his hand before he could hide it. The black ink was viscous, like blood. I tried to look more closely at it, but it vanished within seconds, as though I'd hallucinated the entire thing.

"What is happening to us?" I murmured.

"Every time takes so much more," Rune said.

"Using magic is killing you," I insisted.

"It's killing both of us. How many times do you think we can do this before it's too much? Before we do irreversible damage?"

I traced where the black ink had spread across his hands and then moved my fingers to his face. I swore I could see the glint of blue crystal in his other eye.

"How do we fix this?" I asked. "We can't give up the crowns or the power. We can't be completely defenseless."

Rune opened his mouth, paused, reconsidered. "Get some rest."

"Rune, no, talk to me."

"I will. When you're recovered. When we're both recovered. There are things better spoken of when we're both in better health. If not, there's a risk we may break things worse than before."

He looked scared. But before I could press him for more, he draped a cloak of woven ivy and downy feathers across my shoulders and then pulled away, going to help move the wounded and bury the dead.

I waited until my head stopped spinning before finding Xander and having him lead me to where the worst of the injured were. Marian was already there, using her magic on those with the most life-threatening wounds.

"You hurt?" she said, not looking up from the bone she was mending.

"Nothing you can fix," I said. "How many did we lose?"

"A couple of yours. About five of ours."

Better than I could have dreamed and barely a loss at all. Certainly a good outcome for what we got in return. Still my stomach felt sick.

"Some of the Undersea tried to escape with Bendeti and met his fate," Xander said. "Others tried to flee into the Wilds."

I imagined packs of wolves tracking the fleeing soldiers, tearing them to pieces. I imagined flowers with poisonous clouds of spores clogging their gills and trees snaking roots through their veins that ripped them apart from the inside.

"I don't think we'll have to worry about them," I said.

Marian grinned.

There were about two dozen prisoners of the Undersea under guard at the base of where Rune's throne sat. Cassius guarded them, his sword at the ready.

"They hid when the fighting started," he said. "Rune said to let you decide what to do with them."

I glanced over at Rune. He wanted me to decide because he thought me more capable, he trusted me, or because he thought I'd be more merciful?

As I looked over the prisoners—some of them glaring at me —I wasn't sure which one of those, if any, was true.

"How many of the wildlings that ceded when Rune became High King stayed loyal?" I asked Xander in a low voice.

"Enough," he replied. "But they were of the Wilds. The Undersea has no love for us or our ways."

Yet if these prisoners had hidden instead of fought, then perhaps they had no love of Bendeti, either.

I stepped before them. "Choose one to represent you."

After a lot of shuffling and some muttering, an older, fish-scaled man, so low to the ground he made me think of a crab, scuttled forward.

"I am Nicorso, Empress of Glass." He managed to bow even lower. "I suppose I will speak for them."

"You suppose so?" I said. "Are you the representative or not?"

Nicorso smirked back at the prisoners. "I was the leader of this group, and because I led wisely enough to save their lives, I suppose they think me wise enough to try to do so again." He gave a mirthless grin. "We'll both see if that's true."

I appreciated his honesty. "Your king is dead."

Nicorso nodded. "We guessed that. Which means we now have a queen."

King Bendeti's daughter, the one I'd never met, and the one I couldn't hope to get a read on. Perhaps she was as cold as her father, as cold as the depths. "Will she avenge him?"

Nicorso looked confused at the question, touching the tips of his claw-like hands together. "Many things fall to the next in line. I don't know if a war will be one of those."

That wasn't much of an answer, but I supposed it was the best I was going to get. "And if she chooses to fight us, will *you* fight for her in his place?"

Nicorso weighed his response, and I chose to take that as a good sign.

"We've heard you and the High King of the Wilds have armies who are loyal because of what you've done for them, not solely due to your position. You washed your hands with blood as surely as they did, and your palms are calloused from holding a sword. I respect that, and I know those I lead do too. Bendeti did none of those things, and yet we still followed him. Now, however, I wonder if we were wrong. I don't think it'd be so bad to wait and see if his daughter deserves our loyalty."

Gawdy praise, and a little misplaced, if I was honest. Rune and I might have won the loyalty of some with our penchant for getting our hands dirty. But I wondered if Nicorso and the others knew how strenuous my hold over those who followed me still was.

"If we've truly earned your respect as you claim, then you have a choice," I said. "You can follow us, help us to end anything that would threaten the Wilds, and by extension the Undersea. Or you will be kept at the new High King's palace, under guard. One of yours is already there. I can assure you it won't be comfortable."

"Why would we choose to go with you?" Nicorso said.

I was taken aback. "I just told you. If we don't stop this threat—"

"What I mean is, why would we want to fight for a doomed land? Why would we want to willingly run to our deaths? Others will ask you these questions, Empress. I suggest you have an answer for them."

I wondered when everyone had gotten used to giving me advice on how to run things. I let the uncomfortable silence be my answer. Nicorso grew nervous, shuffling his scaled feet.

"Bendeti was ambitious beyond his borders," he said. "There cannot be the Wilds without the Undersea. Our people were close once—allies more than friends—but there was respect. I wish to see that again. To try to make things as good as you and your High King claim to want."

He's not my High King, I wanted to say, *To me, he's just Rune.*

"We will fight for you," Nicorso said. He gave a bow, and those behind him followed suit. "With claw and fin and roiling current, until our ends, however soon that is."

"Good," I said, secretly relieved. "I'll have some of ours make sure your wounded are taken care of. Once that's done, you will take magically binding oaths and given assignments."

Nicorso lingered as those with him scuttled off to get tended to.

"We've heard of you, the one not of the above or the Below." His eyes scoured my crown. "We're not the only ones who will need to make our final choice in who to serve. And soon."

I kept my expression straight, trying not to show how much the words shook me. "I'll keep that in mind."

Nicorso grinned. "Do that. And let us hope we both make the right choice."

"You okay?" Xander said a minute later, after Nicorso had left and I remained where I was, lost in thought. I forced myself to nod.

"If you're comfortable with it, if *she's* comfortable with it, have Zuri speak to them when we get back to camp," I said. "They may trust her more since she's from the Undersea."

Xander frowned. "Or they may despise her because she's with me."

"I guess there's only one way to find out."

The damp and chill were starting to get to me. My shivering worsened as I stiffly made my way to where Rune's throne had once been. It remained as it had the last time I'd seen it, torn asunder by Rune in his desire to transfer all the power of his position to his crown and to him. It'd been a gutsy move. It made him more dangerous and more vulnerable in equal measure.

He's been vulnerable since the day he met you. You were, are, his blade. You will be his downfall.

I tucked myself deeper into the cloak, though it didn't do much more to stave off the worsening chill. To distract myself and keep my teeth from chattering, I called over Kelar. He didn't look any worse following the fight, maybe a few more splintery bruises along his arm but there was no haunted look of one who'd recently done a lot of butchering.

"Are you fast?" I asked him.

He looked up from where he'd kneeled, somewhat confused. "Slower than some, faster than most, Empress."

"I need you to return Below. Check Grislehaut's chamber and tell me if the water has stopped rising. Tell me how the chamber is doing."

I was grateful that Kelar didn't question why I wasn't having my nonexistent spies doing this but instead answered, "As the Empress wills it" and was gone.

Despondent with exhaustion, I watched the flurry of movement in the Hollow, readying myself to rejoin them, to do what I needed to as a ruler and dreading the thought of it.

"If you wish to catch hypothermia, there are quicker ways to do it," Marian said.

She shoved what looked like a half-rotted, shriveled chili into my hands.

I took a grateful bite of the pepper root and nearly groaned as sweet heat radiated through my body, to the tips of my fingers and toes. The ends of my hair began to steam.

"You're both terrible at that," Marian said. "Taking care of yourselves," she continued at my questioning look.

"I told Rune to get some help," I said.

"And did he listen?"

"Of course not."

Marian rolled her eyes. "See? He'll go until he drops. As you would. It's disgustingly noble."

I continued chewing on the pepper root, swallowing past the dirt taste that coated the inside of my mouth. Nicorso and the rest of the Undersea had been taken back to Rune's palace. The empty pool leading to the Below had already been covered with green, the hole I created sealed, and I had no doubt that after a few good rains it would fill again. Xander joined us, and the three of us sat in silence for a long while.

My eyes kept getting drawn back to Rune, and each time they were, I pulled the edges of the cloak he'd draped over me tighter. I wondered who he'd plucked it from or whether he made it right then and there. Mostly, I wondered *why*.

"It's weird," Marian said, breaking the long silence.

"Isn't it, though?" Xander said, grinning.

"What's weird?" I asked.

Marian nodded to Rune. "Weren't you paying attention?"

I looked at him again. "He's just giving orders."

"Not now. Before. You were the first one he checked on, and I saw how fearful he was the moment you didn't immediately emerge from the pool."

"We're allies," I said, carefully choosing the words. "If I die, then things will be a lot harder for him."

Marian gave me a sad look. "I sometimes forget just how good a liar you are. Just don't do it to yourself. In Mog Moren I saw Rune reaching out, loving, caring for so many people, and each time they were torn from him, and each time the callouses over his heart grew a little thicker. He's trying again, and I'm glad."

"Because you have Cassius," Xander said, tone light. "You don't have to be so jealous anymore."

Xander laughed as Marian hit him. "So? That doesn't make it any less true."

Marian's words didn't make me feel any better. I wasn't an idiot, and like Marian said, I couldn't continue pretending Rune didn't feel *something* for me, and I for him.

I pulled my knees to my chest. "It doesn't matter how Rune and I may or may not feel. All we ever do is hurt each other."

"Because that's what you learned," Xander said. "It's what you thought you had to do in order to stay safe. Hurt them before they inevitably hurt you. And that repeats, over and over and over again."

"And what's going to make this any different?" I said. "How did you learn to let Zuri in?"

"I suppose at some point you have to be open to getting hurt again," Xander said. "And I didn't know if it would work out with Zuri. I just knew that I cared for her. Maybe I was a bit desperate at first. Sometimes you lose so much you'll latch onto anyone, but for us it worked out."

"I don't think I'm brave enough to risk it," I said softly, speaking mostly to my knees.

Marian bit her lip, until I supposed the cutting words she wanted to say slipped back down her throat. "Whatever I wanted between Rune and me wasn't love, not really. We needed each other to get through what we went through, but it could never last beyond that. For you two, I think it *has* to last in order to get through what's coming. And this," she gestured down to Rune. "In all the times I wanted to be with him, I've never seen him act like this."

"Rune's trying, you know, Val," Xander said. "To be better. For you."

He'd been trying. When I allowed myself to actually focus on all the little changes he'd made, when I looked past his anger at what I'd done and saw what he was trying to do, he'd always been trying.

I pulled my knees tighter to my chest, tucking myself farther into the cloak. "Should I let him?"

Marian seemed confused. "Should you let him be better? Only if you want him to be, I guess. Only if you feel brave enough to risk it."

It didn't matter what I wanted. It mattered what was good for him, for us, for the Wilds. If him becoming more vulnerable to be better for me got him hurt, I wasn't sure I could ask that.

My legs were starting to lose circulation, and the sudden heat of the pepper root was making sitting still somewhat unbearable. I also felt I needed to thank Rune. For trying, at the very least.

I stood. "I'm going to—"

Kelar returned, only slightly out of breath.

"The chamber?" I asked.

"Sea water's still flowing into it," Kelar said, and my heart sank. "And the chamber is..."

He grimaced, and I knew how bad it must be. "Bendeti assumed this would happen," I said. "He had a failsafe to make sure the magic didn't stop with him."

"We could talk to the new queen of the Undersea," Xander said. "See if she'll put a stop to it."

I shook my head. It would take too long to reach her, and longer still to get an audience. If she would even deign to meet those who'd murdered her father and didn't try to kill us on sight. But there was one more party who wanted Grislehaut freed.

"Until we can figure out how to keep Grislehaut's chamber from breaking, we can work on killing Father Dumas," I said.

"You think that'll actually help anything?" Marian said.

It couldn't hurt. Father Dumas had been the start of this. Maybe facing him would be a way to finish it, somehow.

At the very least, killing him could be *some* solution, if only the answer about how to satiate my revenge for Joshua.

"I've heard he has heart-gem weapons," Xander said. "Wildling magic won't be much good against those."

That had been bothering me, too. Another problem for another time; time we were rapidly running out of.

"I want to see Grislehaut."

I hadn't heard Rune land beside me.

"I already spoke to him," I said. Spoken to him and nearly lost myself to his magic. With the chamber breaking, his influence was likely stronger now. I couldn't ask Rune to get any closer than necessary unless we had a solid plan.

"You talked to him, yes, and nothing changed," Rune said.

"And you think your silver tongue could convince him differently?" I grumbled.

"Not at all. But I doubt I could make it worse."

"You underestimate yourself," Marian said.

Rune nodded. "Perhaps. At the very least, I need to know truly what we're up against, before he's an unapproachable, relentless being of rage."

"Might be too late for that," I said.

Rune's smirk was dangerous. "Still."

"We can handle things up here," Marian said. "Go do what you need to."

I couldn't shake the feeling that this was the *last* thing we needed to do. Still.

"Fine," I said, before I could talk myself out of it. "Let's get this over with, then."

I gestured for Rune to follow, and together, we went to visit the god.

CHAPTER SIXTEEN

"If you wanted to get yourself killed, you should have let me do it first and saved us the trouble," General Tenia said.

Rune raised an eyebrow at me. "Care to explain?"

"Later," I said wearily. I raised my hand, and the light from the crystals lining the tunnel flared brighter, making it easier for us to make our way down. With the original path we'd taken to see Grislehaut nearly underwater, I'd had to ask General Tenia for a way through the upper tunnels, those closest to the Wilds and easiest to approach from above.

She'd been surprised when I'd told her that I'd killed King Bendeti. She'd been even more shocked to find Rune with me. Between my request to visit Grislehaut again and the High King of the Wilds by my side, she likely thought me the stupidest Empress to ever live.

"I meant to thank you, High King Rune, for allowing Those Below into your Wilds," General Tenia said, though it sounded like she was speaking through gritted teeth. "They're settling in nicely."

"It was Val who convinced me," Rune said. "But you're welcome."

General Tenia looked even more dour as she nodded at me. "Of course. My thanks, Empress."

The gratitude felt as cold as the surrounding stone, but I accepted it all the same.

The upper chamber eventually funneled us into a downward sloping tunnel. General Tenia stopped at the end, where it funneled narrower still into the dark. "This is as far as I go. I'm not foolish enough—"

Her eyes cut sharply to me. "What I mean is, if the Empress wishes to flirt with death, that is her choice."

"She's not the only one who enjoys it," Rune said.

I thanked General Tenia and was shocked again when she gave a curt bow, seemingly without having to remind herself to do so. "I'll await you above."

Rune was smirking as we continued to descend. "I think she likes you."

"You mean she maybe, perhaps, might consider *not* killing me next time she has the chance," I said.

"That's basically the same thing."

I rolled my eyes.

Far sooner than I expected, I found saltwater sloshing at our ankles. Farther down was the unmistakable sound of rushing water, draining somewhere deeper.

"Not good," I said, trying to keep the panic from my voice. "What if he..."

"If he was out, we'd know, I'm sure," Rune said. He brushed past me and kept moving into a wider part of the tunnel where the water rose to our knees.

He stopped, his body going rigid.

"What is it?" I said warily. "Do you see something?"

Rune didn't answer.

"Rune?" I demanded. "What do you—"

He turned, and my heart dropped into my stomach. His hand had started to unwind as though someone had pinched a tab of his skin between their fingers and started peeling it back. His face had begun to distort and dissolve into grains like sand, drifting into nothingness.

"I take it this is the god's doing?" he said.

"Get back!" I yelled. I wrenched him bodily back to me. I touched his hands, his arms, his face, as though he were a sand sculpture I could hold together if I just moved fast enough. After far too long, his form started to solidify once more.

"What are you *doing*?" I hissed. "You... You... This isn't some beast of the Wilds you can subjugate through sheer force and threats." I placed my knuckles against my forehead, trying to calm my pounding heart. "We're up against something that can't be physically beaten, Rune. I don't even know why I agreed to bring you here."

Rune's eyes were uncharacteristically wide, though his mouth was cocked in a familiar impish smirk. "I think it was worth coming down here just for your reaction."

"Don't. Don't make this about us when *you*—"

An overwhelming presence slammed into my thoughts, shoving me to the back of my own mind and taking control. I felt my body straighten up, felt intentions that turned into words move my lips to speak.

"At last, the High King of the Wilds."

Rune's smirk turned into confusion, which shifted into a glower. My panic pitched higher. Grislehaut wasn't free yet, and even still he'd easily batted my mental resistance aside like an errant fly.

"Whatever you're doing to her, I recommend you stop," Rune said.

"And if I do not? What would you do?" From my mouth,

Grislehaut's question sounded legitimately curious, as though he couldn't imagine what strength someone like me or Rune could possibly have.

Rune took a step forward, his gold-red eyes glowing with compulsion. "*You will leave her—*"

It felt as though a pickaxe had been lodged in my mind as Rune's magic tried to tear Grislehaut's influence away. A raspy scream escaped my lips, and I dropped to one knee. Rune knelt, reaching for me.

"Val? Did it work?"

"Careful, High King," Grislehaut said. "Her body, like yours, is oh so fragile. If I press it only a little, it may break."

Rune's hand halted inches from my face. His jaw was set tight in barely concealed rage. "Judging by your strength, I'm assuming that you're nearly free."

"Almost. Almost. I am shattered. I am in pieces. And I will fill the hole those pieces left with everything else." My arms moved as Grislehaut raised them to the surface. "With everyone else."

"And what is it you want?"

"This Empress asked me something similar. I will give you the same answer," Grislehaut said. "I want—"

Her. Only her, came the whisper beneath his whisper.

"Everything to become nothing," Grislehaut said.

If Rune had heard what I had, he didn't show it. "I can't allow you to do that."

"You won't have a choice." From behind my back, I could feel Grislehaut draw a crystal knife from my arm. "But you are a hinderance. That is why I was so happy that you'd come to visit."

I tried to wrestle back control of my body. I tried to scream at Rune to watch out.

Grislehaut moved closer. I slammed my thoughts against

his hold again and again. If he managed to— I couldn't bear it if he—

In desperation, I pulled on the magic deep in my gut, so much that my body temporarily failed from overload. Grislehaut let out something that wasn't quite a scream, wasn't quite a roar.

He lunged toward Rune moments before I came back to myself. Too late to stop the knife falling toward Rune's chest.

He sidestepped and I collapsed. With one arm holding me, Rune thrust the other out. Roots exploded at the far end of the tunnel, crisscrossing so tightly I doubted there was space for even air to get through.

My lungs felt cut to shreds, my mind as though it'd been pierced with needles. When sensation returned to my body, I found Rune cupping my face, searching my eyes.

"You're back," he said. "Only you."

"Only me," I agreed. I could still feel the stirrings of my magic deep inside, but it was waning, as was the disgusting feeling of Grislehaut's influence. I shuddered as I sat up, suddenly unbearably cold.

"We can't keep doing this," Rune said sadly. "We can't continue to be too weak to fight him."

"I don't see any other choice," I said stiffly. "Unless you have some grand, fantastic plan to gain more magic you'd love to share with me?"

When I looked at him, his gaze was thoughtful, a little guarded. His eyes snapped to the end of the tunnel, eyebrows slashing down. "Time to go. Now."

Tendrils of Grislehaut's blue magic were already leaking between the roots, feeling their way toward us.

I leaned a little too heavily on Rune as he helped me up. And if I was trembling as we moved back to the surface, then I could blame it on the cold instead of fear.

Rune had made a room in the palace especially for me, a spacious once-apartment now repurposed in green. A bed of soft willow bark took one corner. In another corner was a small garden of dahlia, bleeding heart, honeysuckle, and stone crop, their collective scent easing the thumping ache in my head.

Grislehaut's intrusion into my mind had left a bitter residue. I'd cleaned off in the room's spring, combed my hair so hard my scalp was left angry. I stared at the garden of flowers and tried not to think too hard about Rune growing these especially for me; if he'd done it anywhere else; if he hadn't, what did that mean; and what did I *want* that to mean, and—

Something tapped at the open window.

A raven with feathers black as pitch sat on the iron-wrought railing of the balcony. It clacked its beak together, regarding me with its gold-red eyes.

I straightened, hand drifting toward my forearm. The Undersea had proven that no defense was impenetrable and there were many ways to try to kill someone.

"Is there something you want?" I asked.

The raven cocked its head. It opened its beak and a man's voice came out, clear as though he were standing in front of me.

"It is an honor to make your acquaintance, Empress of Glass. And now I must request that we meet in person."

Whomever had sent this might be watching me through the raven's eyes, as Raquel the beastmaster could do. I kept a neutral expression.

"Who are you, and why would I want to do that?"

"Who we are to each other remains to be seen. I had a number of names, but now I'm merely the General of the Last Survivors."

Using a raven meant it was highly unlikely they were from the Undersea, and if it was King Bendeti's successor, then most likely she'd have used a far grander form of communication. Perhaps this was another Lord like Tannis and Sulien, vying for control of their small piece of the Wilds.

"We must meet," the general repeated. "Follow the raven. Tell no one. Come alone."

"If I was laying a trap, that's exactly what I'd say," I answered.

The raven let out a gurgling croak. "Though we are just outside the border of the High King's Wilds, I'm sure, should something happen, he'd know. Though, to hear the Empress of Glass unnerved doesn't seem fitting from what we've heard about her."

"You won't goad me, in case you were wondering."

"Follow the raven," the raven repeated and took off.

The last time I'd foolheartedly gone to meet with someone unknown it had led me to Mother Mal. Whether that was good or not was up for debate. Still, my run-in with Grislehaut had opened a new yearning for solutions. I could at the very least see what this other general wanted.

Or, of course, I could be walking into a trap.

WITH ABSOLUTELY NO intention of going alone, I found General Forcheck and told her about the invitation. Her eyes widened with delight, and she gave a throaty laugh.

"General of the Last Survivors? Is that what he called himself?"

"Sounds like someone you know," I said.

General Forcheck chortled like she was in on some secret

joke. "In a manner of speaking. Consider your midnight visitor a personal friend of mine."

"A friend?" I repeated, incredulous.

"True, true, I have few enough of those. But rather, I have enemies that are dead and those who survived me long enough to earn my respect."

This meeting was sounding more and more serious to me. I wanted to insist we get more wildlings or some of my troops, but General Forcheck didn't seem all that worried. And besides, whomever this other general was, I wanted them to talk. Bringing a force prepared for battle typically scared some enough to do so, but it could also scare them into silence.

General Forcheck was already summoning a path for us to walk, something few other wildlings could do outside of Rune, and I hurried to follow her through to the other side. We arrived in an unfamiliar grove of trees beside a dark meadow.

"You need to wait here so I can make sure it's safe," I told her.

General Forcheck cackled and walked ahead. The raven was already waiting for us, perched on a branch above.

Grumbling, I muttered, "Cloak me," to Erebus. Erebus growled as he did so. The bird cocked its head as I bled into the shadows.

I skirted through ferns and fronds until I could make out the shape of leafy tents and hammocks. They truly were just outside the border, judging by the way the trees and beasts hovered at its edge, watching, waiting for them to make a move inside. Despite the raven finding me, Rune's caution had increased even more since the Undersea attack, and he was taking no chances. I wondered what toll it was enacting on him.

Right across the border was a stand of large growth trees with hundreds of glowing insects affixed to the trunks, lighting a collection of wood-woven chairs in soft light. I was surprised to see Tannis and Sulien flanking a wildling man sitting in one of the chairs.

His gold-red eyes were overlarge, pupils swollen nearly to filling them, and the edges of his face were rounded like an owl. The lines in his bark-rough skin gave away his age. Not as old as General Forcheck, but old enough to know tricks of his own. Old enough to be a formidable opponent.

Beware the old in a world where most die young.

I crept to the edge of the meeting place and dropped Erebus's shadow. "I'm here."

Tannis jumped. Sulien cursed. The older wildling merely smiled at me, looking amused.

"I see you listened and came alone."

"I see you didn't," I answered. "And I didn't exactly come alone, either."

Right on cue, General Forcheck hobbled into the clearing and sat, knees popping, into the chair across from the man. She slapped the tops of her legs with her cane, grinning. "Caldre, you elusive grub! I had hoped they hadn't put you in the ground yet. That was always *my* goal."

Caldre laughed. "The General of the Last Survivors once again meets the General of the Killing Green. I'd heard the High King here had put someone impressive at the head of his armies. I'm glad to see it was you, Narita. Still getting your fill of bloodlust?"

Narita cackled.

"So you do know each other?" I asked.

"Back before Narita was exiled, we nearly killed each other more times than I could count," Caldre said.

"And in the times our rulers would call for peace we'd drink and toast and gnash our teeth, waiting for our chance to do battle with each other again," General Forcheck agreed.

"I would fight alongside no one else," Caldre said. His eyes slid to me. "Almost no one else. But that remains to be seen."

"What do you want?" I asked.

Caldre gestured to Tannis and Sulien, who looked as though they were having to bite their tongues to keep from blurting out something. "The same thing the other Lords wanted, though they went about it the wrong way. They underestimated your fondness for the High King."

The way he said *fondness*, all insinuation, made me bristle, but Caldre continued, "We want a place in these Wilds, free from strife."

"You could have made it easier for everyone, but chose not to," Sulien snapped at me.

"You wanted me to kill Rune," I snapped right back.

"And don't you?" Caldre said, raising an eyebrow. "If not, don't you at least want control over him, to make sure he never has the chance to hurt you again?"

That was exactly what the other Lords had counted on and what I'd wanted once, too. How wrong I'd been. Now I would try something different: trust. Though Rune and I had the ability to cut each other deeply, I had to trust that we wouldn't.

If that trust was misplaced because of my foolish feelings for Rune, then I would gladly bear the pain of their consequence. I only had to hope that Rune's feelings were reciprocated enough that I wouldn't regret it.

"You can't control Rune," I said. "Just as you can't control me."

Caldre gave me an indulgent smile. "I am well aware. But Rune was your enemy first. Wouldn't it be easier to strike now than lose the chance to strike at all?"

"You speak so freely about striking against the High King, in front of the one he trusts to command his armies," General Forcheck said.

"And I *trust* that you haven't forgotten what your loyalty to the Lords you served before got you," Caldre said. "Stripped of your position, your family shamed, and you with an extended stint in Mog Moren."

"Summed up perfectly," General Forcheck answered, unshaken. "My High King is different. He earned my trust through blood. Perhaps I'd like to hone his army on you and your kin and truly make you the last survivor."

"We didn't come here to start the slaughter anew."

"Good," I said. "Because Rune and I don't have time to deal with any distractions. We're the only reason the Wilds haven't been overrun."

"The Empress of Glass has reasserted herself as a king killer only recently," General Forcheck said with some delight. "If you offer her anything less than favorable terms, she might try to add you to those ranks. Though I would ask to have the first chance at it."

"I almost missed your threats, General," Caldre said. "And things are only holding together for now. Until the god arrives."

"We have a plan," I said, but I didn't sound convincing, even to myself.

"That is something we could help with," Caldre said. "We could add our forces to yours to face your final enemies. And in return, you give us a place to call our own. We wish to rule over only our small spaces, giving our allegiance to the High King. He can bind us with oaths and he can bind us by blood, but we will do what's necessary to make this a new Wilds, a better Wilds."

Oaths and blood? What an incredibly rash thing to say, especially when dealing with those who could exact both easily.

"You're desperate," I said.

For the first time, Caldre's cool façade dripped away, and I saw the anger smoldering in his core. "Of course we're desperate. In our Wilds, in the place humans once called Sacramento, tyranny has replaced proper rule. The High King governs with fear and death. Lords who don't give in to all demands find themselves torn apart by the green. Their rivers are poisoned. Their loved ones dragged out in the middle of the night and their throats slit. Great beasts that only the High King controls prowl the deep places, swallowing any who manage to escape. We..."

He gestured at the tents.

"...are those who escaped. We only want to ensure that *this* High King and *this* Empress aren't the same as all the others. Make no mistake, had we our way, we'd have no ruler but ourselves."

Despite the harshness of his words, I appreciated them. There was something disarming about someone who was so clearly in it for their own self-interest.

A flicker of movement at the tents behind Caldre drew my attention. Luella, Olette's mother, peered out. My mind froze. My breath hitched. Rune told me she'd found a new Wilds, but I'd never known which one until now.

Then like a specter, she was gone, and I was left choking on a useless apology. Caldre was watching me shrewdly.

"What is the exact price for your allegiance?" General Forcheck said. "Forgive me for not believing you come offering the lives of those who follow you without specific demands."

"We have a few," Caldre said. "But we would ask those directly of your High King. Now that we see the Empress is open to reason, we ask that Rune meet with us next time."

"And if he doesn't agree to what you want?" I said, composing myself. "You'll go after me, or him?"

Caldre held my gaze, unblinking. "I want you to know that

what the Lords did here doesn't need to be repeated. We don't want bloodshed. But we have seen what power can do to those unwilling to check it. I have a deal for Rune alone, one he might find favorable."

"We'll think about it," I said.

"You do that," Tannis said, finally getting a word in. "We'll be seeing you and Rune soon."

"Time to go, I think," General Forcheck said as I swelled with anger. "Best to hold those words until they're tempered by reason."

"If you and Rune don't return ready to be reasonable, then I hope you're as bloodthirsty as they say," Caldre called as we left. "You will need it, for us, and for them."

CHAPTER SEVENTEEN

As General Forcheck and I returned to the palace, I felt as though I'd spent the night rolling in mire mud, dirty and sure that everyone could smell the guilt on me.

We have a deal for Rune, one he might find favorable.

No way anything Caldre had to offer wouldn't come without serious stipulations. It was another knife for me to juggle, and with each one I grew closer to letting them all fall.

I sought out General Forcheck in her room. As with her other one, it was sparse with belongings. Gardenias and peonies dominated the walls, and an ivy roof that grew to block out the rain and receded in the sun tinkled with chimes and birdsong. The air smelled strongly of the tonics General Forcheck liked to brew.

"I need your council," I said to her. "Should I tell Rune of the meeting? He'll learn of Caldre eventually, but right now I feel..."

Traitorous. Filthy.

General Forcheck hobbled over and poured two cups of tonic. Before I could politely decline mine, she shoved it in my hand. "When the time is right, I trust you'll both tell everything. You have a way of revealing all to each other eventually."

I wasn't sure what to make of that. She either meant that I was naively trusting or couldn't trust my own judgment enough to keep things to myself. Or maybe it was a compliment. I was terrible at taking those even when they were given in earnest.

She must have seen the frown on my face because she hit me on the back, hard enough to dislodge a lung. "Buck up, Empress. To become a leader is to make the tough decisions and trust you're strong enough to endure the results."

Still, while once I'd had no qualms about going behind Rune's back if it accomplished what I needed, somewhere along the way I'd stopped thinking that withholding things affecting us both was okay.

"You have an awful lot of trust in us," I said.

"More than you have in yourself," General Forcheck answered. "I and many others have had someone we thought loved us keeping secrets that hurt us in the end." She raised her cup. "Think of it this way: even the worst confession is better than never having said anything at all. And you may just find my High King has a few confessions of his own for you."

My drink sloshed as I swirled it, mulling that over. Maybe she was right. I needed to find Rune first before this could eat away at me anymore.

I winced as I downed the tonic, but at the very least, it filled me with warmth and the heady foolishness that was required for what I was about to do.

Rune wasn't in the courtyard with the other wildlings shuttling weapons and supplies out of storage. He wasn't in the glen with Cassius training for our next battle. He wasn't with Marian or the others in the planning room, hidden among the curling hallways of the palace's interior.

With each place I looked, my anxiety grew. I didn't believe he'd run off to do something dangerous without telling me, but wasn't that what I had done?

Soon I found myself at an enormous sprawl of gardens, in what might once have been the parking lot of a school, the asphalt and light poles long overgrown. A garden seemed redundant in the Wilds, but there was more order here, the loving touch of someone who'd taken great care to ensure everything was where it should be. I walked through a long archway of poisonous night blush, vibrant red dragon's heart, and soft, velvety petals of dew kiss.

"There you are," I said.

Rune sat atop the archway, one knee pulled to his chest, his other leg hanging over the edge. Catching sight of him made me temporarily forget why I'd sought him out in the first place. He'd cleaned the blood off from the last battle and changed into a moss-green coat tight around his shoulders and pants that almost mimicked human fashion, stylish but with the intent to move and fight. With his hair raked back from his crown, face cast in the glow of nearby moon lilies, he looked like my most wondrous nightmare.

"I looked all over," I said, exasperated. "What are you doing *here*?"

He smirked. "What could I possibly be doing *here*, in the lush gardens I created, in a palace I formed from root and branch, relaxing after a hard day's killing. Is it that difficult to believe I simply wanted some tranquility?"

I gave a playful laugh. "Not you. Never you."

"Please, as though you're any better."

Properly chastised, I used vines of honeysuckle to leverage me up to sit beside him. There were a few other wildlings walking at the edges of the garden, murmuring in low voices to each other. None of them wandered any closer.

"You want the truth?" he said, giving me a rare sheepish smile. "I was hiding."

The confession felt real. Vulnerable and unguarded by barbs. I liked it. "What could you possibly have to hide from?"

The sheepish smile turned brittle. "More than you would think."

"I'm sure. So what's the problem, really?" I pressed.

"I used to have no trouble hiding my thoughts," Rune said, exasperated. "But I never could from you. You have a way of seeing right through me like no one else."

"Oh," I said, disarmed. "I wasn't doing anything special. It just seemed... I always thought it was obvious what you were trying to say..."

Rune laughed. "I've flustered you. Good. That happens so rarely I've found I enjoy it when I do. I've been thinking about Grislehaut," he said. "About our magic's connection to the Below and the Wilds. About all that's left still to do."

"And?" I asked. "You saw what Grislehaut is capable of. My magic did nothing against him. Yours only slowed him down. Short of killing Father Dumas, I don't know what else we can do."

"We have to be desperate."

I laughed darkly. "I don't know about you, but I've been desperate for a long time."

"When you took the throne, I was furious at you," Rune said, and my laugh fizzled out. "Not because of what you took from me, but because of what it's done to you. I was..."

He lifted one of his arms and turned it back and forth. I'd run my hands across them once, feeling the raised bumps of his numerous scars. "I'm already so broken that whatever taking the throne of the Below could do to me couldn't possibly make me much worse. But I would have saved you from that. Little did I know, you'd willingly throw yourself atop the pyre," he said with some chagrin. "I continue to miscalculate you."

"The last thing I wanted was to hurt you," I said softly.

Rune's expression was totally unguarded. He looked beautiful. In that moment, I wanted to draw close and kiss him. I wanted to show him how much he meant to me.

"You didn't hurt me, not as badly as you think," Rune said at last. "I was wrong to treat you as I did. But when you came back to me, I thought it possible we could recapture what we had once... That there was still a chance..."

He smoothed the unwrinkled tops of his pants. "Yet I couldn't bear getting close again, not if it would hurt you more. But now we're desperate and both hurt, so what's the harm in hurting a little more?"

"What are you getting at, Rune?" I said. "Just say whatever it is you're thinking."

He looked uncertain. He looked *scared*, and I knew I'd found the real reason he was hiding up here, hiding from me.

I moved closer. "However crazy your plan is, you can tell—"

"Marry me," Rune said.

It felt as though I'd been hit with Bendeti's whirlpool, tossed over and over again with no sense of which way was up or down.

My mouth hung open wide enough for a stray moth to flutter inside before I managed, "You're serious."

"As a severed artery, yes."

"You want us to... You mean we'd..."

"That's twice I've caught you off guard," Rune teased. "You're thinking we're terrible for each other, but what if that terribleness is just the thing we need?"

"I wasn't thinking that at all," I admitted, finally regaining my senses. "You're not making sense. You don't really want that."

"What would you know of my wants? Likely as little as I do. Neither of us are good at sharing how we really feel, but I want to be better. Val..."

He pressed closer, expression serious. "If I'm wrong, if I've screwed it up so badly that you feel nothing but contempt for me, then say it. I've been wrong so many times in my life, what's once more?"

"No, that's not—*why*?" I managed "Why marriage?"

"Why indeed," Rune said, relaxing as though this were a safer topic. "Before the last High King was murdered, before the Sundering, marriage was carefully watched. Just as the humans of old married for political alliance, so too we married to pool resources and power. Literal power, allowing both who participated in the bond to pull from their combined magics.

"Sotera was going to marry you off to Bendeti because she knew there was power in such an alliance. The crowns we wear are tied to us, as intrinsically as magic is tied to the Wilds and the Below. Right now, that power is split. But if we unite...

He looked at me. "If we do this, we'll have access to our full magic. Enough to fight against Grislehaut. Enough to not have to be afraid."

"It's an alliance," I said slowly. "Like being allies. It can be undone once we do what we need to."

"If you want to see it that way, yes."

Did I? I wasn't sure. My thoughts were a tumultuous mess at the moment.

"Why not just ally with each other?" I said, the words spilling out fast. If I kept talking, it would drown out the other thoughts springing to mind, mostly about how marrying Rune wouldn't be nearly as bad a punishment as he seemed to think it was. "Isn't it enough to say I'll fight with you and you'll fight for me?"

"We are allies. And it's not enough. There's power in marriage. Power in the words of forgoing others for one. I am not just choosing you, I am *not* choosing others, and this way we, our magic, is bound inextricably. It's a merging of magic, as much for alliance," his eyes darkened, "as it is for love."

"You don't know what you're asking," I said.

He sighed. "Maybe not. I doubt we both understand the consequences."

"Implications," I corrected. "Consequences makes it sound like a terrible thing."

A smile flickered at the corner of his mouth. "Indeed. I knew how to care for another once, Val, without reservation or fear, to fully trust without hurting someone else. If you agree, I won't pretend it will be perfect. But I *will* try, every day, if you let me."

He took my hands, clasped them tight, as though if he let go even a little, I might slap him, or stab him, or maybe worse, kiss him. "It's been so long that my heart is scarred, rotted, and weak, but I am willing to give it to you."

He moved my hand over his heart gem. Power radiated from it, through my fingertips, down to my core, where the crystal of my bones sang with its harmony.

Once, not that long ago, I would have gladly carved that heart gem out of his chest. Now he was offering to give it to me in an entirely different way.

Rune looked a little startled as I leaned forward and softly, tenderly, brought my lips to his. He didn't deepen the kiss but let it linger, meeting me only where I met him. Somehow this soft, small kiss was more intimate than any we'd shared before.

His eyes were alight when I drew back. "Is that a yes?"

The warmth building in my chest began to cool. My old fears rose to the surface like one of Bendeti's leviathans, and I felt uncomfortable, insidious vulnerability creeping in.

"Let me think about it," I said. That would give him time to reconsider if he was serious. It would give me time to understand how cataclysmically my world had shifted and make a choice when it wouldn't be affected by the striking gold-red of his gaze. "Please."

"Of course," Rune said. "Always."

He didn't sound distraught, only hopeful. And even after we broke apart, I didn't pull away from him, and I didn't leave.

CHAPTER EIGHTEEN

I drifted in the dark.

There was no telling which way was up or down. I could feel cold and I could see black, but I also couldn't feel or see anything.

Then there was a bright flash. A tortured scream. In my flickering peripherals, a blue glow had begun to illuminate where I was, emanating from crystals along the ceiling.

I was Below. And with mounting horror—as the crystals became more defined—I realized I was in Grislehaut's chamber.

Panic clamped my insides with a vice grip. Though I was almost certain this was a dream, it didn't make being here any better. To me, dreams were incorporeal things outside of reality, untouchable and intangible. Those rules likely didn't matter to a god, one whose power was outside of anything I could ever imagine. If Grislehaut noticed I was here—

There you are.

I was helpless as Grislehaut easily battered down my mental defenses and slithered into my deepest thoughts. No matter how much I fought, I could only watch as the unraveling started: first the tips of my fingernails, the keratin unwinding layer by layer. My skin was next, peeling like an overripe fruit, revealing moist flesh, blood, tendons, and beneath that, glowing crystal bone.

Mine, Grislehaut hissed. *All mine.*

"Val! Take my hand!"

Impossibly, Rune was above me, reaching down through a crevasse in the ceiling. It was frame for frame the exact pose that had been seared into my memory the first time Sotera had taken me Below. His face was even covered in blood as it had been, eyes wild and desperate. The tips of his fingers grew closer. "Quickly! Before it's too late!"

My own unraveling hands stretched for his. "I can't," I gasped. "I can't reach!"

Rune looked sad. "That's because you're not really trying."

She's mine.

I couldn't move any closer to Rune as Grislehaut's presence finished taking over.

I couldn't fight this alone.

I didn't *want* to do this alone.

I wanted help. I wanted *Rune's* help, through the good and the bad of it. Despite all we'd done to each other, he was here, now, for me.

But when I managed to reach for his hand again, Rune was nowhere to be found.

There was never really any chance, Grislehaut purred, and I screamed as I was dragged further into the dark.

Sharp pain barked through my knees. When I opened my eyes, I found myself on the ground beside my bed. The last stirrings of my dream—my nightmare—drifted away like thick smoke, just as dark and equally noxious.

I slowly propped myself up on my elbows and tried to get

my breathing under control. I was here. I was okay. Maybe not *okay*, none of us were with Grislehaut still awakening, but I wasn't dead. Yet.

The morning sunlight warmed my chilled body as I stood shakily to my feet. I wasn't down there. I was here. I was safe. And there was still so much to do.

But as I finished dressing and headed down to meet the others, I couldn't shake the feeling I hadn't really escaped the nightmare.

"You look..." Marian's lips tilted into a sour frown. Her eyes skirted over me before sighing. "Rough."

"You were going to use a different word," I croaked, mouth dry.

"I was, but I said what I said."

I would take *rough*. Looking rough meant I didn't look broken or defeated. Both things I felt.

Cassius smirked and refocused on the map of the Wilds stretched across the table. It had been modified to show the gaping hole Sotera had left in Seattle and where Father Dumas might be, sequestered to the outskirts of what little remained of the city.

Rune looked at me from across the table. It seemed he was going to say something, but General Forcheck chose that moment to hobble in and the discussion turned to where danger might strike from next and how hard. I had no idea the number of worshippers and fighters Father Dumas might have at his command, but if we couldn't stop Grislehaut, it wouldn't matter. He'd win either way.

"For once we have the initiative," Rune said. "What a

strange feeling, not having something directly breathing down our throat."

General Forcheck *hmmmed* from the back of her throat. I couldn't help noticing there was a force absent from the map, just at the edge of Rune's territory.

"Something I'm missing?" Rune's gaze swept to each of us. "I called you here because you don't simper or hide the ugly reality. I trust your judgment."

You have a way of revealing all to each other eventually.

Rune had confessed his true feelings for me—or at least something like them—and left himself vulnerable in a way I wasn't sure he'd done in a long time. The least I could do was reciprocate.

"There is another Lord, here." The words left me in a rush. I placed my finger on the outskirts of Rune's Wilds. "General Caldre. He called a private meeting with me last night. He wanted to know if I'd align with him."

When I dragged my eyes up to see Rune's reaction, there was struggle on his face. He'd feared I took the throne to use against him, and that same fear seemed to be trying to take control. After a moment of silent deliberation, he drew away from the table, looking curious. "And did you?"

"Did I what?" I asked. I'd been so worried about how he might react I'd lost the conversation.

"Did you want to align with him? *Did* you align with him?"

"No. He wanted to speak to you, too. But I told him that I would consider it."

Let me think about it. Please.

I was skirting around so many questions these days, questions that needed answers sooner rather than later.

"I wanted to see what he offered you," I added.

"You are the Empress of Glass. I don't control you, and I don't make your choices," Rune said, and I couldn't help feeling we weren't just talking about the other Lords right now. "General Forcheck, it seemed you knew about our midnight visitor, too."

"Indeed, my High King," General Forcheck said. "An old adversary. One who could be an even more potent enemy, should he decide it."

"And if he does?"

"Then we beat them. Or we die," General Forcheck said, not hiding the hint of a smile. "It is the same with every battle, and every war."

Rune grimaced. "Of course it is. Then it seems like I'll be meeting with him whether I want to or not. The last thing we need is to remake the mistakes of the previous High King. Cassius, I need you—"

Pitius appeared at Rune's back, barely rustling the leaves at her feet. "My Lord Rune, I have news."

"Not good, I'll bet," Rune said.

Pitius grimaced. "I'm afraid not. Father Dumas has collected those worshippers still loyal to him and are moving them to the edge of the chasm."

"Maybe they'll all jump in and save us the trouble of killing them one by one," Marian said. "But I personally was looking forward to slitting that priest's throat myself."

Cassius's brow crinkled. "They'll be exposed out there. It's desolate. The surroundings have been flattened and scoured of almost every building. We can't easily reach him without being noticed, but why would he...?"

"He's going to try to help Grislehaut break free sooner than before," I said, certain I was right. "Or, at the very least, he'll try to stop us from reaching him. We can't get to him from Below anymore. The only way we might be able to do anything to him is once he rises from the chasm."

"Is that right?" Cassius said. "How do you figure?"

Before I'd fallen into my nightmares, I'd been thinking it over last night, tossing and turning as I usually did instead of sleeping.

"The last time Rune and I visited Grislehaut, his presence was more corporeal than before," I said. "I'm guessing the chamber trapping him Below doesn't just keep him in place but also disperses his essence. So the higher he rises from Below and leaves his prison..."

"The more he takes on physical form," Cassius finished.

"And the more we can hurt him," Marian said.

I didn't think it'd be as easy as driving a blade through his heart. Even if he was more physical than before, something that could bleed, he was still a god.

"Can we confirm this?" General Forcheck said. "Empress, can your priest of the Below let us know if anything like this has ever proven to be true?"

"Maybe." I could ask, but if Tibald's track record for revealing secrets was anything to go by, I wasn't confident about getting a useful answer.

Rune listened to all of us impassively before raising his head from the table. "Regardless of what form Grislehaut takes, I doubt Father Dumas and his worshippers are doing anything now except trying to make our situation worse. General, how many wildings can we get ready to attack?"

"As many as we need to match his force, unless he found allies we weren't aware of," General Forcheck said. "How many won't be slaughtered by whatever magical weapons those crafty humans have cooked up? Impossible to say."

"Still, muster those we can," Rune said through gritted teeth. I had no doubt that he, like me, was thinking of the magical weapons my former heart-gem dealer Rylan had helped the DFA craft. The weapons had still been a work in progress last we'd run into them, but that hadn't stopped

Father Dumas from negating Rune's magic and nearly killing us both. I shuddered to think what Father Dumas might be wielding now.

If we do this, we'll have access to our full magic. We won't have to be afraid.

"Val?"

The others were staring at me. Rune's eyes narrowed, as though he knew exactly what I'd been thinking. "Problem?"

"We need more soldiers," I said. "Ones who don't have magic that will be affected by Father Dumas's weapons."

"I don't see from where," General Forcheck said. "If your predecessor hadn't seen fit to bury half your kingdom and lead her army into a suicide invasion, then perhaps." She gave me a wry grin. "Or maybe you've learned to conjure soldiers from stone."

"I'll ask the humans taking residence in the Wilds," I said. "I know some there, I can talk with them."

"The humans," Marian scoffed. "The ones who hate you, you mean?"

"Not all of them hate me," I said. Just most.

"Still, what makes you think they'd listen to you?"

"I don't know if they will, but I have to try. And anyway, I need to..." I needed to tell Peyton about Joshua. I couldn't hold that off any longer.

"If they're going to believe us enough to fight with us, you'll have to tell them everything," Rune warned.

"I know."

"Are you sure?" Cassius said.

Of course I wasn't. I wasn't sure of anything anymore.

CHAPTER NINETEEN

Following Sotera's attack, the Department of Fringe Affairs and any government in Seattle had collapsed along with the city. Other than the lingering remnants of the DFA, the only semi-organized group were the Worshippers of the Mother Tree, who quickly made the surviving parts of Seattle dangerous to anyone who wasn't with them. Those who didn't want to be drawn into more conflict had fled here, to Castle Rock, the only human town within the Wilds themselves.

Erebus bled onto my collarbone to escape the light as I came across the first encampment on the outskirts of town: rows of enormous tents and shelters built from overhanging, overlarge leaves and the interiors of fire-scoured trees. I could hear people murmuring and the occasional burst of laughter as I drew closer and then skirted around the outside.

I needed to find Peyton without drawing attention. Easier said than done. There had to be a few hundred people in this camp alone, and I couldn't exactly stroll right through, hood up. If my face wasn't already recognizable to some, my magic and the wildness about me had long since made others stop thinking I was entirely human.

A branch cracked nearby. I stayed in the shadows as a figure walked by scanning with a flashlight. A patrol. Even in Rune's Wilds, it was dangerous, or they didn't trust him enough to be safe.

But as she came closer, I recognized her. "Gracie," I said, stepping into view.

The flashlight beam jerked to my Wild-spun cloak. Gracie squinted. "Your High King said he wouldn't bother us out here. Just because you don't like it doesn't mean you have permission to bother us."

"And if I'm here to visit a friend?" I asked.

The light rose to my face. There was a sharp intake of breath. "Val!"

Leaves kicked up, and she threw her arms around me, holding tight. And if I held on to her a little longer, it was because I missed her, not because I feared I'd never see her again.

"I'm looking for Peyton," I said.

Gracie gestured back to the glow of the camp. "She's with the others who used to be part of the Worshippers of the Mother Tree. Once word got out that Father Dumas and some of his lackeys were part of what happened to Seattle, many people didn't trust her. Wanted her away from the rest. She's not a prisoner, just being watched."

It made sense. Still, it pained me to know that Peyton was essentially being held in isolation.

"And the DFA?" I asked. "How many of them are here?"

Gracie grimaced, and I got the impression the extrication from Seattle hadn't been as bloodless as I thought. "Couldn't tell you. Not a lot. But one of the women who leads them visits

Peyton every so often. Said she knows your stepbrother, Joshua. Leah, I think?"

The knots in my stomach began tightening. She'd been the one person I dreaded seeing above all others. I wondered what she'd do if she saw me. I doubt she'd be as understanding as Joshua was before he'd asked me to end his life. "Is she here now?"

"I don't think so," Gracie asked. "That reminds me, did you find Joshua?"

The entire ride here I'd thought of how best to break the news, what words to say. "I need to see Peyton. And it'd be best if Leah didn't know I was here."

Gracie's lips tightened. "Oh. I'm sorry. Really."

I nodded, not trusting myself to speak.

Gracie led me through the well-worn paths around the outskirts of the tents, in the deep shadows of the trees and out of the glow of fluttering bats and fireflies.

"I'm sure you already know since you're working with Rune, but things have been unstable here," Gracie whispered. "We're trying to get a working government going again, but a lot of people think the DFA is being too overbearing. They try to keep control by reminding people how much danger we'd be in if they weren't there. Though this last week there haven't been as many of them to throw their weight around."

"Why not?"

"Some defected to Father Dumas. The rest tried to take back what remained of Seattle from his worshippers." Gracie shook her head. "Peyton begged them not to do it. But..."

"Let me guess," I said. "Father Dumas hoarded weapons."

"Lots," Gracie agreed. "A small army's worth, and not just any weapons. Some magical ones. Guns didn't do anything against them."

Of course.

We stole across a neighborhood street overshadowed by trees. Sidewalks were buried under sprawling roots, slender, gurgling springs split houses, colonies of mushrooms grew over rooftops.

"How's Rune?" Gracie asked, surprising me. The last time she'd seen him, he'd broken into her apartment, threatened her constantly, and then vanished into the night along with me. I figured that never seeing him again would be too soon for her.

I settled on, "He's fine. Alive."

"I still try to wrap my head around him. I want to see him as that obnoxious guy who took over my house for a couple days, but I can't do it. He visited Castle Rock once, back when we first arrived. Out here he's..."

"Something different," I said.

"Dangerous," Gracie added. She blushed, shooting me a furtive glance. "And beautiful. But you already knew that, didn't you?"

It was my turn to blush. "He's always been dangerously alluring. All the wildlings are."

"Not like him. There are none like him."

How many times had I repeated those very words to myself? Rune was the same and wholly different than any human or wildling I'd ever met. And he could be more to me. He'd *offered* to be more to me.

Gracie was watching my face. "Do you remember what I said to you on my balcony?"

Guys like Rune, human or not, they don't change. He may feel safe, but he's dangerous.

"I remember," I said.

"I still feel that way."

It was as much of a warning as Gracie was going to give. But what if we'd both changed, and I hadn't seen it?

We reached a group of tents at the end of the street, and Gracie led me to a tent made of heavy canvas and painted green.

“Is this Peyton’s?” I said.

In answer, Peyton emerged to talk with someone. She looked drawn and tired, but alive. A couple tents down were people wearing DFA gear. They’d likely pitched next to the former worshippers to make everyone feel better.

Among the DFA I spied Leah, wheelchair bound, sitting around a crackling fire with a beast roasting over it and a pile of ripened fruit collected nearby.

I felt nauseous. Of course she’d be here, next to the one person I needed to speak to.

Gracie squeezed my shoulder. “Be careful, Val. It was good to see you.”

I told myself I’d talk to Peyton the moment Gracie left, but five minutes later, I hadn’t moved from my spot. It was only after Peyton walked to the other side of her tent that I slipped around the shadows and stepped out where Leah couldn’t see me.

Peyton let out a startled cry I hoped no one else heard and then clutched me, sobbing quietly.

“You hadn’t come back, and I thought... I thought... I never should have asked you to go after Joshua. If I’d known... But you’re here, you’re all right. Did you find—”

“Father Dumas is collecting his forces, and we need the support of the DFA to break them up before he makes things worse,” I said before she could go on.

Peyton used the heel of her hand to wipe at her wet cheeks. “Val, the DFA isn’t ready for a fight. There are barely enough of them to keep order here, and even if we had the numbers, their weapons won’t do anything about Father Dumas.”

"Even if it's a show of force, there has to be something they can do," I insisted.

"I agree, but why would they listen to me?"

That had been plaguing me since I'd hastily thrown this shoddy plan together. How was I supposed to convince them to help while still staying safely out of range of those who hated me?

"Tell them the High King and Empress are making a push to take back Seattle. If the humans want to take back their home, they'll help. You were with the worshippers once. You know more than anyone how dangerous Father Dumas is."

"Which means I was part of the organization that killed their friends and took Seattle." Peyton stared at the fire, chewing her lip. "Val, where's Joshua? I've had such terrible nightmares since I found out he'd been taken. Did you find him? I need to know—even if he's not..."

The cold air clamped down on my throat until I felt as though I couldn't breathe. "Joshua's dead." I held in a sob. "I'm so, so sorry."

No matter how bad I'd imagined this moment, seeing the sheer devastation on Peyton's face was infinitely worse. "Did he suffer?"

"No. I made sure of that."

"You...You had to..."

"There will be more like Joshua if we don't stop Father Dumas," I said, hating how much I had to push on, had to drive the knife of anguish deeper into her heart. "You were a former worshipper, but you're also Joshua's mother, a man who was a leader of the DFA—"

"Was," Peyton said quietly. "Dead heroes can't speak, even if it's through their mothers."

Please, Val. Please.

"The DFA see me as worse than a traitor," I said. "Rune

could order them, but I want the humans there willingly. We need to do this differently if things are going to change."

"I can't ask them," Peyton said. I could see her folding in on herself, weighed down by anguish. "Now that he's... Oh my baby, my baby..."

And then, because everything else was unraveling, there was a crunch of dirt beneath wheels and Leah came around the tent. I was shocked to see her eyes full of tears.

"So. He's dead. And you killed him?"

The fire crackled. A small animal screamed somewhere close by. I opened and closed my mouth a few times, trying to piece together some explanation that wouldn't make things even worse. "It was quick. I made sure of that. He *wanted* it like that."

"He wouldn't—he never would have—Joshua wasn't a coward!" Leah snarled. "You hated him. You wanted him dead the moment you started working with those...those... *beasts.*"

"Leah." Peyton fearfully glanced at the trees.

"I loved him," I insisted. "I *loved* him. It wasn't a perfect love, but no matter what you think of me, you have to believe that."

Leah was struggling out of her wheelchair. Peyton, wide-eyed, lunged for her.

"Leah, you can't—"

"Get off," Leah hissed, throwing Peyton's hand aside. The heart gem dangling around Leah's neck began to glow, coating her legs in a thin film of light. She took an awkward, trembling step toward me.

"You *hated* him," Leah said. "Don't tell me otherwise. But you know the part I can't get over? No matter how much you hurt him, how many times you betrayed him and every single human in Seattle, he never stopped trying to make things right between you. He truly believed you two could work together again."

A strangled laugh escaped her throat. She took another step. I didn't move as one of her hands gripped the front of my jacket. "He loved you, and you stabbed him through the heart."

"Leah—" Peyton warned.

Leah's fist slammed against my jaw. I stumbled, but she kept a tight grip on my jacket, using it to steady herself and draw back again. Her next punch split the skin beneath my eye. Warm blood ran down my face.

"He—loved—you—and—you—let—him—die!"

I stood there and took every blow, knowing that as much pain as Leah inflicted on me, it wasn't close to what she was feeling. It wasn't until my face and neck felt like one solid, bleeding bruise that the magic in her heart gem gave out along with her legs.

Leah slumped to the ground, enormous sobs wracking her body. "Why did he still love you enough to keep fighting? Why didn't he just come with me when he had the chance and let everything else eat itself?"

More blood dribbled down my lips as I said, "Because he believed there was still hope to stop all this. Just as I do."

Peyton gently pulled Leah off me and held her close as Leah continued to cry. A few of her soldiers came running around the tent. They quickly assessed the scene and raised their guns at me.

"You need to leave," one said.

I slowly raised my hands in front of me. Whether it'd been my plan or not, I couldn't waste this chance.

"The High King of the Wilds and Empress of Glass are moving to take back Seattle from Father Dumas," I said loudly. "If you want any chance of reclaiming your home, you'll help us out."

Their guns didn't move. "I said leave, now," the lead solder repeated.

"I'll try to convince them," Peyton said quietly to me.

"Thank you," I said.

"Val...do you think we actually have a chance?"

How easy would it be to lie and reassure her that everything would be just fine, no matter what?

I'm not strong enough to do what's needed.

"With the humans fighting, we have a better one," I said. "But there are no guarantees."

Peyton gave a wan smile. "I guess there never really was."

Leah's quiet sobs followed me as I left. Even long after, I couldn't get the sound of her anguish out of my ears, the feeling of anger behind each and every blow.

I couldn't help thinking that, if this was how badly it hurt to lose the one you loved most, I wasn't sure I wanted any part of love after all.

It didn't take me long to navigate through what remained of Seattle and find where Father Dumas had settled.

Mere minutes after Sotera's attack, Bendeti's tides had come rushing in, scouring the ground with sea and leaving a shallow saltwater marsh in its place. Despite this, Rune had managed to spread the Wilds' influence and gain a foothold on the mainland. Thick outcroppings of trees, like wooded islands, had sprung from the north and south and closed in on the derelict city day by day, drying the ground as they went. Streets untouched by both forest or sea wended through crooked carcasses of buildings and cars. A fine layer of dust coated everything, sometimes so thick it hadn't been too difficult to find freshly made footprints and, from there, the worshippers camp.

As I circled around it, the urge to sneak in and try to kill Father Dumas right then and there was a ceaseless chant in my head, nearly impossible to ignore. I had to remind myself that trying to kill Sotera before the last battle had only made things worse. That, and Father Dumas had magical weapons. Even if I'd been at full strength, they still would have been a problem.

So I stayed out of sight whenever patrols of worshippers—clad in military-style gear instead of their usual robes—swept past. I was here to see the chasm. And I needed to understand what Father Dumas was up to.

But after fifteen minutes of slipping through abandoned buildings-turned-hovels and listening in on a number of conversations, what they were doing here hadn't become any clearer. I'd just started to move again when voices startled me. I lunged into the half-opened door of a garage just off the street, moments before Father Dumas and a few other worshippers crossed it. My vision turned red.

He still wore his cloth cap, the gray thread matching his beard, but a bulletproof vest had replaced his robes. I assumed his group was returning from where the chasm was.

Scuffling feet behind me. The snort of a stuffy nose.

A worshipper, maybe the one who'd holed up here, barely had time to enter the garage before I was on him delivering a strike to his sternum that left him gurgling for air. My next blow dropped him to the concrete hard enough to crack his skull. Swift and silent.

Not silent enough.

When I crept back to peer out, Father Dumas was looking my way, a frown on his face. He waved the others on.

"I want to contemplate for a moment."

I nudged the tip of the fallen worshipper's boot farther out of sight as his companions moved on, leaving Father Dumas alone in the center of the street.

"I'm assuming that's you, Val," he said, his voice carrying. "None of the wildings would dare get so close, at least not without threat of severe consequences."

The urge to throw myself from cover and drive Sliver through his gut pounded against my resolve. My sword remained half out of my arm, begging me to draw it.

Father Dumas sighed. "I know why you're here. I truly am sorry about Joshua. And for you as well, though I'm sure you don't want my pity. The truth is, no matter what, I'm as destined to be the villain in your eyes as you were to be the key. You don't know how fervently I prayed that it wasn't you. Your poor stepmother had already lost so much by the time she found you, and I couldn't bear to do anything to make that worse. Yet true belief demands a terrible toll."

Father Dumas clasped his hands behind his back, eyes skyward in what he probably thought was a supplicating pose. "Do I wish you dead? Of course not. Is your death necessary? Very much so. It will come soon, but until that time, you have one last part to play."

He continued across the street, looking back once more. "Perhaps it's not even you, Val. Perhaps I was wrong."

He left, leaving a clear path to the edge of the chasm, as though coaxing me to make a run for it. I knew it wasn't a trap; it was a challenge. He thought his plan safe and dared me to try to stop it.

I tore myself away from delusions of killing him and hurried on while I had the chance. When I reached a vantage point overlooking the chasm, I stopped, momentarily struck dumb.

Floating land—like islands in the sky—had dislodged themselves from the earth and circled lazily over the abyss, like vultures waiting to feast. Atop them were enormous trees, their roots still grasping bits of earth, slabs of concrete with spears of metal and pipe sticking out of the bottom.

I knelt and sank my fingers deep into the dirt until I felt the electric-wire touch of the Below's magic surge to me.

I drew from it. I drew past the pain in my gut telling me to stop, past all the alarms in my head that said I'd already taken too much.

Then I directed all of it at the chasm.

The earth groaned. The shoreline of Elliot Bay sloshed as tremors shook the ground. The edges of the chasm started to move inward as I directed my hands closer to each other, as though I was doing one long slow clap. My arms shook. Sweat dripped down my back.

I was the Empress of Those Below, the Empress of Glass. I had power over the earth and that beneath it. What Sotera had done created a scar on what was once my home. I would see it healed. I would see Grislehaut trapped again.

It's not enough, Empress.

Grislehaut's voice was a taunting whisper. My eyes flew open. Wisps of blue magic were seeping through the cracks at my feet. I tasted sweat on my lips, mingled with copper. Something in my nose burst, and blood flowed down my face, staining the front of my jacket. Still, I pressed on, desperate to see it closed.

It will never be enough, Empress, Grislehaut promised.

The hold on my magic snapped like a strained wire suddenly cut. What felt like an enormous weight crashed down on the back of my neck. Darkness blurred my vision. My knees went out.

I knew no more.

CHAPTER
TWENTY

I awakened to someone shaking my shoulder.

For a moment, disoriented in the dark and cold, I thought I'd been pulled back into my nightmare.

Then Sliver was in my hand, the tip angled toward the chest of the person who'd woken me.

"Easy, Val," Xander said. "Have a good nap?"

I lowered Sliver with a groan and sat up. I was startled to see a worshipper face down nearby, an arrow expertly shot through their throat. I blinked at them and then at Xander. "What are you doing here?"

"I was about to ask you the same thing."

It was difficult to tell with no city lights, but it didn't look like the edges of the chasm had closed even a little. What I *could* see were sluggish coils of blue magic rising from the Below, even more numerous than before.

"You didn't come back, so Rune asked me to help look for you," Xander said. He smirked. "Seems I'm back in his good graces enough he's asking me to fetch things, not that I mind. We have to go. I'm pretty sure the worshippers are sending another patrol around. Even as stupid as they are, they're bound to find us eventually. Did you get what you needed?"

"Not even a little," I said. "I couldn't do it. I *can't* do it."

Xander hauled me to my feet, keeping my hand clasped tightly in his to steady me. "It was you and your belief that gave me another chance. You can't back out now."

Loud voices were coming our way, circling around on either side. Father Dumas had given me one final, futile chance to stop him, and now he intended it to be my last.

I looked at the perfectly intact chasm.

Rune's offer—his ridiculous, insane, tempting offer—drifted through my head again, as seemingly harmless as the blue magic drifting from the chasm.

Marry me. Marry me, and we could become even stronger. We could ensure that nobody we loved ever got hurt again.

That wasn't how it worked. No strength in the world could ever protect everyone.

Yet I wanted it. I wanted *him*. I'd thought it better to stay safe with what was uncomfortable but familiar, like an old blanket; it might have been ratty, smelly, and didn't keep me warm anymore, but I'd held it tightly, unwilling to give it up and risk finding something better.

It was time to burn it. It was time to let it go. I *had* to. Marrying Rune was just an alliance. It didn't mean anything.

Not unless you wanted it to, a smug voice whispered. *Not unless you're brave enough.*

"You asked for help before," Xander said, as though reading my thoughts. "If you can do it once, doing it again can't be that bad, can it?"

"No." *Yes. Very much, yes.* But I didn't have much of a choice anymore. "Let's get out of here."

One way or another, it was time to bring this to an end.

WHEN I RETURNED to the palace, I was surprised to find Rune and the others waiting in the courtyard. A pack of snow-white wolves waited with wildlings on their backs. Rune himself sat atop the alpha. She blinked slowly at me. *We meet again,* she seemed to say. I jerked my head in greeting.

"What's going on?" I asked.

"Caldre's asked to meet with Rune," Cassius said. "He—whoa." His jaw fell slack. "Val—what—"

Rune turned. In one smooth motion he slid off the alpha and was tilting my face toward the nearby sconce of everfire to see better. It was only then I remembered what Leah had done to me. Judging by Rune's furious expression, I must have looked a fright.

"I trust you inflicted far worse on whomever did that?" Rune said.

"Some was self-inflicted," I admitted.

Rune didn't seem to know how to answer that. "I'd appreciate if you joined us, Empress. I'm sure Caldre will make many interesting promises, and I'd hate for you to miss holding him to them."

Bone-tired weariness dragged at my body. "Give me a sec."

I found a gurgling stream that cut through the palace's lower floor and knelt, shooing away the Nauplins gathered in the reeds at the edge. With chirps of fright, they skittered away, and I grimaced at my wavering reflection. Dried blood coated my lips and streaked my cheeks, starting to flake like a rash. Purpling bruises had taken residence beneath my eyes.

I washed the blood off as best I could. Marian waited for me as I returned to the courtyard. Without asking, she started using her healing magic on the worst of my bruises, and I felt the swelling lessen with each passing second.

"I hope it was worth it, whatever you did," she murmured.

"I'm not sure," I said. "I guess we'll know soon enough."

She gave me a strange look but didn't press. Both of us returned to our wolves and the procession took off, Rune and I in the lead as the wolves flowed through the tree like frothing rapids.

All too soon we were stopping. Caldre stood waiting in a small depression hemmed by flowers, each as big as my head. Above, sleepy flocks of midnight-black birds perched, a few watching us with their gold-red eyes.

The wolves took a few turns around the depression before stopping in front of Caldre's group and allowing us to dismount. Once done, they paced at our backs, baring their teeth every so often as though to remind Caldre's entourage how quickly they could tear them apart.

"High King Rune." Caldre bowed, and I was impressed that there wasn't an ounce of fear in his face. "You have quite a different entrance than your empress."

Rune smiled dangerously. "She doesn't need gawdy displays to know who's in charge. I don't either, but my esteemed general assured me that some would like the spectacle."

Caldre gave an affirming nod at General Forcheck. "It can be a powerful deterrent to bloodshed and worse."

"And what would deter you?" Rune asked. He made a show at peering around Caldre to the collection of wildlings at his back. Thankfully, Luella and her guilty gaze wasn't among them. "What do you want from me?"

"You are High King," Caldre said. "The only want I have is to serve—"

"Simpering doesn't look good on you, so don't waste breath doing it," Rune snapped. "You know about me, General of the Last Survivors, so you likely know my upbringing and some of my strife. I disdain games as much as I disdain what the old Lords did to the last High King. You have a price for your loyalty. What is it?"

Caldre seemed to measure Rune, and I got the suspicion that this was exactly the sort of response he'd expected.

"Revive the Council of Loam," he said.

"I did," Rune answered.

"And I disbanded it," I said. "Violently. They wanted to plot against Rune instead of advising him. If you also plan on using the guise of a councilor to set up a way to depose the High King, then we might as well kill you now and save everyone the trouble."

"Revive the Council, give us representation," Caldre insisted. "Though oaths can be broken, bind us to them. Give us control over our own destinies. As long as you rule justly, as long as you aren't so terrible a High King as the one we ran from, we will serve you."

"And you'll decide just how terrible I can be?" Rune said.

"Trust," Caldre said, "has to go both ways, my High King."

"*Your* high king? Already?" General Forcheck said, delighted. "Very clever, you old log wart."

Caldre gave a wan smile. "I was ambitious once. I admit I would have killed and slaughtered to take what I thought belonged to me. No more. I crave peace. For me. And for my granddaughter."

As though on cue, a woman stepped forward from the crowd. She looked as delicate as a drop of dew, features pale and flawless and glistening. Gold capped the tops of her ears, jewels strung her neck, and spider's silk lace patterned up her arms.

She sank to one knee in a perfect bow so delicate she didn't even rustle the grass. "My High King Rune, a pleasure."

Rune stared, waiting. A painful twist had started in my gut.

I could vaguely see where this was going and didn't like it one bit.

"I know you are yet unmarried, Rune," Caldre said. "You ask what my other request is, and this is it: marry my granddaughter, Wren."

Xander's eyebrows rose so high they threatened to disappear into his hair. Rune's wildlings whispered amongst themselves. The sour sensation in my gut worsened.

"That's a bold request," Rune said, as though he hadn't already made the very same proposal to me. "Marriages are ways to shore up alliances, to keep power strong. As High King, who I choose is more important than most."

"And if you are waiting for another such alliance, then by all means, let me hear about it," Caldre said. "But others will ask, and I can assure you you'll find no better match. Marry and cement your rule. It would make you and your magic more powerful. Make you *both* more powerful."

"Or entrap me," Rune drawled.

For the first time, Caldre looked uncertain. "She wouldn't—The Wilds are—"

"Are only as strong as its ruler—or rulers—or so I've been told," Rune said. "And do you think Wren is strong enough to endure me?"

Wren's head remained bowed, though her hands were starting to tremble.

"Are you saying there's someone else?" Caldre said.

"I'm saying it's a bit sudden, and a bit archaic, to be trading future wives for favors," Rune said. "Stand up, Wren."

She did, quickly scurrying behind Caldre.

"If I'm to rule differently," Rune said. "If I'm to *trust* my subjects, as you say, then that has to extend both ways, not by binding me through her."

He was stalling. Being cagey. I found it difficult to draw breath.

"I see this as an official alliance," Caldre said. "It would be an assurance that you'll follow through on your promise—"

"And will she force me if I don't?" Rune sneered. "Will she put a knife to my throat and demand it of me? I can tell you from experience that's an effective tactic, but I don't see her—"

"Without this, I can't be confident in fulfilling *my* end of the alliance!"

The clearing fell silent. Xander gripped his bow tighter. The wildlings at Caldre's back tensed. Things had dissolved too quickly. Rune couldn't deny Caldre entirely without good reason, or risk Caldre giving him nothing. But if he agreed...

"Are you saying you won't do it?" Caldre said.

Rune's jaw was set, the muscles of his neck tense.

"High King Rune," Caldre went on, "if you can't agree to my one proposal without good reason, then we have nothing—"

"He can't marry her," I said.

The weight of dozens of pairs of eyes shifted to me. Cassius was frowning like he'd missed the joke.

"And why is that, Empress?" Caldre said coldly.

All feeling had left my body. Rune was looking at me in confusion. Then disbelief, as he realized what I meant.

What would you know of my wants? Likely as little as I do.

"Because," I said. "Rune's already promised to me."

CHAPTER TWENTY-ONE

Shocked whispers erupted from those gathered. Xander was staring at me, open-mouthed. Marian merely smirked, as though to say, *About time*.

My eyes sought Rune again. Though he was the one who'd suggested it, I was suddenly terrified to look at him, to hear him proclaim that I was lying or that he *had* offered but changed his mind.

A wide, beaming smile, exposing the tips of his slightly sharp teeth, split Rune's face. His eyes were alight with a combination of wickedness and something else. Joy, that was what it was. Pure, unbridled happiness as I'd never seen in him before.

It took my breath away.

"Yes," Rune continued, shifting back to Caldre. "I'm already taken."

General Forcheck cackled. "Woe to your plans, Caldre!"

Caldre frowned. He looked at my hand and then Rune's. "Is it official?"

"Mere technicalities," Rune said with a shameless wave.

"The important thing is that I can't marry your granddaughter, sacrifice as she may be."

Caldre drew himself up. His face began to color with anger. "I insist. If you can't give me any assurance—"

"We will discuss the terms in detail once we don't have a god breathing down our necks," Rune said. "If you want to live in these Wilds, you have to ensure the Wilds live first. And you can try to kill me before that, but while we *may* not win without your help, without me and Val, I can assure you that we won't.

"I want to see loyalty," Rune went on. "But I understand that's earned. Until we come to a more formal agreement, *I give you my word, the word of the High King, that I will do as you requested to the best of my ability.*"

He was obviously being careful with the wording, leaving things vague enough that, should Caldre change his demands, Rune could reasonably forgo his promise. By the purse of his lips, I could tell Caldre knew it too. Nevertheless, the trees stirred; flowers and underbrush leaned in, as though drawn by his words. Rune looked a little tired by the end. Caldre looked a little satisfied.

"I suppose it will do," he said. "For now."

"It will have to do, because that's all you're getting out of me for the moment. Maybe you'll be lucky and I'll die in the battle and save you the trouble."

"I do not wish that, my High King," Caldre said, bowing at last.

"Almost all those who meet me want me dead at some point," Rune said. "There's time yet for you to change your mind."

The wolves emerged from the underbrush and lined up behind him once again.

"We will call on you," Rune said. "I expect you to be ready."

He swept back onto his wolf and made a move for all of us to be off.

"I'll follow in a moment." I looked at Caldre. "I have something else I wish to discuss. Alone."

After a moment's hesitation, Rune nodded. Caldre stepped aside, beckoning me into their camp. I drew into an enclosed tent with a leaf-canopied bed in one corner piled with a number of dandelion-puffed pillows. A couple chairs sat before a pit of everfire and a table covered in sliced fruit and drink.

Wren entered right after me and, before I could say a word, set about pouring a couple glasses of the dark liquid into two goblets.

"Please, drink," she said, handing me one.

I thanked her but didn't dare sip. Wren smiled as though she'd expected that.

"It's not poisoned. See?" She poured a thimbleful into another glass and downed it. After a half minute, her face hadn't changed color, nor did she start frothing at the mouth.

"My grandfather takes special pride in killing those he dislikes face to face, either in battle or in a duel," Wren said. "He'd be ashamed to kill you in such an underhanded way."

"That's...strangely reassuring. Thanks," I said, taking a shallow sip at last.

"I'm happy for your engagement," Wren said. "Or are you already married?" Her eyes strayed to my hands, and I realized I had no ring or anything else that would indicate I was bound to another.

"It's complicated," I said.

"That's an understatement." Caldre burst into the tent. He immediately grabbed the second goblet and took a swig, eyes piercing me. "Your announcement was a surprise. But none seemed so surprised as you and Rune."

While I struggled with how to answer that, Caldre whispered something to Wren. She hurried out, and Caldre watched her, his gaze softening.

"Hopefully I didn't take away from her happiness," I said.

"Please," Caldre said. "Both of us know High King Rune wouldn't have made her happy, and she's far too delicate to not break beneath his force. Her mother was also a Lord with a lot of power and a convenient death that left it all up for grabs. Even now Wren's many siblings are slaughtering each other back in the Wilds we fled. I wished to spare her that."

"And marry her off to the High King of another Wilds, one with rumors about his cruelty?" I said.

Caldre gave a barking laugh. "So that was your benevolence stepping in to save her?"

I didn't feel the need to grace that with an answer.

Caldre tipped his goblet back until the last drop was gone. "Tell me, do you truly care about Rune?"

"I do." That much at least wasn't a lie.

"Enough to bind yourself to him?"

This was entering territory I hadn't yet figured out for myself, not to mention felt comfortable enough discussing with him. "I'm not here to discuss my relationships, but to make another assurance: you shouldn't be reluctant to enter an alliance with Rune. If he's unwilling or unable to follow through with his promises, then as his wif—as High Queen of the Wilds, I will ensure they get fulfilled. But I want your promise of allegiance to me as well as him."

Caldre took his time settling into one of the chairs and crossing a leg. I hated how at ease he appeared. I should be making him more uncomfortable. I should be making him afraid.

"Here's why you're really asking me for allegiance: because at your core, though you claim to care about him, you don't trust him," Caldre said.

"Yes I do," I said automatically.

"Which is why you're here saying you're going to fulfill all his debts should he not follow through." Caldre poured himself another drink, not bothering to offer me any. "Words are one thing, Empress. Actions are another altogether."

"Do I have your allegiance or not?" I said through gritted teeth.

But before Caldre could answer, Luella entered the room. She stilled when she saw me, before quickly recovering. "You wanted to see me?" she said to Caldre.

"Yes, I was hoping you'd refill this wine for me, please," Caldre said, looking right at me as he asked. I clenched my fists hard enough for my nails to bite into my palm. He'd seen me watching her. Perhaps he'd inquired after the history between us.

If Luella was confused about what she was being asked to do, she didn't show it but picked up the carafe and poured more wine into Caldre's goblet.

"Thank you, my dear," Caldre said when she was done. "That will be all."

Luella bowed and started to leave.

"I'm sorry about Olette," I burst out. "And I'm sorry I wasn't the first one to tell you."

Luella took a trembling breath before affixing a fake smile on her face. "It's a relief to know she's not suffering anymore. I think I see her sometimes, you know, walking through the trees. I think I must be going insane, but then...nothing in the Wilds is ever truly lost, is it?"

After Luella left, Caldre steepled his fingers, watching me. "An excellent example of how the Empress keeps her promises. I wonder if the High Queen will be better?"

My blood surged, red hot. "I told Luella not to leave Olette with me. I *told* her it wouldn't end well, that she—"

But while I was blaming Luella, I was really mad at myself. Not only for failing, but for agreeing to it at all.

"No amount of power can keep everyone safe," I said. "And no amount of promises can guarantee anything."

I gave a small bow, one I hoped came off a little rude. "But think of this, General of the Last Survivors: You'd rather have my promise of peace than my promise that there won't be any of your survivors left if you cross me."

I swept out before he could get the last word in. Rune waited, alone, in the depression where we'd had the meeting.

"I hope your talk with Caldre was productive," he said.

My rage still simmered, but I managed to give a nonchalant shrug. "As well as I could expect."

"Good. I sent the others ahead," he said. "You and I have something unfinished."

My mouth was suddenly dry. Stomach churning, I mounted my wolf, and as Rune and I took off, my surroundings became a passing blur as incomprehensible as my thoughts.

Eventually, Rune's alpha wolf gave a small chuff, and we slid through a stand of spruce and into a meadow of silky grasses. The peak of Mount Olympus loomed just over the treetops to the northwest. After I dismounted my wolf, the pair disappeared back the way we'd come.

Rune and I were truly alone.

Rune was running a blade of grass between his fingertips nervously, and suddenly my heart had begun to pound hard enough I was sure my ribcage would fracture.

"I'm hoping you weren't telling Caldre that we were married just to save me from the fate of uniting with his granddaughter," Rune said. "Otherwise, I'll feel like an enormous idiot."

He smirked, a little sheepishly. "But if so, then I would

gladly accept the save. It would be just another thing we protected each other from."

"I agreed because I..." One moment I knew what to say, and the next it flitted out of my head. "I can see now we need an alliance if both of us are going to survive."

"An alliance?" Rune rolled the words over on his tongue. "Yes, I suppose we need one of those, don't we?"

"That's all it'll be, of course," I said. "Combining our magics to stop Grislehaut."

Rune moved closer. I blinked and found myself before him, as though the grasses and ground beneath my feet had carried me forward.

"Do you want to know something funny?" Rune said. "I can tell when you're lying. It took me a long while, far longer than any other, to figure it out. You look slightly down and to the left when you're being untruthful. It's a subtle tell—I doubt any Lords or gods you've spoken honeyed words to have noticed."

They hadn't. But he had. He had watched me that closely, as closely as I had him.

"And do *you* want to know something funny?" I said, feeling suddenly bold and not to be outdone. "You lightly threaten and dismiss when you're nervous about something. You won't eat eel, no matter how many times Raquel catches it for you, and you try to hide it when he's not looking. Like me, I've seen you breathing in the air after it rains because I think it's one of your favorite smells. And sometimes, when you're pretending to be mad at me, but are secretly pleased, your nose scrunches just slightly.

"And you try not to look at me when you really want to, because I think you're scared of what it means and how you feel, like me."

As much as my confession had stunned me, it'd stunned

Rune even more. His mouth hung slightly open, before eventually curling into a wicked grin. "All my tricks revealed. And are you still scared?"

"A little," I admitted.

Rune stepped closer still, or maybe I did. I was becoming less aware of my body with each passing moment.

"Good," Rune said. "Being a little scared of something means it's worth doing. I'll ask one last time: is this what you want? Truly?"

"Do we have a choice?" I said. "Otherwise, we won't be strong enough to do what needs to be done."

"At risk of sounding as maddening as Mother Mal, there's always a choice," Rune said. "I'm offering, but it's your decision whether to take it."

What I wanted was to be known. Understood.

Though I knew it impossible, if I was feeling particularly hopeful, I wanted to be loved. If only loved out of necessity.

"Rune, I want to marry you."

He gave another smile full of unbridled joy, so much it made my heart hurt. He took my fingertips in his, the touch radiating up my arm.

"So what do we do now?" I asked, voice coming out a little breathless. "Is there a ritual? A ring?"

"Words first, I think," Rune said. "I'm...not the best at gawdy speeches. I've only been to a couple wildling weddings, but that was a long time ago, and more violence than tenderness has replaced those memories. But I can try to remember. I think I have to remember. If not I..."

I couldn't believe it. He was blathering. He was *nervous*. Maybe even as nervous as I was.

"Just try your best," I said, encouraging.

Rune swallowed. Nodded.

"By the power of my heart gem
By the blood in my veins
I will stand beside you.
Until nothing of the Wilds remains."

I could feel the power he invoked within the words settle over us both, an invisible thread intertwining us tighter and tighter.

"I don't know any vows," I admitted. "And I've never been to any weddings."

"All's the better, for how dull they are, unless someone is trying to kill a member of the wedding party," Rune said. "You don't have to say anything if you don't want."

But as though conjured, words sprang to my lips:

"I will be your light in the endless dark.
And though I might fracture, shatter, and break,
I will remain to you as endless as the deepest chasm.
By your side forevermore, even as the gods awake."

"Foreboding," Rune said. "But I like it."

I waited for something to happen. Maybe for the earth to rumble its approval or an enormous spring of water to erupt from the ground and a menagerie of animals to march into the clearing carrying bouquets and tossing flower petals.

"Most of the union's power is in the unseen," Rune said, as though reading my mind. "But not all."

My left hand tingled. I looked down as green lines, inked darkly as tattoos, wove through our fingers and across our palms. Halfway across, the lines transitioned from a vibrant Wild green to a soft blue. The pattern on my hand continued where it met his, unwavering and unbroken.

"It's done," Rune said softly.

I thought my face would split from how wide my own stupidly ridiculous smile was.

Rune looked startled. "I don't often see you so happy, especially not when you look at me."

"I smile at you," I protested, the tips of my ears heating. "When you aren't actively driving me insane, I'm sure I smile at you."

"Not nearly so often as I'd like. It appears to be something I must constantly work to remedy—"

I kissed him, as gently as I had the first time he proposed, and that shut him up. I kissed him until we'd each had our fill, for now, and as one we knelt, our foreheads pressed together, our breathing—slightly ragged—in tandem. My entire body was alight with the feel of his energy and heat, relishing in the sensation of, for the first time, not fighting what felt right.

"We should try to reach Grislehaut now," I said. "While we still have the chance."

"I'll be your anchor," Rune said.

His hands rested atop mine, and as one we pressed both to the ground. The Below's magic sang to me, a chorus that had been muted every time before this. The splitting pain that normally accompanied using my magic was nowhere to be found, replaced by the wellspring of the Wilds and Rune's presence.

"If I'm lost, pull me back," I said.

"Always," Rune promised.

I opened myself up and pushed my magic down. It seeped like groundwater through the earth until it brushed against Grislehaut's chamber. Without hesitation, I started to weave threads of magic over the gaps in the prison and tightened them, amplifying the enchantments keeping Grislehaut trapped. I worked in a frenzy, knowing that at any moment—

Grislehaut found me. His burning rage seared through me like a heated blade.

"You dare," he thundered. *"You DARE—"*

With Rune's magic anchoring me, I didn't falter until the last of the enchantments were bolstered. Only then did I retreat, Grislehaut's fury following.

I came back to myself right as my body gave out and slumped into Rune's arms. He cradled me as though I were truly made of glass, lowering us both until we lay beside one another on the slightly damp ground. It had started to drizzle, and with tender fingers, Rune pushed aside the wet hair on my forehead, cupped my cool cheek.

When I could move once more, I focused on his eyes. Though we'd both used an immense amount of magic, I didn't feel like death, and I couldn't see any black ink dripping from Rune's one eye or a blue glow in the other. Whatever curse Sotera's crown had cast on him was gone.

"I bought us a little more time," I said. "I don't know if it'll be enough."

"It'll be enough for now," Rune said. "It has to be. We need to strike against Father Dumas soon."

But neither of us moved for an achingly short time, lost in this place where, for just a moment, everything felt right.

I almost fooled myself into believing it would last forever.

CHAPTER TWENTY-TWO

Seattle looked worse than I remembered.

I stood on an overlook alongside Rune, General Forcheck, and General Tenia, trying to figure out how best to move our forces. Under the gunmetal-gray sky, the waves of Puget Sound lapped the shoreline. The chasm scarring Seattle seemed bigger than it had before. Or maybe that was just my fear manifesting.

"Are you surprised Caldre actually answered my call?" Rune asked. He nodded below us, where Caldre was summoning paths for us to walk across the water to the mainland. Nearby, wildlings and Those Below were getting armed, armored, and heading out under their own instructions.

"Caldre's formidable, and almost worse, he's honorable," General Forcheck said. "We're both too soft. It's probably why we're both in the situations we are. He'll play his part."

"And what is our part?" General Tenia said. She deferred to me, though I could tell she didn't like it. "Empress?"

I wondered if she knew I didn't have a clear answer and was only asking to make me look bad. "Father Dumas will try to do...*something* to fully awaken Grislehaut. We stop him from doing that."

"And then you'll quell the god?" General Tenia said.

I didn't look at her. "Yes."

General Tenia grunted. "I suppose that's as good a plan as any, minus useful details. If you know anything more, I wish you'd consult your general with it."

I caught Rune looking at me amidst discussions with General Forcheck and Cassius. We'd barely gotten any time alone the last couple days. I hadn't bothered hiding my hand and knew that those who hadn't been at the meeting with Caldre had wondered what happened between us. I didn't feel like explaining. Not yet. Not until *I* wrapped my head around it.

Movement at the edge of the trees drew my attention, and my jaw dropped as humans walked out. Some were dressed in black body armor and carrying guns. The rest held swords and knives. They looked ragged, but they looked ready.

As they approached, my eyes found Peyton, and she gave me a flicker of a smile. Leah was in the lead, sat atop a bristle-furred beast a little smaller than the wolves we rode, eyes firmly fixed on Rune. I drew closer to him, as though my mere presence would dissuade any possible attack.

"We're here to help kill the worshippers of the Mother Tree," Leah said loudly. "Since our gracious host of the Wilds needs our help, then we'll answer."

"And get your home back in the process," General Tenia said. "Don't pretend this isn't mostly for your benefit."

"We'll take all the help we can get," I said before everyone could start arguing. Leah didn't even glance at me.

Rune's eyes lingered on Peyton, and for one terrible moment, I wondered if he was still thinking of how she'd betrayed me and all that she'd put me through. Even I'd only just recently managed to forgive her. I couldn't be sure whether he held that same forgiveness.

"You'd fight your own kind?" Rune said at last.

"Please," Leah said. "As if you wildlings haven't been doing the very same thing. How many did you slaughter to get to where you are now?"

Rune's grin was malicious. "Enough. It was necessary."

Leah nodded. "This is necessary. We want vengeance, and so we're here."

"Good. Vengeance is a more potent loyalty than anything I can offer."

He gestured to General Forcheck. "Confer with her. She'll tell you where you need to go. If this works, all of Seattle is yours again and we'll help you rebuild. And I hope, when that is done, you'll consider a truce between us."

Leah sneered. "One thing at a time, High King. First, we have to survive before we start lying to each other again."

"Of course. And for you, a gift from the Wilds, to show my goodwill."

Rune waved his hand. Thin, strong tendrils of roots sprang from the ground and gently wove around Leah's legs like braces, tightening until they were snug.

"They can be easily removed," Rune said. "Simply touch them and will your intention."

Leah gaped at them, before tenderly sliding off her beast. The roots grew rigid, supporting her weight with each wobbly step. Tears gathered at the corner of her eyes, but she schooled her mouth in a hard line.

"I got this injury while fighting wildlings. I won't forget that with a few pretty gifts. But if you have nothing but power and time, we have more wounded who could use your help."

"After the fighting's done," Rune said.

I tried to catch up with Leah as the DFA and humans split off, but Peyton intercepted me.

"Now's not the best time," she said. "It was a close vote to come help the wildlings, but Leah's orders are tenuous at best. Don't do anything that might change her mind."

I watched Leah vanish into the crowd of humans who had gathered to hear from General Forcheck. I wondered if they thought this scene as surreal as I did.

Peyton gave me a smile tinged with sadness, crow's feet gathering at the corner of her eyes. "Some advice you already know: against Father Dumas, you strike hard, you strike fast. Don't let him get away with any more. I know firsthand how he can spin words, how he can manipulate his way into getting what he wants. Don't let him. Kill him the first chance you get."

"If I can."

"You can. You have to." She frowned at the green and blue lines crisscrossing my left hand. She turned it over, and my stomach clenched. "What are these?"

"An enchantment. For protection," I lied. I might be an Empress, but she was still my mother in almost every sense of the word, and this was so much more than sneaking a guy into the house or entering the Wilds after she'd told me not to. I wasn't sure how she'd react to finding out I'd married our once sworn enemy.

"Well, I hope it helps," Peyton says. "I hope it keeps you safe."

I glanced at Rune, who was giving orders to some wildlings. "I hope so, too."

As I left to go help with the preparations, I caught Peyton looking between Rune and me, as though trying to piece the puzzle together, a frown tugging the corners of her lips.

THERE WAS little time for self-doubt when preparing an army. I shuttled between the makeshift planning area—tucked within a small copse of sweet-smelling pine—where I marked everyone's forces on the map, to handing out more weapons, to then helping Cassius in his final preparations with those he'd trained.

"I worry for them," he confessed after we'd sent off the latest group, their arms laden with weapons and greenery-stitched armor Rune had crafted. "I don't trust some of them to not impale themselves on their own sword."

"They're all we have," I said. "And you did all you could."

"And yet it might not be enough." Cassius gave me a tight nod before rushing away to help others.

I got so caught up in preparations I didn't realize how many hours had passed until the overlook was dark. Only when there was nothing immediately pressing for me to do did I sit on the edge of a log. My head spun immediately, as though fatigue had been waiting for this moment to strike. My empty stomach roared its disapproval.

"They'll hear us coming from miles away if you don't fix that."

General Tenia loomed over me, and for one terrible, exhaustion-induced moment, I thought she would draw her cudgel and try to beat me to death right here, in front of everyone.

But she was frowning down at me with an expression that said she couldn't quite make sense of me, either.

"I lost track of time," I admitted.

"Hmmm," General Tenia grunted and turned to look around. She'd prepped and sent off most of Those Below, and the clearing was now far emptier than it had been. "It's too bright up here. Too loud. I prefer the solemn caves of the Below. There were chambers you could go where the magma ran into water and it would steam, turning everything warm. There were places where you could be truly alone."

"I thought all of you wanted to be free," I drawled. I lifted my hands to the sky. "Well..."

The fleshy part of General Tenia's jaw twitched. "I'm happy. But I'm lost. Long ago we were promised a place above. But we've been shut away for so long everything's moved on. I don't think the rest of the world knows what to do about us anymore."

"Then that's for you to decide," I said. "Things are changing. Not always for the better, but most things are moving that way. They can be better for you, too. I'll try my best to ensure they will."

General Tenia wore an inscrutable expression. "I actually believe you will," she said at last. "Go get some food and rest. You'll be no good to us half-starved and weak."

"Are you giving me an order?"

A smirk flitted across her face. "Those Below respect you, Empress. *I* am starting to respect you. I hate that I am, but when have feelings mattered when it came to war?"

"I'd rather you actually liked me, but I'll take respect for now." My body ached as I stood, reminding me of how long I'd been on my feet. "And maybe one day you won't want to stick a knife in my back."

"One day..." General Tenia mused. "I'll take care of the rest. Go."

Rune's palace was mostly empty. The long hallways of the private half where the sleeping chambers were echoed my footsteps. Mica chandeliers cast long, lonely shadows along the walls. I wondered if this wasn't too different than the solemn caves General Tenia longed for.

I turned a corner and bristled.

"What are *you* doing here?" I demanded.

Sulien was admiring the far wall: a mosaic of flowers, ferns, mushrooms, and slender bits of bone magicked together to form the image of a grand landscape of the Wilds, a view that in real life took my breath away. I wondered when Rune had put that there.

Sulien turned, smirking. "Why the hostility? We're *allies* now, aren't we? Unless you've at last considered my and Tannis's offer and want to depose Rune for good. Oh, but I forgot..."

His eyes drifted to my hand. "You *love* him. That's why you got married, isn't it?"

I clenched my fist, tightening the marriage bands. "I'm surprised you're here and not with your master Caldre like the dog you are."

Sulien stepped toward me, and without a thought, a crystal knife was in my hand, glittering dangerously. Anger flashed across his face. "You can try to manipulate Rune in whatever way you'd like, but we will get what we're owed *without* the High King in place."

"Do you know what happened to the Lords who were in power before Rune took the throne?" I asked. "Keep talking and find out."

Sulien didn't flinch, and for not the first time, I cursed that I couldn't make him more afraid.

"How does it feel, being connected to the High King?" Sulien said, voice ringing with bemusement. "I heard you were raised human, with your human ways and human sentiments. You have no idea what you've done to yourself, do you? Human marriages are for *love*, at least that's what I've heard. But wildling marriages are the start of a new battle with new rules. Rune's been desperate before, and he must be desperate now, using you to sacrifice yourself and leave him free to take what he wants."

Sulien was trying to plant seeds of doubt, and I uprooted every one. In some ways I still might be tricked, but gone was the girl who believed every terrible whisper about Rune.

"What does it feel like, Empress?" Sulien said, stepping closer still, until, with barely a thrust, I could drive the crystal knife through his heart. "What does it feel like being connected to Rune, to the Wilds?"

The corridor was filled with nothing but our breaths and the weighted silence waiting for my answer to fill it.

"Like a piece of me has found its place," I answered honestly.

Sulien cocked his head. "You're of the Below, crafted in the dark and the deep. Do you think Grislehaut feels the same, like he's missing a piece?"

"I have no idea what he might be thinking."

"You see, unlike you and everyone else, Tannis and I don't believe an alliance will be enough to stop this. I'm very aware of what slumbers beneath the earth. You've deluded yourself into thinking that more power is the answer."

"And what *do* you believe?" I asked.

"That Grislehaut will destroy these Wilds, and only those who are strong will survive to claim what remains. But to do that, Rune can't be here."

Sulien nodded at my knife. "Your marriage won't protect you. When the time comes, will you actually have the strength to do what's necessary?"

His eyes followed my knife as I raised it at him. "Leave. Now."

Sulien gave a soft laugh, and I had a terrible foreboding that he wasn't just telling me these things to get a rise. He was sending a message.

"Goodnight, Empress. And may your dreams be as nightmarish as what you face."

I WAS FALLING, falling, falling through the dark. Air ripped at my clothes, clogged my ears, and whistled through my teeth as I opened my mouth to scream. I couldn't force a breath as the darkness zipped by, total and complete.

From beneath me, a blue glow began to lighten my surroundings. Another futile scream wrenched itself from my mouth as the enormous maw of a beast, composed entirely of blue magic, rose from below, opening its jaws to swallow me.

"Grab one, Val!" Rune yelled.

His vines were reaching after me, trying to stop my fall. I rotated in midair, only too aware of the mouth I plummeted closer to every second. I grasped for the vines.

"I can't!" I yelled.

"You can," Rune said. "But you won't. Not for me, and not for yourself."

He was wrong. I wanted to be saved. I wanted to be with him, not consumed by this enormous beast.

But whenever I reached out, my hand stopped halfway, as though knowing what I really wanted was below me, in the gaping jaws of the beast—

"Val."

I jerked awake. Through the blurriness of my tired eyes, I could make out the dim lights of the palace kitchens. I vaguely remembered coming down here after encountering Sulien. I'd started picking at a few things to eat and then lain my head down and...

Most of the food that'd been left out had been picked away, as though wildlings had come in and out while I slept, not daring to disturb me. I wasn't sure whether to be grateful or worried about that.

"Here," Marian said, shoving a cup into my hand. She watched as I slowly wrapped my fingers around it.

I sniffed the drink and recoiled at the bitter smell. "Let me guess, this is from General Forcheck."

"One of her latest brews," Marian agreed. "Drink it."

I took a sip and held down vomit until the worst of the flavor passed and a zing of contentedness filled me. Behind Marian, Idwal, one of Rune's spies, flittered around the kitchen, silent as a cloud of smoke, collecting wedges of over-ripe fruit, near-stale bread, pickled root, and chilled slices of carved beast. He placed one of the plates in front of me and offered the flash of a smile.

"You have a bed, you know," Marian said. "A shared one now, apparently. In case you forgot."

I choked on my bite of meat on bread. Marian smirked.

"I'm sorry for not telling you before," I said.

"You seemed just as surprised as everyone else. Rune included."

"Do the others who weren't there already know?" I asked.

"Only everyone," Idwal said, and I suppressed a groan. He gently patted my hand. "Gossip, especially that about Rune, grows as tall as trees and twice as thick as weeds. As hard to trim, too."

"Though I'm sure you and Pitius just couldn't *wait* to spread it, Idwal," Marian drawled.

Idwal smiled sweetly.

"What...do the rest think about, you know, us?" I asked.

"Do you care?" Marian said.

I did, more than I wanted to admit.

"They think that you're the Empress and he's the High

King," Marian said. "And that you're going to save us. Or that we're all going to die."

Idwal finished putting together another couple of plates. He lifted both to me with a, "Long live the Empress," before flitting out.

Marian shook her head. "Spies. They're more trouble than they're worth. If you're seriously worried, then I know the wildlings are curious about you and Rune, not hostile to the idea. Most of them think it's solely for an alliance than anything more."

"But you know better," I said. "You think I'm an idiot."

"I was surprised. There's a difference. I knew you two had a thing for each other, far more than he ever had with me." She watched me push the pickled root around my plate. "Do you love him?"

Did I love him, did I care for him, what was I to the High King? Everyone seemed to have the same question, and I only wished I had the answer. I'd asked myself the same thing a hundred times and a hundred more in the few days since I'd married Rune.

"Does Rune know?" Marian went on, as though my silence was answer enough.

"I haven't talked to him about it," I admitted.

"Of course you haven't. Both of you would have to be dying before you admitted one true thing about the other."

"That's not... I mean..."

"Tell him. Before it's too late. I can't pretend to understand your relationship. I don't think *you* even understand it. But something about it works. You haven't killed each other yet, and you're better together."

She took my plate and tossed the scraps out the small window where it was picked up by skittering creatures. "Go to bed."

I eased back from the table. “Thanks, Marian.”

“Val?” Marian said.

I stopped at the kitchen doorway.

“You and Rune have nothing over each other anymore. You’re in this together, until the end, the way it was meant to be. Do you feel stronger?”

“I do.” I thought of my nightmare, of Grislehaut’s maw, widening enough to swallow me and the entire Wilds. “I’m not sure it’ll be enough, though.”

Marian’s expression darkened. “I hope, for all our sakes, that it is.”

CHAPTER TWENTY-THREE

Sleep still wouldn't come.

After tossing and turning for a couple hours, I threw the blanket off and padded into the quiet palace. The wind hushed through the hallways, tinkling chimes on the ceilings and stirring the glowing bats fluttering through the porticos.

I was surprised to find myself outside Rune's room. I hadn't even checked if he was there on the way back to mine. There were no guards outside. Like most other places in the palace, he'd conjured powerful enchantments to ensure no one could do us harm.

I approached the door and it unlocked itself, the enchantment recognizing who I was. Heart in my throat, I reached out for the handle.

Tell him. Before it's too late.

How could I tell him something I could barely admit to myself? Still, I eased the door open.

Rune wasn't there. His bed lay undisturbed. From outside his open window came the rustle of nocturnal creatures, the groan of trees shifting their roots, the cry of distant beasts.

I stood in the center of his room, wondering if he, like me, hadn't been able to sleep. If he, like me, had been stuck the last few days between the torturous feeling of wanting to be with him and staying away to try and make sense of my swirling emotions. Was he keeping himself busy, all to avoid being around me?

An alliance, I told myself. *Nothing more.*

Call it what you want, Rune's teasing voice answered. *We both know what it is.*

I continued to the lower levels of the palace, where the breezy hallways turned to chilly damp stone and earthen networks of root-lined tunnels. Down here, the palace had begun to intermix with iridescent lines of blue crystal. The Below slowly mixing with the above.

I found the memory room full of floating crystals, one thing I'd managed to use my magic to bring to the surface before the entire Below had been submerged.

The room hummed when I stepped inside, a faint rumbling that resonated through my chest.

The earth remembers.

Was this the reason I'd been having such vivid, terrible dreams lately? The magic in here might have seeped into my head, trying to tell me something. I hadn't searched through any more of Sotera's memories, but maybe now they could quiet the nagging doubts about Grislehaut, the ones I'd had since Rune and I visited him.

I pulled one of the floating crystals to the left, rewinding to where I'd left off.

"What have you done?"

Though I was prepared for it, Sotera's voice still jolted me. From the memory, the crystals had conjured one of the rooms in the palace, perhaps the very one Sotera had locked me in before.

She hurried to the frosted windows. With a swipe of her hand, they became clear, and she peered outside. *"What have you done?"*

"What I must," Empress Lavena, her grandmother, snapped. "What was necessary. We try it now."

The memory dimmed, and only after I'd moved the crystal a little to the right to fast forward did their hologram-like images appear around me again.

I knew immediately where we were.

Sotera and Empress Lavena stood in the vast desert of the Below, beside one of the dozen gargantuan columns, its stone pock-marked and reaching so high up into the dark I was certain they supported the very surface.

"What if you bring it all crashing down?" Sotera murmured.

Empress Lavena turned and slapped her, eliciting a *crack*. When Sotera, stunned, pulled her hand away, small fractures bloomed on her cheek.

"I see now why that husband of yours does as he does, to silence your pitiful mewling," Empress Lavena said. "If what I do brings it all down, then we'll be crushed mercifully quick rather than withering away year by agonizing year. And if you can't be useful, then at least be quiet."

Sotera cradled her cheek as Empress Lavena began chanting under her breath. Before her was the ball of magic I'd seen before, coalesced into a single white sphere with ribbons of blue rippling around it. As her words picked up, the ribbons glowed brighter. When they were bright enough to hurt my eyes, she slammed a hand against one of the pillars.

The earth rumbled. Small fissures opened like cracks in dry skin, swallowing mouthfuls of sand. Empress Lavena pressed harder against the pillar, arm trembling.

"It's not yours," she muttered. "Not anymore. I took it fairly."

Silence descended. The ceiling remained intact. The pillars looked as solid as ever.

"Empress!" A guard ran up and knelt in front of her. "You have to come now. It's—It's—"

"Enough," Empress Lavena said, dropping her arm. She glowered high above, as though imagining the light and fresh air the universe was destined to keep from her. Then she scooped up the ribboning ball of magic. Sotera flinched as her grandmother held it out.

"It's time for you to be strong for once," Empress Lavena said. "Continue using it. Unlock its secrets."

She cradled Sotera's cheek, the same one she'd just brutalized. "*Free* us."

The memories blurred as I scanned to find the next, my head spinning. Terrible understanding was dawning on me slowly, like the blare of an oncoming train growing progressively louder, but there were still a few missing pieces.

I watched as Sotera tried to work her own magic on the crystal. How at first she resented it, ignored it, but then found there was something soothing about it and the promise of freedom it offered.

As she worked, she told it stories: about her grandmother and her expectations; about Those Below and how trapped they were; about the cruelty of her husband, a sharp man with an even sharper fist.

As she spoke, the ribbons of magic responded. During the few happy memories Sotera recounted, they fluttered in delight, and during the many horrifying tales, they wrapped around her wrist, as though trying to console her.

I was in the middle of watching Sotera coaxing the ribbons to grow when the doors to her chambers were thrown open.

Empress Lavena stood between them, panting as though she'd sprinted all the way here. Outside was in chaos, with Those Below rushing back and forth and the palace rumbling, though strangely Sotera's room hadn't so much as budged.

Empress Lavena noticed it, too. Her eyes narrowed on the un-cracked walls and then down to Sotera, huddled close to the ribbons of magic.

"So you haven't been entirely useless. Grislehaut is still trying to awaken, but this is the last time. I will see him sealed away for good."

Sotera was on her feet. "He'll kill you!"

"Then I'll die doing what I was supposed to."

"I won't let you—"

Empress Lavena leveled an enormous crystal sword—the same one Sotera had carried—at Sotera's chest.

"You will become Empress if I fail. Your job—your *only* job —is to free our people from the Below. Unlock the magic's secrets and bring us above. Guards! On me!"

"Grandmother—Empress!" Sotera raced after her.

The doors shut, leaving the ball of magic alone, its ribbons fluttering to an empty room. I waited for the next memory to start, but after a minute or two of nothing happening, I fast-forwarded. One day. Two. Three. A week. The ribbons continued reaching out as though searching for someone to hold on to. Eventually it stopped trying, and they curled sadly back within the ball of magic.

Further and further forward I went. Still the room didn't change, and I wondered for a horrible moment if this was all the memories the crystals had to offer.

Until one day I blinked, and where the ball of magic had been was now a small, naked figure, no bigger than a child, its bones made entirely of crystal.

I stared at it. The crystal child looked around. It moved to one side of the room, then the other, before settling in the corner. The doors burst open again and Sotera stumbled in.

Her eyes were wide, as though she'd witnessed something she could never unsee. Blood covered the front of her dress, and she held a sword in one hand, also covered in it.

This she cast aside and sank to the floor crying, which turned into erratic, bubbling laughter.

She looked up and saw the ball of magic was missing. She leaned forward on her hands and knees. "No—"

Her eyes found the crystal child and grew wider still. "It's not possible."

She got to her feet and cautiously approached the child. "What are you? This is... What *are* you?"

Shouting sounded from down the hall. Muffled voices yelled, "In here, the closest room."

The doors burst open again, and guards carrying Empress Lavena shuffled inside.

"Here. Right here."

They lay her gently on the bed, and I blanched at the extent of her injuries. Her entire body had been shattered, as though she'd been thrown bodily against stone and stomped on a few times. The edges of her were blurry and beginning to unravel, and whatever parts of her were flesh bled, quickly spreading black silt across the sheets.

"Grandmother!" Sotera cried, forgetting the crystal child and rushing to her grandmother's side. Empress Lavena opened her working eye. Her gaze immediately went past everyone and rested on the corner where the crystal child lingered. It then snapped to those surrounding her, as though afraid they'd notice.

"Get out, all of you, save for my granddaughter."

"My Empress," one of the guards protested. "You need healing—"

"Get out! You can't heal a dead woman."

With shuffling feet and muttered words, her guards left.

Empress Lavena stared at the child and then Sotera. "I've been busy. Grislehaut is sealed away, for now. I've bought you time. Did you waste it?"

"What did you take from Grislehaut?" Sotera said. She drew closer to her grandmother's side and gestured to the child. "This isn't simply magic you siphoned from him, and he's not *just* angry at being sealed away. You took something from him. What was it?"

"He's sealed away now," Empress Lavena repeated, sidestepping Sotera's question. "It won't last. He'll want to be free even more."

"I need to know—"

"I'm dying, girl. Are you going to waste my last moments peppering me about things you don't understand, or will you say to me the things you've always desperately wanted to?"

Empress Sotera knelt beside the bed and took her grandmother's shattered hand. Her grandmother jerked it away, swatting weakly at Sotera. "I have treated you lower than dirt. Don't coddle and revere and pretend you *love* me. *Hate* me, as you should. Have some self-respect and use that hate to make you strong. Maybe, if you'd had an ounce of a spine, that wretched husband of yours wouldn't treat you so. Speaking of which, who's blood is that?"

"As if you don't know," Sotera said, voice monotone. "It's the blood of one husband who will never treat me poorly again."

A cracking smile split Empress Lavena's face. "It's about time. Then you are ready to do what needs to be done. Use the magic I gathered."

Sotera's eyes flickered to the child. "I don't know what it is anymore."

"It is cherished. It is *our* cherished, and it will be our salvation. Use it, and become strong..."

Empress Lavena gave a last gasping breath. A sound like crackling ice filled the room as her entire body seized up. Sotera rested her forehead on her grandmother's chest where the last dim light of life within her faded.

After a long moment, Sotera stood and approached the crystal child. It didn't shy away, not when she knelt, not when she hugged it.

"You're our cherished," Sotera murmured into its shoulder. "Just like she said. You will save us all."

Now the room shook, worse than ever before, as though the entire Below was ripping apart and taking the palace with it. Sotera was on her feet in an instant.

"Stay here!"

She dashed back into the hallways. The door briefly closed behind her, before bouncing back open.

Though it had no expression, I could feel the terror emanating from the crystal child. I moved closer to the image of it and held out my hand, as though I could reach back through time and memory and comfort it. It didn't want to be alone. It wanted to be anywhere but here, where people's screams echoed, and the world felt like it was falling apart.

It ran, and I found myself pulled with it, jerked along with no control over the memories. A steady pressure built in my head, as though the surrounding crystals had stopped drawing from Sotera's memories and were now rummaging through mine, the new Empress of Those Below, collected for anyone who took my place.

The crystal child ran through the palace, which was in such chaos nobody paid it any attention. It ran through the cold and the heat. It ran through the darkness, the dim glow of its body lighting its way. I felt its fear and confusion growing with each passing second. It had no clue what it was, but it knew it had to get to the surface.

It had to be free.

Eventually it slipped its tiny body through the cracks of the earth, through vents rising up, up, up, until it reached a small crevasse lined with needle-like crystal, barely big enough for even its tiny body to scrape through.

It emerged in the Wilds.

Both the child and I stumbled to our hands and knees. My head was screaming in pain now. What I saw in these memories was drawing something up from deep, deep inside my mind, and the two images were merging with agonizing intensity.

I smelled something sickly sweet and coppery. The crystal child had stumbled across bodies. The blood covering them was still wet, the flesh already overgrown with fungi and partly gnawed away by small beasts. Those same beasts crowded in the trees nearby and among the brush, their beady eyes staring, waiting for the child to leave so they could keep feeding.

Without knowing why, the crystal child reached out and touched the flesh. In seconds her entire body was covered in it as though it had always been there, and the memories in the crystal and the memories in my head converged with shattering force as I found myself looking at—

Me.

The child that was Val stumbled through the trees until I could make out a town peeking through the parted leaves. A town I *knew,* the memory hazy and distorted by time, but familiar all the same. Gray stone, cut sharply into square blocks, crumbled among spewing piles of metal.

The child Val shivered from the cold. She was covered in blood and bare strips of cloth from the bodies, and the toll of running and finding herself in this new form was enacting a terrible toll. She collapsed, and I nearly did as well.

"Is she dead?"

It was Rune. His scrawny, childish arms poking out of a filthy shirt. His eyes—gold with flecks of red—peered closely at my collapsed form. The child Val blinked up at him and Rune gave a lopsided grin filled with teeth that were slightly sharp and a bit crooked.

"Nope, not dead."

I watched, openmouthed, as Rune pulled a large leaf from a nearby tree and clasped it between his slender fingers. The edges of it glowed, and he pulled at them, rotating as he did so. In moments, the leaf was big enough that he could drape it over my younger self's shoulders.

I watched as Rune tried to leave and I caught his hand. Maybe I'd wanted to thank him. Maybe because I'd felt so alone and powerless and confused, as confused as I was now.

When our hands touched, I felt rather than saw the sharp buzz that traveled up our arms. Rune's eyes widened. Then he gently withdrew his hand from mine, splitting into another crooked-toothed grin.

"Careful, little fox. Getting too close to things like me is going to get you hurt."

And then he was gone, and I was watching as a younger Peyton kneeled in front of me.

"Hey there, I'm Peyton. What's your name?"

I wrenched my hand away from the crystals, and the room went dark.

For a minute or an hour, I lay curled on the floor, trying to control my panting. My head felt like a hundred knives had been stuck into it. I wanted the memories playing over and over again to stop, but this wasn't the crystals showing them; they were here, in my mind. They'd *always* been here.

I couldn't make sense of it. How had Sotera and her grandmother created me—

The knives sank deeper, and I let out an involuntary whimper. I wasn't that...that...*thing*.

You have crystal for bones, a small voice taunted. *You thought you were just one of Those Below? Don't be stupid.*

Was I Empress Lavena's daughter? Had someone crafted me using Grislehaut's magic? Or was I more than that? Sotera had spoken to me, and through that I had become something sentient. Something that was taken from Grislehaut to use as a weapon. Something that Grislehaut had been desperate to get back, willing to destroy the entirety of the Below in the process.

What if you're not the only one who feels like you're missing a piece?

The knives sinking into my brain stopped, leaving me clear to stare at the naked truth.

Empress Lavena hadn't just stolen some of Grislehaut's magic. She had taken part of him.

I was part of the god of destruction.

CHAPTER TWENTY-FOUR

I paced the memory room, barely noticing when I almost knocked my head against one of the floating crystals. I'd replayed the scene I'd witnessed a half dozen more times, trying to pick a line here, a glance there, that told me I was wrong, that I'd misinterpreted everything.

I was Val of Those Below, Empress of Glass, clothed in human flesh.

I was part of Grislehaut. A being Sotera, with her words, must have filled with emotions, given life...*somehow*, before I escaped to the surface.

I put my fists against my eyes and let out a long breath. This wasn't the end. This wasn't over. I still needed confirmation, and then I could see how wrong I was, and maybe I could find Grislehaut's weakness and this would all be behind us.

Nearly an hour after I'd summoned him, one of Those Below arrived with Tibald the priest in tow. Tibald cautiously entered the room.

"Empress. I'm glad to see you not only saved an esteemed

room of your predecessors, but maybe you're using it to learn from their mistakes as well."

"Look at this," I said, and started to replay the memory. Not even a quarter of the way through, Tibald hadn't so much as flinched, nor shown any reaction except moderate indifference.

I drew my hand from the crystal and the memory faded. "You've seen this before. You were there, weren't you?"

Tibald weighed his words, and everything about his appearance seemed a bit slanted now. The sunstone scabbing his skin shone a little brighter. The crystal freezing part of his jaw didn't seem so pronounced. It was as though he'd shed a shoddy overcoat, and a half-dozen details I'd never noticed before came together to make him appear far more capable than I'd thought.

"I was there that day, and many, many days before it," Tibald said. "I was there when Empress Sotera took her first breath of silty Below air. I was there when her mother did the same, and her grandmother, and many of our rulers before that. I was there for them all, so yes, I have seen that memory."

The already cold room suddenly felt frigid. Tibald regarded me curiously as I took a step back. "Empress?"

"Are you...like Mother Mal? Are you a god?"

Tibald gave a reedy laugh. "Hardly, Empress. I am merely a priest of Those Below, not a force of nature or fate. I'll admit I've been blessed with a long life rather than my body seizing where I stand. I am here to do my duty to whichever empress has the throne. To guide them into what is best for the Below. And, in this case, what is best for everyone."

I didn't entirely believe him. But even if I was wrong and he was hiding what he truly was, what did it matter? Unless he could snap his fingers and solve everything this was still up to me—to us—to fix.

"Grislehaut once talked about being shattered and in

pieces. He meant me, didn't he? I'm a piece of him. What did..." A dry lump gathered in my throat, and it was difficult to swallow. "How did Empress Lavena get me?"

"She used an ancient magic, one she didn't pass on to her granddaughter. She thieved part of Grislehaut's very essence."

"Why him?" I asked. "Why did she have to use part of the god of *destruction*?"

Tibald blinked as though the answer were so very simple. "Because he was *there*, Below, with them. You have to understand—though I know you were raised human and may not be as familiar with our legends—Grislehaut was one of the first gods to be quelled by the Forming, that time when the Houses and the Lords came together to drive back the great Wild beasts and trap or kill the gods terrorizing them.

"You speak as though she could have picked a better, more benign god to steal from. Like many of the gods, Grislehaut is not good or bad, he just *is*. His power, Empress Lavena had hoped, would be just as sufficient to escape our underground prison as any other, but he also was the closest and the gravest threat. He, like all of us, has a part to play in this cosmic, divine game."

If it was a game, then I wanted to quit. I was tired of being yanked around like a pawn. I was tired of never getting a moment's peace before another Lord, another ruler, another grasping, power-hungry being tried to ruin what we'd created. I wanted it all to end.

"How am I..." I gestured to myself, unable to properly form the words. "How did I come to be?"

"That is the great mystery, isn't it?" Tibald said in an infuriatingly calm tone. "Maybe Grislehaut yearned so much to be free he found a way to turn you into a vessel that could escape. Perhaps Sotera's words took on physical shape, desperate to be like her. Or perhaps gods were once not unlike mortals, and the part of Grislehaut Empress Lavena stole simply shifted back to something much like it was before."

That was what Mother Mal had said happened to Olette. She'd been just a little girl once, but now had been chosen to become so much more. I wondered if she thought it was a blessing or a curse.

"You seem distressed," Tibald said.

"You *think,*" I growled.

"In a way, nothing's changed. I will admit, I'd hoped when I showed you this room that it would grant you the insight you needed."

"Why didn't you just tell me? I'm your Empress, don't you think I had a right to know?"

"Some things," Tibald said, "are better discovered on your own. If I'd told you and offered you the solution, you wouldn't be as eager to take it. But now that you've seen it for yourself, you know what needs to be done."

When he is one, he will sleep. Joshua's words hadn't meant much at the time, but they were starting to make a terrifying amount of sense now. It took me a couple times to manage, "If it's true I'm part of Grislehaut, then if I found some way to become one with him again, will it end this? Will he go back to sleep?"

I was happy to see Tibald thinking. It made me feel as though he didn't actually have all the answers and, like me, was making this up on the go.

"Grislehaut yearns for freedom, but in a very real sense, I think he simply yearns to be whole again. What a terrible thing, to be alone and in pieces. I do think that once he has the missing part of himself that he will be quelled. You must become one, once more."

"And when that happens, I'll die," I said matter-of-factly.

"You know the answer to that, don't you? I think you've

known from the very beginning. Everything you've done, consciously or not, has led you to this moment."

I couldn't believe that. All the times I'd felt an unwavering calling to go back into the Wilds to collect heart gems; meeting Rune and becoming his blade, and then something so much more; encountering all those who would fall as my enemies or become my friends.

All of that couldn't simply lead to this. It was impossible that all the choices I'd made had, in fact, been meaningless in the end.

"I'll have to think about it," I said. "Knowing what happened, knowing what I am now, I should be able to come up with a solution."

"One you haven't come up with already?" Tibald said.

I nearly punched him in his old, splintery face. "You've done what I asked. Now leave."

"You may not believe me, but I think you are a good ruler, Empress of Glass, and I don't want you to die. But, in some ways, you were never supposed to live at all, so maybe this is how things were meant to be."

The memory room felt oppressively heavy after he left. The crystals glittered as they passed, as though they were laughing at me.

"I'll call once I need you," I said to Erebus.

With a comforting growl that vibrated through my chest, his shadow dripped from my arm down to the ground two stories below. I watched his form, darker than the surrounding night, bleed into the trees.

I wouldn't call him again. That was as much a goodbye as I was willing to give.

All day I'd existed in a fatalistic fantasy, a thousand different scenarios of what might happen once we faced Grislehaut playing on repeat in my head. As though I was General Forcheck overviewing the field of battle, I'd dissected each encounter with him and tried to think of things we hadn't yet tried.

No matter how much I thought and agonized and plotted, every single road led to one outcome.

Every single outcome told me the same thing: if everyone else was to survive, I couldn't.

If no power of the Wilds, the Lords, our marriage, or the Below could stand against Grislehaut, if nothing mortal could stand up against a god, then only part of that same god had a chance.

You know the answer to that, don't you? I think you've known from the very beginning.

The moment I'd made the choice, a sort of numbing peace had settled over me. Not happiness, but acceptance; the relief that came from surrendering to something I couldn't hope to win against. With the others still dealing with preparing for our attack on Father Dumas, I'd covertly began sending pieces of my life away one by one. Erebus was nearing the last of what I could do. He'd become unwaveringly loyal these last couple weeks. It'd be better he return to find his master mysteriously disappeared than share my fate.

My legs hung off the edge of the balcony. Fireflies danced overhead, and the palace and Wilds surrounding it were lush with silence. I wasn't foolish enough to think it was a peaceful one. This was the calm before the breaking storm.

I felt the prickle of Rune's approach even before he said, "There you are."

"Here I am," I answered. It wasn't that I'd avoided him all day. We'd both been busy in our own ways. But I'd yet gathered up the courage to tell him what I'd discovered. I still wasn't sure I would.

Silent as a gentle breeze, Rune settled beside me, letting his long legs dangle next to mine. I waited for him to speak, but he seemed content looking out over the Wilds. It was still startling to see him look so...calm. Comfortable. I'd been getting glimpses of this new side of him the last couple days. Given more time, perhaps I'd get the chance to see more—

A painful ache stormed through my chest.

"I'm just resting," I said. "Don't feel like you need to keep me company if someone else needs your attention."

"Everyone needs my attention, always," Rune said. "But I find doing nothing with you is better than doing something with anyone else."

My fingers found and intertwined his. As the night deepened and my recent discoveries threatened to overwhelm me, I found myself blinking back tears.

Rune looked over at me. "Let me know what's made you shed tears, and I'll make them cry twice as much. Unless the one who did so is me." He tapped his chin. "I'm trying to think of anything recent I've done that could make you so distraught. My presence, perhaps?"

I wiped the tears back. "You're not *that* bad. This is something else."

"Would you like to share it with me?"

I really did. I knew I couldn't. If every inch of me recoiled at what I had to do, I couldn't begin to imagine how Rune might react. And if returning myself to Grislehaut was what I had to do to save all of us, then I couldn't risk him standing in the way.

"I can leave you to your thoughts."

Rune started to stand, but I held his hand tighter. He gazed down at me, eyes glowing intensely in the night. I didn't want to be alone. I wanted to be with him, to show him how much I didn't want to lose him and how I didn't want to be apart.

"I'm sorry," I said.

Rune's eyes narrowed. "What do you have to be sorry for? We've said it so many times to one another, and we'll say it many more, that I'm having trouble thinking of any one thing."

I was sorry for what I hadn't told him yet. For how badly I'd hurt him, no matter what I did.

"I don't know," I said, shaking my head. "I just want...I want..."

But he seemed to be able to fill in the blank. He gently pulled me up and put my hand over his heart gem. Its warmth radiated through my entire body.

"This is yours. Now and forever. You never had to carve it out, but you stole it regardless."

"That is... So incredibly cheesy," I murmured, but I was smiling.

Rune grinned back, all wickedness and delight, and then it was as though we were two magnets drawn to one another and my mouth found his.

I was no longer in control.

I pushed him back toward the bed and he gladly fell, taking me with him, the two of us connected, still furiously kissing. His hands started gentle but grew firm, roughly grabbing me as though to keep me in place. Mine roamed his chest, his back, along the muscles of his arms. They pressed and drew away, as though I was running my hands through the thorns of the circlet in his hair. Cautious, unsure, but wanting. Equally painful and pleasurable. I could feel power building up inside me and recalled the last time I was lost like this, how much I'd hurt him.

"Rune, we shouldn't—"

In one powerful move, he rolled us until he was on top.

One hand caught mine and seemed to absorb the power within me until it wasn't a concern. Until nothing was a concern except his nearness and the continued nagging voice that I shouldn't want this, couldn't want this.

Why not? A small voice said. *He's yours, and you are his.*

But what if he knew? What if he knew what I had to do?

Then all the better to have this one last bit of happiness.

Yes, but—

Any further arguing vanished as Rune moved from kissing the corner of my lips down to my chin and then my throat. A small whimper escaped me.

"Are you scared?" Rune's voice was so soft I wasn't sure whether it was reality or part of my wondrous fantasy.

I opened my eyes to find him staring down at me, lips kiss-swollen, an expression of pure, vulnerable terror on his face.

"Tell me that what we did wasn't a mistake," he said almost desperately. "Tell me that this is right and things will all be for the best."

In that moment I knew exactly how he felt: my emotions stripped bare and exposed.

"Val—"

I rolled him back over and kissed him again.

"I don't have answers, but I do have you," I said between kisses. "And you know me, and I know you, now, and forever."

What a terrible thing, to be alone and in pieces.

I wasn't alone. Not anymore.

Rune seemed to grow more sure after that, and within moments the heady drug of his kisses was making it difficult to think. My hand paused over his heart gem. The power within me yearned to pull from it until there was nothing left, until he was nothing but a husk.

"I don't want to hurt you," I whispered.

"You already have, *we* already have, in so many delicious,

terrible ways," Rune said. "But we survived each other. And we will continue to survive. Together."

He would survive, at least. I would make sure of it.

Tears streamed down my face, and I leaned into him, lost in his touch. My tears were sorrow at what was coming, but I was also more grateful than I could voice.

Because if I was never meant to live, then I was glad that I'd lived even a little bit with him.

CHAPTER TWENTY-FIVE

The next morning found me around the planning table with the others. General Forcheck and Caldre chatted casually about the grand campaigns they'd led, gleefully recounting the numerous times one nearly killed the other. Xander was gathering up the rest of the maps to bring to our new position outside Seattle. And if I snuck a few surreptitious glances at Rune, who cast many barely concealed, heated gazes in return, and if the others noticed, then who could blame us?

"We've prepared as best we can," Marian said, dumping the last of the maps into Xander's arms. "Any longer and our allies may feel we're stalling and that Rune doesn't like to get his hands bloody."

"We wouldn't dare want to give them that idea," Rune said.

"I'm still not set on your grand plan," Caldre said. "You aim to stop Father Dumas, but then what?"

"That would be our dear Empress's time to shine," General Forcheck said. "With her magic over the Below, if we can get her to the edge of the chasm, she might be able to close it up."

Caldre's frown deepened, and though I completely understood why, I didn't enjoy seeing it. "And you think this will stop him?"

You must become one, once more.

"Maybe," I admitted, not willing to explain that I'd already tried that exact tactic and it had failed miserably.

"Maybe," Caldre repeated.

"Perhaps you have other doubts to voice, General," I said. I stared at him, not forgetting the thinly veiled threats Sulien had passed along to me. I thought now, as I did then, it likely wasn't only Sulien and Tannis who were behind the grave warning.

After a long moment, Caldre gave a conceding nod. "I've said all I need to."

"Good," Rune said. "What will be done will be done. No more. No less. General Forcheck, General Caldre, you and your forces will meet me there—"

Footsteps preceded a wildling appearing in the doorway, out of breath. His eyes flickered between me and Rune, seemingly trying to decide which one of us was more in charge.

"Speak, breathless one," General Forcheck said.

"A worshipper, from Father Dumas," the wildling said. "He's here in the palace. He says he has a message."

"His surrender, I'm sure," Rune said. He directed the wildling messenger to go on ahead. "We'll meet him."

Minutes later, Rune, General Forcheck and I stood outside the eastern edge of the palace. The worshipper—a skinny man with a twitchy disposition and the barest hint of whiskers on his chin—shuffled his feet nervously, surrounded by wildlings.

"My hospitality is so close," Rune said, gesturing to his palace. "And yet you stop out here."

The man swallowed. "It's as far as I need to go. I have a message from Father Dumas."

"His nerves make *me* nervous," General Forcheck muttered.

"Strange, you'd think he'd believe that the god they're so insistent on awakening would protect him."

"Let me guess," Rune said to the man. "Father Dumas wishes to give up? To send Grislehaut back to the depths where he belongs?"

"He wants to meet," the man said.

"Of course he does."

"He's trying to stall," I said. "He knows we have nothing to talk about, so he wants to buy more time before Grislehaut breaks free."

"And yet the closer we are to him, the easier to drive a blade into his throat," Rune said.

The worshipper's eyes widened. "This would be *peaceful*—"

"That would be considered peaceful, by our standards," General Forcheck said. "Alas, if only Father Dumas didn't expect us to do just that."

Against Father Dumas, strike hard, strike fast. Don't give him the chance to do anything.

"We—" I started.

"The humans have also agreed to meet with him," the worshipper bumbled.

"You talk about them as though the worshippers aren't humans themselves," Rune chuckled. "As though you don't break just as easily."

"Father Dumas urges you to meet. He says he has something to return to you."

"Does he?" Rune said, curious now.

The worshippers gulped, but I saw Rune had come to the same decision in that moment that I had. If the humans were willing to listen, and if this really was the best chance we were going to get to learn of Father Dumas's schemes and get close enough to inflict real damage, then we had to take it.

"We'll meet him in a few hours," I said.

The worshipper's shoulders slumped with relief, and he scurried back off into the trees.

Rune was frowning. "This feels like a mistake."

"Diplomacy has always felt like a mistake to me, my High King," General Forcheck said. "I suppose that's why I'm not ruling."

"If the meeting goes south, we always have the diplomacy of knives and teeth," I reminded him.

Rune's face split into a devilish grin. He summoned over one of the wildlings. "I need either Pitius or Idwall here. I want to know Father Dumas's whereabouts."

"They haven't come back from when you sent them out the first time," the wildling said.

Rune's brow furrowed. "Interesting. Send them to me the moment they do."

"Some advice, my High King," General Forcheck said. "You'll be leading an army into a grand battle against a god, not some rag-tag group out to slay a king. You need armor befitting your power. Cassius can help you craft it."

"Sounds exhausting," Rune said.

"It might save your life," I said, exasperated. "Yes, General Forcheck, we'll do that. We should have done it before."

I ignored Rune's smirk and General Forcheck's delighted look as we went to the palace armory.

Weapons had been fastened to the wall with delicate roots. Pieces of half-crafted armor lay piled in corners and strewn around, the result of hurriedly arming so many wildlings.

Marian and Cassius were sitting together amongst the wreckage, laughing, as they stitched together hardened bark armor plating and trimmed it with iron. There was a lightness surrounding Marian. A brightness to her eyes, an upward curl at the end of her lips. All things that, for once, didn't vanish when she looked up and saw us.

"Almost time?"

"Armor first," I said.

Marian nodded at Cassius. "Ask him. You wouldn't think it with how thick they are, but his fingers are much defter."

Cassius smirked at the teasing and stood. "Give me a moment."

I knew each wildling had a different connection to the Wilds, a different talent. I was most used to Rune's command over all things within it, Marian's control of ice, and Raquel's sweet talking of beasts. Cassius, for all his skill with fighting, had an eye for beauty.

From the shards of the armory, along with some choice materials—roots and glass from Rune, gems from me—Cassius wove a chainmail of roots intertwined with silver, gauntlets of glass and metal ivy, breastplates edged with teeth and made of reinforced obsidian so smooth it seemed that any bullet or sword would glance right off. When he was done, I couldn't help letting out a delighted gasp. It was one of the most beautiful things I'd ever seen, a marvel of craftsmanship that combined the best elements of both our worlds.

"It's stunning," I said. Cassius beamed, and Marian, if it was possible, smiled even wider.

"Try them on, make sure I got the size right," Cassius said.

Despite the material, the chainmail was feather-light, as were most of the other pieces, as though they'd been enchanted. It was easy, even by myself, to slip them on and fasten them tight. I turned in the mirror, admiring the girl who looked nothing at all like the one who'd worn ratty hoodies as she slinked through the Wilds. For maybe the first time, I could truly imagine myself an Empress.

"No helmets," Cassius said. "Everyone will see the crowns.

Everyone will know who you are and who they should kneel to."

"It's a bit gawdy, don't you think?" Rune said. When Cassius stared at him, Rune broke into a startingly boyish grin and patted him on the shoulder. "It is excellent. In the unlikely event something does pierce it, I'll die looking beautiful."

"You will not," I said firmly. As though to reinforce my words, blue crystal grew along the edges of his armor, further protecting him.

"Perfect," he said. He continued to praise Cassius. He laughed, and joked, and even teased, and I began to see glimpses of it: a lightness surrounded him, too, the same as Marian.

This happiness was what I wanted for him. And because I was part of the reason he had it, that made what I needed to do all the more painful. It was a shard of glass lodged in my heart, piercing ever deeper with every passing hour.

"Val?"

Rune was looking expectantly at me, and I realized he'd asked me something.

"What?"

"Are you ready?"

His expression was so unguarded that for a moment my secret nearly slipped from my lips. More than once I'd tried to tell him. This morning, as I watched his face while he slept. Earlier today when we ate in comfortable silence in the garden. During the small respite after the first meeting with the generals. He, out of everyone, would understand what sacrifice meant.

But he, out of everyone, would try to protect me, even if it cost him his life.

That was something I couldn't risk.

"I'm ready," I said. "Let's go."

Rune took my hand after the others had filtered out, holding me back. His gaze had darkened in that conniving way I knew meant he saw right through me. “You’re nervous about more than just the coming fight.”

“There’s something else,” I admitted. “But I’ll figure it out.”

He brushed strands of hair off my cheek. “Maybe we made a mistake, being together,” he murmured. “Because now, even with all this armor on, I find myself more vulnerable than ever before. I hate the thought of you being in more danger than you need to be.”

“We both understood the cost,” I said.

Tell him, my mind screamed. *Tell him, tell him, tell him*—

Rune kissed me, tenderly, slow. That kiss was a promise, one I knew he couldn’t fulfill.

“You can’t protect all of us,” I whispered. “And you can’t protect me from everything.”

“But I can try. I *will* try,” Rune said.

The shard of glass sank further into my heart.

Our camps were set up on the southwestern part of the Seattle chasm, in the rubble of what were once townhouses. As we emerged from the path Rune summoned and made our way to our fern-woven tents, I overheard Gracie grumbling that she’d once had a townhouse just like these, one she’d spent hours decorating to make it her own.

“I guess it’s not *too* bad,” she said as I passed. “They could still be salvaged, once all this is over. At the very least, the property values should be historically low.”

Halfway to the tent, a human figure pushed their way through the wildlings. It took me a second longer than it should have to recognize Peyton, her face flushed, eyes wide.

"What's wrong?" I said, all my worst fears surging to the forefront of my mind: we were too late and Grislehaut had broken free; Leah had changed her mind and was going to try to murder me.

She found me and rushed over. "Is it true? They're saying that Father Dumas called a truce. That you're planning to meet with him."

"It's—"

She took my shoulders and practically shook me. "*Strike hard, strike fast*, remember? You promised me. The only reason he wants to meet is so he can get something from you. You *must* stop him before he tries something. You *must*."

I'd already considered a dozen different scenarios of that exact worry and hadn't yet come up with *what* Father Dumas could want that we had or that I could give him. And even if we were to try to strike first, it would be extremely difficult, outside the Wilds as we were, and with the magical weapons we knew Father Dumas had. Rune was weaker out here. *I* was weaker out here, and Father Dumas likely knew this.

"We're going to see what he wants first," I assured Peyton. "Whatever he's planning, we won't let him do it."

"And no truce or vows of protection will keep him safe from me if he decides to make a move against us," Rune said.

"He doesn't want peace," Peyton insisted. "He's up to something. Kill him now, while you have the chance."

Shaken, I tried to assure her as best I could, but Peyton continued insisting that we strike before we even met with him. I assured Rune and the others that I'd join them in a bit and then gently took her arm and pulled her aside to calm her down. Over her shoulder, Gracie was helping Leah and others from the DFA move supplies between tents. Leah caught my eye, and her face twisted in a scowl before she rolled away.

"Neither you nor Gracie should be here, Peyton," I said. "If

Father Dumas really is going to try something, if he's really as dangerous as you think, then I want you as far away as possible in case things... In case I can't..."

"Oh, Val..." Peyton rested a cool hand on my cheek, and for a moment I was taken back to when I was a child, so overcome by the sights and sounds of the world I could barely function.

"Focus only on me," she would say. "I know things can be overwhelming but focus only on me. You're safe here. You're loved here."

She'd been the first example of unconditional love I had ever experienced. Even now, when the fate of all we had rested in my hands, it felt good, if only for a moment, to be reminded of that.

"I've already talked to Gracie, and we're not leaving," Peyton said. She let out a shaky breath. "I have a lot to make up for, Val. To you, to myself. If I run now, I'll live the rest of my life regretting not doing more. If something happened to you and I wasn't there to at least try... You understand, don't you?"

My heartbeat drummed faster. "You don't need to prove yourself or make up for anything. I forgive you."

Peyton smiled sadly. "You might have, but I haven't. Not yet. Maybe after this I'll feel better. Don't worry. I'm not a fighter, and neither is Gracie. We won't be in the thick of it. There's a medical segment of the DFA who are there to make sure any injured get the help they need. We'll be safe."

"Empress."

General Tenia appeared at my elbow. She jerked her head to where Rune and the others were waiting. "We need to go."

Peyton's hand lingered on my cheek until I pulled away. I'd gotten my stubbornness from her, and no amount of pleading would change her mind. "Be careful," I begged. "I'll check in on you and Gracie after this."

I could feel General Tenia's eyes on me as we walked back to the others.

"Is there a problem?" I challenged, sure she'd found something to fault me for. "Anything amiss?"

"Everything's as ready and going to plan as could be expected," General Tenia said. "I was just recalling a time one of the Lords of Those Below, a cousin of Sotera, tried to wage war on her. His betrayal was short-lived, and he was captured quickly. Much like Peyton, he re-pledged himself to her and begged forgiveness. Sotera sent him to the front lines in the ensuing battle and only when his body had been pierced by a half dozen spears did she accept his apology."

"And you agreed with her?" I said. "You think I should let Peyton die for what she did?"

"I am continuously struck by how *un*like Sotera you are. And how much I am growing to like that."

For perhaps the first time, it was impossible to miss the measure of respect in General Tenia's voice.

"Until the battle, Empress," General Tenia said, before peeling off to attend to Those Below.

After a stunned moment of disbelief, I joined Rune near the front. Those we'd chosen to join us for our temporary truce with Father Dumas were armed and waiting. With my nod to Rune, we began moving through Seattle's remains toward the agreed meeting spot.

Long before we reached it, Rune held up a hand. We'd arrived on one end of what had once been Pioneer Square, so narrow it was perfect for an ambush. Brownstone buildings barricaded us on either side, their shopfronts blown out as though a bomb had been dropped.

"You actually came," Father Dumas said.

He blocked the other end of the square. As we warily approached, he opened his arms and gave us a welcoming smile that chilled my bones. "Seems you brought enough soldiers to start a fight."

"Are we supposed to pretend that you didn't?" Rune said, eyeing the nearby buildings.

"Of course not," Father Dumas said. "I brought gifts."

The pit in my stomach widened as some worshippers dragged up two figures, their hands bound, and forced them to kneel at Father Dumas's side. Pitius and Idwal, bruised and bloody, their mouths stuffed with cloth. Idwal's head sagged while Pitius's eyes pleaded with Rune to forgive them for being caught.

"Now that I have your attention," Father Dumas said. "Why don't we talk?"

CHAPTER TWENTY-SIX

Father Dumas gestured to the building interiors, where I'd commanded General Tenia to cover our flanks, and then to the rooftops where Rune's wildlings crouched, waiting on his orders. "I see the idea of peaceful negotiations is lost on you, High King of the Wilds."

A muscle feathered in Rune's jaw. "I would have considered it," he said, "until you threatened my own. Now I'm determined to put your body in the ground as soon as possible."

A few worshippers fanned out behind Father Dumas, magically glowing weapons in hand.

"Remember what he did to Sotera, Rune," I muttered out of the corner of my mouth. "We have to be smart about this."

Rune followed my gaze. In addition to the military fatigues and bulletproof vest—in lieu of his priestly cloth and cap—Father Dumas wore a metallic gauntlet encircled by a dim magical light. In the other hand he clasped a sword not unlike the scythe I'd seen in Rylan's workshop, the kind that oozed sick magic and killed anything of the Wilds it touched. I was sure if he managed to hit Rune with that, it'd be disastrous.

"I'd like to speak to you two. Alone." Father Dumas gestured to the center of the square, equidistant between our two sides. It'd be close enough for Father Dumas to strike if that was his plan. It'd also be close enough for me to do the same. Perhaps the best chance we'd get.

"Fine," I said.

I kept my eyes firmly on Father Dumas as Rune and I met him in the center, keeping just out of reach of any surprise attack.

Rune jerked his chin toward Pitius and Idwal. "You will release my wildlings, now—"

"Empress Val," Father Dumas said, chuckling. "*Empress* Val... I left you alive to see the end of the world you helped bring about. I see you've used that time productively." He sighed wistfully and held a hand at hip height. "How much has changed. I remember when you were only this high."

"You mean back when you started poisoning Peyton's mind and manipulating me for your own purposes?" I asked. "Have I turned out like you imagined, or did you hope I'd be dead long before this?"

Father Dumas gave a smile that managed to be far more unsettling than reassuring. "Yes, you're a great deal more *alive* than I thought you'd be by this point. You were supposed to awaken Grislehaut and meet an unfortunate end elsewhere. But now..."

His eyes flickered from Rune and my matching armor to the lines crisscrossing our hands. His eyes briefly widened, and I had the terrible fear we'd given away something vital.

"Why did you awaken a god?" Rune said, voice thick with barely concealed anger. "Especially the god of destruction. If you wanted to die, you need only have asked me and I would have gladly granted your request."

"Your threats are useless and tiresome, High King Rune,"

Father Dumas said. "I did it because this world needed a do over. Those Below, the wildlings, the humans, they're all the same. They've all been fighting since the very beginning, and all of them have reasons they think they deserve everything it is they want."

He waggled a finger reproachfully. "And no matter how noble you think your cause is, they'll continue fighting, even if you manage to defeat me and lock Grislehaut away again. It's a lost cause, whichever way you look at it."

"So that's it?" I said. "You give up without even attempting to make peace?"

"I do wish you were as quiet as you were as a child, Val, so you didn't blurt out such stupid things. We *have* tried. Over and over we've tried and gotten nowhere. Joshua tried. Despite how each of you were at the others' throat, in the end he wanted peace. And look where that got him."

His eyes glittered. "What was that like, watching him gasp for air, listening to him pleading for you to—"

"Shut your mouth," I snarled. "You won't survive this. Grislehaut won't care if you helped free him."

"My dear, *none* of us will survive this. My followers have accepted that. Now." Father Dumas moved aside so we could see Pitius and Idwal. "I have two of your rats we caught sneaking around. They were good, swift and silent. But these heart-gem weapons are useful for more than just fighting, and it was easy to subdue their magic and bring them to their knees." Father Dumas tenderly caressed the hilt of his sword. "Such fine craftsmanship. And no way to make more."

I blanched. "You mean Rylan—"

"We had him craft as many as would be useful, infused with heart gems from your lovely wildlings, High King Rune, and then we killed him. If there was any way to counteract their magic, it's gone now."

Father Dumas raised the gauntlet, the edges of it glowing. Pitius and Idwal jerked, then collapsed, writhing in pain. Their muffled screams couldn't cover the sharp snapping of their breaking bones.

I caught Rune as he lunged forward. "I want to kill him as much as you do," I whispered fiercely. "But he didn't bring us here to talk, he brought us here to bait us, to get us to lose control."

"I know," Rune growled. "But *why*?"

I hadn't figured that out yet. And the longer I wasted trying, the worse things would get.

"Am I boring you two?" Father Dumas said, watching us. "Perhaps another demonstration would be more interesting."

Pitius and Idwal were pulled to sitting. Pitius screamed as she was forced to rest on her broken leg. One of Idwal's bound arms was bent at a sickening angle.

Before I could protest, or plead, or forget my own warning and attack Father Dumas myself, the worshippers plunged magic-laced daggers into their sides.

Pitius collapsed, twitching as veins of black spread across her skin. Idwal sagged forward, face covered in black lines that swelled near to bursting within seconds.

"When I asked Rylan to make us weapons that could fight the magic of the Wilds, the most I hoped for was a way to cut back the green," Father Dumas said. "But these... These are far more effective than I could have ever dreamed."

My vision colored red. A thrumming magic hummed in my core, building even stronger. Forget my own warnings. Father Dumas wanted something, but I'd ensure he was dead before he could get it.

"Rune—" I started.

Rune's smile was cruel and fixed on Father Dumas. "I think whatever little game you've been playing is at an end. I have tried to be a better High King. I have tried to play nice. But for you, Father Dumas, you're special, and just for you I will be the monster that humans have so long believed me to be."

I hadn't noticed the vines slithering between the cracks in the brick until they ensnared the worshipper who'd stabbed Idwal. He didn't even have time to scream before flowers exploded from his mouth, his ears, his nose.

The worshipper beside him tried to flee, but a tree erupted from the nearest building and clubbed him to little more than a red splatter on the pavement.

"Attack!" I yelled to our side. Crystal rose at my command to cover Rune and me as sporadic gunfire took chunks out of the pavement. An enormous root-woven hand plowed through the building to our right and nearly grabbed Father Dumas as he nimbly dodged out of the way. I tried to hold him in place by turning the stone he stepped on into the consistency of quicksand, but again and again he evaded, all while the battle exploded around us. Those Below clashed with worshippers who'd found their way to a higher vantage point while Father Dumas distracted us. Humans and wildlings moved as one, trying to close in on the other side.

Rune tried again to ensnare Father Dumas's legs in vines. He simply severed them with his sword, and they withered to black. He continued backing away, waiting for our next assault.

"He's not attacking back," I growled. "*Why* isn't he attacking back? Isn't this what he wanted?"

"Don't worry about him just yet," Rune said. "We need to get Pitius and Idwal out of here."

Neither wildling was moving. I felt queasy as the black lines of ichor thickly swelled across their bodies. I coaxed the ground to gently undulate, carrying them back to our side and the rest of our forces.

"Get them to safety," I shouted at some of Those Below who'd reached Pitius and Idwal. As they dragged them off, I summoned another crystal shield and dragged Rune behind it.

"We need to get to Father Dumas. Trust me?"

The bloodlust in his eyes faded somewhat. He planted a quick kiss on my lips.

"As you trust me," he replied.

We split. I sprinted toward the right side of the square, leaping the remains of an iron-wrought fence and sliding across cobblestones worn smooth. Ice coated the interior of the nearest shop as Marian led a small group of Those Below against some worshippers. Xander was able to down a couple of worshippers who'd taken the roof, but more than I'd anticipated took their place. This wasn't just Father Dumas trying to catch us off guard. This was an all-out assault.

A worshipper finished driving a sword through a wildling's stomach, and I drew Sliver and stabbed him through the back and twisted, severing his spine. I checked that the wildling was already dead before moving on. My senses were already numb against the carnage. I knew there'd be death. I'd *always* known there was going to be death. Now, I had to find the one person I wanted to deliver it to the most.

I spotted Father Dumas at the far side of the square, surrounded by a couple worshippers guarding his flanks. I managed to sink two crystal knives into the throat of the worshipper on Father Dumas's left, but Father Dumas knocked the next two I threw aside, reacting faster than I thought possible.

"There you are," he said. "I thought I'd lost you."

"Not quite yet," Rune said.

Roots grabbed the worshipper on Father Dumas's right and yanked his so hard into the ground there remained nothing but a pool of blood.

Sword raised, Father Dumas backed up as we closed in on him. The barest hint of a smile tugged the corner of his lips. "Try, try as you might, you can't seem to kill me."

"I don't think we've tried hard enough," I said.

As though we'd planned it ahead of time, Rune and I moved in perfect sync. Father Dumas deflected my crystal blade and shoved me aside as more crystal tried to skewer the lower half of his legs. He knocked back Rune and spun away, deft as a dancer. The magic oozing from his weapon gave me a rancid feeling in my stomach. But no matter how much he threw us off guard, he didn't press the attack.

"He's stalling," I said to Rune, clutching a stitch in my side. The magic seeping off Father Dumas's weapons was slowly wearing me down.

Rune didn't look much better; perspiration drenched his face, creating long red streaks where it met blood. He wiped the worst of it out of his eye. "Once more."

I pulled from deep within, drawing forth spires of crystal that scattered nearby combatants and systematically closed on Father Dumas. Another of Rune's enormous root-woven hands wound through the spires and reached for the priest.

"That should do it," Father Dumas said.

He sidestepped and plunged his blade into the palm of the enormous hand and then withdrew and sliced straight through the nearest column of my crystal.

Rune cried out at the same time a sensation not unlike being stabbed ripped through my chest. I stumbled back, grasping desperately for a wound, but there was no blood and no gash. A moment later both Rune's root-woven hand and my crystal collapsed into dust and ash. Father Dumas's sword pulsed brighter, like a star he'd plucked from the sky, swollen with the power Rune and I had inadvertently given him.

"It was more difficult to goad you into attacking me with

everything you had than I thought," Father Dumas said. He turned the sword over in his hand, admiring it. "Once, I could have simply threatened those you cared about and forced you to let down your guard. You've both changed, and not for the better. But no matter."

He raised the sword high, and before I could wonder at what he planned to do, he plunged it into the earth.

A chasm split the brick and tore apart the brownstone buildings on either side. A chasm of a different kind seemed to split my head, bringing me to my knees. By the time the worst of the pain cleared, I could feel the last remnants of my magic shackling Grislehaut fall away.

Free, he hissed. *I am free.*

The thin ribbons of blue magic leaking from the splitting ground grew thicker. Father Dumas laughed. Whether due to my splitting headache or the shaking earth, it was difficult to get to my feet. Rage, red hot and violent, filled me to the tips of my fingers. I leveled Sliver at Father Dumas as he turned, balancing on the precipice of the chasm.

"Strike me now, Empress of Glass."

Screaming, I lunged forward and sank Sliver into his chest, driving it up to the hilt. Father Dumas never stopped smiling, even as blood bubbled at the corners of his lips and his lungs gurgled wetly as he let out a final breath.

I withdrew Sliver, and he stumbled back. "It is done at last," he murmured.

I watched his body tumble end over end into the chasm—dissolving with each passing second—until I lost what little was left to the darkness.

I stood there, cursing myself. I didn't feel better. What we'd done hadn't been enough. He hadn't suffered enough. We hadn't stopped him.

"Move, Val!"

Rune grabbed me around the waist and pulled me to safety right as the ground where I'd stood gave way.

"Come back to me," he said, taking the sides of my head in his hands and forcing me to look at him. "We need to get out of here."

Focusing on any one thing sent more shard-like pain into my skull. Rune didn't let go until I could look at him without pain.

"There you are."

"Here I am," I murmured.

Rune pulled me up, my feet unsteady. Across the chasm that now split the square in two I could see what remained of the worshippers fleeing. The earth continued to crumble away in every direction. Within moments there wouldn't be any solid ground to stand on.

"Back," I croaked, throat coated in dust. Then louder, "General Tenia, get everyone back, now!"

She obeyed without hesitation, as did General Forcheck when Rune gave the order. I managed into a stumbling run as he and I fled toward the other end of the square. The collapsing earth bit at our heels, promising nothing but an endless fall if we faltered. I ran, not daring to look back, until it sounded like the worst of the destruction slowed and I allowed myself to turn.

Father Dumas had used our magic to transform what had once been Pioneer Square into an abyss. Within its depths, ribbons of blue magic rose in ever-quickening numbers where it dispersed into the air like birds free of their cage. The bodies of wildlings, Those Below, and worshippers rested at the edge of the chasm, threatening to plunge in. I planted my feet and called on the power Below.

Close, I urged the chasm. I pulled upward, the strain curling the tips of my fingers. *Close and keep him there. He can't get free. He* can't—

Like the air expelled from a laugh, a forceful wind erupted from the chasm. It swept me from my feet and slammed me bodily against the brick. I wheezed, trying to get air into my lungs. I had to get up again. This might be my last chance to do anything.

And then Rune was there, cradling my head. With his free hand, he continued trying to cover the ever-widening chasm with vines, sutures to close the gash in the skin of the earth. The veins in his neck bulged. His jaw clenched. But no matter how much he tried, the vines simply snapped and fell away. His shoulders sagged, exhausted, before he helped me to my feet, and together we slowly, achingly, continued making our way back to our side.

"We need to get farther away," Rune said. "There's no telling how far it'll spread."

"Or how long we have left," I said, panting. "Let's bring together the survivors and—"

I risked another glance back. My blood froze.

Peyton stood near the edge of the chasm, lifting one of the wounded that had nearly fallen in.

"No. Peyton—"

I took a step toward her, the warning dying on my lips. She couldn't be here. I'd *told* her to stay back.

If I run now, I'll live the rest of my life regretting not doing more.

Peyton finished helping the wildling to his feet. An enormous cut ran from his shoulder to hip, and each faltering step back to us was agonizingly slow. She met my eyes. Her face was smudged with blood and earth. But despite that, she smiled.

"Go!" she called. "Don't worry, Val, I'm right behind—"

One second she was there, and the next she was gone,

leaving only crumbling brick to mark where she'd been. It took a few seconds to realize I was screaming her name. Another few to feel Rune straining to hold me back from plunging after her.

"No, Val," he snarled. "There's nothing you can do! She's gone, she's gone."

Only when I stopped did I hear the earth giving way, leaving nothing but Peyton's last smile and the realization that I'd never told her I loved her one final time.

CHAPTER TWENTY-SEVEN

The survivors made their way farther inland toward the eastern Wilds, to a vantage point that overlooked the worst of what Father Dumas had done. A new, dark scar had diverted from the main chasm and carved itself through the remnants of Seattle, the ribbons of Grislehaut's magic thickening with each passing minute. Father Dumas's final trick. Peyton's tomb.

Only when what remained of our forces had settled in did I sink to my knees at the edge of the cliff. Everything inside me had been replaced with little more than air, as hollow as the chasm. My legs had become stiff and immovable. Not a moment later, I felt someone tug on my arm, urging me up.

"You need to get a hold of yourself," General Tenia whispered, not unkindly. "Things may only get worse from here, and there are those who may leverage such a tempting opportunity to take control."

She nudged her head to Caldre and, beside him, the Lords Sulien and Tannis.

"What would they lord over? Rubble?" Even my voice sounded hollow.

General Tenia's gaze was piercing, and I thought how, not all that long ago, she would have gladly had me on my knees just like this, if only to make it easier to cleave off my head.

"I'll be all right in a moment," I assured her. "Thank you. Please go see that the others are all right."

She gave me a concerned look as she left. Rune watched me, only half paying attention to the wildlings detailing the damage of the aftermath.

We will bend, but we will not break. We survive because we must.

After another few deep breaths, I stood and joined the others: General Forcheck, General Tenia, along with Rune, Marian, and Xander. I looked for Pitius among Rune's most trusted wildlings, but of course...

"You know him best, General Forcheck," I said. "How likely is it that Caldre would use this turn of events to his advantage."

General Forcheck thought about that longer than I'd have liked. "He's too clever by half and a nightmare on the field of battle. But as I said he's honorable, which is a shame for those who want to win, and those who want power most of all. I truly believed him when he said he wished for a different Wilds. He'll keep his promise to support you, High King Rune."

"Even still, I'm sending him deeper into the Wilds and keeping a large contingent of my soldiers near the palace." Rune looked at me. "You mean to stay here."

It wasn't a question.

"I'm staying until I find a way to stop Grislehaut," I said, feeling as though I was repeating the same bad joke, and everyone knew it. "General Tenia will take Those Below back to the palace, too. But leave a few of them to hold off any lingering worshippers."

General Tenia's mouth had fallen open. "My Empress, everything is lost. We have a day, maybe—"

"Less," I said with certainty. "Hours."

"Hours, then, until Grislehaut is fully free and everything becomes nothing."

"There is no running, and there is no fighting, but until the very end I will do as I'm commanded," General Forcheck said. "My High King."

She gave a long, formal bow and hobbled off. After a long moment, General Tenia did the same. Her gaze was a kaleidoscope of colliding emotions: confusion, disgust, respect, and ultimately resignation.

"I won't forget this," she said, before following after General Forcheck.

"Marian, Xander—"

"We're staying," Marian said. She gestured to her leg. "I've never liked running from a fight, and I'm even worse at it now. Cassius will stay, too, if I ask him."

Xander gently touched my arm. "You came to me for help, and that's what I'll do. Until the end." The scar on Xander's cheek seemed to shine more starkly as he met Rune's eyes. "I will follow both of you to whatever end. However that comes. From *whomever* or whatever that comes."

"Then we're glad to have you," Rune said. "I will give General Forcheck temporary rule. She'll keep things in line until we return."

Until you *return*, I thought. *Just you.*

"You should go, too, Rune," I said.

Rune scoffed. "I have solved many problems with violence, sheer determination, and an inability to stay dead like I'm supposed to. I don't see how this is any different."

My plan involved him not being around. If he was, it would only make things impossibly difficult. "I'm Empress of Those Below. I can find a way to stop Grislehaut without you."

"Another way you haven't figured out before? Please, enlighten me."

"I just think it'd be better—"

Rune's eyes flashed. "Of course you do. Just like the dozens of times I thought it'd be better to intercede when you wanted to risk your life, the times I resisted coddling you in safety. But I didn't because that would be insulting, just like you're insulting me. We're weapons refined in strife, Val. And like a knife, you work best when free of the sheathe."

I inched back as he approached and brought a hand tenderly to my cheek. "If you think you can send me away when things are toughest, then you're gravely underestimating me. Our marriage has amplified our magic, and I plan on seeing its limits before this is over."

I nodded numbly. It'd been pointless to ask, but I'd never forgive myself if I hadn't tried.

"Thank you. All of you," I whispered.

Peyton's final smile flashed through my head. I felt the encroaching anguish building at the edge of my mind, waiting to drown me in sorrow.

All of them would stay. And I if I didn't fix this, all of them would suffer.

My stomach twisted with dread as I went to see how Idwal and Pitius were doing. They'd been deathly still when I'd seen them getting ferried to safety. If they were lucky, they'd died quick.

The overwhelming scent of mint and eclipse flower filled my nose as I entered the small underground cavern. Someone gave a wet cough. In the gloom, I made out Marian kneeling beside a girl who'd had her arm severed at the elbow. Red slicked the leaf-lined bed beneath her.

There were so few of the injured in here. Normally I'd be happy about that, but I knew it was because so few had actually gotten away.

Marian finished staunching the blood and wrapped the girl's stump. She stood and saw me. "There's nothing you can do," she said softly.

"I know. I just wanted to... To..."

To what? To not be alone? To remind myself of a fraction of what more would happen if I failed? "I can try to heal some of them—"

"No, you can't. You always sucked at healing magic, and I doubt that's changed now that you're Empress."

"How are Pitius and Idwal?"

Marian's face softened. "Pitius is bad. I don't know what sort of twisted magic that bastard put in the knife, but..."

She stepped aside, and I could see Pitius's form prostrate on the nearest bed. I'd missed her at first since her skin was so covered in veins of black she blended into the background.

"My god," I muttered.

"Death would be a kindness," Marian said.

I almost couldn't bear to ask. "And Idwal?"

Marian just looked at me, and in the corner behind her I noticed flowers covering the shape of a small body. A shroud had been pulled over his head.

"Why did you come here, Val?"

I turned away, my throat tightening. Marian's hand rested on my shoulder.

"That came out wrong. I suck at saying what I mean, almost as much as you suck at healing. I used to think I'd become so hardened against death that it didn't hurt anymore.

But it doesn't get any easier; we just get better at hiding it. That woman, Peyton, she was like your mother, wasn't she? She meant a lot to you?"

There was nothing I wanted to talk about less than that. "I'm going to go visit the humans," I said.

"I don't think that's a good idea."

"I asked for your help, not to make decisions for me," I snapped.

Marian yanked her hand away as though burned. "I only meant—"

"Do you have a better idea? Do you think we should all run and hope everything will sort itself out? If I had any other choice, don't you think I would have—"

The stench of eclipse flower and grubber's root was making my head spin. The more I blathered, the more Marian's eyes narrowed, and I had the sudden horrible fear that she saw through to what I meant to do.

"I'm just saying, don't do anything rash," she said. "We might be united with the humans, but things just went from bad to worse. I wouldn't put it past them to try sticking a knife in your back when everything gets crazy."

"Like I tried to do to you, once upon a time?" I said.

Marian grinned. "I actually liked that about you. Still do."

She took my hand and gave it a gentle squeeze before returning to Pitius's side.

"Rune and I are staying near the chasm until we figure something out," I said. "Tell Cassius thanks from me when you see him again."

"Tell him yourself later," Marian called. As I left, I saw her cast a worried look at me over her shoulder.

I left the safety of the trees and made my way to where the humans were camped. The eerie blue dusk light seemed distorted and physical, settling like a film over piles of brick, concrete, and metal rubble. A threatening silence permeated everything.

I wasn't surprised to find that most of the humans had left, but as I approached the camp, a familiar figure limped out on a pair of crutches. I could feel her glare in the dark.

More than that, I could see the pistol, glinting as she pointed it at my chest. The world held its breath. Neither one of us moved.

"Are you going to do it?" I asked after a long beat.

"I should," Leah said. "It'd be the least you deserved after all the people who died because of you. Peyton's dead. You killed Joshua. Your family's gone, and you're responsible."

I almost wanted her to pull the trigger. I wondered if a bullet would be enough to kill me or if I was too far removed from being a human for that to work anymore. Leah seemed to be debating, too. Her arm began to tremble with the strain of keeping the pistol pointed at my heart.

"You need to leave with the others," I said. "If you believe anything, believe that I don't want you to get hurt."

"And where would I go?" Leah said. "Way I hear it, there won't be a single stone or blade of grass once Grislehaut's done with it."

Without dropping the gun, she took a wobbly step, using one of her semi-functioning legs to prop herself up. "It should have been you that died. All of this would have been prevented —they would still be alive—if *you'd* have died."

You could fix that, I wanted to taunt. *Just a few pounds more of pressure on that trigger and you can do what no one else has been able to yet.* I was so tired of having everything be my fault. I was especially tired of Leah acting like she was the only one who'd ever loved my family.

Leah's arm trembled even worse, and with a roar of rage, she threw the gun and cursed at the ground. "When this is over, if we survive, I recommend you stay out of the human world. You won't find welcome here."

I'd known that from the moment I'd chosen to help Rune. But before I could tell her, Leah limped away, and the eerie silence covered me again.

THERE WAS no point in making a grave for Peyton. What right did I have to mark the death of one I'd loved when so many others had lost their loved ones?

Moreover, a grave would immediately be lost. If not among the endless piles of rubble, then from the ground giving way when Grislehaut finished emerging.

I couldn't tell how close he was to doing that. The chasm lay below me. Bits of floating land circled it like the planets in a solar system. The chasm had opened wider in the hours since Father Dumas had cast himself in, no matter what I did.

No more, Grislehaut seemed to taunt. *I won't be held down anymore.*

That left me only my final, terrible, option: I had to go to him. My eyes rested on the jagged sides of the chasm, awash with light.

To stop him, he and I had to become one again.

"Can I join you?" Rune said.

I nodded and he sat. He peered down at the chasm, the light cutting sharp angles in his face.

"I know I threatened to kill her once, but I'm sorry about Peyton," he said. "I never truly wanted her to come to harm. And the closer I grew to you, the less I wanted that."

"I know," I said hollowly.

Being married now, it felt odd to be this close and not touching him. I leaned into him and Rune shifted, allowing me to sink against his chest. There was so much I wanted to explain but I couldn't conjure the words.

"We will find a way," Rune said. He squeezed my arm. His chin brushed the top of my head. "We'll find a way to send him back."

He raised our clasped hands. With his finger he traced the lines of our union from his wrist, across the tops of his fingers, to where they connected with mine, intertwining and curling and becoming one. "Our power, combined. Together."

"Together," I lied, feeling as though my heart was being ripped out.

After a long moment of silence, Rune said, "There's no one around but me. It's okay to let go."

His assurance gave me the permission I'd kept from myself. Fat, ugly tears rolled down my cheeks. Rune pulled me closer as I wracked with sobs, and with him holding me, I cried and cried until I felt nothing anymore.

CHAPTER TWENTY-EIGHT

After I'd spilled all my tears, I told Rune I wanted to be alone a little while longer. He seemed reluctant to leave but at last placed a tender kiss on my forehead and bled into the darkness back toward our camp. I waited until I was sure he was gone before I hurried into the Wilds.

I hadn't been sure of many things following Father Dumas's surprise attack, but I was surprisingly sure of what I was doing now.

Thanks to my marriage with Rune, I had a newly revived connection to the Wilds, and it was easy to slip through the tangle of trees. I thought hard about where I wanted to go—and the being I wanted to find—and the fronds, vines, and mist parted, creating a path straight to a gently bubbling waterfall. The falling screen of water resembled glass, and though I had to contort myself a little to dip to its height, I knew this would lead to the Halfway.

I paused, unsure of how to cross. The last few times Hob, Mother Mal's wrinkled assistant, had ushered me through. The last time Rune had used his magic. Now I wondered...

I tapped into my own Wild magic and stuck my hand through the waterfall. My hand felt cool but not wet and vanished through to the other side.

Taking a deep breath, I contorted myself the rest of the way through.

I startled as I stepped into the scarred woodland glen. Unless I was misremembering, the enormous tree in the center —woven with cutting veins of lapis blue—had doubled in size, pushing the clearing's boundaries. The ghost-white trees had gained a slight flush of color, and even the ever-night sky, the ultimate indicator that this place existed between places, had the barest tinge of blue, as though the events in our world were bleeding over into it.

"What's going on?" I muttered. A gentle breeze stirred the lowest branches of the Mother Tree, shivering the leaves. I turned to follow it as it trailed whispering fingers over the top of the grass before reaching the edges of the surrounding trees. A small figure stood half-hidden within, watching me.

"Olette?" I said, astonished.

I hurried to the edge of the trees in time to see a woman much too old to be Olette walking away. In one hand she carried a thinly woven lantern full of everfire. A gentle, haunting tune hummed through my ears. I wanted to hear the end of that song, to join her wherever it was she was going.

"So you've accepted your part at last," Mother Mal said.

Mother Mal had emerged from the now even more enormous trunk of the Mother Tree, and its roots lowered her to the forest floor. Her all-too-human eyes peered down her long skull face. "You haven't come to plead or beg or make promises you don't intend to keep, all to squirm out of what you know needs doing, have you?"

"Not this time." I looked for the woman again, but she'd vanished.

Mother Mal looked around. “I don’t see the High King here, ready with his flattery and silver-lined words. But perhaps he used all of those on wooing you. Congratulations on your union.”

I rubbed my thumb against the back of my hand. “Thanks,” I said, unsure of how to take that. Mother Mal was difficult to read at the best of times, but now more than most I wished I could. I was sure there were a dozen things she wished to say regarding my and Rune’s union.

“Tell me, why have you come?” Mother Mal said.

“I thought you knew everything,” I said.

Mother Mal’s skull parted in a feral grin. “I want to hear you say it. To see whether you truly understand.”

I shook my head. “You knew from the very beginning. You knew...” Of course she had. Despite her vague answers and insistence that she didn’t take sides, Mother Mal had never been wrong, even as she let us believe we were in control.

“Things have a way of happening the way they are meant to,” Mother Mal said. “I asked you once before, and I’ll ask one more time: will you give up the seed of the Wilds?”

“Why give it to me at all if you were only going to take it back?” I asked.

“I simply offered it to you. *You* made the choice to—”

“To take it. Yeah, yeah.” I’d heard this tired rationale before. I stepped closer. Maybe it was because I was focusing on it, but I seemed to feel the seed more strongly in my chest, pulsing with life.

“What if this kills me?” I lay a hand over where my heart fluttered, like a caged bird desperate to break free. “The seed feels like a part of me, like it’s supposed to be there.”

“It was, at one time, yes. Now it must return to where it’s meant to be.”

Just as I was supposed to return to where I was meant to

be. Fitting, I supposed. And if removing the seed started to kill me, then what was the difference? I'd be dead soon enough anyway.

"Okay, it's yours. But..." I took a deep breath, sure I wouldn't like the next part. "How do I give it back? It's kind of stuck—"

Mother Mal braided one of her hands together into a sharpened point and plunged it into my chest. I sank to a knee, unable to even scream as her hand expanded and wrapped around the seed. With barely a sound, she plucked it out.

There came a growl above me. The wet drip of something cold landed on my forehead, and the smell of damp forest floor filled my nose.

I opened my eyes to find myself on the ground. Erebus hovered over me. The chin of his muzzle, overgrown with mist-soaked moss, dampened the strands of my hair as he nuzzled me.

"Hey there," I croaked. "I thought you were— Have you been in the Halfway the entire time?"

No thanks to you, Erebus seemed to growl.

"He's loyal." Mother Mal sat perched on a nearby tree root. Her long, slender legs were pulled into a cross-legged position, the billowing moss of her clothing settling over her. At her feet was a freshly tilled spot of ground with a small mound in the center where something like a single seed might have been buried.

I stood and checked over where Mother Mal had stuck her hand in my chest. No marks, but the sensation of having my ribcage wrenched open wouldn't be leaving in a hurry. "You could have given me a warning."

"I could have," Mother Mal agreed, in a tone that told me this would have taken the fun out of it.

"What happened?"

"You gave up the seed and the power it provided."

I shivered. "Does that mean..."

I knelt and placed my palm to the ground. The Wilds' magic greeted me immediately, and I let out a relieved breath.

"Your union to Rune ensures you will always have some connection, though it may wane," Mother Mal said.

"So why take the seed at all?"

Mother Mal merely stared at me. Erebus shuffled closer, and I scratched him behind the sprigs of mint that made up his shoulder blades.

"It is easy to hold onto power and claim you need it," Mother Mal said. "It is far more difficult to give it up. You have done what is needed, Empress."

"Great. Thanks." I crouched next to Erebus. "I need you to stay here with Mother Mal."

Erebus chuffed, and I felt the liquid cold of him trying to attach to me. With great pain, I shrugged him off and held the two vines on either side of his head to keep him in place. "*Please*, Erebus. It'll only be for a little bit. Just until I return."

Mother Mal watched me. I had no doubt she could see through my lie.

Erebus's physical form collapsed, and his shadow crept to the darkened spaces beneath the tree roots. He gave a longer, sulking growl.

"Will this work, Mother Mal?" I asked. "Am I just throwing my life away, or will rejoining Grislehaut actually fix anything?"

"I can't give you any finalities."

"Please. You're the queen of finalities, or fate, or whatever you call it. If we're all doomed, I'd like to know."

Mother Mal peered up into the broad tree branches. They seemed to have reached even farther out in the short time I'd been here. "Though Grislehaut was my child, he was an unruly one. You have been missing from him for quite some time. There's no telling what he'll do, or whether he'll be quelled."

As vague and useless an answer as ever. "Protect Rune, no matter what happens. If you won't protect him because of who he is to me, at the very least protect him because he's High King of your Wilds."

"I will do what needs to be done," Mother Mal said.

I looked again into the trees, seeking the mysterious woman I'd seen before, but there was nothing except the growing blue light. Erebus gave a mournful, low howl as I walked out of the glen.

Despite missing the seed, it was still easy to use the Wilds to cloak me, and all too soon I'd slipped past Rune's sentries and returned to our camp. The blue light emanating from the chasm was even brighter now, a miniature sun rising from Below. I wouldn't have to wait long. A couple hours, maybe.

Rune had coaxed two trees together, creating a soft, private dwelling cradled in their branches. I stopped in the doorway, brushing aside the curtain of blossoms. A dim cluster of fireflies fluttered near the roof.

I shouldn't be here. I should already be heading to the chasm, using time to my advantage. But the thought of leaving without seeing Rune one more time was more anguish than I could bear.

"Come here, Val."

The gold-red of Rune's eyes glinted at me from the mosswort bed just big enough for two. He extended a hand from beneath the silken covers. "Val—"

I took a step back, and his eyes narrowed.

"I should—" I started.

I tried to think of something I should be doing, something that could extradite me from this situation without making Rune more suspicious.

"After all we've done, it's nice to know there are still things that make you nervous." Rune was smirking playfully, and I felt my cheeks heat. "Val. Please."

"We can't rest. We have—I have—"

"You need to rest now. There's nothing more that can be done at the moment."

I shook my head, holding back tears. The confession of what I was going to do threatened to break free, stronger than ever before. I was so caught up holding it back that I didn't notice Rune get out of bed until he gently took my arm. He guided me as we slipped beneath the covers together and he held me close.

It took more than a few minutes for my tense body to relax. I closed my eyes, swearing it would be for a moment, and awakened in a daze. It was still dark save for the ever-present blue glow. One of Rune's arms remained wrapped around me. The rest of him had rolled over in sleep.

I turned my head to watch him. Once, I'd swore the only time he'd seemed serene was in sleep, and now he seemed even more serene than that. His eyelashes fluttered slightly. His mouth hung barely open as he took deep, unfettered breaths.

I wondered if he was dreaming about what he'd do against a foe such as Grislehaut. What he thought *we'd* do.

I brushed a strand of hair away from his forehead. The dark and the quiet laid bare the realization I'd had for a while but refused to acknowledge until now.

I loved him.

I loved him as sharply as a glass blade.

I loved him as savagely as a Wild beast.

I loved him with all of me, whatever I was, in the same way I was sure he loved me.

Rune stirred as I stifled a hiccupy laugh. How much I'd hated him made this all the crazier. I loved him more than I ever thought possible, and I wished I didn't, because that only made things infinitely more difficult.

Fate was playing one final joke on me. Because of all the terrible things Rune had done to others and all the terrible things he'd done to me, the worst by far was making me love him.

CHAPTER TWENTY-NINE

The earth rumbled in my bones as I slipped out of bed. The pseudo-dawn blue had grown brighter. As I stepped to the curtain of blossoms and peered through, I could see from this vantage point that the wisps of blue from Below were beginning to take physical shape, swirling more pieces of earth high above the chasm.

I lingered just behind the curtain; breath stilled in my lungs. I felt like a stage performer on opening night, the light from the chasm the spotlight that would show my greatest, most terrible, act.

I would have one shot to do this. And if I was wrong and it didn't work... Well, I wouldn't have to worry about that.

"You're still up."

I froze as Rune spoke right behind me. I moved my hands beneath my armpits to hide their shaking.

"I couldn't sleep," I said.

"I doubt you even tried."

He stepped closer, boxing me in. His gaze felt as though it were prying every secret I had from my ever-loosening lips.

"What are you really up to, Val? You're never without one of your tricks." He smirked. "And I should know. It's one of the most delightful things about you."

"I just couldn't sleep," I insisted.

Rune's eyes flickered between me and the forming Grislehaut. "I've been thinking a lot about what we might do about him. Like you, I've been digging, trying to come up with something."

"Is that right?"

"It is. And in my searching I came across the memory room, the one you brought up from Below. The one you spent an awful lot of time in and emerged looking distraught."

My mouth had gone dry. He'd noticed. Of course he'd noticed. "I was looking into the past, trying to find something we could use."

"As did I," Rune said. "And when I did, I discovered so many interesting things."

I looked sharply back at him. "You… But you couldn't…. Only the Empress…"

Rune held up a hand. From within glowed an ethereal blue light. "Like your burgeoning powers of the Wilds, I found that with our marriage my control over the Below growing, too. It took some time and patience, but eventually I could use it. Enough to unlock the floating crystals in that memory room. Enough to question that priest of yours. I watched what Sotera's grandmother did. I saw what Sotera created. But I wonder…"

I couldn't move as he drew even closer. "What conclusion did *you* come to when you saw that? What plan did you connive?"

Again, his eyes moved to Grislehaut, and then back to me. "Whatever it is, I doubt it's one I'd like."

I cleared my throat. "You're being paranoid."

He cocked his head, smirking without mirth. "Am I?"

"Yes. I'm going to check on the others."

He caught my arm as I tried to step away. "Val... You looked slightly down and to the left. You're lying."

I closed my eyes and then turned and hugged him, throwing him off guard.

"Wha—"

"I'm sorry," I murmured into his ear. "But I knew you'd try to stop me."

"Val, what are you—"

He staggered back and had to steady himself as crystal encased his feet, immobilizing him. His expression hardened. "If you think sacrificing yourself to that god will— Val!"

But I was already leaping from the tree, my knees smarting as I hit the ground. Rune was shouting after me, but I poured on the speed, trying to put as much distance between us as I could, trying to get the rushing wind to block out his voice. I'd only bought myself a little time. If Rune really had gained some power over the Below, then it wouldn't be long before he'd free himself.

And indeed, as I cut left down a rubble-covered street, I felt the ground shift beneath my feet. When I glanced back, it was as though the very Wilds had uprooted themselves to pursue me.

Don't follow, I urged uselessly. *Stay behind where it's—*

A root-woven hand burst through a building and tried to grab me. I sliced through it. From the corner of my eye, beasts grander and more terrible than any I'd seen before closed in on either side. Vines spewed from the cracks in the ground and tried to hold me in place, but I used my own magic to force them away.

"Go back!" I shouted at the ever-encroaching Wilds. "Rune, stop, you can't come after me!"

I could see him, a furious speck atop the shoulder of one of the beasts. What did he expect to do if he caught me? Confine me to my room? Keep me a prisoner for my own good?

As a wave of green crashed down, I cut right down an alleyway and let it slam past. I sliced through a chain-link fence and emerged panting, a stitch in my side, on the next street over. The chasm was just ahead.

The Wilds were already pivoting to follow me. With a shout, I drew my hands up, and a wall of crystal three stories high shot toward the sky and created a wall the green crashed against. The beast Rune rode on slammed itself against the wall, launching Rune onto the nearby rooftop where he didn't even break stride. He was already close enough to where I'd be able to hear him. It wasn't his compulsion magic I needed to worry about, but his pleading.

Whatever your plan is, I doubt it's one I'd like.

Rune hit the ground at the same time I kicked off to the chasm. As I drew near, I could feel its pull like a black hole increase, tugging my clothes, my skin, my very bones closer. The surrounding rubble had been scoured of all definable features, all of it being erased piece by piece.

"Val!"

I didn't hesitate when I reached the edge of the chasm but leapt onto the nearest floating piece of land as it hurtled by. It bobbed slightly when I landed, and I took a moment to steady myself. Behind me, Rune had just reached the edge.

"Stop following me," I called. "You know this is the only way!"

"You seem to think so, since you didn't want to talk to anyone about it!" Rune snarled.

"You've seen the memories! You and I both know we couldn't have come up with anything better!"

I couldn't hear his scathing response as the land I stood

atop orbited out of earshot. Ahead, I could make out my path over the center of the chasm. A half dozen leaps and I'd be there. Rune's form was growing smaller by the second. I cupped my hands over my mouth.

"I love—"

He jumped. The stupid, wonderful idiot jumped after me, but I could see he would come up short. My heart dropped.

But at the last second a vine shot out of the floating island and pulled him up. Almost immediately he was jumping to the next island and the next. I had no doubt that if he reached me, he'd do everything in his power to ensure I didn't go any farther.

Breathing ragged in my throat, I took a running start and leapt to the next island—one so small I was forced to spin my arms to keep balance—and then leapt to the next. A low buzzing like a swarm of locusts was building in my head, becoming more pervasive by the second. I risked a look down and recoiled, the few contents of my stomach threatening to come up.

Far below, I could make out the clear edges of Grislehaut. He was a god with no discernable features, and yet it wasn't hard to make out his enormous gaping maw. Two powerful legs dug into the sides of the chasm as step by gargantuan step he leveraged himself up. I could feel his presence fill my mind.

"Has my Mother sent you? Are you trying to stop the inevitable?"

"I'm here now!" I shouted into the swirling wind. I had to duck as a piece of steel nearly took my head off. Wind howled in my ears, so loud it was hard to think. "I'm here now, and I know what I am. I know what you're missing! Take me and leave everything else alone!"

"Val!" Rune's voice was growing closer. I was running out of places to jump.

Desperately, I leapt to the last floating island I could reach, hanging just over the center. It moved right before I landed, and I had to claw my way atop it, fingers bleeding as they dug into the rock. At last I pulled myself to standing and walked to the edge.

"I'm here," I called down to Grislehaut. "I'm what you need."

I drew Sliver and held it over him. From here I was lost. How did I return to a god? Especially a god that didn't seem interested in having me back. I'd start with what I knew.

I gritted my teeth and sliced the inside of my forearm down to the bone. When the blood was flowing freely, I turned it over, letting the stream of crimson get whisked away by the wind. I nearly passed out as I peeled back the flap of skin to reveal my crystal bone. Its glowing blue was nothing compared to Grislehaut's vibrant form.

"I'm part of you," I whispered. "Please. Please make it end."

Grislehaut roared, and the entire world seemed to roar with him. The edges of my body had begun to blur, dissolving piece by piece. The skin along my hands peeled back layer by layer, until I could see more of my crystal bone peeking out beneath.

"He doesn't want you," Rune said over the worsening wind as he landed behind me. "Surely you knew he never had any intention of going back to sleep."

I closed my eyes, took a deep breath. "That's why I have to force him to take me back."

Rune gave a harsh laugh. "And when that fails, then what? I'll be here without one of my most powerful allies—without my wife? Val, you'll... You'll *leave* me?"

I refused to turn around. The second I saw Rune's devastated expression, all I'd struggled to do up to this point would come undone. Rune's hand gently closed on my upper arm, as though any harder and he feared I'd skitter away like a frightened rabbit.

"There will be another way," he said.

"I've tried—we've tried—and they haven't worked."

"Then we haven't tried enough!" he said. "We'll seek stronger powers. We'll leave these Wilds and try again—"

"It'll be too late. You know it'll be too late."

My body started to teeter over the edge. Rune's grip tightened.

"When we said our vows, were you lying? Did those words mean nothing to you?"

By your side forevermore, even as the gods awake.

"I didn't know what I do now, Rune. I never would have said them if I'd—"

"Did. You. Mean. Them?" he snarled.

More of my skin had peeled away, and the tips of my fingers had dissolved into long streaks of tan. I was easy to make out Grislehaut's form, bigger than thought, bigger than my worst nightmare. I could feel him battering at my mind. This time he meant to destroy my mind and discard the shell of my body, making it impossible for anyone or anything else to stop him.

"I promised I loved you," I said at last. "And that will never change."

I turned and kissed him. Rune's shocked mouth took a moment to form against mine. His grip tightened, suspecting another trick.

He was right.

With my free hand, I slipped the amulet from my pocket—the same amulet the Lords had wanted me to use on Rune from the very beginning.

They were getting their wish.

I broke the kiss and whispered the words to activate the amulet against Rune's lips.

He went completely still. Now I looked into his furious eyes and drank in the beautiful devastation on his face one last time. Already his power was eating away at the amulet's.

So, with the precious few seconds I'd bought, I pushed off him, stepped to the edge of the island, and threw myself down toward Grislehaut.

CHAPTER THIRTY

Time, for only a moment, seemed to want to remind me how monumentally stupid I'd been and that I should reverse this. Go back a few seconds prior when I'd been holding Rune. When he'd promised we'd find another way. When I'd confessed I'd lied.

But of course there was no going back as time resumed its terrible, frantic pace, and I plunged toward Grislehaut. I managed to angle myself headfirst, and my stomach moved to my ankles. Over the air circulating through my ears, I thought I heard Rune's distant roar of rage, and I could only hope that by the time he broke free of the amulet this would all be over and he wouldn't see any point in plunging after me.

Come on, I urged as Grislehaut grew closer. I covered my eyes with a thin film of crystal to escape the blinding wind and readjusted my trajectory.

"You dare?" Grislehaut's voice slithered through my mind. *"I won't accept you. You will have no power over me."*

Grislehaut's mouth opened. More of my skin peeled away

by the second, and I wondered, had anyone been watching, if my entire body were glowing.

Go back to sleep, I urged. *Be whole again.*

"This world will be mine. I will devour it all..."

Crystal fins along my arms gave me scant maneuverability, and I tilted my body, aiming for his one enormous eye. Ribbons of blue magic and my bones were blending until the two were indistinguishable. I had the horrible thought that I would dissolve to nothingness before I reached him or would fall right through and shatter Below.

Then I tightened my focus, and my form tightened along with it. My brain felt as though hands had gripped both hemispheres and were trying to rip it apart. I had to hold on a little longer. Grislehaut's eye—as big as a city block and filled with ceaseless rage—was affixed on me.

"You cannot—she cannot—after so long, I won't be quelled—even if Mother demands it. This world—You won't—"

Then his eye refocused, and he was seeing me, really seeing me.

Seeing me as Rune did. Seeing me as who I really was. Seeing all parts and loving me regardless.

"I'm sorry," I whispered to the wind and tasted salt from my tears.

I drew Sliver again. The ribbons of magic wrapped around me until I saw nothing but blue. White light. I tried to think of something. Feel something.

But nothing was there. I wasn't there.

I wasn't anywhere.

I wasn't.

"Welcome back, my heart, my soul."

...Am I...

...Am I...?

....

...

...Cold... And dark, just like the... Just like the...

....

I feel nothing but the cold and dark.

CHAPTER
THIRTY-ONE

It took ten seconds for Rune to break the amulet's hold.

Ten seconds before he was able to crush it into dust.

Ten seconds where he hadn't been able to stop her.

He'd known she was up to something. It'd been more than the halting silences between her words. More than how her eyes would dart away when she got too close to sharing what it was she was going to do. He'd discovered the crystal chamber harboring Sotera's memories far too late. But though he'd eventually uncovered what Val believed would save them all, Rune never thought... He never believed she'd...

He threw himself to the edge and watched her fall, feeling as though a piece of him had been ripped out and was falling along with her. Her body glowed, brighter and brighter, until he had to cover his eyes.

A roar shook the earth itself, and then the magic that had been swirling around his head began to stagnate. The floating islands of land they'd both leapt across to reach this point were slowing down.

Still Rune didn't move except to let out a wrenching sob. He couldn't see her anymore. It couldn't be... She couldn't be...

It didn't matter if Val had chosen this. Didn't even matter that Grislehaut was receding back into the earth and the pressure that had built—pressure he hadn't even realized had taken over—was receding along with it. It didn't matter that her plan had *worked*.

Something crashed below him, jarring him from his agony. One by one the floating islands, free of the magic that'd kept them aloft, were plummeting to earth. Where he was standing began to stutter and fall, and Rune was forced to launch himself over the edge before it collided with an island below, leaving nothing beneath his feet but open air.

At last, purpose. Val wouldn't have wanted him to throw his life away, and Rune hadn't chosen to. But as he hurtled downward with no hope of stopping his fall, all he felt was a profound loss of control in the most glorious way. Gone was all choice. Everything he was and had ever been held suspended in this weightless moment.

He closed his eyes.

Something slammed into his gut, and the air was punched from his lungs. The sharp, hot pain of a few cracked ribs radiated up and down his spine. He groaned and the pain continued to spread. Maybe it was more than a few ribs. Maybe he'd ruptured something, too.

When at last Rune stumbled to solid ground, he found he'd landed on a thick tree root. It was one of dozens that had burst through the chasm wall, slowly reaching across to cover the abyss. Rune grimaced, putting a hand to his stomach. He looked up as a shadow covered him.

The Mother Tree was no longer in the Halfway. Somehow, Mother Mal's home had spewed out from beyond the space between spaces and entered into their world. Inch by inch its enormous canopy, bigger than anything Rune could have ever hoped to conjure, continued blotting out the sky, displacing everywhere that Grislehaut's magic had taken.

Rune followed the path of the root he stood on, noting how out of all the others it just so happened to have been directly beneath where he'd been falling, noting how it flexed and gave just enough that it cradled him as he hit it rather than killing him on impact. Mother Mal always spoke in half-truths and false promises, but Rune could only believe that had been intentional. Mother Mal had *saved* him.

"That meddler," Rune growled. "That damned meddler."

But now that he was here, another thought took root and sprouted. The last time he and Val had been in the Halfway, Mother Mal had asked Val for something. A seed. What if...

The very moment he thought this, the earthen wall at the end of the root crumbled away, leaving a suspiciously arched pathway, just big enough for him to walk through. Rune started toward it, every breath excruciating. But if the pain helped him forget that Val was gone, that he'd lost her—

No. He hadn't lost her yet. He might have only been grasping at phantom solutions, but until he had nothing left, he would keep trying.

Rune ducked through the earthen opening and stumbled into the Halfway. He didn't even question how it led him here, but he immediately limped to the base of the Mother Tree at the center of the clearing. The ground beneath the ever-broadening canopy was as dark as the sky before a thunderstorm.

Mother Mal sat perched atop the roots at the base of the tree. She looked like she'd been expecting him.

Of course, Rune seethed. She'd likely planned this from the very beginning.

"Val has offered herself as a sacrifice," Rune said, the words burning the back of his throat. "But she came here before that, didn't she? You wanted something, and she gave it to you at last."

Mother Mal uncurled a slender hand to indicate a lump of dirt at her feet. "Freshly tilled and planted. But it needs cultivation."

Rune stared at the dirt. He'd heard many legends of the Wilds: tales of honor and sacrifice from his father; tales of horror and murder that Vanesi tormented him with before he went to sleep; and then there were the tales of the strange and impossible, spun by Mother Mal from the moment they'd met her.

"What will you do now?" Mother Mal repeated.

Rune fell to his knees and plunged his fingers into the dirt. He called on all the strength as High King of the Wilds and poured the magic deep into the earth. He gave everything away until he was empty, and still he gave more until the broken parts of him were screaming at him to stop. When he at last opened his eyes, he realized he was screaming, too.

He collapsed onto his back. When the pain subsided enough, he turned himself over to see if anything had happened.

The lump of dirt hadn't changed.

"You have to help me," Rune said through gritted teeth. "You wanted this."

"As did she," Mother Mal said. "How badly do *you* want it?"

Biting his tongue to stem the pain, Rune stood and gave the earth more magic, until he could barely keep himself upright.

"That's...everything I have," he gasped.

"Good," Mother Mal said. "Then the rest is not up to you. And you have another task to attend to." Her skulled face turned toward the entrance of the clearing. "As you can see, now that I'm no longer hidden in the Halfway, it didn't take long for the pests to get in."

Rune managed to his feet and found Tannis waiting for him. Her dress had been replaced with armor not unlike his. Her sandy hair was tied back into a tight braid. In one hand she clutched a mace bristling with cactus spines and thistle. She drew closer, circling him.

"It was far more difficult to find you than I thought it'd be," Tannis said. "Although, I'd hoped you would make my life easier and die along with your stupid beloved. But here we are."

"Here we are," Rune agreed. "And because I'm weakened you think to try your luck?"

"Wouldn't you, my *High King*?" Tannis said. She raised her mace. "Your victory will be short lived. And once you're gone, we'll take everything that's owed to us."

Had he ever been so foolish as her? Rune hoped not.

Whether emboldened by her own hubris or with how frail Rune guessed he must have looked, Tannis darted forward with little care, swinging the mace at where his head had been. On instinct, Rune called on the Wilds but too late remembered he'd depleted everything he had; it was sluggish in answering. Tannis's mace pricked the narrow space between the armor of his shoulder. Rune danced free, speckling blood across the grass before pulling his glass knife. She laughed.

"What a paltry little dagger!" Tannis hefted her mace. "Let's see how good you really are without your magic."

She came at him again, swinging over and over, each strike growing closer than the last. Rune's ribs screamed as he was forced to spin out of range. Not fast enough, and the mace met one of the crystals lining his armor—the same crystal Val had insisted he add—and deflected off.

Rune couldn't help grinning. Even when Val wasn't here, she was still watching out for him.

Tannis leveled the mace at his throat. "I'm not going to

play around until you're strong enough to fight back. I think it's time to end this."

"I agree," Mother Mal said.

The pool of life and death bubbled to sudden and alarming life, spewing some of the liquid from the dark half onto Tannis's back. She screeched, flailing around. The smell of burning flesh filled Rune's nose as steam rose from where it touched her skin. She desperately tried to wipe it off, only spreading it more in the process. Exhausted as he was, Rune spent a precious few seconds staring at her.

"What will you do now, High King?" Mother Mal asked. "Will you act?"

That was exactly what Rune planned to do, and he scooped up the mace Tannis had cast aside and, in one brutal swing, bashed her head in. Tannis's screams fell silent as she flopped ungracefully to the ground.

Without thinking, Rune drew his knife and stood over her. If he was out of magic, there were other ways in the Wilds to get it.

He sank the knife into Tannis's cooling chest and, in a couple savage slices, carved out her heart gem. It was deep red and smeared with blood, glowing strongly from within.

Rune's head was starting to spin as he limped back over to the seed and dropped the heart gem next to it. He couldn't be sure, but he thought the heart gem flared a little brighter. With this, he could bring her back. With this, things could be as they once were.

"Some things aren't up to you," Mother Mal said.

"Please," Rune said to the sky. "*Please*."

The ground remained unchanged.

CHAPTER THIRTY-TWO

Everything was cold and dark. I found myself in a…in a—

Tunnel

—tunnel. One that went nowhere. One that went somewhere. Even if it did, I wouldn't know where. Oppressive darkness pushed against me from all sides. I stumbled over rocks. A frantic stress gnawed at my gut.

Had to get out. Had to get to… Had to get to…

Them. Him.

I turned another corner. A dead end. I doubled back, turned another corner. A dead end. A dead end. A dead end.

Around and around I went. Every turn a dead end. The panic built until I felt I would explode from it.

Then I saw a—

Light.

—light. Shining from the end of another tunnel. I stumbled toward it until I could see the light was a—

Lantern.

—lantern held by a woman. Her face looked painfully familiar, like the image of someone I'd once known, but now so terribly unfocused they looked entirely different. She seemed only a little older than me but reminded me of someone young. The light illuminated her flowing silken dress. The entire outline of her body shone with an ethereal light. Almost like a—

Goddess.

—goddess.

“I’m lost.” I didn’t know why I said the words, but I knew they were true.

The woman smiled and held out a hand. “I will show you the way.”

The moment I took her hand, all the stress of trying to get out melted away. The pain vanished.

She tugged me down the tunnel until it wasn’t just her lantern that was casting light, but something up ahead. My tongue was thick in my mouth, trying to form words I didn’t know.

“Where are—"

The clearing I suddenly found myself sitting in was entirely surrounded by trees so thick I couldn’t see to the other side. A tree more enormous than any of them sat in the center, its branches providing a—

Roof.

—roof overhead.

I fidgeted, my crossed legs feeling as though centipedes and spiders were crawling up my skin. But though I could fidget, I couldn’t move my legs more than that. They didn’t hurt, not exactly. Nothing hurt. Even if it did, I wasn’t sure I’d recognize it for what it was.

The edges of the clearing had begun to thicken with ribbons of blue magic. These wended around the tree trunks, leaked from the ground. Something about it made me think of *seething*. It seethed, and it wanted in.

"You tricked me," the voice growled, and I knew, somehow, that it was growling at me. "You *tricked* me. It doesn't matter what my sister says, or my Mother. I'll devour you, and then I'll devour them all."

"You can't have her, not anymore," the woman with the lantern said, emerging from the darkness of the trees. "What of yours she once was has been returned, and what is left of her isn't yours to take."

I stared at the woman, not fully aware of everything, but aware when the name—

Olette.

—Olette popped into my head. She looked like her mother, Luella, older but without the weight of sorrow dragging her down.

"Olette," I said.

The woman smiled, and the unfocused image of the person I'd once known became clear. The smile was so full of warmth, tenderness, and reassurance that everything would be okay that I felt my squirming insides settle. The seething blue magic at the edge of the clearing receded.

"I am Olette as she would have been," the woman said. "That path was closed off to me, and now I am Rhasahlyn."

"The spirit of *gentleness*," the seething magic sneered. "Rhasahlyn who comforts. You won't comfort me, though. You won't quell me as you once did."

The name stirred a memory, one that flitted through my head and was gone just as quick. The name Rhasahlyn being repeated by someone—a boy?

I waited for his name to pop into my head, but nothing came.

"I'm sorry, Olette," I said, sure it was the right thing to say. "I'm so sorry for what happened to you. I'm so sorry for what I did." I paused. "What did I do again?"

Olette—Rhasahlyn—smiled again. "I am at peace, the same peace I bring to others. I have been gone so long there has been little of that to go around in these Wilds."

The ever-encroaching blue magic seemed to recoil like vagrant mist as she approached it. She reached out and through it.

"You can't silence me, sister," the seething blue magic murmured. "One day I will be free again, to do as I was created."

"But not now," Rhasahlyn said. "Now you must sleep." The magic dimmed. "You are whole now. Return to your slumber and be at peace, brother. Be at peace."

The seething blue magic vanished, and when it was gone, I could see farther within the trees, see ghostly white figures in a quiet, solemn procession. All of them were moving toward a light on the other side. It was too bright to stare at for long, but all the same, I felt compelled to lift my feet and walk toward it.

A gentle hand took my arm.

"Not yet," Rhasahlyn said. "One day you may go with them, but there are those who are waiting for you elsewhere."

I stared at her. Were there? I couldn't imagine who she was talking about. I couldn't think of a single thing that made any sense.

Something softer than a whisper but louder than a thought rustled the branches.

Please. Please.

Rhasahlyn knelt and gently hugged me. "You poor creature. You are nothing more than a shell, full of memories and thoughts that are both yours and not."

"Oh," I said, not having a clue what she meant. "What do I do, then?"

Rhasahlyn drew gentle fingers across my cheek. "You must wake up now, Val. You must wake up and you must live."

CHAPTER THIRTY-THREE

My eyes flickered open. I lay on my back, looking upward at...at...

Trees.

Trees. That's what loomed above me. At least I thought that was what they were. Thinking of anything before this moment hurt. I wasn't even sure what I *should* think about, only that if I tried to remember it, it wouldn't be there.

The next instant, the trees were replaced by a boy's face, covered in something dark—

Dirt.

—and something smeared red—

Blood.

He had gold-red eyes and a face I didn't know—

I knew that face. I knew that I knew it, though I didn't know *how.*

The boy reached down. His hand hovered over my cheek, unsure.

"It worked," he murmured. Something wet and clear dripped from his eyes. "She's back."

He vanished from sight. "She needs rest," he said.

"You drained yourself to revive her," someone else said. "You should be resting, too."

"I could have done more. It wasn't enough."

"It will be as it will be. Do you trust me on that?"

A long silence. "It was you who saved me from going in after her, so I will, for now. I will trust that, for once, things will get better."

"I am honored by your trust, High King." The voice sounded chiding.

The boy—

Rune.

RUNE.

—reappeared over me. This time he brought his hand down and let it rest on my cheek. He held it there like he wanted to scoop me up but was holding himself back. I wanted to reach up and curl my fingers around his, but I couldn't move. I could do nothing but stare and *exist.*

"I'll be back," he murmured. "There's so much that needs doing, but I'll be back, every day."

I'll be here, I wanted to say. A deep wellspring of emotion bubbled up from somewhere deep inside. Emotion for him, though I couldn't decipher what it was. *I'll always be here.*

He left me with the lingering sensation of his fingers on my skin.

Time passed in a blur of sleeping and waking, with the only marked difference that a little more of me returned every time I awoke. New words for things sprang to mind, and soon names joined them.

Rune. Marian. Xander, Pitius. General Forcheck. Joshua. Peyton.

They were names, nothing more. I hoped, soon, memories would come attached to them.

Each time I awoke, Rune was there, just as he promised.

"Do you remember who I am?" he asked the second time.

"Rune," I replied.

His smile was bright and blazing. "And who am I to you?"

I thought of his name, but like all the rest, nothing came attached along with it. "You're Rune," I repeated.

"Give her time," Mother Mal said. Still, Rune's devastated face stayed with me.

Eventually I stayed awake longer. One hour. Two. I discovered I lay at the base of an enormous tree, curled in the center of a flower with petals wrapping me like—

Blankets.

—blankets. I sometimes heard Mother Mal talking to a knee-high creature with a wrinkled face.

Hob.

And to Rune.

I felt reborn and put together piece by piece like a...a...

Puzzle.

—puzzle.

One day, when Rune came and sat on the edge of the flower, I couldn't take my eyes off him. I wasn't sure what he was to me, only that he was important. I knew so little still, but I knew that face.

I grabbed his hand. He looked down, surprised.

"Help me remember," I said.

He seemed hesitant at first. Then slowly he crawled to lay beside me, his eyes never leaving mine. He didn't move—barely breathed—as I traced his cheeks, his lips, the edges of his eyes. His thumb rubbed the green lines intersecting across my hand, mimicking the lines on his.

"I don't know *who* you are, but I always knew you," I said. "Does that make sense?"

"No," Rune admitted. "But I'll be here until you remember. I will *make* you remember."

He told me about himself, and about me, and how we met, and what we did. And the more he told me, the more things returned. Sensations came back, memories, too.

Then one day I awoke and knew who I was. Val, Rune's blade. Val of Those Below. Val, once part of Grislehaut, now no more.

Val the Empress of Glass, wife of Rune the High King of the Wilds, the King of Thorns.

But mostly Val. Just Val.

THE FLOWER PETAL blankets were smooth against my bare skin. I blinked at the blue sky peeking through the thickened canopy. My head spun as though I'd stumbled off a tilt-a-whirl, and only after I'd blinked a dozen times did the thoughts settle. There were still memories missing, still things I knew I was forgetting. I trusted they would come back in time.

I sat up, throwing my legs off the edge of the flower. My feet kicked a large stone. A heart gem, empty of magic and dull colored. My tongue felt like sunbaked bark.

As though it'd heard my thoughts, one of the petals unfurled near my head and water trickled out. I drank from it greedily until my stomach felt swollen.

"A little at a time," Mother Mal said. She perched atop the roots at the base of the tree, Hob at her feet. "You've been deprived of many physical things for a long time. In some ways you've been deprived of them forever. Don't hurt yourself by doing too much."

A million questions swirled through my head. I settled on, "What—"

A fit of coughing took over as the simple word seemed too much. Mother Mal waved a hand and Hob, squeaking with delight, scurried off.

"I remember being led here by someone," I said after the worst of the coughing subsided. "She... She looked like..."

"As I said, Olette has become my child, Rhasahlyn, the Spirit of Comfort. She knew you and brought you out of the darkness. Her spirit is free now as it hasn't been in a long, long time."

This wasn't making any sense, but one thing I remembered very clearly was that asking questions of Mother Mal would only make me more confused and very likely frustrated.

"Olette—Rhasahlyn—she made Grislehaut sleep. Is he...?"

Mother Mal patted the roots. "He slumbers beneath. And he will stay that way, for all our sakes. But that is not what you wished to ask."

"It worked then," I said, my excitement growing. "I returned to Grislehaut and I... I..."

I looked at my arms, my legs. The rest of my bare, but very physical, body. Grislehaut was gone and I was still here. Somehow.

One of the flower petals broke off, and I wrapped it gratefully around me. "You saved Rune. What about the others? Are they okay? Did Grislehaut—before I quelled him, did he—"

"I did what needed to be done," Mother Mal said.

"I don't understand. How am I *here*?"

Mother Mal merely gestured to the base of the flower. It had sprung up from a lump of dirt. A memory flashed through my head—one where Mother Mal took something and planted it in the exact same spot the flower now grew.

"That was the seed I gave you," I said slowly. "It did this. But how?"

"The earth remembers," Mother Mal said. "The seed I gave you remembered. It rooted itself deep within and germinated, and over time it became all of you. It was watered with your emotions and tilled by your memories. The sunlight of who you were helped it to grow until it had imprinted every piece of you. Almost every piece."

"Imprinted," I echoed. "Does that mean... Am I not—"

"You are," Mother Mal said firmly. "You are all that you're meant to be and nothing more."

What might have been a wave of existential crisis rose to pull me under, and I in turn barely pulled myself out of its reach. Still it frothed beneath, waiting for me to slip.

"You gave me the seed," I said. "Which means you wanted me to come back."

"Another wanted you back more."

"But why did *you*?" I insisted. "I didn't think you liked me that much. At all, really."

Mother Mal drew herself up to her impressive height. "You are terrible at reading others. In many ways what you had become was my doing. I only did my small part to rectify that."

I stood from the flower and almost immediately collapsed. Again and again I tried to stand, but whatever the seed had managed to grow back thus far hadn't included strong muscles or the coordination to walk.

"Things will return, but they take time," Mother Mal assured me.

"I don't want time." I scanned the ground. I couldn't feel the magic of the Below or even that of the Wilds. "I can't feel anything. I need to—I have to—"

I found a rock, the edge slightly jagged, and raised it above my forearm. Just as I was about to bring it down, a tendril of Mother Mal's arm shot out and stopped me.

"You are no longer part of Grislehaut. You no longer have crystal bone. You are part of all things now. A little of the Below, a little of the Wilds, a little of humanity."

Mother Mal plucked the rock from my hand, and I sank to the ground.

"Will my magic also come back with time?" I managed.

"Perhaps," Mother Mal said. "Perhaps not. Some things aren't meant to be."

"That's literally all I was. From... from my bones to my crown to—Without that, what am I?"

Mother Mal looked down her bony skull at me, and I swore, for perhaps the first time, I saw what might have been tenderness in her eyes. "You are you. Just you. Just—"

"Val!"

Rune stood at the clearing entrance, mouth agape. I could only stare right back at him, a thousand different emotions colliding in my head.

"Me," I whispered.

He crossed to me in a blink, slowing as he knelt to my level. His eyes took in the cast-aside rock, the scratches along my arms and legs. "Hob told me you'd come awake for good. How do you feel?"

I pulled the flower petal tighter around me, suddenly cold and a touch embarrassed. "I could use a little more covering." New memories popped into my head, those of Rune and I together, sometimes so close and so intimate I blushed further. "Though...I remember you didn't mind so much the times I had nothing on."

A wicked grin spread across Rune's face. "You're not wrong about that."

With a twist of his hand, a Wilds-spun cloak appeared over my shoulders. I stared at it, in awe of how easily he'd conjured it. Had I been able to do that once? Maybe, but now...

"You're not finished healing," Rune noted.

"Not everything's come back," I admitted. I looked up at him, at the intensity of those gold-red eyes, and felt stirring emotions that fit within me perfectly. "But I know you."

"Good," Rune said. "Then we'll start from there."

At Mother Mal's insistence, and against my many arguments, I stayed with her for a time longer, discovering the basics of how to exist in my new body. It was strange to relearn how to walk, as though I was a newborn giraffe. My muscles seemed determined to stay weak, but eventually they too returned. I wouldn't be winning any fights anytime soon, but at least I might be able to walk out of here on my own. I itched to see the world outside the glen, the one I'd left behind, the one that had narrowly avoided total destruction.

Rune came every day, bringing more changes of clothes, Wild-grown food, well-wishes from friends who wanted to see me.

"Eventually," Rune always assured me. "They'll be there when you're ready."

Other times, the two of us sat side by side, not saying a word. Once, he took my hand and gently ran his fingers up and down mine.

"I've been waiting to ask until you were better whether you wanted to break our marriage," he said.

I looked up at him, startled. Tons of memories from the human world had returned during my time here, and I certainly remembered what *that* meant. "Are you talking about divorce? I thought we had to wait at least twenty years and grow apathetic to one another before we did that."

Rune scoffed. "As if I could ever grow apathetic toward you. No, it's more like I'm asking once again if you want to bind yourself to me. Look."

He turned my hand over and traced the lines intersecting across its back, the ones mirroring and interlocking with the ones on the back of his. "The lines are faint. Something about being revived in a new body has lessened the bond. They can be renewed, strengthened. Or, if you'd like..."

He cleared his throat. "There is no desperate need for an alliance between us anymore, at least not an alliance that can't be formed through treaties or other kinds of vows. If you don't wish to be bonded to me anymore, then all we'd need to do is dip our hands in a mixture of the silver leaves of a glintbush, nightblush, and the first dew of a new morning."

"Is that all?" I drawled. "I'm sure we can pick all of those up at the local supermarket."

The corner of Rune's lips quirked. "It is perhaps a bit laborious. But not so much as being bonded to someone you don't truly care for."

"What makes you think I don't care for you? That I don't love you?"

Hope spread across Rune's face. I thought about why I'd chosen him in the first place. The reasons were muddled and hadn't yet fully returned, but I knew we'd married for far more than just an alliance. I trusted him. I loved him. I chose our union for *him*, not just the power being together had offered.

"We'll renew our vows," I said, clasping my fingers in his. A small knot of shame curled in my stomach. "And when I can recall everything, I'll explain why I left you the way I did."

"Oh, we'll be talking about that," Rune said, a dangerous glint in his eye. "You can be sure."

But as he kissed me gently, rather than dreading that conversation, I looked forward to it. We still had so many things to say to one another. I could only be grateful we'd get the chance to say them at all.

"I'm ready," I assured Mother Mal.

As her assessing gaze roved over me, I stood a little taller, trying not to show any lingering weakness. I still tired far too quickly and still had nightmares of plunging into a dark chasm with nothing but the great eye of a god waiting Below.

But I'd lost count of the days I'd been here. It was time to leave and face whatever of the world remained.

"I expect to see you again," Mother Mal said. "For while Grislehaut might be gone, there are many things left undone."

"I'll be back," I assured her. But hopefully not for a while, and hopefully in better condition.

I followed Hob out of the clearing, through a waterfall, and out the other side into the Wilds. Mist coated my arms and gathered at the tips of my hair.

"I'm sorry to see you go," Hob said. "Mother Mal has been so lonely since the others left."

Left. As though the great snake Kaffa and the watery creature Xin had wandered off somewhere instead of being murdered. I looked back into my reflection in the waterfall, trying to imagine Mother Mal showing any emotion to their loss other than mild detachment.

"You'll need to take care of her, then, Hob, until we can come visit," I said.

Hob clutched the ends of his beard in his wrinkled fingers. "Goodbye, Empress of Glass."

I wasn't sure that title was accurate anymore. Still, I gave him a gentle, somewhat awkward pat on the head. "Goodbye, Hob."

Only when he'd left did I realize I had no idea where to go. Memories of the Wilds were still coming back to me slowly, and my surroundings were unfamiliar. I tried tapping into my Wild magic before remembering it was gone, too. A sense of profound loss welled up, and I stifled it before it could take over.

The fronds beside me twisted into a path, and Rune stepped through. He came to a surprised stop when he saw me and then broke out in a smile.

"Come on," he said, stepping back into the path and offering me his hand. "I have something to show you."

I'd missed many things about the Wilds, but I didn't miss the nausea-inducing path we walked. Soon, though, we stepped out from the darkness between places and emerged on an overlook.

Since remembering what I'd done, I'd asked Mother Mal many times to tell me what remained of the human world. Now, the answer lay in full view before me.

The Mother Tree no longer existed solely in the Halfway. It burst from the center of the Wilds, so enormous it didn't seem to fit within reality, a full-sized tree mistakenly placed among miniature toys, its canopy covering everything beneath.

"You saved them," Rune said. "All of them."

Across the inlets and isles, past where Port Orchard had once been and the sluicing curve of Elliot's Bay, were the remains of Seattle. The dark scar of Father Dumas's chasm and Sotera's attack were still there, and the rubble appeared smoothed over by Grislehaut's magic.

But in the south, in what remained of the human world, sat a large encampment, alongside half-constructed buildings.

I squinted. "What's that beside them?"

"The Wilds," Rune said. "The Wilds are helping them rebuild."

The more I took in, the more my confusion grew. Though there was still a long way to go before this new Seattle rivaled the former's glory, they'd still made far more progress than I could have ever imagined. "How... How long was I..."

Asleep? Dead? Gone?

"Out. How long was I out?"

"Six months," Rune said. I nearly staggered. So long and yet not, since I hadn't expected to come back at all.

"A lot's changed since you were gone," Rune said. "The Council of Loam can explain it better."

I was still staring dazedly below as Rune took my hand and led me through another path. We emerged on a worn asphalt street, now smoothed over with greenery. We approached the coliseum-looking structure at the end. From the entryway, I could see there were over half a dozen people inside, assembled around the calcified stump of an enormous tree. My breathing came in tighter gasps.

"When you're ready," Rune said, leaving me beneath the entryway.

"He joins us at last," General Forcheck said. "My High King, just because you *can* show up late doesn't mean you always *should*. You may even try being on time once and startle everyone."

"I had a pressing matter to attend to," Rune said.

Marian snorted. "Everything's a pressing matter. What could be so important—"

She turned and spotted me still lurking in the shadows. A hush fell over the room as the others noticed. Then Marian let out something between a half-choked sob and cry of jubilation, and I staggered back as she limped over and threw her arms around me.

"Rune, that jerk, said you weren't ready to see anyone," she sobbed into my shoulder. "He kept promising you were all right, but we couldn't see you, so we weren't sure, I wasn't sure..."

"I think he just wanted to keep me to himself," I said.

Marian squeezed me tighter. "I'll give him hell for that later."

And then I was being swarmed. Faces became a blur: Xander, Cassius, Raki.

General Forcheck pounded me on the back hard enough she nearly broke my spine, saying, "You can't stay dead. I like that."

At some point Marian managed to grab my arms again, chastising me. "I can't believe—if you *ever* do something like that again..."

Xander was grinning so broadly I feared his face would split.

A small wisp of a girl appeared at my hip.

"Pitius!" I cried, hugging her.

"Val," she replied, voice whisper-soft. "I'm so glad you're back."

I didn't hold onto her long; she still felt much too frail, and there were still faint lines of black scarring her pale skin.

"If we're all done with the reunion, we have things to discuss," someone said coldly.

Leah hadn't moved from where she stood around the table, beside an older human man who looked alarmed at the celebration taking place.

"As touching as this is, we've all been aware Val was alive for a while," Leah continued.

Rune glared at her but eventually waved his hand. "Agreed."

"Don't worry about keeping up with everything, Val," Xander said. "We'll fill you in later."

They reassembled around the table. Leah gave me a curt nod that I returned, and I was grateful for even that. It would likely be all the acknowledgement I'd get from her.

When this is over, I recommend you stay out of the human world. You won't find welcome here.

Xander's warning about not needing to follow along was nice but misguided. Once everyone began speaking, I couldn't have followed if I tried. All too quickly, I found myself growing tired as the meeting droned on.

I sank to the floor and rested my head against the wall, listening as they discussed the new Lords that would help keep peace in the Wilds. I wasn't all that surprised to hear that Marian, Xander, General Forcheck, and Caldre had been gifted some dwellings of the old Lords and land to rule over by themselves, answering only to Rune.

All those who were loyal. All those who deserved it.

"My Empress?"

I opened my eyes to find the council was breaking up. Leah and the older human man were already gone. Caldre and General Forcheck were in an animated discussion while the rest of the wildlings lingered. Rune spoke with them but kept shooting glances my way.

I looked up to find General Tenia before me.

"Did I miss anything good?" I asked. "Besides the last six months?"

The corner of General Tenia's lips quirked. "We might all be on the council, but like any council, it's mostly expelling hot air and very little progress—No, don't get up."

She knelt to my level as I started to stand. She gave a small bow and then looked unsure. I guess it might have been difficult to know what to say to me, given that I was supposed to be dead.

"The ones who saw what you did say you were like a falling star," she said.

I laughed. "They need to get their eyesight checked. I can assure you it wasn't nearly so graceful."

"They'll write poems about this, and songs," General Tenia insisted. "Your name will be legend among Those Below and beyond."

I cringed inwardly. After enough excitement for three lifetimes, and a dozen more after that, I craved something I rarely got: peace and quiet.

"I only wanted to check, what is your command?" General Tenia said.

"My command?"

"Now that you're back, what would you like me to do?"

My mind went totally blank. "Have you been leading Those Below since I've been gone?"

"I have. But now that you're returned—"

"Keep leading them," I said, and it was as though a great weight had lifted from my shoulders.

General Tenia looked bewildered. "I can't keep... It was just until you returned..."

Once upon a time, I would have done anything to take more power and had fought viciously to keep what little I had. I'd wanted the power in order to not be hurt again, and to hurt others. And while I still wanted to defend myself and protect those I loved, I wasn't the same person I'd been before. Literally.

"You should keep leading," I repeated firmly. "I'll be close by if you need, but you know Those Below best. You love them, and you'll do anything they need to make sure they survive. If you don't want to lead, give them a choice on who'd they'd like instead. But I'm sure they'd choose you again."

I got to my feet, ignoring the tingling pins and needles in my legs. "We can figure out the specifics later."

I was shocked to see grimy tears leaking from the edges of General Tenia's one crystal eye. She gave a low bow.

"Thank you, Emp—Val. Thank you."

Rune found me outside, staring up at the trees and marveling at the variety of different colors and birdsong.

"Things might have changed, but meetings are still tedious," he said.

"I'm not going to be Empress of Those Below anymore," I said.

Rune didn't look the least bit surprised. "That's good, for you'll be busy ruling a different kingdom."

That was what I'd been worried about. "Rune, I have nothing to offer them. I don't have my magic. I can barely fight. I feel—" *Brittle. Fractured. Half-formed.* "Off."

Rune gently took my face in his hand. "That's strange because it's not what *I* see. I see it now, that same fire, that same sharpness as before. We may not have to rule with blood, but you will show your teeth if the need arises, I'm sure of that."

I drank in his words. If he could have that much confidence in me, then surely I could spare a little for myself.

On impulse, I kissed him, and it was as though the final piece of the puzzle of who I was fell into place at last.

CHAPTER THIRTY-FOUR

My official coronation, or re-coronation, or wedding, with all the fanfare that came with things like that, took place a couple of weeks later.

The pessimist part of me said that whatever tenuous alliance that held everyone together, whatever afterglow of good will following Grislehaut being vanquished, would wear off by then.

So I was surprised to find King's Hollow packed. It had changed; the seawater had been drained away or soaked into the earth, the dead removed, and Rune's original throne, split down the middle during Sotera's first attack, had been refashioned into two separate ones.

The ceremony was held at twilight, with thick cloud cover and a canopy strung with glittering lights and delicate baubles of glass that didn't look all that different from shards of blue crystal.

I leaned over to Rune and muttered, "Fitting."

He noticed where I was looking and smirked. Dressed in an actual suit jacket of green and pants lined with bits of silver silk like spider's webs, he looked the picture of alluring and dangerous.

"Lest we forget what was," he said.

I didn't think we could ever forget. And as I stared at the blue crystal, I couldn't help feeling they weren't just for me.

Below us, a smattering of Those Below lined up behind General Tenia. They were those who had broken to the light of the surface, free of the oppressive damp and dark of the Below. Though Sotera did terrible things, it was difficult to reconcile those acts with the girl I'd seen in the crystal memories, the one who only wanted to please and do right by her people. She, like me, had been forged into what she became.

And so, if only for a moment, her name would be on my mind tonight.

After everyone filled the clearing, the official ceremony began. Tibald the priest stepped up the dais, cradling a silk pillow with two crowns resting atop it.

"To Rune, the King of Thorns, High King of the Wilds: in the face of this new age, we reacknowledge your sovereignty as the Wilds' one true ruler. Kneel and accept your crown."

Rune did so. Tibald raised the crown—a circlet woven with jeweled berries, gold, and snarls of ivy laced with silver—and placed it atop his head.

My heart began to pound as Tibald turned to me. The pressing stares of all those present seemed to magnify tenfold.

"Once our Empress of Glass, now our Queen of the Wilds. In this time of new beginnings, we acknowledge your sovereignty, as well as your union. Kneel and accept your crown."

Legs feeling as though they were cinder blocks, I did. Tibald rested a similar crown—this one including flecks of obsidian and crystal—atop my head.

"Rise, High King and Queen," Tibald proclaimed.

There was smattering of applause as Rune took my arm

and we stood to face everyone. Some wildlings perched in the branches let out whoops.

Rune held up a hand, and the applause died. "That was a pretty speech. Mine, however, will not be, and I will keep it short. Like my wife—" He paused, as though turning the word over on his tongue. "Like my queen, we have lived a long time with blades rather than understanding. It does not matter who you are, if you wish to move forward in peace, as we do, then we will always be open to you. We will try to change from the violence of our past."

He looked at me as though I had something to add. I found I did.

You will show your teeth if the need arises.

"Peace, as my husband says," I said. "But..." I let the word hang, a blade over a neck. "Bloodshed where necessary."

My eyes scanned over the Lords, over Leah. "*Don't* make it necessary."

Rune wore a chilling smile that only a fool would dare challenge. He clapped his hands and flowers burst to life at the base of the throne, and the dour mood lifted. "Enough speeches!"

It might have been the end of speeches, but I still had to stand before the throne, waiting for everyone to come up and swear their loyalty to me, the new queen, or to introduce themselves.

There was General Forcheck, knees popping as she knelt and slyly slipped one of her tonics into my hands.

"The strongest yet," she said with a grin. "To celebrate later."

There was General Tenia, leading a procession of Those Below. Behind her was Garrett of Castle Rock, wiping away tears in his eyes and blubbering how he'd always dreamed of this day. Behind him were some children he'd brought, their eyes faintly glowing blue.

Caldre was next, broad-shouldered Sulien at his back, sulking and refusing to meet my eyes.

"My queen," Caldre said, bowing. "May your rule be as magnanimous as your radiance."

I gave him an indulgent smile. "Caldre. And now that we're all safe, may your loyalty be as stalwart as your words are pretty. But where is Lord Tannis?"

Caldre's faint smile vanished. Sulien tensed.

Rune's voice was chilly, "After I used my Wild magic to bring you back, I was left less than able. Lord Tannis thought to take that chance to remove me."

"Ah," I said.

"Yes," Caldre said soberly. "She found you were not so weak as that."

"And I hope you learn from her mistake," Rune said.

Giving an even deeper bow, Caldre hurried off, Sulien lurching after him.

"We will need to watch him," I whispered to Rune. "Do you think the wolves will still listen to me if I ask for their help?"

"They'd be fools not to," Rune said. "Already scheming, are we?"

"Scheming sounds derogatory. I'm taking precautionary measures."

"Believe me, I meant it as anything but an insult."

Someone coughed, and I found Marian smirking at us. "If you could spare a bit of your time, my High King and Queen."

I hugged her while Rune clasped Cassius's arm. Both of them were dressed in similar finery of a dress and coat, which was probably the most shocking thing I'd seen all day.

"I hope, if you're not too busy ruling and everything, you'll come to our wedding," Marian whispered in my ear.

It was then that I noticed the faint lines intertwining her hands, matching those on Cassius's. Lines I figured would darken with their vows. "Of course," I blurted out. "I wouldn't miss it."

Beaming, Marian and Cassius moved on, leaving me with a much less welcome face: Leah, with a small entourage of humans, all dressed in sharp military attire.

None of them moved to bow, or nod, or give any sort of acknowledgement. The way some of Leah's soldiers were glancing at her told me *they* didn't even know what she meant to do.

I'd retrieved Joshua's body shortly after leaving the Halfway. The magic within the currents of the Undersea had somewhat preserved it, but he'd still been unbearably difficult to look at, and I'd returned him to her in a beautiful, closed, rosewood coffin that Rune had created himself. I'd told Leah to bury him wherever she wanted—be it in Seattle or in the Wilds—and I would join her if she wished.

She hadn't reached out to me since.

"Leah—" I started.

As though jerking from a trance, Leah gave a stiff nod and about-faced.

"Whatever you think of me," I called after her, "you'll always have friends here."

Leah didn't make any indication she heard me, but before I could mull over her silence, a woman clearly from the Undersea had taken her place. She was as pale as sea salt, with long blue hair moving ever so slightly, as though caught in a current. She fidgeted, clearly unused to being the center of attention.

"I am Dreya," she said in a voice as coarse as sand. "Daughter of King Bendeti."

I stared at her for a moment, processing this. "It's, uh, good to meet you."

"And you. I know my father had quarrels with the Wilds and the Below, but I'm here to promise an alliance rather than war."

She might have been understating things a bit, but I got the gist. Rune gave a stoic nod. "We would gladly accept that."

Dreya nodded and started to hurry away.

"The Council of Loam once had a representative from the Undersea, didn't it?" I asked Rune.

He looked surprised, but quickly caught on. He raised his voice. "The Council of Loam would once again have a member from the Undersea, Queen Dreya, if you desire it."

She paused and gave another harried nod before blending into the crowd with her entourage. I untensed a little, feeling as though I'd diverted potential disaster in some small way.

The introductions, pledges of loyalties, groveling, and apologies continued until it all became a blur, and I lost track of time and faces. Though we hadn't asked for it, people left piles of gifts for us. All of them seemed ridiculous: freshly slain beasts, impractically ceremonial swords and armor, gemstones that were too gawdy even for royalty, and especially for me. And if it wasn't wildlings trying to curry favor with elaborate presents, then it was humans leaving even more impractical gifts like a blender and bread maker, as though the palace of the Wilds would have outlets. Still, whether given out of fear or true respect, I smiled and was grateful all the same.

Within the hour my feet had gone numb, and I itched to readjust the crown now digging into my scalp. It was only when the procession had petered out and plates of Wild delicacies and drink came out did Rune offer me his arm.

"Now for the most dangerous part: small talk."

We threaded through the crowd, me taking in the occasional looks of awe from those who hadn't come up to the throne. Some from the Council of Loam tried to corner Rune into talking about one nagging issue or another, and more than once Caldre tried to beseech me to be allowed to go Below and recover what was there.

I only half-listened while the other half of my mind drifted off. Everything was as perfect as it could be. Yet the missing magic I'd once had left a gaping hole that was becoming increasingly difficult to ignore. As though I was seeing only part of the wonder of the world that was actually around me.

Still, I should have been grateful, even having lost that. Most had lost much more. I was alive. I was here.

I felt a light tug on my arm.

"Want to ditch this?" Marian said.

Rune was still talking with one of the representatives of the Council of Loam, a bored expression on his face, his gaze often shooting to me. There were still plenty of guests mingling in small groups. It didn't seem like they'd be leaving anytime soon.

"Aren't we kind of required to be here?" I said.

Marian raised an eyebrow. "Do you want to be?"

"Not really."

"You're High Queen. You can do whatever you want. Abuse your powers for once."

A giddy lightness overtook me. This might be the last time in a while where I'd be able to get away before the reality of the position I'd assumed kicked in.

I made a subtle motion to Rune.

"Apologies," he said. "I'm afraid I'm being called to a meeting I can't miss."

Those from the Council of Loam looked put out as he swept over. Before we could be dragged into another conversation, and almost the moment we stepped free of the crowd, Rune summoned a path.

We came out in what was now Seattle, on a narrow street thick with green growing within and around the buildings. A few people noticed us, and I quickly took off my crown. There would be plenty of time for wearing it later, I was sure. Tonight, of all nights, I wanted to be Val. Just Val.

I was surprised when Rune led us down the street to a little café, as though he knew the layout well.

"You're not the only one who changed in six months," he said when I gave him a surprised look. He held the café door open for me. "There are things in the human world that aren't that bad."

"Like coffee," Cassius said.

"And mayonnaise," Xander added. Zuri on his arm, skin flushed with fresh seawater, wrinkled her nose at him.

The café interior was half glass observatory, with the other half leading directly into looming Wild trees. There was plenty of plush seating, couches, silken hammocks, warm air, the scent of spice, and muted conversations. Regular humans doing regular things. Only a couple people looked our way when we came in, and of those who did, their gazes didn't linger. They didn't seem afraid of Rune, and I wondered if, to them, he was just another wildling. To them he wasn't the vicious High King, and *I* was nothing but one of them.

I could get used to this.

We took a seat and were brought menus. I couldn't stop looking around. From the half-human, half-Wild café, to Rune —my husband and the High King—to how the humans seemed perfectly content to sit beside beings whom, until a little over a year ago, they'd feared more than almost anything. It felt as though I'd been plucked from my real life and dropped into a dream.

"Is this all you hoped for?" I asked Rune.

He peered over the menu at me. "Nothing is perfect. But it's pretty close."

"I'll take it, whatever you say," Cassius said.

Our food came, and Xander tried to get Zuri to sip cappuccino and nibble on toast with avocado they only recently started getting shipped up here again. Cassius tried to teach Rune one of the board games the café kept on hand, one with little soldiers as pieces, while Marian rolled her eyes at each of Rune's moves.

"You can't brute force your way through everything," she said.

Rune just gave a wicked smile.

"Val?"

I jerked. Xander was looking at me, brows furrowed. "Everything okay?" he asked.

I hadn't realized I'd been staring at the trees outside the café. For just a moment, I'd sworn I'd seen the flash of a woman in a silken dress pass through, her outline shimmering with light. Something about her was painfully familiar.

A strange sensation stirred in my gut. A buzz that seemed to radiate from my very bones traveled up my arms.

"Fine," I said. "I'm totally fine."

And yet when the others went back to their game—Rune's gaze lingering on me longer than the rest—I got up without another word and left them behind. The trees seemed to beckon me into their quiet embrace as I walked away from the warmth and light. I could hear voices in the branches. Gentle, laughing, and happy.

I knelt. Without knowing entirely why, I pressed my palm to the dirt.

Butterflies erupted in my stomach as I felt it: lines of magic, like strings I could pluck. They were all around me. They'd always been there and were revealing themselves to me again.

"Are you okay?" Rune said.

A green bud struggled to break free from the dirt and wrap around my finger, holding tight. It was small, it was weak, but it was there, and I knew, given time, it could grow into something mighty. That was a promise.

I looked back at Rune and smiled. "You know, I think I will be."

The End of the Savage Wilds Series

Want more action, magic, and romance? Check out my other books!

Get notified about new releases, exclusive ARCs, cover reveals, giveaways, and more by **joining my author newsletter.**

Please Leave a Review

I can't thank you enough for choosing to read my books! Every single review helps me find new readers and continue doing what I love: writing great stories for you to enjoy. If you get a second, could **you leave a review or star rating?** Thank you so much for your help and support!

Get notified about new releases, exclusive ARCs, cover reveals, giveaways, and more by **joining my author newsletter.**

instagram.com/seanfletcherauthor
facebook.com/seannfletcher
bookbub.com/profile/sean-fletcher
amazon.com/author/seanfletcher
goodreads.com/seanfletcher

MORE BOOKS BY SEAN

Savage Wilds Series

Savage Wild Hearts

Savage Wild Souls

Savage Wild Gods

Legacy of Dragon Series

Dragon Born

Dragon Lost

Dragon Unleashed

Dragon Blood

The Heir of Dragons Series:

Dragon's Awakening

Dragon's Curse

Dragon's Bane

Dragon's Fate

Paranormal Outcasts Series:

Elemental Outcast

Elemental Trial

Elemental Queen

The Darkness Within Series:

Called by Darkness

The Cursed One

Enemy of Magic

The Dark Prince

The Mages of New York Trilogy

Mage's Apprentice

Mage's Trial

Mage's End

ACKNOWLEDGMENTS

It takes an author to write a book, but as always it takes a village to make that book readable. For *Savage Wild Gods* I have this village to thank:

To my beta readers, Lana Turner, Marie Reed, and Andrea at Hot Tree Editing.

To James T. Eagan at BookFly designs for the incredible cover.

To Tia Bach for impeccable proofreading.

And to my fans, of course, who support me, visit me at festivals and conferences, message me about different books and characters, keep up on my going-ons, and in general give me a target to write for.

About the Author

Sean Fletcher is an award-winning and bestselling fantasy author across multiple age ranges and subgenres, with over thirty books in more than five different series, many of which have hit #1 in their categories. Since writing and pitching his first book at fifteen, he's forged a path through the publishing industry, continuing to hone his craft and expertise at a premier literary agency before becoming a full-time author, speaker, and editor.

When not jotting down highly enjoyable lies, he's often doing something most people find masochistic, like cycling long distances, hiking high mountains, and indulging in more sweets than is medically advisable.

Stalk him on social media or his author newsletter to learn more about his upcoming releases.

The setting, characters and story used in this book are completely fictitious and come from the author's imagination. Any similarity to real persons, living or dead, is coincidental and are not intended by the author.

Fletcher, Sean
Savage Wild Gods (The Savage Wilds Book 3)
Denton, Texas
1. Young Adult Contemporary/Dark Fantasy

ISBN (hardcover): 978-1-963248-00-5
ISBN (paperback): 9798884885042

First edition published May, 2024

www.ingramcontent.com/pod-product-compliance
Lightning Source LLC
Chambersburg PA
CBHW030514030826
49196CB00027B/124